# Dance of Desire

★★★★½

" (DANCE OF DESIRE) . . . is a fast-paced tale,
and Kean successfully uses all the senses to drag
readers in. The secondary characters, from the
servants to the peasants, are finely drawn, too,
and serve to bring this tale to life. SENSUAL"

—*Romantic Times BOOKClub Magazine*

Saphire Imprint
Medallion Press, Inc.
Florida, USA

Dedication:

*For Megan, whose beautiful smile always warms my heart.*

*And for Mike, my Knight in Shining Armor.*
*I cherish each day with you.*

Published 2005 by Medallion Press, Inc.
225 Seabreeze Ave.
Palm Beach, FL 33480

The MEDALLION PRESS LOGO
is a registered tradmark of Medallion Press, Inc.

Printed in the United States of America

Library of Congress Cataloging-in-Publication Data

Kean, Catherine.
  Dance of desire / Catherine Kean.
    p. cm.
  ISBN 0-932815-35-X
  1. Great Britain--History--Richard I, 1189-1199--Fiction. I. Title.
  PS3611.E15D35 2005
  813'.6--dc22

                        2004026145

Acknowledgements:

*I could not have succeeded in my writing journey without my dear friends and fabulous critique partners — Nancy Robards Thompson, Teresa Elliot Brown, and Elizabeth Grainger. You are amazing writers, and I truly cannot thank you enough.*

*My heartfelt thanks also to Alicia Clarke and Cheryl Duhaime, who have read every word I've written and are always enthusiastic; to Amanda Lord, the best sister in the whole wide world; and to David and Shirley Lord, rare and beautiful people who taught me to strive for my dreams. You never failed to encourage me, and I am very proud to be your daughter.*

# Chapter One

"I DO NOT LIKE THIS WRETCHED SCHEME, MILADY."

Lady Rexana Villeaux shivered in the icy night wind that whipped into Tangston Keep's forebuilding. "I know, Henry, but 'tis the only way to get the list of traitors."

She drew against the stone wall, into the shadows at the bottom of the stairs. Bawdy laughter and the music of lute and drum carried down into the passage from the great hall. As she smoothed the veil covering her nose and mouth and the silk over her head, tiny bells tinkled at her wrists. The jewelry's weight pressed upon her skin, a foreign sensation.

She inhaled a shaky breath. Would her deception succeed?

In the dim light, Henry glanced at her, his gaze worried. Rexana's belly clenched into a knot. She must not succumb to fear. She must focus on her task. Her brother's life depended on her. Dear, impetuous Rudd, the only family she had left.

Wiping her sweaty palms on her embroidered skirt, she started up the stairs.

Henry strode beside her. Torchlight flickered on his silvery hair and shadowed the grim set of his mouth. "I hope your hot-headed fool of a brother appreciates the risk you are taking to save his arse."

Rexana shot Henry a sharp glance. "Mind your tongue. He is not your pupil in the tiltyards any longer, but master of Ickleton Keep. Your lord."

"With respect, he is fifteen and very much a boy." Henry wagged a finger, callused from years of wielding a sword. "I still remember the day your mother and father presented him to me, all pink, squished, and noisy as a pig's fart."

Her heart squeezed. "Henry!"

"You are right. 'Tis no time to speak of such matters. May your parents forever rest in peace." Henry's eyes darkened. With a scarred hand, he caught her elbow, halting her just outside the light spilling in from the hall. "Milady, look at you. An earl's daughter, dressed like an infidel whore. What madness convinced me to let you go through with this?"

She swallowed a sting of irritation. Heaven above,

she did not need his permission. When would Henry cease treating her like the child he had bounced on his knee and hand-fed expensive sweetmeats? "Not madness, Henry. Fate. The girl who plays the Saracen's lover in the local mummer's troupe would have entertained the sheriff —"

"Except she fell ill." Henry nodded. "I helped her through Ickleton's gates, then summoned the healer."

"A boon, that her costume fit me well enough."

He snorted in clear disapproval. "Nay, a curse."

Rexana looked down at her stiff fingers, darkened like her body with thin layers of flour and mud. "The girl knew of no one to take her place, and it provided us a way to get through Tangston's gates. Henry, we *must* find the missive that lists the names of sworn traitors. The one the sheriff intends to send to the crown."

"Because somehow Rudd's signature is on the document." Henry sighed. "Could the maidservant who fled Tangston be mistaken about what she overheard? She was half mad, ranting about the sheriff's barbaric ways —"

"Her dead sire swore fealty to my father. Moreover, she is a friend of Rudd's. She had no reason to speak false." Cheers and laughter erupted in the hall and, with a shudder, Rexana looked toward the noise. "Rudd is not involved in the rebellion stirring against the crown. I will not see him ruined by accusations of treachery."

Henry touched her arm. "Please. Must you dance? We will find another way to save Rudd."

"There is no other way." Rexana curled her clammy hands into fists. "I can delay no longer. The others know what to do?"

"Aye."

Footfalls echoed in the corridor. She glanced past Henry to see four musicians approach, men loyal to her and Rudd. They willingly risked their lives this eve. For that, she would be forever grateful.

Rexana's pulse began a painful thunder against her ribs. Her fingers flitted to the delicate gold brooch pinned to her bodice and hidden by the garment's fringe. An arrow wrapped with a flowing ribbon, a gift from Rudd a few sennights ago. A reminder of the bond forged between them one snowy day, and why she must not fail.

She pulled from Henry's grasp. As the mummer had instructed, Rexana removed her leather shoes. If she did not fully accept her role this eve, she would never deceive the barbarian sheriff.

Gasping as her bare feet connected with cold stone, Rexana pressed her shoes into Henry's hands.

"Milady —"

"Rudd would try to save me," she said softly. "And I am indebted to him in more ways than you could ever understand."

Blinking away stinging tears, she stepped into the hall.

Fane Linford, High Sheriff of Warringham, sipped his wine and glanced across the vast, smoke-hazed hall. Every nobleman in the county, it seemed, had accepted his invitation to this feast. They celebrated his return to England as well as the position of authority granted to him one hot, bloody morn at Acre by King Richard himself.

All, that is, but a significant few.

His gaze drifted to the lute player sitting near the fire who plucked out a song. More musicians, strangers to Fane like the majority of the guests, moved to the hearth with their instruments.

A rough voice rose above the hall's noise. Fane's eyes narrowed on the harnessed black bear which stood on its hind feet, turning in a circle as its trainer shouted commands and flicked a stick. A crude if not effective display of a master's power over his minion. A display Fane intended to emulate when he crushed the rebellious lords rising against the crown.

"A clever bear," said Lord Darwell, seated at Fane's right.

Setting aside his silver goblet, Fane reached up to pull a lock of ebony hair from his eyes. "I preferred the fire eaters who performed earlier. I admire a man who risks his own demise, but is still fully hale afterward."

Darwell scratched his thick, graying beard and laughed as though uncertain how to respond. "You have a point."

"One of many I learned on crusade."

A flicker of unease crossed Darwell's face, quickly replaced by a mix of curiosity and admiration. "You spent many months as a prisoner of the Saracens, did you not? I must congratulate you. I understand the siege of Acre last year would never have succeeded without you. I doubt my son would have returned."

A chill rippled down Fane's spine. With his eating dagger, he speared a morsel of roasted quail and shoved it between his teeth. "I only did what was necessary."

"How did you manage to stay alive amongst the infidel? Did you not spy for the king?"

The chill spread. Deepened. Fane forced a smile. "A warrior has his secrets." He chewed the meat, poorly spiced like most of the fare he had recently tasted. With wicked intensity, he craved a fiery mélange of turmeric, cardamom, and cumin, and the perfume of eastern food.

Darwell chuckled. "Secrets? Mayhap a woman?" After taking a noisy slurp of wine, he slid sideways until his elbow pressed against Fane's arm. "Are the rumors true?" he asked in an eager, hushed voice. "Did you really fornicate with a Saracen wench? What was it like? Did you enjoy it? Did she —"

"As I said, a warrior has his secrets." Fane stifled the urge to grab Darwell by the front of his tunic and growl in his face. Every lord he had met since his return to this cold, wet country had wanted to believe in his depravity. Even when they commended his heroism, he saw disgust in their eyes. Darwell hid his distaste better than most.

With a grin, Darwell straightened and eased away. "One day, you will tell me the truth. When we have drunk each other under the table and trust one another as friends."

Fane laughed. Hellfire, he did not have to disclose his past to Darwell or any man. One day, his peers would look upon him and speak to him with genuine respect, accepting him for who he was. It would take time to build the necessary alliances and destroy the canker undermining loyalty to the crown — far longer than the three sennights he had resided at Tangston — but Fane had long ago mastered perseverance. His allegiance to the king had sustained him through days when he longed for death. He would ensure the crown's victory in Warringham.

Shrugging aside his thoughts, Fane glanced back at the bear. The animal completed its circle. Grunting, it dropped back to all fours.

Applause filled the hall. Darwell cheered.

As Fane clapped and thanked the flushed-faced trainer, he noticed movement near the forebuilding's entrance. Light glittered off the embroidered costume of a dancer. Eastern garments accented her figure and floated like cobwebs as she wove her way past the far tables.

Fane's breath caught in his throat. Memories . . . .

Leila's lithe, oiled body gilded by lamplight. The cloying smell of burning incense. Torture. Imprisonment. Living each day as though it were his last.

The sapphire ring on his right hand glowed as blue as the dancer's garments. He grabbed his wine and gulped a mouthful. It tasted like sand.

What insanity had possessed him to grant the eager-to-please steward full control over the eve's entertainment?

He should send the dancer away. Immediately. But others in the hall had already noticed her. If he dismissed her now, even discreetly, he implied displeasure, disastrous for a woman who earned her livelihood through recommendations of her good performance. The poor wench probably depended on this eve's coin to put food in her belly and feed her children.

Nay, God help him, he could not send her away.

Beside him, Darwell blew a sigh, then squinted at the left side of the hall. "I have not seen young Rudd Villeaux yet this eve. Did he not plan to attend?"

Dragging his gaze from the dancer who hesitated in the shadows, fingering her veil, Fane wiped his lips with his thumb. "I received word from him earlier this eve. He cannot come. Pressing matters of estate."

"A pity, his parents' deaths. He is young to have the responsibilities of lord."

"They died recently?" Out of the corner of his eye,

Fane watched the dancer stretch her slender arms over her head, preparing her body to perform. The men at the tables behind her grinned, pointing to her navel, and he bit back an inexplicable pang of annoyance.

"The earl and his wife were buried six sennights ago. Both killed by sickness." Pouring more wine from a silver jug, Darwell said, "Did you know the Villeaux's are distant cousins of the king? No purer blood in England. The son is a handsome enough lad, but the daughter —"

"Daughter?" Fane murmured. The dancer rubbed her arms with her hands. Was she chilled from standing in one of the drafts wafting through the hall? Or, was she anxious about performing before him? His mouth curled into a bitter smile. Had she heard the subversive gossip that called Fane the failed son of a once-powerful earl? That named him a ruthless infidel? Regrettable, that some of it was true.

"Her name is Rexana." The name tumbled off Darwell's tongue with undisguised appreciation. "Exquisite. Fair of face with breasts like —"

Fane tipped his head to the nearby fruit bowl. "Oranges?"

With a chuckle, Darwell uncurled his hands. "Finer than your costly oranges." He shook his graying head. "I am a fool to speak so, when I pray my son Garmonn will marry her. 'Tis Garmonn who is friends with Rudd Villeaux and who went on crusade," he added with a sly smile. "Mayhap you will speak favorably of my son when I petition the crown for the marriage?"

"Mayhap." Pushing aside his goblet, Fane reached for the bowl and speared a dried fig with his eating dagger.

"Wedding Lady Rexana will permit Garmonn into the most respected court circles," Darwell said eagerly. " 'Twould be a great honor. What father would not want the best for his son?"

Resentment stung the back of Fane's throat, but he quickly cleared away the foolish emotion. Years ago, he had vowed not to feel even an inkling of remorse for the final, bitter confrontation with his sire. Futile, to wish that dark day had been different. The old tyrant was long dead.

Keeping his tone noncommittal, Fane said, "I will consider your request. Though she sounds so exceptional" — he plucked the fig from his dagger — "I am tempted to wed her myself."

Disappointment clouded Darwell's eyes. He opened his mouth to speak, but a tabor's strident hammering curtailed his words.

Fane glanced up. He froze.

Lifting her hands high in the air, fingers curved outward in invitation, the dancer slunk between the rows of tables. She twirled into the open space in the hall's center.

With slow, sinuous movements, she began to dance.

Each step brought Rexana closer to the dais. To the dark skinned man with wild black hair and eyes that glittered with frightening intensity. To the barbarian Sheriff Linford, who held her brother's fate like the fig caught between his fingers.

She silently cursed her stiff limbs. Her body was no stranger to creative expression. Yet, when she danced in the meadow, she had only the birds, still water, and ancient willows watching. There, she danced for herself.

Never for a man.

A shiver tore through her. She must focus, draw upon her heightened emotions, use her anxiety, sorrow and fears to enhance her performance.

She must not fail.

Ignoring the appreciative stares of the noblemen around her, she whirled across the space directly before the sheriff. Dry rushes scratched against her feet, an odd sensation. The pungent scents of dried basil, fennel, and rosemary floated up from the floorboards. Cool air brushed against her naked stomach. She fought the urge to cover herself.

Raising her lashes a fraction, she glanced at Linford. He was not watching! He conversed with Lord Darwell whose tongue, as she well knew from past feasts at Ickleton, always loosened after a few goblets of wine.

Disquiet swirled inside her. Curse Linford! Did the rumors not claim that he enjoyed eastern courtesans? Why, then, did he ignore her?

She spun in a graceful turn. Still, he did not watch.

Frustration bubbled in her throat. By the saints, she must distract him, otherwise Henry would not be able to slip into the sheriff's solar to find the missive.

Too many lives depended on her. Most of all Rudd's.

Rexana cast the musicians an urgent glance. *Faster*, her mind cried. As though sensing her urgency, the drummer nodded, quickening the pace. She threw out her arms and stamped her feet. The tiny bells at her ankles chimed.

Whirling even nearer the lord's table, she thanked the holy saints that the poor lighting and dark cosmetics would hinder Darwell from recognizing her. As would the veil and head covering, she silently reminded herself. The musicians had commented earlier how thoroughly all her features, except her eyes, were concealed.

Spurred by a burst of confidence, she drew close enough to distinguish the sheriff's deep, slightly rough voice. Close enough to see the tanned plane of his cheek and the hard, sensual curve of his mouth. Close enough to speak to him, if she dared.

"Look at me," she whispered, "*Look at me*."

Linford glanced up. Over the floating veil, she caught his gaze. His eyes were brown and shadowed by wickedly long, black lashes. His wary, perceptive gaze slashed into her with stunning force.

She stumbled, caught herself, and disguised her falter

with elaborate turns. As she spun back to face the dais, she saw Henry edging his way to the stairwell.

Oh, God.

Fear sharpened her breaths. Her gaze shot to Linford. He had not seen Henry. Laughing at a comment from Darwell, Linford turned the fig slowly in his fingertips. The sapphire ring on his hand glinted as he tossed the fruit into his mouth, then stared directly at her.

So, she had captured his attention.

A spark of satisfaction warmed her. With a smooth swivel of her hips, she dropped to the rushes. The drummer faltered, then resumed his frantic pace. *Do not fail me*, she prayed.

With catlike movements, she crawled across the coarse rushes. The tang of crushed herbs, rotting food scraps, and mildew filled her nostrils. Never in all her years had she been this close to a hall floor. Her mother would have swooned with horror to hear of such an occurrence.

A blush stung Rexana's cheeks. Resisting the urge to scramble to her feet, she rose up on her knees, arching her spine to flaunt her bare skin. She must focus on her goal, not her fear. No one recognized her. No one would ever know of this incident. Once Henry had the missive, she could forget all about this eve.

Curving her arms in an elegant move, she straightened and rose to her feet. She peeked at Linford through her splayed fingers. His gaze met hers. He slid another fig between his teeth, chewed, then licked his bottom lip.

She glided toward him.

He resumed talking with Lord Darwell.

A scream burned for release. Stubborn, stubborn man. She had piqued his curiosity. Now, how did she keep him enticed? How did she hold the interest of a savage?

Heady anticipation shimmered through her. She must think like a barbarian. Act the part of an infidel courtesan. Play to his desires. Reveal the wildness trapped in her soul.

*Dance, Rexana*!

Closing her eyes to the faces around her, she focused on the tabor's rhythmic beat as well as the plaintive melody. Reminded herself that Rudd's life hinged upon this moment. Stretched her body and limbs farther than she ever had before.

The ankle bells tinkled.

*Step. Whirl. Step. Sway.*

Fear, anxiety, and longing bloomed inside her, feelings she had known well since childhood. The schooling of a titled lady left little time for chasing beetles or butterflies, or for picking bouquets of stringy wildflowers.

Her parents had expected her to accept her noble duty. She had done so. Bravely. Willingly. She had loved and trusted them. Now, they lay buried in the hard earth.

Dance, Rexana! Step. Whirl. Step. Sway.

He was watching now.

The silk brushed against her legs, a sensation similar to the breeze wafting through the grasses near her secret pool.

There, surrounded by the quiet majesty of trees and weathered rocks, she allowed the stifled voice inside her to cry out.

There, lifting her hands to the sun, she absorbed the power of the vast blue sky and the soil beneath her feet.

Surrendering to the passionate howl inside her, she danced.

She reached her palms upward. Aye, just like that.

Step. Whirl. Step. Sway.

Rexana dared another glance. Linford stared as though he could not look away. As though her dance seduced him.

She rolled her head and shoulders in a slow, sensual arc.

Exhilaration flooded her mind.

Her steps quickened.

The familiar cry hummed through her body. Heightened her senses. Infused her heart and soul with a heady blend of joy, confusion, and . . . yearning.

Her body arched.

Spun.

She danced as she dared near the pool, where no one could see, with only her reflection to laugh at her folly. In those moments, she felt more alive than at any other time in her life.

As she whirled in wild momentum, she heard the music slow. The dance was ending. Too soon!

She would summon the musicians to begin another song. She lowered her arms. Blinking away the haze of bittersweet memories, Rexana dipped her head, then extended her arms in an elegant finale.

The last strains of the music stopped.

The hall fell silent.

Utterly silent.

Her breaths, obscenely loud, rattled in her throat.

Why had the chatter and merriment halted?

She raised her head a fraction. Her pulse kicked against her ribs. Darwell sat alone at the lord's table, his cheeks flushed and his jaw gaping.

Not five paces to her right stood Linford, his arms crossed over the front of his tunic. Half masked by smoky shadow, his face revealed no emotion.

She rubbed her trembling hands over her belly. What had happened? Had Darwell recognized her? Had he told the sheriff her identity?

Fear shot through her. For herself. For Henry and the musicians. For Rudd.

Tugging her veil closer about her face she took two startled steps back.

"You will not run away." Linford's mouth tipped up in a half smile. He crooked a finger. "Come here, little dancer."

Fane scowled as the woman's eyes widened with panic. Why did she want to flee? Because of the shocked murmurs spreading through the hall? Because of the rumors about him? Or because no man had dared to confront her after a performance?

Her chest rose and fell in a frantic rhythm. Perspiration beaded on her throat and dotted her bronzed skin. He looked lower, at her breasts swelling against the embroidered silk bodice. Beautiful. A generous handful of warm flesh. Breasts as big as . . . oranges.

His hardened loins stirred.

With effort, Fane wrenched his gaze from the dancer's cleavage to meet her stare. She had not moved, but stood as still as a carved stone statue. He sensed her reticence, strong as the sensation that virtually hummed in the space between them. She would cross to him. Of that, he had no doubt. Whatever the rumors, he was Warringham's sheriff, appointed by the crown. By virtue of setting foot within his keep, she owed him that gesture of respect.

"I am waiting, love."

She swallowed and made a small sound of distress. His gaze narrowed on her face. Her nose, mouth, and chin were concealed by the veil. Were her lips full and red? Was her nose slim or angular? A woman of mystery. Mayhap deliberately so. Her eyes were rimmed with kohl, heavily lashed but . . . emerald green. Unusual, for a wench of dark skin and eastern blood.

Frowning, he glanced at the cloth covering her head, but the fabric lay flat against her temples. He doubted her hair flowed thick, glossy, and black like Leila's.

His hands tightened into fists, even as he snuffed a sting of anger. Foolish, to take offense. This woman was an entertainer, a wench of English blood acting a role. She did not understand the nuances of eastern dance. He had recognized that the moment he saw her move.

As though sensing his displeasure, the woman tipped up her chin. She started toward him, each step articulated by the chime of bells. Ah, but how she moved.

Torchlight skimmed over her slender shoulders and down the planes of her firm stomach. She glided toward him as though she approached King Richard himself. Head held high, she radiated the poise and elegance expected of the highest noble courts.

Who was this woman?

She paused before him. Almost in afterthought, with the barest hint of resentment, she lowered her gaze to stare at his tunic. He sensed the tumultuous emotions warring within her, threatening her self-control. The same fierce emotions had reverberated in her dance and touched a note deep inside him. Her heart had spoken.

It echoed the profound, primitive bellow of his own tormented heart. Before her dance had finished, before he could stop himself or consider the consequences, he had walked around the table, stepped off the dais, and crossed to her.

Steeling his wayward concentration, Fane drew in a breath. She smelled of violets. Sweet. Delicious.

"An interesting dance you performed this eve," he said.

"I hope it pleased you, milord." Her very English voice sounded slightly husky and breathless. The way a woman sounded after she had been kissed. *Focus, fool!*

Shoving aside the distracting thought, Fane muttered, "I never saw a dance quite like yours in all my years in the east."

She stiffened. The bells at her wrists jingled as she clasped her hands over her stomach. "I was instructed in this fair country. I admit I have never danced before a sheriff of such . . . authority, milord. Your esteemed reputation —"

"Ah." With a firm hand, he reached up and touched the edge of her veil. As his fingers tried to drag down the shimmering fabric, she jerked away. He frowned. "You fear me, little dancer?"

Beneath the sweep of her lashes, her eyes sparked. "I do not."

"Yet, you turn your face away and refuse to look up at me. You are indeed frightened. Or you hide secrets from me."

Her green eyes glittered in the torchlight. Lovely eyes, darkened with anger, confusion and distrust. Eyes that revealed the passion within her.

"I am honored you wished to speak with me," she said with the barest quaver, stepping back, "but I must leave now."

His jaw hardened. "You cannot. I have not dismissed you."

"I do not need —" Her sharp voice faltered.

Fane's lip curled in anger. She did not need to finish. He heard her unspoken words. *I do not need your wretched dismissal, barbarian.* A treacherous thought for a peasant who fed herself through the coin earned from her dance.

As though sensing his displeasure, her gaze softened. So, she was wise enough to bite her tongue and try to pacify him. "I believe the jugglers are to perform next. I do not wish to delay the rest of the eve's celebrations," she said. Glancing at the musicians, who stood staring at her as though awaiting a superior's orders, she added, "Your guests will grow restless."

*As I grow restless, woman, in your presence. As my blood stirs, and my pulse thickens, and my soul hungers for more of your dance.* "You will stay."

She gasped, a sound of utter indignation.

Before she could dart away, he caught her hands. Raising them to his lips, he kissed her fingers, feeling the tremor that coursed through her. As he released her, he drew the sapphire ring from his finger and pressed it into her palm.

"A token of my appreciation, and my interest." He trailed his thumb down over the veil to her lips. "You will stay, love, as I command. By the end of this eve, we will know each other very well. And I will know all of your secrets."

# chapter two

A SHUDDER RAN DOWN REXANA'S SPINE. How could she refuse Linford's gift and proposition without causing grave offense? At all costs, she must avoid creating a commotion as well as any disastrous consequences for herself, Rudd, and her loyal friends.

Turning the ring in her damp fingers, she looked down at the sapphire. A large stone, set in delicately etched gold. No doubt worth the equivalent of a wealthy lady's dowry. Did he favor all his women so generously? Did he pay for her body — or the secrets he expected her to reveal?

Fear tingled through her to the tips of her toes. She would never betray Rudd. Nor would she offer herself to a stranger. A barbarian. Yet, even as she steeled her resolve, a strange excitement surged. Forbidden interest, coaxed to life by his hungry gaze. Wanton curiosity.

What would it be like to taste Linford's sinfully curved lips? To feel his fingers skimming over her skin? To sense his breath upon her belly?

As though he tried to read her mind, Linford's eyes narrowed a fraction. Mentally squashing her thoughts, she averted her gaze. Her parents, a blessing upon their departed souls, had expected her to remain pure for her noble husband and the sons she would bear him in love and honor. By God's holy rood, she wanted to keep this vow.

But Rudd's life was more important than her virtue.

Her fingers tightened on the jewel. She had no other way to protect Henry and win time for him to find the missive, but to accept Linford's offer. From what she had heard of the sheriff, she doubted she could simply refuse, hand back the ring, and walk out of the hall. If she declined, he might toss her over his shoulder and carry her off to his private chambers, as she had heard was the custom of hot-blooded infidels. Dread and excitement trembled through her.

Conversation began to fill the hall. The sheriff's interest in her was already inciting gossip. Turning her head a little, Rexana glanced at the musicians. The drummer met her gaze, scratched his cheek, then shook his head. The signal. Henry had not yet returned.

Anticipation buzzed in her veins like a swarm of

bees. Until Henry had the missive, she must act her role to the fullest. Like the courtesan Linford thought her to be, she must tempt. Seduce. And, if necessary, yield her body to him.

Curving her mouth into a smile, she raised her lashes. "Your gift is most generous, milord." Panic swelled up between her ribs. She struggled to ignore it.

"The stone is of high quality." With strong fingers, Linford clasped her hand. He tilted it sideways, so light gleamed off the sapphire's polished surface. "It is exquisite," he murmured, "as are you."

"You are equally generous with your flattery."

He smiled. His palm cradled her hand. How neatly her fingers fit into his. His breath fanned across her brow and, as he leaned closer, she caught the scents of spices, red wine, and sweet figs.

Pleasure tingled inside her, swiftly followed by caution. So easily, she could be swayed by his intriguing scent and false praise. Spoken in a husky whisper, his words had glided off his tongue with the practiced smoothness of a rogue skilled in the art of seducing women. Foolish, that her heart had fluttered.

Yet, no man had ever spoken to her with the passion underscoring his tone. Certainly not Darwell's son Garmonn, who courted her with all the charm of a randy bull.

Blocking out the memories of Garmonn, she thought of the arrow brooch. Why she always wore it. Why, even if it cost every last bit of her courage, she was honor bound to save Rudd.

Linford's callused thumb brushed over her wrist. A caress. As she feigned a coy giggle and glanced back at him, she noticed a servant setting fresh jugs of wine on the lord's table. A plan floated into her mind. Reassurance flooded through her like cool, refreshing rainwater. She might not have to yield her virtue, after all.

If she kept her wits about her, she could ply Linford with drink as she laughed, teased and tempted him. When his eyes rolled back into his head and he toppled over in a drunken stupor, she could slip away. Leaving his gaudy bauble behind, of course. He would gain naught from her but a sore head.

A delighted laugh bubbled in her throat.

He gently squeezed her hand. "You accept my offer?"

"Aye." She withdrew her fingers from his. Turning her hand over, she slipped on the ring. The gold band was too large, but it did not matter. She would not wear the jewel for long. With a lazy shrug, she eyed the stone. "How could I refuse?"

Grinning, he lowered his mouth to her ear. "I am pleased I did not mistake your craving for adventure, or your wild and lusty spirit." As he exhaled, his breath blew over the silk covering her ear. Her head spun.

*Wild and lusty spirit?* She gulped. "You are indeed . . . most perceptive."

"And ravenous." His mouth curved into a wolfish

smile that blazed its way through her entire body. Her sheer silk garments suddenly felt tight and unbearably hot. Before she could protest, before she could refuse, Linford took her hand. He drew her toward the dais. Toward the vacant chair beside his.

Toward Darwell, who looked on the verge of recognizing her.

Alarm burst inside her. She tore from Linford's grasp.

He turned with the predatory grace of a stalking cat.

"One moment, milord," she said, keeping her face averted from Darwell's probing gaze. "I . . . ah . . . must speak with my friends. Reassure them all is well. They may be concerned." Gesturing to the musicians, she started toward them.

As she neared the tables, a bead of sweat ran between her breasts. What if Darwell called out her name?

Two steps, then Linford caught her elbow. "Do not worry. My steward will speak with them."

"Still, I should —"

With gentle pressure, he turned her back to face him. "Why do you hesitate? Do you intend to deny me?"

Her blood chilled at the hint of warning in his voice. Laughing softly, she straightened the bells at her wrist. "Of course not. I am weary after my dance, 'tis all. The musicians usually see that I rest before we undertake our journey home."

Before the last words had left her lips, Linford flicked his hand. A balding man in a red woolen tunic shot to his side.

His face somber, the man bowed with excessive flair. "What is your pleasure, Sheriff Linford? Shall I tell the other entertainers to begin?"

"Winton, show this woman to my solar. See that she is made comfortable."

Staring at the steward's shiny, bowed pate, Rexana swallowed a desperate moan. *The solar!*

As he turned away, Linford added, "I will join her as soon as I am able."

"As you wish, milord."

Bowing to Rexana, Winton thrust out his arm. He pointed to the stairs that rose along the hall's far wall and ended at a wooden platform.

The stairs Henry had climbed moments before.

Was Henry still searching Linford's chamber?

She half turned toward the sheriff, half formed a protest, but her courage wavered. He already suspected her enthusiasm. She could not risk further arousing his distrust, or lingering in the hall when Darwell might guess her identity.

Her belly ached. Her mind raced with visions of Winton opening the solar door and Henry springing to his feet before an opened chest, a parchment in his hand.

Clearing the nervous squeak from her throat, she

cast Linford what she hoped was a seductive smile. Aware of his gaze trailing down her bare back, she tilted up her chin, then started after Winton, who marched past the crowded tables with brisk efficiency. As she walked, she forced her proper, ladylike steps into loose-hipped strides. Made her body sway, as the dancer had instructed, in a manner that promised and enticed.

She must find a way to warn Henry. She would save him and Rudd from the sheriff's clutches.

And herself.

As a quartet of nimble male and female jugglers ran toward the dais and began to spin brightly colored balls, Fane chewed another fig. Sticky residue clung to his fingers, and he licked away the essence. Would the dancer's skin taste as sweet?

His loins roused again, a distracting press of flesh against his wool hose. Drying his hand on the tablecloth, he forced himself to concentrate on the jugglers' feats. He must be patient. Once he knew the outcome of this night's carefully laid scheme — planned earlier with his trusted men-at-arms and now unfolding leagues away — he could attend his physical needs.

And hers.

What an unexpected turn of events, to meet her this eve.

The delicious memory of her filled Fane's mind. As he looked at the jugglers, he mentally slipped off her head covering, veil, bodice, skirt, and dancing bells until she stood naked before him. Ah, God. His gut twisted. He fought to keep himself from rising from the table to charge after her.

He sighed and gritted his teeth. Never had he been so drawn to a woman, even Leila. This dancer intrigued him. Enticed him with her mysterious allure, one that seemed an odd blend of temptress and veiled innocent. She was a talented actress. Or, she had a great deal to hide.

Darwell tapped his fingers on the table. "She reminds me of someone."

Fane's gaze snapped from the jugglers. "Who?"

"The pretty wench you invited to your chamber," Darwell said with a disgruntled laugh. "I vow I have met her before. Cannot think where."

Fane toyed with a morsel of fig on his tongue. "She mentioned she learned her dance here in England. Mayhap you saw her perform at a local fete."

"Mmm." Darwell scratched his chin, and gaze darted to the oranges in the fruit bowl. Picking out the largest orange, he turned it slowly in his palm.

Footfalls intruded over the jugglers' antics. Looking past the closest tables, Fane saw two men-at-arms in full chain mail striding toward him. He smiled.

Soon, little dancer. Soon.

The men skirted the jugglers and halted before the dais. "Milord."

Aware of the curious stares from noblemen at the nearby tables, Fane asked quietly, "What news do you bring?"

The taller guard squared his shoulders. His face lit with pride. "We found them, milord. In a tavern several leagues from Tangston."

"Excellent." Satisfaction coiled inside Fane. His instincts had not failed him.

Darwell's eyes widened. "Found who?"

"Lords who conspire against the crown." Not taking his gaze from the guards, Fane said, "Where are they now?"

"The bailey. Soon all four will be in the dungeon, as you ordered."

Fane frowned. "Only four? Surely there were more."

The second guard's face reddened and he shuffled his feet. "The others escaped out a hidden door in the cellar. We tracked them through a corn field, but lost them at the riverbank."

With effort, Fane stifled a flare of annoyance. "No matter. We will capture the others soon enough." He fixed the men-at-arms with a firm glare. "Put the prisoners in cells. See that they are well guarded. I will come to the dungeon shortly."

"Aye, milord." The men-at-arms bowed, then retreated across the hall.

The orange in Darwell's hand thudded to the table. Trapping the rolling fruit with his palm, he said, "This eve, of all eves, you sent men to root out traitors?"

Fane shrugged. "What better time for them to plot? No doubt they assumed I would be too busy carousing with my honored guests to pursue their treachery. They were wrong."

"Indeed." With the barest tremble, Darwell wiped his mouth with the back of his hand. "Well, may I be the first to congratulate you on your victory."

A wry laugh burst from Fane's lips. "I cannot claim victory yet. I must capture the other conspirators. I will not be satisfied until I have them all."

Darwell picked up the orange and tossed it back into the bowl, dislodging the neat mound of figs. "For your sake, I hope the lords you arrested this eve are traitors. What if your guards mistakenly detained innocent men?" He clucked his tongue. "What a wretched scandal that would be. I would not like to be in your position, milord, if you are in error."

Fane's blood boiled. Were Darwell's words a warning? Or, a statement of genuine concern?

His thumb brushed his eating dagger's smooth handle. He needed no reminders of the dangers of the coming days. He had known them before he rode through Tangston's gates to assume his duties as sheriff, but he had confronted death more times than he could count on his fingers and still lived.

He would not fail in his duty to eliminate the corruption in Warringham, even if it entailed the temporary detention of guiltless men. No one he knew had ever died from rankled pride. If his men-at-arms had acted in error, he would extend a suitable apology and make restitution. He would prove that beneath his bronzed skin and barbaric scars, his English blood ran as red as any other lord's in this hall, and that he was worthy of respect.

Fane's fingers closed around the dagger. "I appreciate your concern, but you need not worry. Unless, of course, your fealty is questionable." He raised an eyebrow at Darwell.

The older man's eyes crinkled as he laughed. "Do not be foolish. I am as loyal to the king as any other lord here this eve."

"Those who did not attend? What of them?"

Darwell's mouth tightened. "Garmonn is not here this eve because he is unwell. Will you condemn him, Rudd Villeaux, and others like them who wanted to come, but could not?"

"I assure you, I will not condemn an innocent man."

Perspiration shone on Darwell's pale forehead as he nodded his agreement. His love for his son was admirable. Not all fathers respected the seed of their loins. A painful image blasted into Fane's thoughts like a sandstorm. His sire, purple in the face, condemning Fane's irresponsible behavior. Refusing to heed his pleas. Ordering him to leave and never return, despite Fane's mother's shrill weeping.

A hard smile tilted Fane's lips. A pity, his sire would never see how he had misjudged his "utterly worthless" son.

Glittering fabric near the wooden landing caught Fane's gaze. The dancer? Nay, a nobleman wearing an embroidered tunic the same color as her costume. By now, she should be curled up on his bed, awaiting his pleasure. Fane's blood quickened. Another duty he would not neglect.

Setting aside his eating dagger, Fane rose from the table.

"You must leave, milord?" Darwell's hand fluttered in the direction of the jugglers. "They have not finished their act."

Fane smiled. "I must attend to pressing duties."

Her pulse drumming a fierce beat, Rexana stepped onto the landing overlooking the hall. Laughter boomed from below. As she followed Winton toward a torch-lit corridor ahead, she glanced through the hovering smoke to the jugglers who gamboled before the dais, balancing wooden boards on their heads.

Before she could caution herself, her gaze slid to Linford. His dark, untamed hair gleamed as he turned to speak to Darwell. Even from a distance, the sheriff exuded raw authority and a keen intellect that warned he was a man who would not appreciate deception, especially within the walls of his keep.

She must warn Henry. Quickly.

An idea skittered into her mind.

She hiked up her skirt with both hands and hurried to catch up with Winton. Her bare foot caught on a patch of rough wood. Sudden, sharp pain pierced her heel. "Mercy!"

Winton halted and looked at her. "What ails you?"

She bit her lip against the discomfort. Her plan did not include getting a sliver, but she could use the injury to her advantage. Raising her voice to carry above the hall's commotion, she called, " 'Tis my foot. A sliver, I vow."

*Oh, Henry! Please hear the sound of my voice. If you are still in the solar, hide. Now!*

With a whimper, she raised her foot. If she could convince Winton she needed help to walk, she could delay reaching the solar by a few precious moments.

Winton's face pinched into an irritated scowl. "Come. We can tend your wound in the solar." Turning his back to her, he strode into the passage.

She whispered a curse. The steward was not to be deterred. Well, neither was she. As she limped after him, she fumbled with her bracelet's clasp. "How far is his lordship's chamber?"

Winton pointed to broad oak doors to his right. In the light cast by blazing reed torches, she saw two armed guards. How had Henry managed to slip past the sentries? What if he had not succeeded? What if —

She dismissed her anxious thoughts. A man as clever as Henry would have found a way. A distraction. A ruse. However, if he tried to run from the chamber now, he would be challenged, captured, or even killed.

She had one last chance to warn him.

"*This* is the solar?" She flicked her hand, repeating Winton's gesture. The bracelet flew through the air and smacked against one of the wooden panels, then landed on the floor with a musical clunk. She feigned utter surprise. "The goldsmith told me he fixed the clasp. I will have words with him."

A sigh rushed between Winton's thinned lips. He rolled his eyes, stooped, and picked up the ornament.

*Hide, Henry. Hide! Do not try to run.*

The steward held the tinkling bracelet out to her. "Thank you," she murmured. With a relieved smile, she noted the jewel was undamaged by the fall. As she fastened it around her wrist, Winton depressed the door's wrought iron handles, pushed open the panels, then motioned her inside.

As though a magical box had sprung open, an exotic scent wafted out of the solar to greet her. A reminder that she entered Linford's lair. A reminder of danger, forbidden temptations, and desire. A shiver tingled down her spine.

As she stepped into the shadowed solar, illuminated only by the hearth's orange-yellow blaze, her breath caught in her throat. Glancing about, she braced herself for Henry's bolt for the door. For Winton's cry of alarm. For the rasp of the guards' broadswords and their bellows to "halt." For the imminent confrontation, in which she must aid Henry and somehow keep the missive from Linford's men.

Her gaze fell to a pair of strangely decorated gold candlesticks on the nearby wall shelf. She edged toward them. A candlestick was a wretched substitute for a weapon, but it must do.

Sweeping through the doorway with a flaming reed, Winton began lighting the wall torches. The room's shadows surrendered to a warm glow. Every nerve in Rexana's body hummed. The sapphire ring pressed against her skin as her hands closed around the candlestick's cool gold.

Few places remained for Henry to hide. Did he stand behind the carved wooden screen to the left of the hearth? Was he crouched on the opposite side of the bed?

As Winton skirted the enormous bed, strewn with pillows and an animal skin she did not recognize, she hardly dared to breathe. She watched, the chased metal slick beneath her fingers, as he knelt, tossed several more logs into the fire, then rose and lit the remaining torches. Without incident.

Relief filtered through her. Either Henry remained well hidden, or he had found a way out of the solar.

Easing her rigid grip on the candlesticks, she sighed.

Winton crossed to her. "You will wait here for Sheriff Linford. I will send a maidservant to treat your foot."

"Nay," Rexana said hastily. "I can tend the splinter."

"Very well." The steward's voice turned stern, as though he addressed a truant child. "You are not to touch any of his lordship's possessions. Including the candlesticks."

Rexana managed an insolent shrug. "I am only looking at the odd decoration." With her fingertip, she finished tracing a curved symbol, then lowered her hands.

Winton's visage softened only a fraction. He tipped his head toward the nearby table. "While you wait, you may have wine. Or figs and oranges from the fruit bowl."

After shooting her a final, pointed glance, he strode through the doors. They clicked shut behind him.

Rexana exhaled on a whoosh. She was alone . . . unless Henry had squeezed himself into a corner and awaited a signal from her before he emerged.

Rubbing her arms with her hands, she whispered, "Henry?"

Silence, broken only by the fire crackling in the hearth.

"Henry, 'tis safe to come out. Are you here?"

No answer. She grinned. He was probably on his

way back to the hall to meet up with the musicians.

If Henry had the missive, she did not need to tempt the sheriff. She could regroup with the others and leave before Linford realized she had gone.

The sheriff's parting smile nipped through her mind. She fought a pang of disappointment, for she would not experience his skilled kiss, touch, or breath upon her belly, after all.

Rexana shook her head and dismissed the senseless emotion. She did not crave a barbarian's attentions. Not now. Not ever.

Setting her hands on her hips, she glanced about the chamber. She gnawed her bottom lip. Could she outwit the guards at the solar doors? Mayhap. Yet, Henry had managed to slip out by an alternate route. 'Twould be wiser for her to leave that way too.

Her gaze fell upon the tall, elaborately carved screen which blocked a corner of the chamber. What did the wooden panels conceal? A hidden door? She stepped forward. Pain lanced through her foot. Cursed splinter. No time to remove it. Linford would soon come to his chamber, and she wished to be long gone before he arrived.

As though attuned to her dishonorable thoughts, the fire popped and hissed. Only burning pitch, Rexana reminded herself with a nervous laugh, as the flames flared and cast accusing fingers of light across the screen.

She hobbled across the floorboards. Her feet sank into the brightly patterned carpet near the bed. Ignoring the silkiness, the urge to pause and wiggle her toes in deeper, she approached the screen. Gripping one edge, she peered around.

The fire crackled. Logs shifted and thumped onto the hearth grate, while the blaze roared with a fierce heat.

Behind the screen, a bathing tub, wet from use earlier in the day, rested on the floorboards. Beside it was a small table holding a bowl of water, folded linen cloths, a towel, and a round cake of soap. No hidden door, only an intriguing scent.

Rexana wiggled her nose. What a fragrance. Unique. Exotic. Irresistible. Ignoring the fire's loud snapping, as well as the warning buzz skittering through her mind, she picked up the cake, held it to her nose, and inhaled deeply through the veil. Her eyelids fluttered closed.

"Mmm." Lemon, cinnamon —

"Is it to your liking, love?"

With a startled squeak, Rexana dropped the soap. It bounced off the edge of the tub, banged the opposite side, then fell to the bottom with a thud. Hands pressed over her heart, she whirled around. Linford stood beside the screen. Close enough for her to recognize his spicy musk. He had used the soap when he bathed.

Vivid images flooded her imagination. Him sprawled in the tub, rubbing the soap between his palms. Lathering the cake into a frothy mass. Rubbing it, slowly, inch by wanton inch, over his broad, damp, naked chest.

She stifled another appreciative "Mmm." Oh, mercy.

Their gazes met. He raised one eyebrow in silent challenge, as though awaiting an explanation.

"Milord." She scarcely heard her voice over her hammering pulse. "I did not expect you so soon."

"So I see."

Her gaze shot past him to the closed doors. Too late, she recalled his cat-like stealth which she had witnessed in the hall. The noisy fire had disguised his entry.

Yet, she had only herself to blame for her curiosity.

She looked back at the tub. Laughing, she pointed to the soap which had slid far out of reach. "I hope you do not mind. I have never smelled that particular blend of scents." Her voice quavered and she groaned inwardly. How effortlessly he rattled years of carefully tutored poise. She had not trembled this much when her father had presented her to King Richard.

As though noticing her discomfort, a smile tilted Linford's mouth. "I bought that kind at a bazaar in Cyprus. Worth every bit of coin. English soap is simply not the same."

Rexana swallowed. His enticing male scent, his

closeness, and the assessing glint in his eyes sent chills rippling over her skin. Stifling a swell of worry, she focused her thoughts upon acting her role. She must not foolishly betray herself or endanger the others, or undermine her own plans for escape.

She must tempt. Seduce. Distract.

Linford's gaze sharpened slightly. Her skin prickled with goose bumps. Though he did not touch her, she felt his gaze traveling over her face like a physical caress.

"Why do you look at me so?" he asked.

Forcing sultry warmth into her voice, she said, "Whatever do you mean, milord?"

He laughed softly, but his tone held a hint of derision. "As though I will throw you upon the bed and ravish you like a hot-blooded savage. I promise I will treat you with civility."

"I do not doubt your skills." By the saints, she hoped she sounded appropriately intrigued.

His teeth flashed white, a brazen promise. "Good. Yet, unfortunately, I came to tell you our pleasure must be delayed until later this eve. I have urgent matters to attend first."

"Urgent matters?" Rexana sensed steel behind his words. Had he captured Henry? Did he know of the plan to steal the missive? Oh, God, she must know.

She smoothed her veil and schooled uncertainty from her tone. "What could possibly be more important than pleasure?"

"Traitors."

"Here? In Warringham?" She cleared the catch from her voice. "Who would attempt treason with you as High Sheriff?"

"Indeed." With a faint smile, he closed the distance between them. His gaze held hers with fierce intensity. Her stomach did an unsettling swoop, like a swallow plummeting to snatch a fat worm. Did he suspect her?

He moved so close, his breath warmed her brow. She took a step back. Bumped against the rough stone wall. The splinter bit deeper into her foot, and she winced, even as she forced a giggle. "Surely you do not believe —"

"— that I frighten you? I know I do. You will not fear me once we have coupled. Of that, I am certain." He flattened one hand on the wall beside her head. His expression turned stark with sensual hunger, and he kissed her temple. "I will return to you as soon as I can. I vow upon my honor, I would rather stay here with you than question the traitors, but I cannot ignore my duties to the king." His voice softened, became a warm tingle against her cheek. "Do you understand, little dancer? Until the moment I return, I will be thinking of you, your beauty, and all the secrets we will share."

His words became a throaty murmur, a sound like

a cat's purr. Unable to resist, she looked up into his eyes. This close, they were a decadent brown shade, the color of a mélange of costly spices. Cinnamon. Cumin. Coriander. His lashes dropped on a blink. In that gesture, he promised her a multitude of sinful pleasures. Her skin prickled with delight.

Nay! She should not be tempted by what he offered.

Henry and the others could be in danger.

Linford's fingers skimmed up her forearm in a feather-light caress. Skilled. Sure. A lover's touch. Her flesh throbbed with the contact, even as sudden heat swirled down to her belly. Her breath puffed against the veil.

Disquiet and yearning pulled at her heart, even as his fingers glided up past her elbow. How could one touch elicit such a multitude of sensations? As she willed the muzzy haze from her mind, his fingers snagged the veil's edge. Tugged.

He intended to see her face!

She swatted aside his hand and whirled away, her skirt swirling about her legs. Forcing a petulant tone, she said, "You should not tease me when you cannot stay. Shame, milord."

Chuckling, he started toward her. "Little dancer—"

Her frantic gaze fell to the wine goblets. "A drink, before you leave?" She limped to the trestle table and picked up the jug. Wine splashed over the goblet's rim.

Spattered on the table. Dripped onto the floor with a steady *pat, pat*. Under her breath, she cursed her trembling hands.

Hearing him stride up behind her, she turned and pressed the goblet into his palm. He raised the vessel to his lips.

"To your pleasure," she said in a bright tone.

His lazy smile returned. "To *our* pleasure, love." He took a sip, then frowned. "Why do you not drink?"

Her fingers fluttered to the veil. "I am not thirsty." As she shifted her weight to ease pressure on the splinter, pain shot through her sole. She smothered a gasp. "Later, when you return, we can drink tog—"

His goblet clanged down beside her. He crowded her against the table. The hard edge pressed against the back of her thighs. As his masculine smell enveloped her, and his legs bumped against hers, she wilted to half sitting on the table's edge. She barely resisted bolting for the door.

"You find fault with the wine?" Her fingers clutched the table's edge so hard, she vowed the wood would snap.

"The wine is delicious. I must keep a clear head for the interrogation." He smiled. "Now, before I go . . ."

His hands landed upon her hips. A firm, deliberate touch. His fingers splayed upon her skirt. Then, with agonizing slowness, they slid down the curve of her hips, bare legs, and calves. A thorough, appreciative touch, as though he relished the feel of silk and flesh. A silent, answering cry of pleasure warbled inside her.

He groaned, dropping to his knees before her. She stared down at his unruly hair, the crown of his head scarce a hand's reach away from her.

His fingers brushed her skirt's hem.

She drew a sharp breath. Was he fulfilling some kind of eastern mating ritual? "W - What are you doing?"

He touched her right ankle. "This one, is it not?"

With effort, she forced herself to exhale. "Pardon?"

"You limp. This foot hurts you. Aye?"

She nodded. With gentle pressure, he tilted her grubby foot to inspect it, and she squirmed with embarrassment. " 'Tis naught. Only a splinter."

"It causes you pain. I would be barbaric, indeed, to leave you in discomfort."

She ceased struggling. Odd tenderness blossomed within her. As his face furrowed in concentration and his fingers skimmed between her toes and over her sole, the ache grew.

In the past, young lords had courted her, but she had never permitted them to touch her. Above all, Garmonn. He had begged for her kisses, crudely demanded them once when he had walked with her in Ickleton's garden, but she had refused. No man kissed or touched a lady, except her wedded husband. Now, with Linford's deft hands probing her skin and her flesh shimmering with strange sensations, she appreciated the wisdom of her parents' strict tutelage.

His light touch tickled. She squirmed.

He chuckled, then moved to the heel of her foot. "Ah," he said, "There."

"Is it . . . large?"

"Enormous." When she groaned, he added, "Half a tree."

Rexana laughed. She could not resist.

He grinned. With his thumb and forefinger, he plucked at her sole. A quick pinch. Then, arching an eyebrow in triumph, he held up the splinter.

"Thank you. It feels much better."

Smiling, he tossed the bit of wood aside. With utmost care, he placed her foot on the floor and then rose, smoothing the creases from his tunic. She stared at his tanned fingers, so strong, capable and careful. Her stomach did a queer turn. Was he truly the unprincipled barbarian the gossips claimed him to be? Had they misjudged him?

He caught her staring. His smile changed and, from one heartbeat to the next, sharpened with determination and desire. "I regret I must leave now." Lowering his face to hers, he murmured, "But first, I will have a kiss."

She froze, numbed by a rush of alarm. "Kiss?"

"Kiss. Remove the veil, love."

# chapter three

As THE DANCER SHRANK FROM HIM, Fane fought a frustrated growl. By the barest thread of restraint, he resisted the urge to wrench the slip of fabric from her face. Why did she look at him as though he asked her to commit a forbidden act?

Moments ago, he had sensed her anxiety. He had been patient, leashed his lust, and done his best to soothe her fears. For a brief while, he had succeeded. When he had teased her about the splinter, her eyes had sparkled. Yet, so quickly, the mirth had evaporated and been replaced with distrust.

Uncurling his clenched fingers, he reached out to smooth a hand up her slender arm. A slow caress, without threat. A whisper of touch, as one would handle a violet's delicate, fragrant bloom. She shivered, and he swallowed a surge of annoyance. Did his chivalry mean naught?

As though sensing his impatience, she raised her darkened eyelashes. She looked at him with a hint of coy challenge. "Why must you see my face now? Why spoil the anticipation? When you return, we will explore each other's secrets. We will have all night, and many more nights, if you wish."

Her voice sounded unsteady. As though, despite her provocative words, she had little knowledge of sensual pleasure. Did she pretend to be an innocent? A shy virgin who had yet to experience the pleasures between a man and woman?

Clever little actress. How she toyed with him.

He could not wait to taste her. "One kiss," he said. Inhaling deeply of her luscious scent, he reached for the veil.

"Cease!" She twisted against the table, catching his wrists. Her palms were damp, the tinkling bells cold against the backs of his fingers. Disquiet settled in his gut like a dry, sun-scorched stone. Did she find him repulsive? Nay. When she had laughed and relaxed her guard, he had caught a glimmer of interest in her eyes.

Her gaze was no longer flirtatious but glittering with warning. Her fingertips pressed into his skin with steady pressure. Saucy wench. She dared to tell him what to do? Only now, when he lowered his arms, did she release her grip. Only now did she avert her gaze and show him the respect his position as High Sheriff and noble lord demanded.

He stared down at the sweep of her lashes, noted the stiff line of her body. Suspicion gnawed at his thoughts. There was a reason for her reticence. One he must pursue. "Why can I not see your face? What do you not wish me to discover?"

Her bosom rose and fell on a ragged breath. So, his suspicions were correct. He would know this secret before he left to see the prisoners in the dungeon. He must know, or the nagging mystery would devour his concentration.

"Why do you deny me?" As he wiped brown powder from his fingers, a cosmetic she had used to darken her skin, a thought leapt to his mind. "Is your skin flawed? Do you fear I will reject you because of imperfection?"

"Nay." Her hushed reply quivered in the air between them.

"Then, why?" he demanded. "Tell me now, love—"

A knock pounded on the door.

She started. The bells at her wrists and feet chimed, a burst of sound that shattered the tension between them like a boulder crashing through stained glass. In a graceful shift of limbs, a waft of fragrance, she slipped past him, heading toward the hearth.

Fane cursed.

The knock sounded again. "Milord," a man called.

Hesitating not far from the crackling fire, she pressed a hand to her breast. Did she try to still the wild beat of her heart? Did it pulse with even the barest fraction of the urgency that roared in his veins and fed his rock hard loins? Ah, God. 'Twas madness, to crave a woman so intensely.

Especially when he had important duties.

Resisting the overwhelming urge to chase her, Fane sighed and tore his fingers through his hair. For now, God help him, his need must wait. "Enter," he bellowed.

The door opened. A man-at-arms, one of the guards who had captured the rebels earlier, marched into the solar and shoved the door shut. A purpling bruise marked his right cheek. Fane frowned. He had not noticed the injury earlier in the hall.

The man halted abruptly. His face paled before he dropped to a bow. "I apologize for disturbing you, milord. One of the traitors is being difficult. He demanded to see you. He says no lord of his status should be treated in such a foul manner."

A bitter laugh burst from Fane. "What insolence. Did you tell him he must wait his turn for an interrogation, like all the other conspirators?"

The guard's expression turned grim. "He refused to heed me. He ran for the stairwell, yelling your name. Took three men to subdue him enough to get him inside a cell and chained." Rubbing his jaw, the guard added, "Would have been easier to hit him back, but you ordered us not to use unnecessary force."

"So I did." Fane looked at the dancer. She stared into the fire as though she pondered a difficult dilemma. Light danced over her figure, and his gaze skimmed down to her bottom's curve beneath the clinging costume. Hunger and disappointment flooded through him. His duties might keep them apart longer than he anticipated. How unfortunate.

Scooping up his wine goblet, he took a final sip. The spicy wine, simultaneously sharp and sweet, drenched his tongue. She would taste as exquisite when, at last, he kissed her.

Fane set down his goblet and turned to the guard. "This traitor," he said, starting for the door. "What is his name?"

"He is the late earl's son. Rudd Villeaux."

A cry broke from Rexana before she could smother it. She had feared for Henry and the musicians. But her brother, imprisoned in Tangston's dungeon? Arrested as a traitor?

Horror and disbelief tightened her stomach into a painful knot. Gasping, she clutched the wall. How could fate be so cruel? Rudd would never turn against the crown. He was not that foolish. Young and impulsive, aye, but still loyal.

"Love?"

Linford's voice sliced into her thoughts. *Beware, Rexana. Beware!* Dragging together the strength to respond, she straightened and offered an apologetic wave. "I did not mean to interrupt. I stepped on my sore heel."

His eyes narrowed. "Ah."

She turned back to face the hearth. Did he not believe her? Aware of his intent gaze, she softened her body's sway, pressing one hand against the wall and lazily resting the other on her hip. She wiggled her injured foot as though easing discomfort.

Linford resumed speaking with the guard. Thank the saints!

The fire blazed with fierce heat, yet Rexana's blood ran as cold as a frozen pond. She prayed Henry had found the missive. She must burn it as soon as she returned to Ickleton, before Rudd's life was destroyed by this horrible misunderstanding.

As she partly listened to the men's conversation, wispy smoke drifted up from the flames. Tears stung her eyes. Unable to resist, she lifted her hand from her hip, parted her bodice's fringe, and touched the arrow brooch.

Earlier that day, Rudd had told her he could not attend Linford's feast, despite making prior arrangements to go, because of a matter in a nearby village that would delay his return until late eve. Part of her had been glad, for he would not be able to stop her leaving for Tangston or know of her dance. Part of her had worried that he missed such an important event, especially the opportunity to meet the sheriff. Yet, with all her tasks to complete around the keep before she left, along with the additional ones Rudd had delegated to her, she had not paused to question his commitment. She should have.

The rough wall dug into her palm. What had he done to cause his arrest? Had he accepted another reckless dare from Garmonn? The knot in her belly twisted. She would have to smother her pride and plead forgiveness for Rudd's misdeeds, as she had only last month when he had taunted then set loose a neighboring lord's prized bull. The beast had caused untold damage before being recaptured.

This time, she would have to face Linford, not a cantankerous old lord with poor hearing. She would have to prove beyond doubt that Rudd did not conspire against the crown. That someone else had penned his signature on the missive. That he deserved his freedom.

She brushed her fingers over the brooch's hammered gold one last time. She shoved away from the wall, wiping her eyes before kohl and tears ran black lines down her veil. Whatever she must do to save her brother, she would do it. Rudd was all she had left. She would not lose him.

A touch on her shoulder snapped her from her thoughts. A familiar, spicy musk blended with the tang of burning oak. Linford stood behind her. He had moved silently, like a shadow.

"What ails you, little dancer? 'Tis more than a tender foot." With firm hands, he turned her around and stared down into her face.

Rexana urged herself to relax. Her right arm settled over her belly in a futile attempt to curb her queasiness. "You are wise, milord. My foot's pain is naught compared to my troubled thoughts. I could not help but overhear. I do not like word of treason, especially in this peaceful county."

He nodded gravely. His gaze dropped to the fringe covering her brooch. She prayed the ornament stayed hidden from view.

"I, too, despise treachery," he said.

Behind the veil, she sucked her lip between her teeth. *I deceive you*, a voice within her cried, *but I have good reason. My brother is not a traitor. He should not be imprisoned in your dungeon.*

A questioning smile touched Linford's mouth. "You cried out with such . . . passion. Do you know Villeaux?"

Denial flew to her lips, but her frayed nerves hummed with warning. She would only further pique Linford's suspicions if she tried to speak false. "I am an . . . acquaintance of his."

Linford's eyebrow arched in cool disbelief. Before she guessed his intentions, he reached out. Flicked aside the fringe. Exposed the little arrow bound with ribbon. "Acquaintance?" he demanded. "Or lover?"

Rexana's breath wedged in her throat. "Not lover," she managed to say. As he tilted the ornament to examine it, his fingers grazed her bare skin. Her body trembled.

"Did he give you this brooch?"

Her pulse thundered at a dangerous pace. She forced a shrug. "He gave me the trinket, aye, but he is not my lover."

"Why, then, did he gift you with this? 'Tis a favor? A token of his passionate intent?"

The words grated between Linford teeth. A thrill rippled through her. Saints above, was he jealous? Her tutors had never instructed her how to deal with a jealous suitor. Nor had the mummer advised her on such a predicament. Yet, somehow, she must ease his volatile emotions.

" 'Tis a token of his friendship," she soothed. "Naught more."

To her dismay, the suspicion in the sheriff's gaze did not ease, but intensified. She must be more persuasive. Bolder. She ignored a prickle of fear and caught his fingers touching the brooch. Covered his big, rough hand with hers. His dark lashes lowered a fraction, as though he acknowledged her caress.

"Milord, I have never danced for Lord Villeaux as I danced for you. Nor do I wish to."

Heat seeped from his hand into hers. Sensation flooded through her fingers and swept up her arm. A hot, bittersweet curl of desire. Potent. Undeniable. *Wanton.*

She should never have dared to touch him.

Before she could pull away, Linford half sighed, half growled. "Your words please me. I have no wish to compete with Villeaux for your heart."

"He and I could never be lovers. After all, he is a nobleman. I am a common peasant."

A crooked smile curved Linford's mouth. "You are far from common, love. Villeaux believes this as well, or he would not have given you gold."

Dread hummed through her in a single, shattering scream. Did the sheriff toy with her? Had he guessed her identity? Her hand flew to her throat. She tried to giggle, to dismiss his statement, but sounds and words refused to warm her lips.

" 'Twould please me to have a closer look at your brooch. The unique design intrigues me." Linford's fingers skimmed up and down her arm, an insistent touch. "Remove it, love."

Protest burned within her. Her eyes stung. Blinking away fresh tears, she said, "I cannot part with my brooch."

His smile thinned. "Fear not. I shall return it to you this eve. You have my word."

Her hand dropped from her throat to fist into her

skirt. Numbness swept through her, chased by frustration. If she declined, would she further arouse his suspicions about the relationship between her and Rudd?

She scrambled to hone her thoughts. What would a peasant dancer do? One whose livelihood depended upon the generosity of the man standing before her. Watching. Waiting.

She was not in any position to refuse.

Fighting bitter regret, Rexana reached up and unfastened the brooch's clasp. She dropped the ornament into his palm. The little arrow glinted, a flash of light, before his bronzed fingers closed over it.

Across the chamber, the man-at-arms cleared his throat.

Fane dropped a light kiss on her cheek. "I must leave you now, but I will return as soon as I am able."

*The brooch!* "Milord —"

"I will take good care of your jewel, I promise. Think of me, as I shall think of you," he whispered. "I look forward to the pleasures to come."

He bowed to her in farewell, then turned and crossed to the waiting man-at-arms. The door closed behind them.

Rexana crossed her arms over her bodice. Already she missed the brooch's delicate weight. What did Linford intend to do with it? Show it to Rudd during the interrogation? Demand to know why he gave it to her, as well as his feelings for her?

The solar's silence pressed down upon her. She paced the floorboards. Fie! Rudd would recognize the brooch. He did not know of her dance this eve or the mission to save his honor, so he had no reason to deny knowledge of the brooch. What might Linford do, when he learned the truth? To her? To Rudd?

She pivoted sharply. She could do naught shut away in Linford's chamber. She must think of a way to deceive the solar's guards and escape. Now.

As Rexana started back across the chamber, she caught metal shining on the table. The wine jug.

She hurried to the table, scooped up the heavy vessel, then tossed the remaining wine into the fire. The blaze hissed and belched a cloud of smoke. A shame to waste good drink, but that could not be helped.

As she adjusted her grip on the curved handle, the sapphire ring weighed upon her knuckle. Anger stirred. Why should she not keep the ring, in payment for Linford confiscating her brooch? With a furious sigh, she slipped it off and tossed it onto the animal skin. She had no desire to keep Linford's gift, or to be in any way indebted to him.

After reviewing her plan one last time, she crossed the chamber to yank open the door. Rowdy cheers and music echoed in from the corridor outside. A boon, that the revelry in the hall continued. She had hoped as much.

The nearest guard, a stout man with greasy brown

hair, frowned. "What do ye want, wench?"

Rexana bit back an indignant retort. She must remain in character, at least for a while longer. "Sheriff Linford finished the wine before he left." With a sensuous turn of her wrist, she held the vessel out for the man's inspection. " 'Twould be discourteous of me not to get more."

The guard grunted. "I will summon a kitchen maid."

A brazen laugh rumbled in Rexana's throat as she flattened one hand against the door's embrasure. Leaning forward to display more cleavage, she tilted her head toward the merriment. "All the servants are tending the lord's guests. They are far too busy to see to this little errand. Direct me to the kitchens, good man, and I will fetch the wine myself." Brushing a finger down her veil, she winked at him. "No one will ever know."

The guard licked his lips and glanced at his fellow sentry, who snapped a reprimand. The brown-haired man's grin vanished. "Ye cannot leave. Our strict orders —"

She clucked her tongue. "His lordship will have great thirst when he returns from his important duties. Imagine his fury, when I tell him you prevented me from fetching more wine."

The two guards exchanged glances.

"Are you afraid I will run away?" she cooed. "Why would I wish to? His lordship has offered me riches if I please him this eve, and I intend to claim them all."

Shaking his greasy hair, the guard said, "Come. I will go with you." He pointed down the passage. "That way."

Clutching the jug, she walked down the shadowed corridor. The guard clomped beside her. His unwashed body smelled as strong as the acrid smoke spewing from burning torches along the walls. Rexana gritted her teeth. She must elude this armed oaf at the earliest opportunity. How?

She squinted through the smoke fogging the passage. Ahead, brightly colored tapestries which depicted crusading knights winning a bloody battle against gruesome demons decorated one wall. With a shiver, she forced herself to block out the images and quickened her pace.

"Milady."

The whisper came from the tapestry portraying a hideous, fanged, three-headed beast run through by a crusader's sword. A shriek bubbled in her throat. Did her mind play tricks on her?

"Zounds! Milady, do not scream."

The guard froze. His face crumpled into a wary scowl. "Did you speak?"

Moistening her dry lips Rexana halted. "Nay, good man. Mayhap 'twas a . . . monster?"

The tapestry shifted, as though the beast writhed in its dying moments. The guard blanched. He reached for his sword. Before he unsheathed the weapon, Henry lunged out from behind the hanging and smashed his fist into the guard's jaw. With a grunt, the guard staggered back, struggling to draw his weapon.

Henry kicked him in the shin. The guard bent double. Lunged at Henry. Plowed him back into the tapestry. A cloud of dust poofed into the air around them.

Rexana's fingers tightened on the jug. Ignoring the panic quickening her breaths, she swung her arm high. Brought the jug arcing down. Smacked it into the guard's head with a metallic *clonk*. The guard slumped to the floor.

"Well done, milady." Henry straightened, shoved aside the sleeve of his gray woolen cloak, and scrubbed his hand over his reddened nose. "Pah! Wretched dust."

Rexana hurried over and clasped his free hand. At the familiar feel of his rough, wrinkled skin, reassurance flowed through her. "I am glad to see you."

His eyes crinkled with a smile. "And I you." His gaze softened with puzzlement. In hushed tones, he asked, "Why are you not dancing in the hall? Why do you carry a wine jug?"

A blush heated her cheeks. "I will explain later. You had no trouble slipping past the sentries? You have the missive?"

Henry's smile vanished. "Milady, I do not."

The tapestry's colors blurred before Rexana's eyes.

The breath rushed out of her lungs and she fought to keep her voice lowered. "Oh, God!"

Thrusting up his hands, he said, "I could not find a way past the guards, or another entry into the solar. Nor could I subdue two armed men on my own without causing a commotion." He shook his head. "When they questioned me, I pretended to be drunk. I asked directions to the garderobe. I hid behind these tapestries, waited for one of the guards to need a piss, but —"

"Henry, Linford has arrested Rudd for treason."

The old warrior's jaw dropped. "What?"

"Rudd is imprisoned in Tangston's dungeon. Linford is interrogating him now. The sheriff took my brooch, so I fear Rudd will tell —" Linking her fingers through Henry's, Rexana stepped over the guard's limp body. She tugged Henry back down the passage, heedless of his muffled protest. "We must return to the solar and find the missive. Then, find a way to free Rudd."

Henry pulled her to a halt. "Milady, nay."

She spun to face him, her skirt wafting to stillness about her legs. As she planted her hands on her hips, the jug thumped against her hip, releasing the tang of residual wine. "I do not fear Linford," she said, grateful for a steady voice.

"Mayhap not," — Henry tapped his broad chest — "but I do. I worry for more than my cracked old bones. You must not risk your own capture, or your brother's life, by attempting to free him when the dungeons are crawling with armed guards. Think, milady. What will Linford do when he discovers who you are?"

Frustration swelled inside her. "Henry —"

His tone roughened. "I promised your parents as they lay dying that I would watch over you, protect you. Please. The dangers this eve are too great."

As she held Henry's beseeching gaze, a chill crawled down her spine. The draft, gusting over the floor, brushed over her toes and ankles like thin bone fingers. Was the air as cold in Tangston's dungeon?

"I cannot bear to be without Rudd," she whispered.

Henry patted her shoulder. "You must. For now. If luck is with us, we can meet up with the musicians and ride with them to Ickleton. 'Twill be safest to travel the road together."

A nearby torch spat. Over the smoky crackle, she caught the unmistakable tromp of footsteps.

Had the other guard by the solar heard the scuffle?

Had he decided to investigate?

She glanced at Henry. "Run."

"Wait." Reaching into his cloak's folds, Henry withdrew the leather slippers she had bought on a visit to market with Rudd. Blinking back tears, she set the jug on the floor near the fallen guard and yanked on the shoes.

As she straightened, Henry tossed his long cloak around her shoulders, then drew the hood over her face. The garment smelled of smoke and horses.

The footfalls grew louder.

Henry pulled her to a lope. "Keep your head down," he said over her chiming bells. "I will find the bailey."

"How?" As she ran, she fumbled to unclasp the noisy bracelets. Stuffing the first into the mantle's pocket, she said, "Do you know the way?"

Henry shot her a worried glance. "While I look, you pray."

# chapter four

His hands balled into fists, Fane stepped into the dank stairwell that led down to Tangston's dungeon. In the shadows ahead, the man-at-arms massaged his bruised cheek, then disappeared around a curve in the passage.

Fane shrugged the tightness from between his shoulders. After escaping General Gazir's hellish eastern prison, he had hoped never to set foot in a dungeon again. A foolish thought for a High Sheriff. 'Twas a necessary part of his duty.

His boots clipped on the uneven stone stairs. The darkness thickened. Memories scuttled out of his mind's farthest reaches, the place that hurt a thousand times worse than a scorpion's poisoned sting. A tremor raked his body. Again, he felt chains biting into his wrists. A whip lashing his back. Knives, hooks, and other wicked instruments of torture, too horrible to envision, cutting his flesh. His stomach churned.

Rough voices floated up from the dungeon and wove into his thoughts. He forced the memories aside. The past would forever haunt him, had irrevocably scarred him, but did not alter his immediate obligations to the crown. Leila had respected his loyalty to his English king, which had burned in Fane's soul and sustained him through unspeakable torture. She had told him so. He would not fail Leila's memory. Or himself.

A smile touched Fane's mouth. The sooner he questioned the traitors, the sooner he returned to the dancer that fate had brought to his hall. A delicious thought.

The brooch shifted in his grasp. Its warm surface touched his palm. A peculiar design, an arrow wrapped with a ribbon. What was its significance? Why had she looked so stricken when he asked her to remove it? What was her true relationship to Villeaux?

She had denied a love affair. Fane's instincts told him that was true. Yet, he must understand the link between her and Villeaux, even if seduction was required to get the information.

An even more delicious thought.

He would enjoy unveiling the woman hidden behind the glittering façade. As he had vividly imagined in the hall, he would slowly disrobe her, from veil to tinkling ankle bracelets. Afterward, he would explore her slender body. Taste her. Prove to her that he understood the wild cry of her dance.

Together, they would forge unforgettable, sensual memories.

He hurried down the last stairs. His boots hit dirt. The stairwell opened into a vast chamber, patrolled by men-at-arms. The air smelled of damp stone and mold. Brushing aside a lingering memory, Fane strode into the cavernous room and assessed the three lords who sat in sullen silence within one of the cells. As he turned away, Kester, the stocky, seasoned captain of the guard, bowed his graying head, then offered a wax tablet scratched with notes.

"We have their names, milord, as you ordered. None of the prisoners will discuss the tavern meeting."

After skimming the information on the tablet, Fane handed it back. "Where is Villeaux?"

Kester pointed across the dungeon to the farthest cell.

As though sensing a confrontation, the men in the other cell muttered amongst themselves. A guard grunted and banged on the bars. As Fane strode across the chamber, silence fell, broken only by the sputter of nearby torches.

He halted outside the cell and stared at the lad fettered to the wall. The guards had removed his fine leather boots, which lay in a heap near the bars, and chained his ankles and wrists. They had put Villeaux by himself to prevent him from causing further mischief. Or so they hoped.

A futile wish, Fane mused, as his eyes became accustomed to the dim lighting. He studied the lad's taut features. This boy was trouble.

Fane's mouth twisted into a faint smile. He narrowed his gaze in deliberate challenge. To his surprise, Villeaux did not attempt to speak, or plead his innocence, or bow his head, or sob, or shiver. His green eyes, remarkably like the dancer's, blazed with defiance.

Aye, this one was definitely trouble.

In the shadowed darkness, Villeaux looked no more than fifteen. His freckled face held a boyish innocence, yet his quick gaze proved him older than a boy. As Fane curled his fingers around a horizontal bar, Villeaux's manacled wrists, barely visible below his soiled tunic sleeves, jerked, and his hands fisted. His spine went rigid. Fane smothered a chuckle. So. The boy had plenty of pride to accompany his foolishness.

The cold metal chilled Fane's hands. He waited. He would not be the first to look away. Uncertainty crept into Villeaux's intelligent eyes before his face contorted into a scowl. Blowing matted brown hair from his brow, he took a step forward. Then another. Iron links dragged on the dirt floor. He reached his fetters' limits, and the chains snapped taut.

A memory shot into Fane's mind. Once, he had been a chained prisoner facing his Saracen captors from the other side of the bars. He shoved away the unsettling thought. He would not draw flawed parallels between his imprisonment and Villeaux's. He would not sympathize with a traitor.

The boy hissed through his teeth. "Are you Linford?"

"I am High Sheriff Linford," Fane said in a brusque voice. "You will address me with respect, Lord Villeaux."

The lad snorted in disgust. "Release me."

Annoyance pricked, yet Fane stifled the emotion. For now. "I cannot let you go. You were caught in a clandestine meeting conspiring with fellow traitors."

"I am no traitor."

"Is that so?" Reaching under his tunic's hem, Fane withdrew a thin, rolled parchment tucked into the belt of his hose. He unfurled the skin. Trapping opposite corners between his fingers, he held it against the bars. "Recognize this document? It lists men who have pledged to overthrow the crown. Here, near the bottom. Your signature."

Sweat glistened on Villeaux's forehead. Beneath a tangle of hair, his eyes turned cold. "How did you find —"

"I have my sources."

Villeaux's mouth tightened. "What do you want from me?"

Ah. The crux of the matter. "For a start, I expect

you to cooperate with the guards. I expect you to answer my questions to the full extent of your knowledge, and to provide the names of every other traitor participating in these plots against the crown."

"Then you will free me?"

"Then we will discuss your punishment."

The boy's eyes flared, as though he found the statement insulting. Then, tipping back his head, he laughed. The insolent sound grated down Fane's spine.

"I see naught amusing in your predicament."

Villeaux's lips eased into a mocking grin. "Do you know the full extent of my late father's influence, Sheriff? He belonged to King Richard's innermost circle of loyal friends and advisors. He personally knew the king's ministers —"

"Your father is dead. A most unfortunate loss."

Anguish clouded the lad's gaze. Jerking his head to one side, he stared at the mildewed wall.

"You are unwise to provoke me, and foolish to waste your young life." Drawing away from the bars, Fane returned the missive to his belt. Anger charged his words. "Do you wish to stand trial in the King's Courts? To be beheaded? Tell me what I wish to know, and I may plead for leniency."

"Burn in hell, bastard."

Fane laughed and smoothed the front of his tunic. "Very well. Do as you will, but I urge you to at least consider the consequences." Dropping his voice to a rasp, he added, "Not just for yourself."

Villeaux's head whipped around. "What do you mean?"

Moisture glinted in his eyes. Tears of humiliation? Regret? Mayhap he was not as immune to persuasion as Fane had first thought. 'Twould be a pity for one so bright and full of potential to be condemned to death.

Choosing his words with care, Fane said, "I am told you recently inherited a large estate. Many villeins and lords depend upon you for leadership. You are also responsible for the welfare of your unwed sister."

"Rexana," the lad said.

"Aye, the Lady Rexana." An image of Darwell's hand, fondling the plump orange, flitted through Fane's thoughts. Mayhap one day soon, he would meet the lovely lady for himself.

Villeaux's gaze sharpened. "If you dare hurt her —"

"I have no intentions of harming her," Fane said easily. "Yet, her fate depends on yours, does it not? If you die a traitor, you stain not only your honor, but hers. The crown will seize your holdings and grant them to another lord. What will happen to Rexana?"

The lad's mouth trembled. His gaze darted past Fane to the other conspirators' cell. "What do you care?"

Fane shrugged. "I have not even met her, yet I vow she is important to you. You would be wise to think of her, if you have not already done so, before you make a final decision on whether to cooperate."

The brooch tilted in Fane's curled hand. A reminder. The warm metal represented a promise. Before this meeting ended, he would have an answer to the question that chewed at him like an annoying camel.

His thoughts turned to the dancer awaiting his return, and desire stirred his blood. He fought to keep his voice controlled. "There is another woman, as well, you must consider." Fane shifted his hold on the brooch, caught the little arrow from pointed tip to feathered fletching, then raised it between his fingers. He held it to the bars.

In the shadowed, smoky light, Rudd's face paled. "Where did you —"

"A fetching wench, aye? Exquisite breasts. Long legs —"

"*Wench*?" Chains clanked, a violent sound. "How dare you speak so of her? God's teeth! Where is she?"

Triumph coiled through Fane. At last, he had found leverage with the boy. Though, he noted with dismay, Villeaux seemed to care more for the dancer than his own sister. "She awaits me in my private solar," Fane said, holding the lad's shocked gaze. "I look forward to seducing her."

Villeaux lunged to the end of his chains. His breathing turned ragged. Furious. Desperate. "Do not touch her, Linford, or I swear to God, I will kill you."

Fane laughed. Leaning one shoulder against the

cell's bars, he dismissed the threat with a flick of his wrist. "The dancer told me you gave her this bauble. What, exactly, was she to you? You see, I have claimed her for my own."

The lad's eyes narrowed to angry slits. "*Dancer?* Your mind is addled. That brooch belongs to my sister. I paid a goldsmith to design it, and gave it to her myself."

Warning buzzed at the back of Fane's mind like a noisy, blood-sucking horsefly. Stunned fury crashed through him, even as he bit out the word: "Sister."

The lad nodded. "Rexana."

Anger roared through Fane, hotter and fiercer than the lust in his veins. His fingers tightened around the brooch. The dancer's exotic mysteries vanished. Evaporated, like the thin smoke from a stick of burning incense.

*Cursed fool!* He had sensed many contradictions in her, yet he had ignored them. He had allowed lust to rule his head — a mistake that, months ago, would have cost him his life.

Villeaux's voice slashed into Fane's thoughts. "How did you get her brooch? What have you done with Rexana?"

A harsh laugh exploded from Fane. "Naught yet." He turned and stalked across the dungeon. The darkened chamber blurred in a haze of angry red.

"Linford!"

Fane ignored the lad's urgent cry, the guards' startled mutters, and the frigid draft that swept over him as he lunged up the stairwell. He thundered toward the solar.

Lady Rexana owed him an explanation.

She owed him far more than that.

"See, milady? I told you we would safely leave Tangston."

Huddled in a corner of the moving wagon, jostled from side to side, Rexana glanced at Henry through the foggy night air. She ignored a prick of disquiet. How foolish to doubt their success. Each grinding turn of the wagon's wheels took them further from Linford's keep. She smiled. "You did. Thank you, kind sir, for your escort as well as your gallantry."

Seated at the front of the wagon, beside the drummer who guided the horse, Henry grinned. "My pleasure, milady." His chest puffed out like a proud cockerel's. "I do not regret asking the kitchen maid the way to the bailey. She was besotted, therefore unlikely to remember a word of our chatter." He wagged his eyebrows. "She kissed most sweetly, as well."

The musicians laughed.

The drummer snorted. "I am glad ye were not tempted ta press yer sloppy charms on the guards at the gatehouse. They would not have let us pass so readily."

More laughter. Henry scowled. Rexana smothered a giggle behind her hand. She could hardly imagine a woman, let alone a grizzled warrior, puckering up to kiss either of the grim sentries who watched all who rode through Tangston's gates.

The breeze blew through trees along the roadside, a sound unlike the wind howling past Tangston's walls. With a shiver, she recalled the agonizing moments when the guards had ordered them to stop. As the wagon had creaked to a halt, her anxious mind whirled. Had Linford discovered her missing? Had he learned that she was Rudd's sister? Had he ordered her detained? She had drawn deeper into the folds of the scratchy cloak Henry had loaned her, tugging the hood over her face. After a few words from Henry, and a bawdy jest from the drummer, the guards had waved them over the drawbridge and onto the pitted road which wound its way toward Ickleton.

The horse settled into a steady *clop, clop*, while the men continued their banter about kissing. Rexana snuggled into the cushions and blankets provided for her comfort. The breeze, heavy with the scent of damp loam, fingered its way under the hood to brush her cheeks. A touch as light as Linford's.

Uncertainty clenched her belly like a fist.

Had they escaped the sheriff? He and his men

might be in pursuit. He might emerge from the night's inky shadows, quirk an eyebrow, and demand to know what made her believe she could ever deceive him.

She buried deeper into the blankets. If Linford questioned Rudd about the brooch, would he answer, or would he realize he must protect her identity? A tiny thread of hope wound its way through her. If he did not divulge her, and she found a way to free him within the next day or two, Linford might never know that his veiled dancer was, in truth, a wealthy, titled lady. A virgin who had never experienced a lover's kiss.

The memory of Linford's hungry stare flickered through her mind. The skin across her breasts tightened. Heated. Her lips tingled, as though the cool night conspired against her and mimicked his kiss. What would it have been like to kiss him? Would he have tasted deliciously exotic?

A night bird flapped overhead with an eerie shriek, startling her from her thoughts. She blushed. How shameful to ponder her desires, when Rudd was Linford's prisoner. She rubbed her lips together to squash the queer sensation. Despite her efforts to swallow it, a moan bubbled in her throat.

One of the musicians touched her arm. "Are ye warm enough, milady? Are ye comfortable? 'Twill be a long journey."

She forced a smile. "I am fine, thank you."

Struggling to ignore her unease, she stared into the

night. Fog wreathed the shadowed bushes and trees, and swirled around the wagon. By the dawn's light, the mist would disappear. As, too, must all evidence of her night as an exotic eastern dancer.

As soon as she reached Ickleton, she would give the mummer a bag of coins in thanks for the loan of the costume. She would also arrange for the woman to be far from Ickleton by daybreak.

Determination quickened Rexana's pulse. First thing on the morrow, she and Henry would begin a plan. She would see Rudd exonerated. And freed.

Hands on his hips, Fane looked around the empty solar. Emotion seethed within him — anger, frustration, cursed desire — but he leashed the urge to throw back his head and roar like a furious beast.

Nervous shuffles echoed in the open doorway behind him. Idiot guards. He had found one half way down the passage, staggering to his knees while rubbing a bump on his head. When sharply questioned, the guard babbled a tale about escorting the dancer to fetch wine, a man leaping out from behind a tapestry, and a blow to the head. When the guard roused, he found himself lying on the floor. The assailant and the dancer were gone.

Fane muttered a foul Arabic curse, a memento from

his Saracen captors. With the help of an accomplice — a trusted servant, no doubt — Lady Rexana had escaped. For now.

He swung around to address the guards. "You." He pointed to the taller man, whose face drained of color. "Go straight to the bailey. Tell the guards at the gatehouse what has occurred. The dancer and her companion are not to leave the keep."

The guard's head bobbed. "Aye, milord."

A menacing growl burned Fane's throat. He glared at the wounded guard, who swayed on his feet as though a strong draft would send him toppling to the floor. "You will inform Kester. I want this keep searched, chamber by chamber. If she is within these walls, I want her found. Bring her to me."

The guards bowed and turned away.

"Later, we will discuss your punishment for disobeying my orders."

Fane slammed the solar door. He sucked air into his lungs. Anger pulsed at his temple, stiffened his fingers until it seemed his bones would snap. When he found her . . .

As he strode toward the hearth, where he had last seen her, his gaze fell to the lion skin stretched over the bed. A blue object glinted on the tawny fur. Ignoring the bitterness burning in his belly, the repressed lust still heating his blood, Fane strode toward the pelt.

The sapphire ring. She had not kept it.

His hand shaking, he slid the heavy ring onto his finger. The sapphire glowed as though lit by a vibrant inner spirit. Lady Rexana's kohl-rimmed eyes had gleamed as brightly.

His jaw hardened. Why had she not robbed him of the jewel, as she had stolen his dreams of a night of sensual pleasure? Did she believe that by leaving the ring, one honorable decision in her ploy of deception, she might save herself from his wrath, or his right to demand an explanation from her own lips?

Fane's eyes squeezed shut. He still saw her beautiful, supple body kissed by firelight. Still felt her skin's warm softness against his palm. Her scent lingered in the air.

Footfalls sounded in the outer corridor. His eyelids flicked open. Did one of the guards return with her? Fane strode to the doorway.

As he wrenched the wooden panels open, Darwell staggered to a halt, his hand raised to knock. "Milord!"

Silently, Fane bellowed. He steeled his voice into firm politeness. "Lord Darwell."

Wheezing, Darwell braced one hand on the doorframe and wiped his brow. "I came to say good eve. My squires are in the bailey, readying my horse for the journey."

The urge to snarl and send Darwell scurrying back down the corridor burned hot in Fane's blood, but he smothered the rash impulse. Darwell's political influence extended to many noble courts. Very foolish, to strain an important and necessary alliance over a woman.

A woman Darwell knew well.

An idea sparked at the back of Fane's mind. The plan rapidly flared with potential.

He smiled. "Must you leave so soon?" Standing to one side, he gestured into the solar. "Would you care to come in? Mayhap for one last goblet of wine?"

Darwell beamed. "My squires will wait. I thank you, milord." Rubbing his pudgy hands together, he stepped into the chamber, his gaze bright with interest. As though in awe of Fane's collected wealth, he stopped and stared.

Fane closed the doors. Mulling his next words, he motioned Darwell toward the fire. "Did I tell you I have discovered the dancer's identity?"

Mopping his cheeks with his sleeve, Darwell giggled like an excited little boy. "Tell me. Who is the vixen?"

Fane's smile hardened. "Lady Rexana Villeaux."

Darwell gasped. "Lady —" He slapped his chest. "Tsk, Tsk. I should have guessed." Cupping his hand, he bobbed it up and down. "Oranges! I am a complete fool not to have recognized her earlier."

Darwell was not the only fool.

As the older lord rattled on about his lack of perception, rage blasted through Fane. His fist tightened around the precious jewel until the gold band bit into his palm. *Why* had she concocted such an elaborate ruse? Did she know of her brother's treachery? Did she support it? Had she aimed to distract Fane and his guards while Rudd attended the tavern meeting with the other conspirators?

A sour taste, as sickening as rotten dates, filled Fane's mouth. Through her highly provocative dance, had she intended to prove the High Sheriff of Warringham to be a barbaric misfit, ruled by lust instead of reason?

By God, he would have answers!

He would not allow Lady Rexana Villeaux to play him for a fool. If word of her deception became known throughout the county, his capabilities as High Sheriff would be in question. One woman — a traitor's sister — would not undermine his efforts to secure Warringham for the crown and to establish peace.

He forced his anger aside, focusing on his plan to snare the lady. He looked at Darwell, who now hummed an off-key tune while wiggling his hips in an appalling imitation of her dance.

Fane cleared his throat. "Milord."

Darwell straightened with a snap and pop of bones. He laughed sheepishly. "My apologies, Sheriff. I did not mean to . . . ah . . . become lost in my thoughts."

"Lord Darwell," Fane said, easing his painful grip on the ring. "You seem a man of integrity. I vow I can trust you?"

Darwell smoothed his skewed tunic. "Aye."

"Before I say more, I must have your solemn vow you will not reveal Lady Rexana's secret."

Darwell's grin wavered. "Secret?"

"That she performed here this eve."

"Ah." With a sly wink, the older lord said, "There is a reason for her disguise, and for dancing half nu — . . . For her enthralling performance." Darwell leaned sideways, as though the crackling flames might suddenly grow ears. "You can confide in me. I swear, I will not tell anyone."

Dragging his hand over his mouth, as though he pondered a matter of grave importance, Fane said, "The crown forbids me to reveal Lady Rexana's role. However, 'tis vital that no one" — his tone hardened — "I repeat, *no one*, learns she performed at tonight's feast."

Darwell's eyes bulged. "A crown secret? O - Of course I shall not speak of it."

"If you do," Fane said with quiet menace, "I must report your indiscretion to the king's ministers. Without question, this would not bode well for you or your sons." He paused for dramatic effect. " 'Twould destroy Garmonn's chances of a lucrative marriage."

Darwell's face whitened. "I swear, upon my honor. Lady Rexana's secret is safe with me."

"Good." Fane blew a sigh and smiled. "May this eve be the start of a long and valuable friendship. I will send for wine, so we may toast our agreement." As he headed toward the solar doors, he said: "While you are here, you must share with me all you know of Lady Villeaux."

Shaking his head in obvious bewilderment, Darwell wiped sweat from his upper lip. "Whatever you wish to know, Sheriff, I shall be glad to tell you."

# Chapter Five

SWINGING HER SHOES IN ONE HAND, Rexana walked through the shadowed glade. As birds twittered and flitted from tree to tree, she willed her weary mind to snap fully awake. Willed her anxious thoughts to clear. Willed her worry to evaporate like the morning mist rising from the deep, gray-green pool.

She dropped her shoes into the grass, then walked down to the water, drew her skirts up about her knees, and hunched down in the mud. As she stared at her reflection, she trailed a finger through the shallows. Her features blurred in a cloud of brown silt. An omen of the uncertain future?

A breeze stirred the pond's surface. She shivered. Her body ached from a fitful night's rest. Snatches of sleep were haunted by nightmares of a gleeful Darwell telling Linford that he had guessed her identity. Of Rudd, blurting out her name. Of the sheriff, his face taut with anger, as he confronted her.

She had awakened at every creak of her bed, every gust of wind past the chamber's shutters. Yet, Linford had not come thundering into Ickleton in the dead of night, bent on finding her. He had not arrived at the gates at dawn.

Mayhap Darwell had not guessed the truth, after all.

Mayhap Rudd remained defiantly silent.

She withdrew her fingers from the murky water. "Oh, Rudd," she whispered.

At first light, she had met with Henry and a few trusted men-at-arms, yet they had not found a way to win Rudd's freedom — apart from battering down Tangston's portcullis and whisking him from the dungeon. Her stomach churned, for lives would be lost in such a rash attempt. She had no desire for bloodshed or battle, most of all against a skilled crusader like Linford.

Moreover, the sheriff still had the missive. Naught prevented him from hunting down, arresting and imprisoning Rudd again.

If Linford ever discovered she had deceived him, he might arrest and imprison her, too.

She tightened her fingers into fists, burrowed them into the silk crushed under her breasts, and tipped her face into the breeze. She must not drain her strength by worrying about herself. How did Rudd fare? Did he wonder if she missed him? Did he have faith she would help him?

The breeze skimmed over her cheeks, tender as a caress. Gentle as Linford's touch. She fought to suppress the sensations his memory aroused: anxiety, curiosity, longing.

Aye, shameful longing.

Overhead, the tree boughs stirred. Whispered. She forced herself to listen. Breathed in the scents of wet earth, marsh plants, and crushed grass. Let the serenity of the pool flow through her soles into her. The ancient rhythms of this place understood. Her tears for her parents had dripped into the clear water. In return, her soul's burden had been lightened. Here, she had danced until she could face the next day. Here, she would think of a way to help Rudd.

Rising to her feet, she untied the ribbon binding her hair, then loosened her braid. She strode up the bank to the grass and, in the familiar ritual, stretched her arms up to the sun. Fingers spread wide, she turned like a dandelion spore drifting in the breeze. Swayed to and fro, like the grass' seed pods. Bowed like the violets quivering in the oaks' shade.

Grasses swished against her skirts. She stretched. Arched. Turned.

Her hair tangled about her throat. Her breathing

quickened. Her mind cleared to accept the glade's nurturing wisdom.

She spun, dipped, and whirled until her chest tightened with her gasped breaths.

Enlightenment eluded her.

Despair cried out inside her like a lost child. Pressing a hand against her ribs, she stumbled to the patch of violets. She knelt and, with shaking fingers, plucked the fragrant purple heads and stuffed them into the cloth purse slung at her hip. Later, she would press the essence from the blooms for scented water, a task to busy her mind and quell the frustration drowning her heart.

She would not lose hope. The answer would reveal itself. She must return to the keep, find Henry, and begin their planning anew. She must not rest until she had a solution.

Wiping her fingers on her bliaut's skirts, Rexana rose, then donned her shoes. Mud stained her gown's hem. A trivial concern, compared to Rudd's fate. With a last glance about the pool, she slipped into the surrounding woods to make her way back to the keep.

Long moments later, she passed through the postern gate and stepped into the bailey. The tension in her belly eased a notch. Mayhap by now, Henry and his men had come up with a plan. Shooing aside a goose which ventured near the open doorway, she secured the door's latch, waved to the boys taking kitchen scraps to the pigs, then strode toward the keep.

She had gone only a few steps when a maidservant ran to her. "Milady." The girl straightened her apron while dipping in a curtsey. "Henry is looking for you. A lord arrived a short while ago. He asked to speak with you."

Dread swooshed through Rexana. Had Darwell decided to visit and ask her about last eve?

Or, God help her, had Linford come?

She forced calmness into her voice. "Who is this lord?"

The maid shook her head. "I do not know, milady. Henry did not tell me, but caught my arm and told me to find you immediately. The visitor brings word of Lord Villeaux."

Rexana's stomach twisted. Linford would certainly have news of her brother. But by now, word of Rudd's arrest could have spread through Warringham's noble households. Could this lord possibly be an ally of her father's or Rudd's, offering assistance? Could this lord provide the answer she so desperately sought? "Where is our guest?"

"In the great hall, milady. Waiting."

"Thank you." Lifting her skirt's hem, Rexana crossed the bailey. Dust stirred at her feet, and, as she neared the stables, she smoothed her hands over her snarled hair. To properly greet her honored guest, she should change her garments and rebraid her tresses

. . . but she must not delay such an important meeting. She would present herself in her disheveled state. Hopefully, her guest would accept a gracious apology.

As she passed the stable, a horse raised its dripping muzzle from a water trough. A huge, magnificent destrier with a shiny gray coat and black mane and tail, no doubt worth a sizable ransom. Who in this county could afford such a magnificent animal?

Armed guards, her guest's escort, sat with their backs against the stable's far wall, their horses tethered nearby. This lord was clearly a man of authority. Mayhap his powers even exceeded Linford's. Anticipation quickened her strides.

Upon reaching the forebuilding, she yanked open the door, then hurried into the stairwell. The door boomed shut behind her. Her footfalls tapped on the stone stairs, the rustle of her silk gown unnaturally loud. Strange. She heard naught from the hall ahead but the hearth's crackling blaze. No conversation. No booted footsteps approaching to greet her.

Only silence.

Sucking in a breath, she stepped into the hall.

Squinting in the room's smoky haze, she strode past a row of trestle tables and searched for the visitor. A tall man stood with his back to her, facing the fire, one foot scratching the belly of an old dog sprawled on the warm hearth tiles. A long black mantle, trimmed in fur, skimmed over his broad shoulders and draped down to the top of his black leather boots.

Misgiving tingled through her. Why did the man not turn to greet her? Had he not heard her approach?

Clearing her throat, she started toward him. He straightened. The elegant gesture, almost deadly in its smooth precision, shot warning through her body. The hair at her nape prickled with awareness. Stunned dismay. Fear.

She stumbled to a halt. His leather boots creaked as he turned to reveal a firm, tanned profile. Curved mouth. Brown eyes that met her gaze with satisfaction and challenge.

Oh, God. Linford.

Fane watched her eyes darken with trepidation. They turned as green as the battle trappings hung alongside swords and shields on the wall behind her. Had she naively thought never to see him again? Foolish little fig.

Her fair skin, scrubbed free of kohl and darkening powders, turned as white as a fresh lily. Her lips pressed into an unsteady line before she seemed to realize her mistake and her mouth eased into a smile.

"Good day, milord." Admirably, her voice revealed only a slight quaver. Holding her head high, as though naught were amiss, she strolled toward him. Her shoes whispered on the rushes strewn over the floorboards, the sound of softly spoken secrets. Did she know he was exceptionally well versed in the art of exposing deceptions? Did she know he intended to unveil all of hers, every single one, before he finished with her?

"Good day to you, Lady Rexana Villeaux." Holding her gaze, he spoke her name slowly, rolling the last vowels over his tongue. She would know she had not fooled him last eve.

For an instant, shock gleamed in her eyes. Then, her brow furrowed into a frown. With a polite, puzzled smile, she said, "You know my name. One of the servants must have told you, for I do not believe we have met."

Laughter bubbled in Fane's throat. What game did she play? Admiration stirred in his gut, tempering his smug satisfaction, as his right hand curled into the folds of his mantle. So, she wished to do a merry dance with his mind, did she? Pretend they were strangers? Pretend she had not danced in front of him last eve and tempted him with seduction?

A smile tilted the corner of his mouth. She could initiate this little pretense. He would finish it.

Playing to her, he dipped his head in a chivalrous bow. "Fane Linford. High Sheriff of Warringham."

"At last, we meet. I am honored."

His smile threatened to break into a grin. Ah, she was clever.

As she neared, he allowed his gaze to drift over her face, to appreciate the features she had disguised last eve. To rattle the dignified, ladylike poise which surrounded her like an iron shield.

Ah, God, she was beautiful. Her hair was not black like Leila's, but golden brown, the color of sweet clover honey which, as a boy, he had devoured by spoonfuls from the pot. Her tresses tumbled over her shoulders in an unfettered mass to brush the narrow indent of her waist. Her green silk bliaut, oddly creased with mud at the hem, skimmed her hips, then fell in folds to the floorboards. His mouth watered. He did not have to imagine the curve of her legs hidden beneath the fabric. He had already seen them. He would never forget.

She moved close enough that he saw dark smudges under her eyes. Fatigue? Worry for her traitorous brother? Fane's eyes narrowed. Did she realize that her brother had revealed her identity last eve? Was this lovely creature an accomplice to her brother's conspiracy?

He would know. He *must* know.

As she glided to a halt, she said, "I apologize for your wait, milord. I regret I was detained by an important matter."

She had stopped several paces from him. Far enough away that she could whirl out of his reach if she so wished, yet near enough to taunt him with the perfume of violets. Another facet of their sensual game. How he loved a worthy chase.

Chuckling, he stepped from the fire's heat. Before she could move away, he pointed to the fuzzy green burrs clinging to her sleeve. "Detained? By a meadow sprite?"

She stiffened, but made no effort to remove the burrs. Her smile wavered only a fraction. "I am sure you understand, milord, that as lady of Ickleton Keep, I have a great many responsibilities. More so now that my parents are dead."

He nodded. "I heard of your loss. My sincere condolences to you and your brother."

Beneath her wrinkled bodice, her luscious breasts rose and fell on a sharp breath. Her clasped hands tightened, yet she did not break his gaze.

"I am told you bring word of Rudd," she said.

Ah, the first glimmerings of a concession. "Indeed, I do."

Her knuckles whitened. As he stared at her slender fingers, he noted the stains under her nails. Curiosity gnawed at him. What had she been doing, before she came to him? Why did she look rumpled, flushed, and desirable in her unruly state?

Fane's mouth tightened on a sudden, ridiculous sting of jealousy. Had she been rolling in meadow grass with a lover? A possibility. One that should not matter to him.

One that *did* matter.

"I regret I must be completely honest about your brother." His tone was sharper than he intended. Behind him, the fire snapped, as though mimicking his words.

"Honest, milord? Whatever do you mean?"

As her question hovered in the air between them, the tension thickened. Pulsed. He pursued his verbal advance. Step by step. "I mean"—he raised an eyebrow—"that I will speak naught but the truth."

Her gaze sparked with wariness. "Of course."

"I expect the same from you."

Her breath rushed between her parted lips. Her hands flew up, fingers splayed as though to ward off his advance. "Sheriff Linford, do you imply that I would try to . . . to deliberately deceive you?"

The shrill womanly indignation in her voice roused the smile he had smothered earlier. "Aye, little fig. I do."

"Little . . . Oh!" She bit down on her bottom lip, as though to quell a scathing curse. Clenching her hands into fists, she whirled away in a blur of honey-gold hair and blue silk and stomped across the hall. Over her footfalls, he heard her say, "I do not appreciate your boldness."

He laughed. "I know." With noisy strides, he pursued.

She quickened her pace. Caught up her skirts. Ran toward the forebuilding's stairwell. Lunging past her, he reached it first. Planting his feet apart, he spun, rammed his hands flat on the walls, and blocked her path. Cool air blew up from the door at the bottom of the stone stairs and stirred his mantle.

Breathing hard, he stared at her.

Hands on hips, she halted well out of his reach. She sucked air between her teeth, then shot him a look that could freeze a lusty man's blood. "Stand aside."

"First, we settle a matter between us."

"If you will not tell me of Rudd, we have naught to discuss." Her eyes flashed a clear warning. A moment more, and she would scream for her men-at-arms.

Caution gnawed at Fane. He could not risk hindering his carefully planned proposition. For now, he must concede to her.

And heighten the game.

With a dry laugh, Fane shook his head. Easing away from the wall, he reached into his mantle to withdraw a small, cloth-wrapped package. The familiar, distinctive eastern scent wafted to him. Flooded him with anticipation.

Holding her gaze, he tore aside the fabric and tossed the package's contents onto the table beside her. "You are mistaken, little dancer. We have a great deal to discuss."

With stunned dismay, Rexana watched the cake of soap slide toward her — identical to the one she had savored in his chamber. Her stomach did a slow, unsteady turn even as her mind raced for words. What did Linford intend now that he knew her deceit?

Her insides froze as he strode to the table. Closer. Closer. He came near enough that his male essence blended with the soap's lemony fragrance. Her nostrils filled with his scent. With the potent aura of man, danger, and temptation.

A tremor rippled through her. Curse her fickle heart. His clean, exotic scent should not be the least bit enticing.

His tanned fingers closed over the soap. As he moved, his mantle's fur cuff brushed her arm. A deliberate touch. She jerked back two steps.

"No more secrets, Lady Rexana," he murmured, his voice surprisingly soft.

Words grated from her lips. "How dare you?"

"Nay, milady. How dare you?"

Her gaze snapped to his. He smiled, the faintest crook of his mouth that implied a wealth of meaning. Recklessness and rebellion sped her pulse. She had not admitted to her deception. She could still feign ignorance of what he implied. Pretend the soap was only soap, and his insinuations as flawed as his barbaric tactics.

As she stared up into his face, hard yet unmistakably handsome, she saw the forewarning glittering in his eyes. He could be equally as stubborn as she. Moreover, he possessed one bargaining tool she did not: Rudd.

Yet, if he knew with certainty she was the dancer, and that she was Rudd's sister, Linford would have challenged her with the brooch.

Wariness undermined her defiance. He had journeyed to the keep for a specific reason. To confront her? Aye. Yet, mayhap he did not have proof she and the dancer were the same woman, but aimed to explore his suspicions. Mayhap he wanted her to betray herself. She must speak with care to learn his purpose.

Lowering her gaze to his hand cradling the cake, she quirked an eyebrow. "What is your meaning, milord? Why do you challenge me with simple soap?"

"More than soap, as well you know."

The caution within her intensified. "I fear I do not understand." The false words weighed heavy as stones on her tongue. "Mayhap you will plainly speak what it is you want, then tell me of my brother."

"Very well. I know your secret, Lady Rexana. I know you disguised yourself as a dancer last eve. I know you performed for me, and that you came to my solar."

She dried her moist palms on her skirt. "Indeed, Sheriff? What proof do you have 'tis so?"

He released the soap, then again reached into his mantle. Fabric whispered, the barest warning.

The brooch landed on the table between them.

The little arrow gleamed against the dark oak. She rubbed her lips together and smothered a choice, unladylike oath.

"Your brother told me this brooch is yours. He had it made for you. Gave it to you himself." Linford's shoulders raised in an indolent shrug. "Lord Darwell also had suspicions —"

A sigh burst from her lips. "Loose-tongued, pompous old —"

"Do not speak ill of him." Linford's smile turned crooked. "He has an excellent eye for a woman's physique. He thinks your . . . attributes . . . are most exceptional." As Linford spoke his gaze heated and skimmed over her bodice, as though he, too, appreciated her generous proportions. Inwardly, Rexana cursed the wicked thrill of excitement that tingled through her to pool in her most private of places.

When he continued to ogle, she barely resisted the urge to slap his arrogant cheek. She crossed her arms over her chest. "Must you stare?"

His gaze, glowing with mischief, slid up to her face. "My apologies, but I cannot help myself. I agree with Darwell."

His words cooled her like icy river water. Flattery? Did he believe she would be influenced by such false words?

Panic flitted through her like a butterfly fighting to escape a rainstorm. Had he sensed the yearning trapped within her? Did he use his skills in seducing women to lure her into a trap of confession? "Why did you come here?" she demanded.

"Ah, the heart of the matter." Leaving the soap and brooch on the table, he crossed his arms, mirroring her defiant posture, then leaned his thigh against the table. "Let us begin with the most obvious question. Why?"

She stared at his hands, firm and bronzed against his mantle's black wool. Beautiful hands, which controlled and manipulated power. Yet, in his solar, he had touched her with gentleness. Fear pricked her. How did she stop herself from crumbling and falling right into his waiting fingers?

"You came for the missive, aye?" he pressed.

Shock jolted through her. When she raised her lashes to glance at him, he smiled like a barn cat which had devoured a plump robin.

Before she could reply, he said, "I was awake long into the early morn, considering your dance. I wondered what would make a lady of your position desperate enough to risk her reputation as well as the respect of her noble peers. Few things, I vow, except her brother's life."

A chill skittered across the nape of her neck. Too astute, this man, for her to reject his words with a simple "nay." Moistening her lips, she said, "If you guessed correctly?"

His soft laughter echoed. "So, my suspicions about the maidservant were correct. Did she ride to Ickleton, then, after fleeing Tangston, and reveal to you what she heard me say?"

His words plunged into Rexana's thoughts like falling rocks. "You . . . you *wanted* her to overhear your words? To learn of the missive?" As shock swept through Rexana's mind, her body numbed. She had just betrayed herself.

As though acknowledging her careless slip, Linford cast her a lazy wink. " 'Twas clear the day I rode into Tangston that she distrusted me and would never swear fealty to me. I discreetly investigated her past, and learned of her dead father's devotion to your family. When your brother's loyalty to the king became suspect . . ." Linford shrugged. "An ungracious plan, I admit, to feed her select information on the traitors, but necessary. I will not fail to root out those who undermine the crown's authority."

"Did you speak true about the list of traitors?" Rexana asked. "Do you possess a parchment that bears my brother's signature?"

"I do."

She rubbed her arms. Fear, outrage, then sickening frustration battled within her. "The missive is forged. My brother is guiltless."

Linford plucked a leaf from his mantle's cuff. "I fear not, milady. Last eve, my guards caught him in a clandestine meeting with a number of other lords."

Anger screamed inside her. "Rudd would never betray the king."

His tone cool, Linford said, "Lady Rexana —"

"I swear so. Upon my honor."

"Your honor," Linford repeated with dangerous

softness. He uncrossed his arms. As he pressed his fingertips on the table, his fur-trimmed cuff whispered down over his wrist. "An interesting point. Might I note you recklessly risked your honor by performing before a crowded hall of nobles?" His mouth slanted into a half smile. "I am curious, love. How far would you have taken your deception?"

She swallowed. Hard. His intense gaze darkened. Demanded an answer. Unease poked at her, but she refused to heed it. She would not yield to Linford's barbarism.

Her chin tipped up. "As far as I felt necessary." Let him believe the worst of her. She did not care. She would never dance for him in his hall again.

"Would you have given me your virtue?"

He spoke softly, without criticism, yet his hushed tone only magnified the question's importance. She shrugged aside an inner cry for caution. "To save Rudd's life, I would risk a great many things."

Despite her resolve, her voice shook. Memories of a wintry day, of Garmonn laughing and aiming his bow into the woods, tore through her mind. Again, she heard poor Thomas Newland's agonized scream. Saw blood spattered on the snow. She closed her eyes against the anguish, horror, and revulsion that rattled her courage.

Rudd had saved her from certain death that day. He had risked his own life to come after her in the blizzard. Found her, half frozen, trying to drag Thomas to safety. She would have perished if Rudd had not come.

Now, she must save Rudd.

As she raised her damp lashes to meet Linford's gaze, his expression softened with admiration. "You must love your brother very much."

"I do." She cleared the rasp from her voice. "Do not mistake me, Sheriff. I will not allow you to persecute Rudd."

A velvety laugh rumbled from Linford. "Ah, love. I vow we can be of service to one another, after all."

His satisfied tone warned her that he danced nearer his true purpose. She spun away from the table. "I have no desire to help you."

"You have not heard my proposition."

Bitter laughter burned her throat. "If it concerns my honor —"

"Aye, yet more importantly, preserving it."

"I do not care what the gossips say." Even as she spoke, a shudder ran the length of her spine. Through one impulsive but necessary act, she had perhaps ruined years of tutoring and social acceptability. By now, Darwell might have told Garmonn and half of Warringham, in lurid detail, how she had danced for Linford in an attempt to seduce him and rescue her brother.

And how she had failed.

Fighting the despair slicing through her, she walked to the hearth and raised her hands to the roaring flames. At her feet, the dog raised its grayed head. It looked at her with filmy eyes, while its tail thumped on the tiles.

Her father had adored this faithful hound which had followed at his heels everywhere he went. Unconditional love. Unfailing loyalty. How could an animal feel what she felt for Rudd? She blinked away fresh tears.

Linford's hands, firm yet surprisingly gentle, came down upon her shoulders. She started. She had not even heard him walk up behind her. Where his palms pressed, a strange, glimmering heat seeped through her bliaut to her bare skin. Tingling sensations rippled across her back, like sparks from the wood popping in the hearth.

She tried to wrench free, but he did not release her.

"I respect your stubborn loyalty to your brother," Linford said from behind her, his breath stirring her hair, "but you should not bear responsibility for his treachery."

"Remove your hands."

As though he did not hear her protest, he murmured, "You are young. Beautiful. A lady of rare courage and intelligence." One of his fingers slid across the silk between her shoulder blades. "A woman of wild, wild passions."

She whirled around. Her skirts tangled with the heavy drape of his mantle and wound about her legs. She stumbled, but his arms caught her. As she fell against him with a shocked "oomph," his hands slid easily around her waist.

Her fingers plowed into the glossy fur trimming the front of his mantle. Her nose hovered a breath away from his stubbled chin. The smell of his warm, male body enveloped her. Taunted her. Enticed her to press her breasts, belly, and thighs even closer. To relish the forbidden physical contact.

Alarm shrilled within her. She must free herself from his hold, before he weakened her heart and mind.

She squirmed. "Let me go."

"I want you, Lady Rexana." Linford's dark eyes, so close to hers, gleamed in the firelight. His breath warmed her cheek, while his hands splayed over the small of her back. "Accept my proposition, love, and I will do all in my power to help your brother."

Trembling with indignant fury, she arched an eyebrow. "How, milord? Do you *dare* ask me to become your courtesan?"

"Nay, little fig. My wife."

# Chapter Six

"WIFE? NEVER!"

As the words shot from Rexana's lips, Fane tensed. He had expected her to initially reject his proposal, yet her refusal still stung like lemon juice running into an open wound.

He must convince her. He would have her for his own.

He stared at her pursed lips, lush, red, and close enough to kiss. If he swept his mouth over hers, would her shocked cry become a moan of pleasure? Would she sigh, then soften in his arms? He imagined the keening sound she would make as he coaxed her to kiss him back, the way her aroused body would shift against his to encourage greater intimacy. Heat flooded his loins.

He had dreamed of such a kiss last eve.

As though attuned to the lust streaking through him with the force of a desert storm, she wriggled in his hold. His arms instinctively tightened around her. He smiled down into her flushed, mutinous face.

"We will wed, love. 'Tis a wise decision for us both. My position will protect you from any scandal that might arise from last night."

Beneath the sweep of her lashes, her gaze turned frosty. "So gallantly you speak. Yet, I vow the greater scandal is for me to wed a barbarian."

He laughed softly. She hurled sharp verbal barbs. Though her words held some truth, he would not let her manipulate him, or sway his purpose. "A boon, then," he said lightly, "that I am not completely uncivilized, after all."

Her eyes flared before she abruptly shook her head. "Milord, I appreciate your . . . offer," she said between her neatly-formed teeth, "but I am not afraid to face the gossips' accusations. Alone."

"Are you certain?"

She jerked in his arms and this time, trod hard on his foot. With a lazy grin, he let her go. She whirled away, halting at the other side of the prone dog to glare at him. "I do not fear you, Sheriff. Nor will you bully me into accepting your offer of marriage. Did you know my father had many friends in the king's court? If I write to ask for —"

"A different husband? The crown will deny your request."

Her eyes flashed like polished gems. "I do not think so."

He calmly straightened his cuff. "Before I left Acre, the king signed a writ awarding me the hand of any English maiden I desire. The king's ministers are aware of this writ." His gaze flicked to hers. "I will petition for the honor of your lovely hand. My request will be granted."

Her jaw clenched. "I shall also write and ask the ministers to intervene on Rudd's behalf."

"They will refuse. I have a missive bearing his signature, which proves he supports the traitors."

As though fighting the urge to lash out and scratch him, she clawed her fingers into her skirts. "Sheriff, your arrogance is most . . . unappealing."

He shrugged. "Yet, well founded. The king has made no secret that he and England are in my debt. He is determined to secure the crown's control of these lands. Here, I am the king's law."

The slender column of her throat moved on a swallow. Her skin looked soft. Flawless. His fingertips itched to explore the tender spot beneath her ear, the side of her neck, her throat's shadowed hollow. He would enjoy discovering her.

"Even if I wished to accept your offer, which I do not," she said, drawing his focus back to her fetching mouth, "I am already practically betrothed."

She spoke with effort, as though divulging privileged information. Anger flamed in his gut. He barely restrained a furious cry. She would not be taken from him. Not this woman, whose passionate heart was so kindred to his own.

"Betrothed? To whom?"

She shivered. "Garmonn."

"Darwell's son," Fane growled.

She nodded, yet she did not giggle or blush like a maiden smitten, and his heart warmed with wicked gladness.

"Marriage between us was discussed when we were children," she said. "You see, Sheriff, I cannot wed you."

Fane sensed her slipping from his grasp like a handful of sand. Yet, he had vowed to finish this game between them, and so he would. Quirking a brow, he said, "You are not formally betrothed. Darwell asked me last eve to support your betrothal to Garmonn. I cannot. I will not, for you will wed me."

In the flickering firelight, her eyes sparked pure fury. "You leave me no choice, then, but to marry you?"

Her stinging tone tempered his triumph. Yet, he managed a smile. She would come to see that they were an excellent match. He would be diligent, gentle and courteous in his persuasion. He would show her the joys and pleasures in the rituals of love. Together, they would create their own unique dance. A dance to last a lifetime.

Turning away from her, he walked to the other end of the hearth. He must give her the dignity of her own space, so she could reach the decision herself. Waving his hand in the air, he said, "Of course, you have a choice. You may refuse. You may tell me to eat my words and never set foot in your keep again. Yet, what I told you earlier stands. I have the power to help Rudd. I am willing to do so."

"To have me," she said, her voice barely audible over the hissing fire.

"Aye. To have you."

"I do not love you. I never will."

The admission, so coolly spoken, cut him like Saracen steel. The insecurities locked deep inside him stirred to life. Again, he heard his father's bellow. *Godforsaken idiot. Leave and never come back. What your mother saw worth loving in you, I do not know.*

Fane bit back an oath. As he stared into the leaping fire, he remembered Leila's exquisite face, her bronzed skin a contrast to the white bedding upon which she lay. *Fane,* she whispered, reaching her naked arms up to him. *Lie with me, and together, like doves, we will both be free.*

Dragging his fisted hand over his mouth, he forcibly blocked out the memories. He would not be devoured by his past. He would not waver from his desired course.

"I regret you find our marriage distasteful, Rexana," he said, turning to face her. "Yet, few ladies have a choice in their marriages. Yours would not be the first to be forged for reasons other than love. Or the last."

"How comforting."

He ignored her icy glare. He reached into his mantle, withdrew a rolled parchment, then held it out to her. "Your signature, milady, and our agreement will be complete."

She frowned. Worry gleamed in her eyes, along with curiosity. The old dog whined. Stepping over its shaggy tail, she walked toward him. "What do you have?"

"A marriage contract. It states that by mutual consent, we shall be wed in three days' time."

She laughed. "Three days! Impossible. What of the betrothal ceremony? What of the banns, which must be published three Sundays in a row —"

"I recently donated a pair of gold candlesticks to Tangston's village church. Penance for my time in the east." He gave a wry smile. "Father John will not be concerned with the banns."

Her cheeks turned an angry red. "You are a man of the law, yet you so readily break it?"

"I told Father John we knew each other before I went on crusade. Since you were not betrothed, we discussed marrying when I returned. I also showed him the king's writ."

"But —"

Fane leveled her with a stern gaze. "Deny my story, if you will, but 'tis your word against mine. Whom do you think Father John will believe?"

Her eyes huge, she stared at the parchment crushed between his fingers. The dog licked its lips and nuzzled her gown's hem. Her expression hardened with sadness and regret.

"Promise me you will help Rudd," she whispered.

"I do."

"Swear it!"

In her damp, glittering eyes, he glimpsed the fire he had sensed the night she danced for him. A fierce heat driven by determination, integrity, and love. If she gifted him with only a fraction of that passion, he would be a fortunate man.

First, she had to begin to trust him.

He pushed the parchment into her right hand. Bowing his head to her, a gesture of utmost respect, he dropped down on one knee. His cloak tumbled over his bent leg to spread behind him on the rush-strewn floor. Straw and dried herb stems poked through his hose into his skin, and the scent of mildewed food wafted to him, but he did not rise. He would not interrupt this important ritual.

Clasping her left hand in his, he looked up at her. "I

swear, Lady Rexana. Before you and God."

Her breath trembled through her lips.

Squeezing her clammy fingers, he said, "Please. Sign."

In the distance, a door creaked open. A blast of cold air whipped over the floorboards. Voices echoed in the forebuilding — a man and woman arguing as they climbed the stairs to the hall. As though recognizing the voices, Rexana started and glanced toward the sound.

Fane rose. Her fingers stiffened in his grasp. She tried to pull free, but with his thumb, he caressed her knuckles. A reassurance. A promise to protect her, now and always.

An instant later, a man-at-arms emerged from the forebuilding. Henry, Fane recalled. The tough old warrior had very reluctantly admitted Fane and his men into Ickleton Keep.

A flustered looking maidservant, her apron askew, hurried at his side.

When Henry's gaze fell to Rexana's clasped hand, he stopped talking. He abruptly halted.

Holding back a grin, Fane met the older man's stare, which darkened with frustration, dislike, and protectiveness. Henry obviously cared a great deal for his lady. Fane guessed he had accompanied her to Tangston last eve.

"Henry," Rexana said.

Offering a polite smile to Henry, Fane said, "Good day to you, once again."

The warrior scowled. "Why do you hold Lady Rexana's hand?"

"I bid farewell to my intended bride."

The maidservant gasped.

Henry recoiled as though shot by an arrow. "What?"

"You are overbold, Sheriff," Rexana muttered, looking as though she would love to throttle him. "I have not agreed."

"You will."

Before she could pull away, before he thought twice and snuffed the mischief coiling inside him, Fane tightened his hold on her. He drew her fingers to his mouth. Her skin smelled of violets. Sweet. Inviting.

He felt her shiver. Her eyes spat warning sparks, but he merely smiled. With lazy intent, he kissed the back of her hand, leaving his impression upon her skin. Once. Twice. Then he nipped her with his teeth. To those watching, the tiny bite would appear no more than another gallant kiss.

Her lips parted on a shocked gasp. Outrage flared in her gaze, then embarrassment and confusion. Did he also see a hint of pleasure? She twisted her fingers free.

"Good day to you, little fig," he murmured.

He turned on his heel, nodded to Henry and the swooning maidservant, and strode from the hall.

"You cannot sign!"

Her palms pressed to the trestle table, head between her arms, Rexana shut her eyes and waited for Henry's shout to fade. Oh, God, how could she have told Linford she was practically betrothed to Garmonn? Loathing shuddered through her to the core of her soul. She would die before she ever committed herself to that merciless oaf.

Weariness pressed upon her heart. Despite her best efforts, she had failed to thwart Linford. Now, she must do what had to be done.

" 'Tis the only option, Henry," she said quietly. "You know it, as well as I."

"Surely there is another. If you spoke to Lord Darwell —"

"Whatever opinion he has of the sheriff, Darwell will not act against a high-ranking crown official. He would be foolish to do so. He could lose his lands, his keep, his fortune." She sighed and felt the morning's frustrations settle deeper into her bones. "Since Darwell is the one who revealed me to Linford, I would rather eat pig slop than ask him for a favor."

Henry exhaled on a growl. "How could he?"

"I know." Nudging aside skeins of hair, she stared at the parchment pinned down with ale mugs and the fragrant soap. Her brooch glinted nearby. She inhaled a calming breath, then, as Linford's essence drifted up to her, dearly wished she had not.

The memory of his kiss shuddered through her. The

back of her hand warmed, as though once again his lips caressed and nibbled her flesh. An indecent heat roused within her.

She blinked hard. *Focus, Rexana!* She must not let Linford's flirtations rule her body or ruin her concentration. Narrowing her gaze, she focused on the missive's lines of black ink.

Behind her, Henry paced. "Why not contact Garmonn?"

Her stomach tightened. With effort, she steeled the disgust from her tone. "He is of a temper to charge into Tangston and challenge the sheriff to a bloody tourney. I do not wish any deaths on my conscience."

"Wait! If Garmonn weds you on the morrow . . . a secret ceremony —"

Beneath her hands, the wood felt cold as a sheeted ice. "Then Rudd will be at Linford's mercy. Rudd will have no one to help him win his freedom. I cannot allow that to happen."

Henry snorted. "You place a great deal of faith in Linford's vow. Can you guarantee he will follow through with his offer to help Rudd? Nay. Since your brother is no doubt innocent of treason — as Linford will discover — you will have bound yourself to that . . . that *barbarian* for naught."

She squeezed her lips together. Dear Henry. Ever loyal to the Villeaux. For his support, she would always be grateful. Yet, she had no other course but to tread the path Linford had set for her. Rudd had risked his life to save her from certain doom months ago, and now she must risk hers.

"Linford will keep his word. I will make certain he does, by becoming his wife." Swallowing the lump in her throat, she traced the parchment's rough edge and skimmed the formal Latin script that committed her in mind and body to Linford.

Her breath caught. "In written word . . . only?"

Hope bloomed inside her. Could the answer be so simple?

Her finger skimmed the neatly penned text, the parchment slightly abrasive against her fingertip.

Henry stopped his furtive pacing. "Milady?"

Excitement thrummed inside her. "What if the marriage is not consummated? Linford and I will not lawfully be man and wife. Correct?" She looked up at Henry, sweet hope pulsing through her. "I can say I stayed pure because I did not truly consent to the marriage. I can petition for an annulment."

With a hearty roar, Henry clapped his hands together. "Aha! In the meanwhile, being inside Linford's keep, you will find a way to save Rudd. Rudd escapes, he is proven innocent, you demand an annulment, and the sheriff is left in a very foul mood."

Rexana laughed. "Exactly."

Hands on his hips, Henry grinned at her. "A clever plan, milady." The warmth in his eyes faded. "But dangerous."

She straightened away from the table. "I am willing to face the danger."

"You are prepared to tempt Linford's appetites?"

The spot on her hand where he had bitten her tingled. In his own crude way, he had marked her as his own. She covered the back of her hand with her other palm, smothered the tingling sensation, and smiled. What delicious irony, that he would never have her as he desired.

"Henry, please fetch me a quill and ink."

# Chapter Seven

THREE DAYS LATER, the morn dawned clear and bright. A perfect day for a wedding. Or, at least, it would be, Rexana thought moodily, if she were to marry a man she loved.

She adjusted her hold on her plodding mare's reins and struggled to calm her jittery nerves. As she had often reminded herself since signing the marriage contract, she had good reasons for wedding the sheriff. She would not lose sight of her purpose. Not now. Not in the coming days.

The morning breeze carried many sounds: the hoof-beats of horses bearing her wooden chests of clothes and personal effects; the snap of the banner displaying her family crest; and the merry tune played by the musicians who walked ahead of the procession to herald her arrival. A few paces in front of her, Henry spoke to one of the men-at-arms who escorted her to Tangston's village church. There, the wedding ceremonies would be performed.

There, in name only, she would become Lady Rexana Linford.

The town gates loomed ahead. The fortress rose on the grassy hill beyond, tall and imposing like Linford himself.

*'Tis the right choice*, she told herself firmly. *Believe it, and you will not fail.*

Henry dropped back so that his horse walked alongside hers. "Not far now, milady." He frowned, as he had earlier when he helped her onto her mare and smoothed her mantle so her bliaut would not gather dust on the journey.

"I shall be fine, Henry."

"Still, I worry." He swatted away a bee that shot up from the wildflowers growing along the roadside. "If you need help, no matter what 'tis —"

Tears clogged her throat. "I will ask you. Thank you."

Shouts came from the gates ahead. Rexana straightened and looked at the peasants gathered on either side of the gates and peering over the stone wall. Curiosity and excitement warmed the faces of the men, women, and children who watched her approach. The enormity of her decision flooded through her, yet she managed a smile. No matter how fearsome her decision seemed, she would persevere. She would win Rudd's freedom.

Children darted toward her, clutching bouquets of wilting daisies and meadowsweet. Leaning down, she took them from their sticky fingers. One day, her womb would bear a babe, but not Linford's child. The thought left her feeling strangely empty. How ridiculous. She felt naught for Linford. Certainly not love.

The men-at-arms moved closer to contain the crush of people. Tucking the flowers in front of her saddle, Rexana followed the musicians through the town gates. More people crowded the streets. The noise, the narrow wattle and daub buildings reaching upward toward the sky, the sea of anonymous, staring faces melted into a blur around her and she kicked her mare forward.

"Rexana." The familiar voice cut above the din. "Here. By the tavern."

A man staggered out of the building's crooked doorway. His handsome face looked unshaven, his shock of red hair unkempt, his rust brown tunic stained and creased. She hardly recognized the young lord. Garmonn.

Her mouth went dry. The last thing she needed was a confrontation with him. Not when she had done her best to avoid him the past few days. She waved, then coaxed her mare onward.

"You refused to receive me," Garmonn called in an overloud, petulant voice. He elbowed his way through the throng. When he reached her side, he stumbled along beside her moving horse. "Why did you refuse me? What have I done to deserve your disfavor?"

He set his hand on her leg. Memories flooded her mind, sending panic rushing through her in a harrowing deluge. He had won her disfavor months ago, but 'twas not wise to remind him now. Forcing a gentle tone, she said, "With only days to prepare for the wedding, I had no time for visits. I am sorry."

"You are heartless." His bloodshot eyes hardened. "Rudd rots in the sheriff's dungeon. You do naught to help him. Instead, you wed that crusading bastard. You should be marrying *me*."

The noise around her quieted. Warning buzzed in her veins, as well as anger. Did he not see how mortifying this was for himself, and for her? Did he intend to cause a scene? "Garmonn —"

"Do not marry Linford." His fingers tightened on her, crushing her mantle and gown. The mare flailed her head, and with a gasp, Rexana struggled to keep control of the animal. "Listen to me." He leaned closer, his lips wet with spit. " 'Tis dangerous —"

"To mistreat my bride," boomed a deep voice. "Unhand her, or you will find yourself in my dungeon."

Her breath caught. The crowd parted as Fane strode

toward her, flanked by men-at-arms, one hand on his sword's grip. Sunlight gleamed on his silky hair and embroidered blue tunic, crafted from the most beautiful fabric she had ever seen. The lavish garment denoted wealth and authority.

She swallowed. "Sheriff Linford."

"Milady."

Her horse snorted, sidestepped. Fane reached up, caught the jingling bridle, and steadied the animal. His gaze slid to Garmonn. "Lord Darwell's son, I believe?"

Garmonn's face reddened. He managed an unsteady bow.

"Your father is looking for you. He hoped you would honor Rexana and myself by attending the wedding ceremony." Fane shook his head. "I vow you should go sleep off your drink."

With an awkward gesture, Garmonn smoothed his tunic. "I am not besotted."

"You reek of tavern smoke and ale." Fane's eyes narrowed. "You have already embarrassed my bride with your foolishness. Leave, before I choose to take exception to your crudity."

"You dare to call me crude, you bast —"

"Leave," Fane snapped. "Now." His hand closed on his broadsword's hilt.

Garmonn reached for the dagger at his hip.

A hush fell over the crowd.

A sickening tightness clawed at Rexana's chest. She stared down at Garmonn, his face a ghastly shade of purple. If she did not intervene, he would attack Fane. She knew well of Garmonn's twisted cruelty.

"Please." She softened her words to remove any hint of insult. "Do as he says. Rudd would wish it, as do I."

Garmonn's gaze held hers. His eyes scorned her, condemned her. Called her a liar. Fear stormed through her.

"When Rudd is proven innocent and freed from the dungeon," she soothed, "I will tell him to come see you."

As though her words eased an internal dilemma, Garmonn smiled, then spat out of the side of his mouth. He sheathed his knife. After casting Fane a last, disparaging glance, he turned and staggered through the crowd.

She sighed. Her shoulders sagged. Past the rushing sound in her ears, she scarcely heard Fane's command to his men-at-arms. "Find Garmonn's horse. Make sure he leaves and does not return."

Guards thundered past. The chatter and music resumed.

Rexana unwound the reins that had somehow become twisted tight around her fingers. Bits of meadowsweet, dislodged from the saddle during the fray, tumbled to the ground.

The mare suddenly eased into a walk. Rexana looked up, to see Fane leading the horse off the main street into an alley cluttered with broken wine barrels and crates. The crowd moved back to allow them room to pass. As men-at-arms stepped forward to control the throng, Fane said, "Do not let anyone follow."

He strode farther into the alley. His tunic glittered and outlined the muscled swell of his shoulders. Lower down, the fabric shifted against his buttocks, suggesting taut muscles and curves. Rexana quickly averted her gaze. She should not notice such things.

"Where are you taking me?"

He glanced over his shoulder. "To the church, love, to make you my wife."

Frowning, she pointed to her right. "The church is in that direction."

"I thought you might need a moment to calm yourself and right your garments." He kicked broken crockery out of the horse's path. "Father John might think I could not wait to sample you."

Her hand froze in the midst of straightening her skirt. Her heart lurched into a steady *thump, thump* and she glared at the back of Linford's head. "You are a rogue to suggest such a misdeed."

Again, he looked back at her. His smoldering gaze skimmed over her mantle before he grinned crookedly. "I am tempted."

A thrill skittered through her. She ignored the

sensation. "You would not dare."

"You misjudge me." He chuckled, a sound of wicked intent. "Then again, mayhap not. 'Tis rumored, after all, that I have few morals."

The horse slowed, then halted. The trill of a flute, laughter, and voices drifted from the distant street. As the sunlight slanted over the buildings and lit Linford's eyes, Rexana's heart slid down into her belly.

Releasing the horse's bridle, he strode to her side. Her embroidered shoe touched the front of his tunic.

Oh, God. What did he intend?

"Have you forgotten the way to the church, milord?" She stared at him. The leather reins bit into her palms — just as Linford had bitten her hand. With shocking vividness, she remembered his mouth's moist heat, and his teeth grazing her skin.

"I remember the way," he said. "So, too, do I recall your skin's warmth. You smell like violets. You taste like a sweet, ripe fig. Irresistible." His fingers brushed her sleeve. "I want to kiss you, Rexana."

She twisted away. "Stop."

"Am I that fearsome? Come. I am to be your husband. Grant me one little kiss. For luck."

*Luck*? Oh, aye, she needed plenty. His sinful smile promised he knew all the ways to kiss a woman and make her beg for more. Did he know she had never been kissed on the lips by a man? Did he know that if she kissed him here, now, she might not want to stop?

Pushing aside his hand, which glided up her arm, she said, "You wish to kiss on the mouth?"

His eyes gleamed with surprise and obvious pleasure. "Aye."

As though caught up in the clandestine excitement, her traitorous pulse quickened. The heady scents of crushed flowers and potent male teased her, tempted her. What would it feel like, to kiss mouth to mouth? Would he taste of exotic spices and wine? Would he —

Mercy! How could she think such things?

She adjusted her hold on the reins as he leaned forward, his gaze hungry and expectant.

"I regret, milord," she murmured, "you will have to wait."

Kicking her heels into the mare's sides, she urged the horse to a brisk walk.

His bold laughter chased her. "Rexana, you vixen. You will make me a happy man." His footfalls echoed in the alley.

He pursued.

She whistled between her teeth. The mare broke into a fast trot. Smiling, Rexana rode out into the market square.

Fane caught up with Rexana near the church. He halted at the edge of the milling crowd. More people than he had expected had gathered to witness the public ceremony held on the church portico, before the wedding party moved inside for the private, nuptial mass.

Breathing hard, he set his hands on his hips and stared at Rexana, still seated upon her mount. The wind had pulled strands of hair from her braid, once smoothly coiled around her head. Her mantle hung askew, and her cheeks glowed from her defiant flight.

He had never seen a woman look more beautiful.

Meeting his gaze, she quirked an eyebrow. He grinned. They were well matched. If she proved equally feisty in the privacy of his solar —

"Ready, milord?"

"What?" Fane dragged his gaze from Rexana, being assisted from her horse by Henry. Clad in full ceremonial robes, and holding a leather-bound book, the priest stood at Fane's side. Shoving aside his lustful thoughts, Fane nodded. "Aye, Father." He withdrew the sapphire ring from his finger and handed it to the priest.

As Rexana removed her mantle and smoothed her exquisite silk gown, Fane walked to her. Henry withdrew a wrapped bundle from her saddlebag. With a hint of reluctance, she shook out the sheer veil and draped it over her hair, then secured it with a gold circlet. Her gaze sharpened as he approached, as though she expected him to follow through with his threat of a kiss, but she did not step away.

He resisted the urge to draw her into his arms and pleasure her with a thorough, soul-wrenching kiss that would sap the rebellion out of her. That particular pleasure must wait.

Capturing her elbow, he propelled her toward the church's carved stone portico. He ignored her squeak of protest.

"I am quite capable of walking on my own." She tugged, unsuccessfully, to free her arm.

"You might try to run away again," Fane said. "We cannot have that, can we?" As he walked, he nodded to Lord Darwell, who stood at the front of the crowd, surrounded by other prominent nobles Fane recognized from the celebration at Tangston. Darwell smiled broadly and waved, yet looked on the verge of tears.

Rexana sighed. "I will not run. I signed the writ and agreed to wed you. I will not relinquish my vow."

"Nor shall I, little fig."

Fane glanced at her. Beneath the veil's gauzy edge, determination glittered in her eyes. Remorse chilled his innards to icy stone. She wanted this marriage, would see the ceremony done, though not for her own pleasure or personal reward. Only for her damned traitorous brother.

Anger soured his heady anticipation. She gave herself to save Rudd, as Fane had known she would. Did she truly expect to receive naught in return? Was she unaware of the profound union awaiting them when she willingly gave herself to him? Together, they would write their dance into the night sky and pinpoint each exquisite step with stars.

He would show her he was no compassionless bar-barian, regardless of her brother's fate.

Father John stood in front of the church's massive carved wooden door, chatting to a lady with her young son. Fane drew Rexana to the bottom of the stone steps. Head held high, her bliaut drifting in the breeze, she stopped beside him. He released her elbow. Taking her hand, he linked his fingers through hers. She stiff-ened, but did not push him away.

Leaning close to her, Fane whispered, "Smile, Rexana." Her veiled hair smelled of sunshine and violets.

As Rexana stared straight ahead, her mouth eased into a ghost of a smile. "I am, milord."

Shaking his head, Fane murmured, "Mayhap if I kissed you, there, on your cheek that is the color of desert sand blushed by dawn, you would not have dif-ficulty smiling."

Her lips twitched.

"Ah. I knew you had a smile hidden away with your dancing bells."

Her fingernails bit into the palm of his hand, a rep-rimand. "You are not the only one in strange spirits. Whatever is the matter with Lord Darwell? I cannot decide if he is bursting with a secret, or about to bawl like a babe."

"He is disappointed, no doubt, that you will not be wedding Garmonn." Mischief warmed Fane's heart. "I also told him you pursued me. Tempted me. Seduced me into proposing marriage."

"*What*?!"

Fane winked, fighting to hold back a chuckle. "A necessary tale. How else could I explain your dance and our quick nuptials without arousing suspicion?"

She cast Darwell a sidelong glance. "He believed you?"

Fane licked his lips. He should not tease Rexana any further . . . but shame on him, he could not help himself. Not when for the first time in days, he tested the hot well of passion inside of her. "After a few elaborations." When her eyes widened, Fane shrugged. "I told him you found my eastern allure irresistible."

"Devil's spawn!"

In mid-sentence, the priest halted. Turning away from the noblewoman and her son, he peered down at Rexana. "Milady?"

Rexana's face turned scarlet. Murmurs and chuckles rippled through the crowd. It seemed onlookers were already nudging elbows and placing bets on their wedded happiness.

Fane's conscience pricked and he squeezed her fingers. He did not care what the others believed. Neither should she. They were destined for one another. He countered her glare with a genial smile.

She looked away. "My apologies, Father, for the interruption."

As the priest resumed his conversation, Fane leaned close to her again. Her hand shook in his grasp, as though she was sorely temped to slap him. "Do not be angry, love. Word spread quickly of our wedding. I had to give an explanation." Fane brushed his thumb over her wrist's soft curve. "You believe I have been unfair, depicting you as a lusty vixen?"

"You misjudge me," she said, her tone cool.

"Nay. I look forward to proving it."

She blinked in a gust of wind, and reached up to smooth her veil. He stared at her profile. She was so lovely. Proud. Independent. Yet, she would come to realize they were two halves of the same soul.

The priest cleared his throat, then tapped his book, a clear signal he wished to begin. Fane met his gaze and nodded. A hush fell over the onlookers, broken only by birdcalls and the wind whistling around the church's walls. The sapphire glittered between the tome's crisp parchment pages. As the priest began to speak in formal Latin, the surrounding world became a blur. Fane knew only the press of Rexana's fingers against his, the rise and fall of her breasts as she breathed. Her breath was his breath. She belonged to him, as he belonged to her.

Rexana's elbow jabbed into his side, bringing him back to the present.

"Take her right hand, milord," the priest said, obviously for the second time, "to say your vows."

"Gladly, Father." Fane clasped her clammy fingers in his, held her gaze, and repeated the words that would make them man and wife. He listened as she tonelessly repeated her vows.

The smiling priest blessed the ring. Rexana looked at it, and her throat moved. Fane's mouth flooded with a bitter taste. Did she think he mocked her with the sapphire, which he had given her before under different circumstances? One day, he would tell her how the ring helped win the battle at Acre and saved thousands of Christian lives. It represented all that was honorable in his past, as well as his future.

On the priest's instruction, Fane repeated a blessing and slipped the ring onto each of the three fingers of her left hand, then settled it on her ring finger. "With this ring," he murmured, "I thee wed."

Her bottom lip quivered. He willed her to look up, to see the truth of his gift to her, but she did not.

It did not matter. He would prove the truth to her.

"You are husband and wife," the priest said. When the crowd clapped and cheered, his face broke into a ruddy grin. "Come inside, now, for mass."

"First, Father, I will kiss my bride."

The crowd tittered. The priest's mouth flapped. "Milord," he said quietly, "that comes later in the proceedings. After I bestow upon you the Kiss of Peace."

Fane gestured to the throng. "Surely these good people wish to see how deeply we are in love, and that our marriage is one of mutual consent."

Rexana gasped. Her gaze shot to Henry, who stood nearby, as though seeking reassurance. Then her expression hardened.

"Rexana—" Fane began.

She wrenched her hand from his. Her eyes blazed with shock and indignation. He had expected to see maidenly trepidation, mayhap even embarrassment, but not willfulness.

Did she resent having to kiss him before a crowd? Or did she disagree that their marriage was one of consent?

Her gaze darkened with challenge, and he grinned. Clever little fig. She dared him to kiss her with all the passion simmering inside him. Dared him to show himself as a lusty, boorish oaf with no morals. Dared him, before the priest and hundreds of witnesses, to show himself as a fool.

She dared the wrong man.

He slowly raised her hand to his lips. He felt the tremor run down her arm, heard her quick inhalation. She watched him through half lowered lashes. With the grace he had learned from watching the king's courtiers, with the civilized restraint he had learned years ago, he pressed a kiss to the back of her fingers. Once. Twice.

As though pulled by an invisible string, she tensed. Expectation flared in her eyes. Laughter bubbled inside

Fane. She thought he would bite her again? This time, he deserved more than a cursory taste. This time, he wanted more.

He smiled, pulled on her hand, and drew her to him. Her fingers brushed over his tunic as she resisted, a slight, sinewy turn of her body. Before she could wriggle away, he leaned forward to cup the back of her head. Anchoring his fingers into her veiled hair, he kissed her soundly on the lips.

The crowd murmured and clapped.

As their lips met, she jumped. A startled rasp came from the back of her throat, as though the contact was not at all what she anticipated.

What did she feel? Astonishment? Pleasure?

He drew back, and her shuddered breath rushed over his mouth. Her tongue darted between her reddened lips, as though to fully explore the taste of him. Or to savor it.

He paused, his mouth close to hers. Her fragrance enveloped him, urged him to look into her eyes. She stared back at him, her breathing uneven. Her ringed hand fluttered between their bodies, even as her slightly glazed eyes looked up at him. In their depths, he read surprise. Confusion. Yearning.

"Another?" he murmured, the hand behind her head drawing her forward.

Laughter rippled through the onlookers. The priest smiled. Shaking his head, he pulled open the church's wooden door.

As though snapping from a daze, Rexana slipped free of Fane's hold. Her arms fell primly to her sides. "You are a man of many surprises, milord."

"There will be more to come," he said easily.

"Of that, you can be quite certain."

Raising his brows, Fane looked at her. Before he could ponder her words, or offer a witty reply, she caught up her skirts and climbed the steps to the open doorway.

He laughed and followed her, his boots rapping on the stone stairs. Puzzlement and anticipation shot through him. Did she intend to surprise him? How? When? At tonight's wedding feast?

Later, when they were alone in their chamber?

Ah, God, he could not wait.

# Chapter Eight

SHUTTING OUT THE WEDDING FEAST'S REVELRY, Rexana picked at the decorations on the marzipan pastry sitting before her on the lord's table. Torchlight glittered on the sugared rose petals tumbling over the delicacy's sides. A riot of sparkles, like sunlight dancing over pristine, newly fallen snow. Too pretty to eat, when her stomach churned with nerves.

Laughter boomed from a trestle table below the dais. Raising her lashes, she glanced at the noisy hall. Fane stood beside a flush-faced Lord Darwell amongst a crowd of other nobles. Fane was telling a tale, something about a huge spider in a crusader's tent, to the obvious fascination of all the men. He gestured with one hand, while holding a goblet of wine in the other.

Torchlight played over his angular face and fine tunic, and her stomach did an unsettling swoop. He was a very handsome man, Fane Linford, High Sheriff of Warringham. Her husband.

She shivered, and a sugary petal crumbled in her fingers. After mass, she had said goodbye to Henry. He had promised to manage Ickleton until Rudd returned, and needed to get back before dark. Fighting tears, she watched him and the men-at-arms ride away. Then, with the musicians playing a jaunty tune, she, Fane, and the wedding guests headed to Tangston Keep.

As Fane elaborated on the spider, her gaze dropped to his mouth. Since their kiss outside the church, he had been exceedingly courteous. He offered her first choice of the roasted meats and delicately spiced dishes. He offered her first taste of the wine—no cheap, watered down market fare, but a costly red. Moreover, he bestowed upon her compliments worthy of the most romantic *chansons*. He spoke as though they had not wed for a purpose, but for love.

Her throat tightened. She snapped her gaze back to the pastry. No matter how much his words had thrilled her, she must uphold her vow to remain virgin. She must deny him on their wedding night, and all the nights after that.

Yet, after that amazing first kiss . . .

Fane's earthy chuckle echoed. She fought the strange warmth swirling through her body, and tried to clear her thoughts. Her gaze fell to the circlet and veil she had removed earlier and set on the table, then the roses, gillyflowers and violets spilling from the oddly shaped gold bowl nearby. Flowers adorned every hall table. More dotted the rushes strewn across the floor. Even more blooms trailed from the wrought iron torch brackets, as though a pagan deity had cast a spell upon the hall, transforming it into a meadow. The extravagance was peculiar, but delightful.

Rexana inhaled the nearby arrangement's fragrance. Reaching out, she caught a violet, half fallen on the linen tablecloth, and her heart flooded with emotion. How her body yearned to dance. If she did, would she conquer her nagging physical cravings? Would she smother the voice inside her, that whispered she would betray her brother if she succumbed to Fane's temptations?

As though drawn by a silent cry, she looked up. Fane met her gaze. His lips curved in a brazen smile as he raised his goblet to her.

Heat flooded her cheeks. Her breasts tingled as though tiny, icy raindrops peppered her skin. The warmth within her quickened, spread, resurrecting the taste of him on her lips. Spicy. Bold. Wonderful.

*Traitor*!

She looked away. Heat skimmed down her spine to her arm braced on the table. The fragile violet lay crushed in her clenched fingers. When had she closed her hand? She did not remember.

She wiped her fingers on the tablecloth. She would not be seduced by Linford's charm. She would not forget that her only reason for going through with the nuptials was to free Rudd. Right now, as Tangston celebrated, he sat in a dungeon cell, alone and —

"Lady Linford?"

Rexana groaned silently. Would she ever grow used to her new title?

Darwell stood on the opposite side of the table.

"Good eve," she said.

"May I congratulate you on your wedding." He spoke politely but an odd light glinted in his eyes. "I wish you and the sheriff a prosperous future."

"Thank you."

He leaned closer, his breath smelling of wine. He grinned like a boy who had been handed a bag of sweets. "I have vowed not to speak of your secret" — he winked — "and I shall not. But I wanted you to be certain. 'Tis absolutely safe with me."

*Secret?* "Milord?"

He patted her hand, clenched again on the linens. "Worry not. A score of trained knights could not beat it out of me."

Panic pounded at her temple. Did he know she intended to get an annulment? Had her intentions been obvious? Surely not. Darwell likely spoke of her veiled dance, and not revealing her identity.

As she mulled her next words, his expression sobered. "You are a courageous woman. I regret you will not be Garmonn's wife. He loves you, you know. He would have fought for your hand in marriage and championed you, if you had let him."

She exhaled a held breath. Thank God Darwell had changed the subject. Yet, relief could never smother the chilling memory of Garmonn's foolishness in the market, or his past cruelty. "Mayhap 'tis better that I wed Sheriff Linford," she said. "Garmonn and I may not have suited one another, after all."

Darwell shook his graying head. Out of the corner of her eye, she saw Fane move away from the table below. Nearby, musicians began a lively song on lute and tabor.

She glanced back at Darwell, who now stared at her with open curiosity. He caught her hand. "Forgive my boldness, but I must ask. Did you *really* seduce Linford and demand that he marry you? Do you really prefer him to Garm —"

"I have left you alone too long, love."

Fane approached the table and set his goblet down with a thud. Darwell released her hand.

Rexana pressed her lips together. Had Fane heard Darwell's words? Not likely, over the music and chatter. Yet, she would be wise to diffuse any suspicion, before she cast unwanted attention upon herself. She picked up the wine jug and held it over Fane's goblet.

"More, milord?"

"Please." As though displeased by what he had seen, he turned to Darwell, who hastily brushed a crease from his burgundy tunic. "I hope you were not frightening my wife with tales of the marriage bed. She looks as pale as an old sheet."

Darwell chuckled. "I did not speak of such matters. I congratulated her on the wedding. An excellent day for Warringham, I vow."

"Ah."

As Fane's gaze once again settled on her, Rexana gulped. She had tried not to think of the physical encounter to come, the intimacy she must prevent. As she poured, light gleamed on the jug. A memory flashed through her mind. Fane kept wine in his solar. Tonight, would she have to bash him on the head to snuff his ardor?

Dread whipped through her. If she did not free Rudd as well and escape with him, she would have to explain herself to Fane when he roused. Not a pleasant prospect.

She concentrated on pouring the drink. Still, when Fane's fingers trailed over her knuckles, her hand jerked.

"You look tired, love. Are you well?"

"Aye."

"Shall we retire to our chamber?"

Before she sloshed wine all over the tablecloth, she set the vessel down. She smiled brightly. "Not yet. I have finished with my pastry. Now, I wish to see our guests. I am eager to begin my duties as lady of the keep and your wife."

"Indeed." He grinned as though her words greatly pleased him.

Darwell bowed low, excused himself, then hurried away.

Pushing back her chair, Rexana stood. She held Fane's heated stare. His mouth still bore a crooked grin, and she frowned. Did he tease her? Surely he realized the importance of her mingling with the guests and playing the role of Lady Linford. This eve, she would be the cultured hostess and bride in love. Her mouth tightened. She would not neglect her part of the pretense to which she and Fane had agreed. Nor would she give Fane one reason to forget his promise to help Rudd.

She skirted around him, heading toward a crowded table where she recognized a few nobles.

The music swelled. The tempo quickened.

Her heart thumped faster. Oh, how she wanted to dance!

Several noblemen and women moved into the open space between the tables, then linked hands to form a circle. They began to dance. Longing swirled inside Rexana. She hesitated on the circle's outskirts. Her body swayed to the rhythm.

Fane came up behind her. His hands slid around

her waist as he murmured against her ear, "Shall we join them?"

His body brushed against hers. Where his palms pressed, her skin burned. Sensual craving flamed inside her, and she trembled. Her feet itched to step to the side, step together, in time to the tabor's rhythm. She yearned to spin, like a bird feather falling down, down, down in a graceful spiral. Her blood hummed with the call of the dance.

Fane's breath warmed her cheek. "One dance, then you can chat with the guests. Aye?"

He moved to her side, holding out his hand. An invitation. A chivalric gesture, underscored by a sensual significance she was only beginning to understand. Was she wise to dance with him? She shrugged aside her unease. She could socialize with some of the guests. And Fane could not whisk her off to the solar.

She drew in a breath scented with flowers and wood smoke, then slid her hand into Fane's.

His sure, warm fingers closed around hers. Smiling, he drew her toward the ring of dancers. The circle parted, she moved into the line, and the gap closed.

Step to the side. Step together.

Rushes crunched beneath her feet. The scent of crushed herbs and petals rose around her, a smell that reminded her of the forest glade. She tried to ignore the brush of Fane's callused palm against hers. His hand's gentle clasp. The graceful way he moved. He stepped and swayed in perfect rhythm, as though he, too, felt the music in his soul. He was magnificent to watch.

With a cheer, the revelers broke apart. Rexana spun around, her skirts floating at her ankles. Excitement thrummed in her blood. Beside her, Fane grinned. He caught her hand again, and the circle resumed.

"Faster," he called, and the other dancers laughed. The musicians nodded.

The pace quickened. Around and around the circle went.

Step to the side. Step together. Turn.

Perspiration beaded between Rexana's breasts. Wispy hair fell into her eyes. Freeing her hand from Fane's, she wiped her brow. The perfume of flowers seemed stronger than before. The hall's smoky darkness seemed more intense. The scene around her blurred.

She closed her eyes, and saw herself dancing near the gray-green pool. Mist cloaked the edges of the clearing. Beneath her feet, dewy flowers opened to the dawn.

Step to the side. Step together. Turn.

Faster.

Step to the side. Step together. Turn.

Her breath rasped through her lips. The day's tension whirled through her like mist swirling in a gust of wind. She raised her hands, reached for the hint of daylight streaming through the mist.

Faster.

Turn. Turn —

She bumped into a solid object. Her eyes flew open. She reached out, halting her fall. Her hands met not a gnarled old tree but a trestle table. The forest vision dissipated, and again she discerned flowers and wood smoke.

She stood in the center of Tangston's great hall.

From the edge of the dance circle, Fane stared at her.

As he advanced toward her, Rexana's thoughts scattered like windblown apple blossoms. His eyes glittered. His broad chest rose and fell. His breathing sounded as ragged as her own.

His breath could be her own.

She heard titters and murmurs. The dancers looked at her, their expressions bemused. Awareness prickled. She had broken the circle. She had yielded to the maelstrom of emotion and yearning inside her. Oh, God, she had been foolish to dance.

Fane halted before her. As though no one watched, as though they were the only two people in the hall, he reached out to catch a strand of her hair. Her stomach did a sluggish turn. His body heat scorched her across the space separating them. For one reckless moment, she longed to press her body against his. To run her hands over him. To kiss him.

"Come, little fig."

His words shivered through her. "Why?" she whispered.

"You know why."

Her pulse drummed an erratic tempo, nothing like the music which had resumed. The table pressed against her, hard and immovable, while her body felt shimmery and weightless.

Dipping his head, he leaned his damp forehead against hers. His thumb stroked over her mouth. "I have waited all day for this moment. As have you." Before she could say a word, he cupped her chin and tilted her head back so she looked into his mesmerizing eyes. "I want all of you, Rexana. Body, heart, and soul. Tonight, at least in body, you will become my wife."

Exhilaration sang through her. As his husky words faded into the noise around them, she stared at his mouth. Wondrously formed. Close. Tempting.

Caution nipped at her. *Beware, Rexana! Do not yield to his seduction. If you do, you will be bound to him forever.*

As though sensing her reticence, he nuzzled her cheek. His hair, soft and smelling faintly of cinnamon, brushed her flushed skin. "I know the passion in your soul," he purred. "Let me release it. Let me show you pleasure."

*Yes*, her wicked body cried. *Oh, yes.*

With effort, she stifled her wantonness. Shame! Too easily she thought of surrender, when she must focus on preserving her maidenhood and saving Rudd.

Rexana pressed her hands against his chest. "Milord—"

He winked. "Later, you may thank me."

*Thank him?* Her jaw dropped and her hands fell away. Was there no end to his boldness?

Laughing, she said, "How arrogant, to speak highly of your prowess in the bed chamber." She pushed away from the table to slip past him.

His arm slid easily through hers, curtailing her escape. "I will prove my skill. This way."

Mercy! How would she keep him at arm's length when they were alone? She glanced at the tables nearby. "Wait. My duties. The guests —"

"— will understand. They expect us to leave early. We are, after all, newly wed."

Fane steered her past the nobles who had formed the circle again and resumed dancing. Slipping one arm around her waist, he guided her toward the landing's stairs.

The crowd parted around them. Bawdy whistles followed.

A scream burned inside Rexana.

"Milord, we will carry you to your chamber," a man called. Footsteps came up behind them, and a tremor shot through her.

"We will help you and your wife disrobe and get into bed," another yelled, as raucous laughter boomed. " 'Tis tradition in this part of England."

Rexana cringed.

As though sensing her distress, Fane chuckled and shook his head. " 'Tis a foolish custom. One I will not heed."

"You do not respect English customs, Sheriff?" a man cried.

The music and conversation faded to eerie silence. Every person in the hall seemed to be watching what happened next.

Rexana swallowed. Would Fane yield to nuptial tradition? Would he defer to his guests, and allow the marriage bed to be public spectacle? Would he choose his guests' wishes over hers? Her stomach twisted into a painful knot.

Fane's possessive arm tightened around her waist before he smiled down at her. "My apologies, sires, but I share my lovely wife with no one."

A relieved sigh whooshed out of her lungs . . . until Fane slapped her bottom.

Laughter echoed through the hall.

She jerked out of his hold to glare at him. "Cease."

His teeth flashed. "Soon, you may scold me properly."

Before she could utter one word, he bent and tossed her over his shoulder like a sack of onions.

"Put me down!"

The laughter swelled. Rexana's face burned. He walked toward the stairs. She shook hair out of her face. Pummeled her fists against his back. Kicked her legs. Twisted.

His laughter rumbled beneath her. "Go on, little fig. Scream. 'Twill give the guests plenty to talk about. Aye?"

# Chapter Nine

REXANA CONTINUED TO STRUGGLE as Fane neared the stairs. He tightened his hold on her silk covered legs. He would never forgive himself if he dropped her head first on the landing. The gossips would never forgive him, either.

Ahead, a wide-eyed Winton moved out of his path. "Milord."

"See that the wine flows," Fane said. "Make sure none of the guests get into the dungeon. The guards on duty have been forewarned, but if there are problems, I expect to be informed."

Winton's gaze darted to Rexana's wriggling legs. "On your wedding night, milord?"

Fane gritted his teeth. "Especially on my wedding

night."

Ignoring Winton's elegant bow, Fane climbed the stairs. His boots thudded on the dry wood, as anticipation thundered in his veins. His mouth flooded with the remembered taste of Rexana. Tonight, he would taste more than her lush red lips. He would savor her breasts. Her hips. Her thighs . . .

He strode into the shadowed passage off the landing. The guards on duty quickly opened the solar doors. Fane relayed instructions, then strode inside. He kicked the chamber doors closed with his heel.

Soft candlelight flickered on the whitewashed stone walls. The fire glowing in the hearth cast its yellow-orange light over the tiles. The bedding had been turned down, the lion skin folded and set on his wooden chest. As he walked farther into the chamber, he smiled. As per his orders, violets scattered over the floorboards.

He halted and set Rexana on her feet. She stumbled back several steps, putting distance between them. She righted her mussed gown, then glanced about the chamber.

Stooping, he picked up a violet, small yet perfectly formed.

"They are everywhere," she said, "even on the bed linens."

He straightened. She had retreated to the window. The night breeze stirred her loosely braided hair and set the candle flames fluttering. The chamber's shadows shifted, danced.

Drawn by her shaky voice, he walked closer. "I know you like violets."

She nodded. The hair across her brow shifted, and she swept it back with her hand. Her bodice stretched taut with the movement. The taste of her thickened in his mouth.

"You try to seduce me."

"You are my wife. I will do all in my power to please you."

Wariness shadowed her eyes. Pausing beside her, he braced one hand on the wall. Moonlight shimmered on her face and brushed her throat and breasts with light and shadow. Desire coiled up from his belly. She was his. Now. Forever.

His fingers curled against the rough stone. He burned to touch her, to glide his hand over her milky skin. To make her arch against him, sighing with pleasure. By the thinnest thread of restraint, he resisted. He had never forced a woman into his bed. He would not start now.

He would be careful. Clever. Oh, so clever. He would overcome her virgin apprehensions, little by little, until she yielded to her passion. In the great hall, he had sensed how close she came to acquiescing. He had seen it in her glazed eyes, heard it in her breath's uneven tempo.

Soon, of her own free will, he would taste violets on

her naked belly.

Soon, they would create their sensual dance.

Easing closer, he tried to slide his arms around her. She bolted like a spooked horse.

"Rexana."

"Milord." She stood beside the bed, her hand fisted into her skirts. Ready to flee.

A wry laugh burned his throat. Mayhap he had misjudged the ease of this seduction.

Shifting his weight to one leg, he casually leaned his shoulder against the wall. He softened his voice. "Come back. I will not devour you."

"You will kiss me," she said, sounding out of breath.

"Is that so terrible?"

Her mouth quivered, before her shoulders thrust back in clear rebellion. "I am not ready to . . . I cannot kiss just yet." Her gaze darted to the bowl of figs on the nearby table. "Are you not hungry? After all that dancing, I am ravenous."

*Ravenous.* If only she knew. A grin curved Fane's lips. "I am starved."

"Excellent." Her skirts rustled as she approached the table. She picked over the mound of fruit. "Fig, milord?"

"A little one. Only it can satisfy my craving."

"Little —" Her right hand, clasping a plump fig, froze. She blushed. "Oh."

"Rexana, let me kiss you. I crave you, as a dying man craves life. I hunger for your glorious taste. Your lips pressed to mine. Your soft body curved against me."

As he spoke, her eyelids fluttered down. Then, as though catching herself surrendering, her eyes flew open.

Satisfaction curled through him. So, she was not immune to his gilded words, the flowery romance of a noble courtier. She wanted a civilized seduction. Slowly, carefully, he shoved away from the wall. "Did you know, love, that you taste of violets?"

"Violets?" Her gaze widened, even as her fingers flitted up to her mouth.

"Aye." He stepped closer. "Sweet, ambrosial, like the finest nectar. When we kiss, your taste floods my tongue. I am the honeybee, drunk on your essence. I taste . . . bliss."

"Bliss?" Her fingertips brushed over her lips.

"Exquisite bliss," he amended on a whisper. "The sweet passion consumes me. Torments me. Devours my sense of reason. I roar inside with wanting you."

She half moaned, half sighed. Her eyelids slipped closed. She swayed slightly against the table, and he quietly crossed the space between them. He halted before her. Close enough to catch her in his arms. Close enough to claim his prized kiss.

Her lashes fluttered. "Milord —"

"Kiss me, Rexana."

Her eyes opened and clouded with doubt. Longing. Resistance.

He touched her sleeve's embroidered cuff. Slowly, gently, he trailed his fingers up her arm. She shivered, stepped back two paces, and stumbled over her gown's hem.

"You want my kiss." Frustration darkened his tone. "Do not deny it."

"I want it," she agreed in a tight voice. At least she did not foolishly try to refute what they both knew to be true.

"Then take what you want." He spread his arms wide in invitation. "I am yours."

Her eyes were as bright as the sapphire on her finger. She did not move toward him or attempt to speak, and his frustration swelled to anger.

"Love."

"I cannot." Her fingers wrapped tighter around the fig, as though the sweet fruit could sap the poison from her refusal.

"You are my wife." The words, hard as stones, ground between his teeth. As he looked at her face, etched with rejection and misery, a thought cleaved him like the blow of a Saracen sword. The luscious taste of her soured in his mouth. "I see now. You find me repulsive," he said coldly, "because of my past."

She inhaled sharply. "Of course not."

His hand thumped on the table. Oranges and figs

bounced from the fruit bowl to roll across the table. "You think me barbaric. Unclean. Unfit to despoil your pure, unsullied English body."

Her face reddened. "Cease!"

Fury and disappointment snapped inside him. Had he really thought her his soul mate? Had he thought her different from all the others? He could not school the bitterness from his words. "We are man and wife now, Rexana. You belong to me. By law, I own your kiss, as well as your maidenhood."

Her eyes hardened to the green of polished glass. Her jaw set, and he heard the *pop* as her nails pierced the fig's flesh.

Had he really spoken such callous words? Would he prove himself to be the barbarian the rumors claimed him to be? He would never win her trust, or her heart.

Cursing under his breath, he moved toward her. "Rexana —"

Her arm swung back. Before he could step aside, the fig thudded against his chest. The earthy smell of ripe fruit exploded in the air around him. The fig dropped onto the toe of his boot, then rolled onto the floor.

Stunned by the force behind her blow, he halted.

Another fig slammed into his shoulder, then an orange. He grunted, annoyance smothering a flare of amusement. "God's teeth."

"How dare you speak cruelly to me?" She grabbed more fruit from the table. "You mean, insolent —"

An orange smacked into his belly, shocking the breath from his lungs. "Ouch. Stop." He strode toward her.

"I think not." A fig whizzed past his ear, narrowly missing his head. Zounds. Did she try to injure him? With fruit?

Incredulous laughter rose in his throat.

She scowled. As she darted past the end of the table, she caught a fat orange. "You smile. You find my anger amusing? Unwise." Her gaze dropped to his tunic's hem. His groin. She held the orange as though it were a dangerous weapon, a determined smile curving her lips. "Beware. I am an excellent shot. I used to shoot targets with Rudd."

Before she took aim, he lunged. He caught her wrist and pried the orange from her fingers. She shrieked. Cursed. Fought like a wild creature while her free hand pummeled his chest. With a growl, he grabbed her other wrist. Raised both arms above her head. Propelled her backward.

"Release me," she spat, twisting in his hold.

"Not until you listen to me." Meeting her furious glare, he tightened his grip on her wrists, enough to secure them but not enough to hurt. She swore again, planted her feet firmly on the floorboards, and resisted the backward momentum. He leaned his body full against her. His legs tangled with her skirts. His belly pressed against her stomach. Her breasts crushed against his tunic until her spine arched. With a frustrated cry, she stumbled back.

One step. Two. She bumped against the wall.

Panting, Fane slid his palms up her wrists to lock his fingers through hers. He pinned her hands above her head, against the stone, and stared down into her face. Her hair snarled over her flushed cheeks and snagged in the stone. Her braid hung in a tangled mess. Her lashes flicked up, and she returned his gaze with icy resolve. Her blazing eyes told him what she wanted him to believe — she would never yield.

She lied.

As he flattened his body against her, she quivered. Her lips parted on a ragged gasp. Her eyelids drifted closed. He slowly shifted against her. Chest to chest. Belly to belly. Steel against womanly softness.

Her breath caught. "Fane —"

He covered her mouth with his own. Tasted her, as he had wanted. Ah, God. Naught compared to her velvety sweetness. To the essence of proud, fierce, desirable woman.

She sighed against his lips. As though the leashed passion inside her broke free, her mouth opened beneath his. Seeking. Hungry. He slid his tongue between her teeth. She nipped him, and he started with the unexpected pleasure. With the blinding surge of lust.

With a muffled cry, she strained against his imprisoning hold. He loosened his fingers. Her hands slid free and plowed into his hair. She held his head firm, kissing him back.

He met her kiss, thrust for thrust, gasp for gasp. She molded against him as though wanting more. Needing more. She smelled incredibly, arousingly good. A possessive groan tore from his lips. Heat seared through him. Tore at his loins. Devoured his thoughts.

He wanted her. Now.

Why deny what they both desired?

With a gentle shove, he pushed her back against the wall. *Here*, his mind screamed. *Lift her skirts. Take her as she begs to be taken.* He squeezed his eyes tight to shut out the nagging voice. Later, he would show her the exciting and creative variations on lovemaking. The first time as his wife, she would have the tender seduction he planned.

Sliding one arm behind her shoulders, the other under her trembling knees, he lifted her into his arms. She fitted easily. Perfectly. Careful not to stumble on her gown's flowing drape, he strode toward the bed. His body tightened with anticipation of their joining. He could scarce wait to see her naked body. To slide into her softness. To feel her arching and moaning against him.

"Fane," she said thickly. Through the haze of lust, he sensed her hand pressed against his chest.

Resistance. Again.

He stifled the groan rising in his throat. Tenderness mingled with his frustration. Of course. She was virgin. She had uncertainties.

As he approached the violet-strewn bed, he pressed a kiss to her brow. "Hush, love. 'Twill be all right."

She pushed more firmly, then kicked her legs. He could scarce see past the froth of pale skin and silk.

"Zounds, woman." His knees hit the oak bed frame. Before he could regain his balance, he dropped her onto the mattress' edge. The bed ropes creaked in protest.

Scooting sideways, she tried to rise. He braced his hands on the coverlet, either side of her hips, curtailing her progress. As her eyes glinted with warning, he pressed a bold, open kiss to her mouth. With a low moan, she melted into his touch, and his right hand fumbled for the ties securing her gown.

Before he had unfastened the first one, she caught his wrist. "Fane, stop."

"I am sorry for my bitter words," he said against her lips, his words punctuated by kisses and nibbles. "I would never take you in anger. Please, believe me."

She drew back, her mouth swollen and red. Tears glistened along her lashes.

"I love you, Rexana."

Confusion and disbelief darkened her eyes. "How can you? We have known one another but a few days."

"My heart and soul belong to you. They have from the moment you first danced for me."

"Nay," she whispered.

His fingers curled into the embroidered coverlet, the silk as soft as a woman's bare thigh. "Make love with me, Rexana. Let us share our passion."

Closing her eyes, she shook her head. Misery lined her beautiful face. "I cannot."

"You mean, *will* not." The wilting violets strewn on the linens mocked him, as did her scent. She did not want his seduction. She did not want *him*.

As though sensing his thoughts, she shivered a sigh. "From the time I was a young girl, I studied to be wife and chatelaine." She returned his stare with one of fierce intensity, while her voice roughened. "My father told me I would wed a nobleman of compassion and honor. A man who would trust me. A man who would love me, and whom I would trust and love in return. Into our loving home, we would bring children."

"What are you saying? I am not noble enough for you?" Fane bit out the words. "Have I not treated you with compassion and honor?"

He leaned forward to brush his cheek against hers. He crowded her with his body. A shameless coaxing, but he could not resist. He needed her. Desperately.

Her fingers knotted in her lap. Her hands almost touched his loins, the hard place that throbbed for her. The place that consumed his focus. He groaned inwardly. If she touched him there . . . Barely able to leash his lust, he forced himself to inhale slowly.

"You ask me to couple with you, to commit an act of love and trust." Her voice quavered. "Yet, I do not trust you. I do not love you."

*How can I? You will persecute my brother,* his mind finished for her. Her earlier words rang sharp in his mind. *I cannot love you. I never will.*

He snorted. "You believe all men and women fornicate for love? Some want only the pleasure." He forced the urgency from his tone, fought the sensation of falling into a deep pool with no way out. "I can give you pleasure. I am not unskilled in the arts of pleasuring a woman." As he spoke, he slid his fingers up into her hair to tip her head back for his kiss.

"To lie with you this way mocks all I have been taught, all that I believe." She turned her face away so his kiss landed on her cheek. "Will you ask it of me?"

He growled against her skin. "Once you have experienced pleasure, you will feel differently." He set his hand on her shoulder, and began to press her back on the bed.

"If you believe so, then you do not love me after all."

He stared at her pale face and the proud line of her jaw. As her words infiltrated his lust-hazed brain, shock and crushing disappointment followed. "You expect me to refrain from my marital rights."

She swallowed, then looked away. "Aye."

The enormity of her demand blasted through him. His blood cried with the injustice. His mind howled. His loins cooled slowly. Painfully.

He released her shoulder and dropped his head. He stared down at her hands, folded neatly in her lap. Her knuckles were white. She sat in stiff silence, as though she were a bow drawn tight and at the slightest provocation she would snap.

Shaking with need, he breathed in the tantalizing scent of violets and woman. He could continue his seduction, woo her passion-drugged senses until she was too aroused to stop him. He could overpower her and force her to spread her thighs, as was his right by law. Yet, the pleasure would be temporary. Afterward, she would hate him.

His eyes closed on a groan. He could never, ever disrespect or force her. He would not mistreat her, as General Gazir had mistreated all the pretty virgins sold into his bed.

Spitting an oath, Fane straightened. He righted his tunic and turned from the bed. Away from her, before the last thread of his control frayed.

Behind him, the mattress groaned. Silk whispered. He imagined Rexana smoothing her bliaut over her shapely legs. He tried to squash the lascivious images romping through his mind. Her naked, laughing, and rolling beneath him. Him suckling one of her incredible, pink-tipped breasts while his hand —

He cursed and strode toward the door.

"Milord?"

Her unsteady voice made him pause. Fane sensed her relief, yet also uncertainty. He dared not turn around. He dared not glance back to see her kiss-reddened lips and tousled hair. He dared not give himself one reason to walk back to the bed, especially to reassure her. If he did, all his honorable intentions would be lost.

"I will not take you now," he muttered, the words painful. *I will think of you though, luscious little fig*, his mind seethed. *I will imagine my hands on your soft white skin. I will envision my body sweating and straining above yours.*

"You are leaving?"

He managed a sharp nod. "Get into bed. If you are wise, you will be asleep when I return."

"Where are you going?"

Hellfire! Why did she ask? She did not care. She only wanted the marriage to save her brother. She had not wed for pleasure or love.

Never for love.

Fane crossed the last paces to the doors. He yanked them open. Without a backward glance, he slammed them behind him.

As the solar doors boomed closed, Rexana slid off the bed. She fell to her knees on the lush carpet. Her gown slithered into a pool around her, and she pressed her trembling hands over her face.

Fane had accepted her refusal. He had not forced her to couple with him. Relief rushed through her like a wave crashing upon a sandy stretch of beach.

Tears filled her eyes. Part of her had not expected him to honor her wishes. Was he not a pitiless savage? A man whose morals had been sullied in desert lands far from England? A warrior who took what he wanted, simply because he wished to?

Yet, Fane had been . . . chivalrous.

The confusion that had pestered her earlier grew. She had sensed his intense arousal and his desire. Why had he heeded her? Did he care what she thought of him?

Muttering an oath, she dug her fingernails into the patterned carpet. She deluded herself. He had stopped because he did not want to rouse nasty gossip. He did not want rumblings that he had foully treated his virgin wife, a distant cousin of the king, a claim that might win her sympathy amongst the nobles who distrusted him. Fane did not want to give them reason to take up arms against him or stir the brewing rebellion. If the nobles took their grievances to the king, and the king believed them justified, Fane might be stripped of his status and his lands.

Her hope fizzled like a fire doused by water. Fane left her this eve because he was a master tactician, a man who understood power. He had not left because he cared for her.

Logs shifted in the hearth. The blaze popped, sending red embers scattering across the tiles. She dried her eyes, and weariness weighed upon her. Fane was a far more complex and cunning man than she had imagined.

Yet tonight, she had accomplished what she hoped. She had resisted and won.

*Fane is gone for now,* her conscience warned, *but he will be back.* Soon.

Rexana glanced at the mussed coverlet. Crushed violets marked the fabric. The stains might never wash out. Memories of Fane standing over her, his hands caressing and his mouth toying with hers, flitted through her mind. She could not suppress a shudder.

The fire's warmth stretched out to her. It echoed the heat, invisible yet frighteningly potent, coursing in her blood. Fane was fire. He had only to touch her, whisper to her, and the flames inside her roared to life.

He must never know how close she had come to surrendering.

His words slashed through her mind. *I will not take you now.* He had told her to be asleep when he returned. What would happen if she were still awake?

Did he infer that if she were not sleeping, she must accept the consequences—and his lust?

She must be sound asleep. Snoring, even, to prove her oblivion.

With jerky movements, she dried her cheeks and stood. She searched the chamber for a night shift, but found none. A nervous laugh bubbled up inside her. The servants had not expected her to need a sleeping garment. They expected her to be naked in bed with her husband, warmed by his body, heated by their love-making.

Shivering in the ghost of a draft, Rexana crossed to the bed, unfastened her gown's ties and let the garment fall to the floorboards. Only her linen shift, embroidered with tiny flowers, protected her from the chill. From him.

She pulled back the sheets, swept aside the violets, and climbed in. Hands folded together atop the bedding, she lay staring at the ceiling. She prayed for sleep.

*I will not take you*, Fane's husky voice seemed to whisper from the shadows. *Yet.*

# Chapter Ten

HIS ARMS CROSSED OVER HIS TUNIC, Fane walked Tangston's windswept battlements. He found the darkest shadows, leaned his shoulder against a squared merlon, and stared down into the fire-lit bailey. The cold stone numbed his arm, yet he did not draw away. He watched the squires, musicians, and serving girls who had congregated around the huge fires. Bawdy jests accompanied by laughter drifted up to him. Ale mugs clinked. The merrymakers cheered him successfully bedding his wife, while he stood alone. Aroused beyond belief. Rejected.

Anger surged through him. He remembered the guards' shocked faces as he stormed out of the solar. He had ignored them. They would never know the marriage had not been consummated with quiet efficiency. Only he and Rexana knew what had taken place. Only they knew she had denied him.

Lust still thundered in his blood and tightened his loins. A strong wind gusted. It pummeled his back, buttocks and thighs, yet he welcomed the discomfort. It distracted him from images of tangled linens and Rexana's nude body.

A bitter laugh rumbled in his throat. She had surprised him with her temper. She had stunned him with her reasons for wanting to remain pure. She had bested him, in a way no other woman would dare.

The wind blew again. Hair snarled into his eyes, and he yanked it away. Giggles rose from the rowdy bunch gathered around the nearest blaze. Men and women sat together on the ground, their ruddy faces warmed by firelight. Others sang or danced to a randy folk tune, played on a lute.

His gaze narrowed on one couple. Servants, he guessed from their garments. As they turned, swaying to the music, the woman stared at the man. Sexual hunger etched her features. She swirled closer. Her body and eyes beckoned. Tempted.

Fane's hands clenched on his forearms. He wanted Rexana to look at him that way. With desire, passion, and the wild heat that he knew burned in her soul.

The song soared. As though caught up in the music, the man grasped the woman's hand. Spun her around.

Pushed her out of the light and into the shadows beside a horseless wagon. His face plunged between her breasts. He yanked up her skirt.

Fane watched, unable to tear his gaze away, as the woman leaned back against the cart, then curled her bare leg around the man's waist. He fumbled with his clothing. His hips flexed. Her mouth parted on a gasp. With frantic urgency, she matched the man's driving thrusts.

A strangled groan broached Fane's lips. He turned away, squeezing his eyes shut against a rush of carnal images. Ah, what he would give to have Rexana pliant. Willing. Eager.

'Twould never be . . . Unless he undermined her reasons for refusing him.

Unless he made it impossible for her to deny her needs.

Or his.

The faintest smile touched his lips. A worthy challenge. Rexana vowed she would never love him, but she desired him. She had admitted so.

Desire could grow into love.

Aye, she must learn to love him, for their souls shared the same dance. She belonged to him. He would never let her go.

Fane strode along the battlement into the wind. The breeze stung his face, yet his heart lightened. He would woo her. Tempt her. Sway her heart and soul until, of her own free will, she yielded. When at last she gave herself to him, she would hunger with the same fever pitch as he.

Ah, a worthy challenge, indeed.

The fire had burned low when Rexana heard murmured voices outside the solar. She tensed, instantly alert. Turning her head on the pillow, she squinted through the darkness at the chamber doors. She twisted her fingers into the coverlet. Waited.

The doors opened, admitting a seam of light.

Rexana shut her eyes.

She sensed Fane's bold presence even before the door clicked shut and his boots thudded on the floorboards. Tension seemed to reach across the shadowed chamber to touch her, like a prowling hand, where she lay on her side in the bed and faced the fire. She forced her breaths into a steady rhythm. Pretended she blissfully slept, when in truth she had fidgeted, plumped the pillow twenty-two times, and rolled from one side of the bed to the other.

Her mind still tormented her with memories of his sinful smile. The desirous glint of his eyes. The taste of his firm, sculpted lips.

Her heart warned that she would regret the deception she had initiated between them.

His footfalls suddenly quieted. He had stepped onto the carpet. With intense effort, she forced herself to stay still. She sensed him coming closer. Closer.

Her nerves screamed with anticipation.

He stopped beside the bed. Behind her. The heat from his body warmed her back. He smelled of night air.

Rexana fought a shiver. What did he intend? Had he come to take her . . . now?

For what seemed an eternity, he stood over her. She sensed his gaze traveling over her shoulder, down her arm lying atop the coverlet, along the curve of her body tucked beneath the bedding. She braced herself for his hand upon her shoulder, for his touch which she feared yet also craved. Her chest tightened until it hurt to breathe. Yet, by some miracle, she managed to remain still.

A moment later, he moved away. He headed toward the fire.

The air whooshed from her lungs.

He halted.

Had he heard? Her eyes still closed, she waited. Listened. She heard naught but the fire's snap.

The silence dragged. By the saints! What was happening? Was he sneaking back to her? Ignoring an inner cry for caution, she raised her lashes.

He stood at the end of the bed. His dark, deliberate gaze locked with hers. "You are not asleep, after all."

She swallowed. "I *was* asleep, milord," she said, coloring her words with a hint of resentment, "until you woke me."

His laughter rang out in the darkness. "Ah, Rexana. Have you not yet learned I can tell when you speak false?" His smile became a white slash in the shadows.

"Very well. I did not sleep. How could I, wondering where you had vanished to?"

His grin faded. "You refused me, wife. You denied me my right. Why would you worry where I had gone?"

His gritty voice pricked her. What did he imply? Clutching the coverlet, she pushed herself up to sitting. His gaze wavered, fell to her lips, then drifted down the scooped neckline of her shift to her cleavage only just hidden by the sheets. Slowly, so slowly, his attention returned to her face.

His jaw hardened. Anger? Disapproval? Did he find her lacking in her state of undress?

Rexana refused to let his blatant inspection distract her from her purpose. "Where did you go?"

"Where do you think I went?"

A horrible thought shot into her mind. "Did you harm my brother? I swear to God, if you hurt Rudd because I ref —"

The coverlet slipped. Fane's gaze instantly riveted to her breasts. With a shaking hand, she caught the bedding and secured it under her arms.

Fane half groaned, half cursed. As though resisting another oath, he looked away and dragged a hand over his mouth. "Trust me, your brother is the last person

I wish to see."

"Then where —"

"It does not matter." Fane turned his back to her. He crossed the chamber, then dropped down on one knee near the hearth to rekindle the fire. He focused on the simple task as though it took extreme willpower to complete.

She stared at the tousled hair brushing his shoulders. His back's rigid line. His well-formed thighs, visible only when he reached for the wood. His tunic shifted. Revealed fascinating bulges of muscles and sinew. Accentuated his masculine power.

Rexana's throat tightened. Any woman with a whit of sense would appreciate his physical beauty.

Maybe another woman had.

The thought clouded her mind like a suffocating fog. It transformed her worry about his intentions into a shock that robbed her breath. Had Fane bedded someone else? She dared not ask. But she must. "Did you lie with another woman?"

He stilled. He laughed, an astonished sound, before tossing a last log into the blaze. Brushing his hands on his hose, he stood and faced her. "Would it matter if I did?"

The answer rang in her heart, loud as a church bell. "I would never forgive you."

Her answer seemed to please him. His grin returned, marked with lazy intent. "I am glad 'tis so, love. I swear to you, upon my cursed soul, that I did not take another woman this night. I have no interest in another." His tone roughened. "I want only you."

He walked toward the bed. Toward her.

Rexana's fingers tightened on the bedding. Her nails scratched on the fabric. "Milord —"

"No more pleading this night, little fig. No more harsh words. No more refusals."

His words numbed her cold. He intended to have her. Now.

She scrambled back against the pillow. She stared down at the rumpled bedding and her hands curled like wilted flowers. Words of protest refused to come. A traitorous excitement unfurled within her. Tempted her. Urged her to lie back and accept what in secret she wanted.

Trembling, she looked up. He reached for his tunic's hem. Holy saints above, she could think of naught to say to delay him. Naught to save her virginity. Naught to keep him from making their marriage binding under law and God.

He yanked the tunic over his head in one fluid motion, then tossed it to the floor. Her gaze dropped to his chest.

All thoughts of self-preservation shattered.

His bronzed skin bore scars. Small, ugly red pocks. The lines of a whip. A ragged, pitted slash rippled down his ribs. Bile rushed into her mouth to drown the pang of excitement and worry. What had happened to him? Who had beaten him? How had he endured such terrible physical torture?

He caught her watching. His eyes narrowed, darkened with unease. Yet, he did not look away. As though daring her to shrink in horror, to swoon with maidenly distress, he reached for the points of his hose. And smiled.

Rexana gulped. She had seen a man's bare chest many times, but none quite as broad or impressive as Fane's. She had swum with Rudd on hot summer days. Never had she doubted her actions. Yet here, in Fane's bed, with him standing over her, those days seemed years ago and desperately naïve.

His fingers worked the points. She stared. She caught her mouth gaping, and snapped it shut. She must look away. Resurrect the ladylike modesty ingrained into her by years of boring tutelage. She must not ogle Fane like a lusty courtesan.

Yet, she could not avert her eyes.

A burning curiosity spread through her. What masculine mysteries hid under the woolen fabric? What made the fascinating bulge between his legs?

She wet her lips with her tongue. He saw. His gaze heated. A strangled moan burst from him. He sucked in a breath, then swore. Violently.

Embarrassment drowned her delicious curiosity, so she shut her eyes. Her cheeks flamed. He had not liked her staring. He had taken exception to her wantonness, thus felt bound to curtail her inappropriate behavior. Her barbarian husband had more honor than she thought.

"Lie back, Rexana. Keep your eyes closed."

Her heart jolted. "Why?"

His mouth tightened. Fury, no doubt, that she did not immediately do as he commanded. "Obey me. 'Twill be easier for you this way."

"But —"

"Do it, Rexana."

His fierce tone shredded the last of her bravado. She fell back. She drew the sheets up to her neck but, on a last swell of defiance, opened her eyes the tiniest bit. Shifting her head on the pillow, she peeked at the hearth. At him.

He had turned his back to her. Firelight and shadows defined the muscled planes of his shoulders, ribs, and his spine's shadowed dip. He was beautiful.

And brutally scarred.

As her gaze skimmed over him, she fought anger and regret. Slashes marred his back, scars far deeper and crueler than those on his chest. These wounds were inflicted not only to cause physical agony, but to break his spirit. Barbaric wounds.

Tears hurt her eyes. She wanted to run her hands over his scars. Soothe them. Tell him, with tender caresses, that she did not consider him any less a man.

Tell him, with words as gentle as her touch, that she hated what had been done to him.

That she . . . cared.

A shiver ran through her. A foolish thought. He did not want her compassion. He wanted her body. He wanted to consummate their marriage and their arrangement. He had told her to shut her eyes so she would not see his imperfections before they coupled. Did he believe she would more easily accept him after the act, because once he had taken her virginity, she was irrevocably bound to him? Did he believe that once he had deflowered her, the physical scars would no longer matter?

A soft pop warned he had pulled free the points of his hose. Her pulse lurched into a faster rhythm. Wariness and curiosity returned, stronger this time. She tried to keep her eyes closed — oh, how she tried — but fascination consumed her. His hands moved to his hips. Fabric slid down over his buttocks. Revealed smooth skin sprinkled with dark hairs. Exposed a scar the size of her fist on his thigh.

Oh, God.

He stepped out of the hose. Straightened. As though sensing her gaze, he said, "Your eyes are still closed, love?"

"A – Aye."

"Good."

As he turned in profile, she snapped her eyelids shut.

A last image, of a flat stomach, a mass of black hair, and bold, hard flesh flared before her eyelids.

Before Rexana could ponder what she had seen, the sheets pulled back. The bed ropes sagged. She tipped toward Fane. She squeaked, ramming her palm into the mattress to prevent her from rolling against him. Flat on her belly, she raised her lashes, pushed up on her forearm and struggled for balance.

"You disobey me. You do not close your eyes."

He lay on his side, the sheets pulled up to his waist, his head supported by one hand. Partly hidden by a snarl of hair, his eyes glittered with promise. Intent. Desire.

"I wish to see what you are about, milord," she said.

He chuckled. Without the slightest attempt at subtlety, his gaze moved to her shift, and her breasts crushed into the mattress. "Ah, Rexana. You are brave, yet I still hear fear in your voice. You will not be so frightened of me on the morrow."

A tremor raked through her, from her neck to the tip of her toes. "Bold words, milord."

His eyebrow arched. "You do not believe I can have you?" His free hand skimmed across the sheets. Closed over her taut, splayed fingers. His palm's callused warmth shot invisible sparks up her arm and fired the wanton heat in her blood.

"I believe you will try." She tried to pull away, but his hold tightened.

"I will try, and I will succeed." His smile turned blatantly sensual. "I will have you. Body, heart and soul."

Her limbs trembled. She began to scoot backward in the bed, but he held her firm. His fingers slid under her wrist. Tightened. Pulled her with gentle firmness toward him. Her shift drew taut over her chest. The skin across her throat and breasts tingled as though he had touched her there.

"Come here, wife. I hunger to taste you."

Excitement buzzed through her like a big, unpredictable bee.

His gaze darkened. Smoldered.

He stared at her lips, then bent his head toward her.

"Fane —" she whispered, an instant before his mouth touched hers. Warm, sure, his lips branded her with his taste, words, and intentions.

He nipped her bottom lip. Sucked it between his lips. She jerked back, but he pursued. Teased. As though she had no say over her traitorous body, her mouth opened like a budding flower worshipping the sun. His tongue glided between her lips. She groaned with the pleasure. With the hunger that flamed deep within her. How could she fight him, when he made her feel like this? How could she resist when, very soon, he would ask her to lie back and yield?

As she drew in a helpless, shuddered breath, he ended the kiss. Drew away. Smiled.

He caught her hands in his. He shook, as though with urgent need, yet he placed a tender kiss on the back of her fingers. "Good night, Rexana."

"Good . . . night?"

He nodded. Set her hand upon the mattress. Patted her fingers, as though he regretted ending their encounter but had no choice in the matter.

He lay back on his pillow, folded his hands upon the sheets, and closed his eyes.

Rexana shook the bewilderment from her kiss-fogged mind. She stared at his handsome face, then the firm slash of his lips which had plied her with temptation. "You do not wish to couple, milord?" Fie! Her body burned like a May Day bonfire.

His right eye flicked open. "You are disappointed? I thought —"

"Nay, I . . ."

He yawned, covering his mouth with his hand. "I am more weary than I realized. 'Twas an eventful day. Do not worry yourself. I have no wish to take you, after all."

Yawning again, he turned onto his side. Faced away from her. He exhaled a long breath and lay still.

Rexana frowned. She stared at Fane's scarred back, and his hair tangled on the pillowcase. Confusion, desire and disappointment swirled inside her with the force of a spring gale. He did not want her. He had rejected her. He had preserved her virginity. She should be delighted, not yearning for him to change his addled mind.

She wriggled back to her side of the bed. The ropes squeaked and groaned. Her shift had somehow knotted itself around her knees so, with a scowl, she sat up, swept aside the sheets, and straightened the garment, eliciting more squeaks and groans. Fane did not stir.

Curling on her side, she watched firelight dance on his hair. Admired the swell of his muscled shoulder, limned by golden light. Dreamed of his wondrous kisses.

Thank the saints, he did not know how she hungered.

Smothering a curse, Fane listened to Rexana's fidgeting. He counted each of the bed's creaks and groans. Wondered, with perverse curiosity, what noises it would make when he thrust into her slick, willing warmth.

God's teeth, his entire body ached for release.

Fane gritted his teeth. Fought the urge to roll over and kiss her until she gasped, moaned, then begged him to take her. He fisted his hands into the sheets. Fought the longing to touch and taste her satiny skin. He squeezed his eyes tight. Fought to ignore the sensual dance his mind invented between her and him.

Valiantly, he leashed his thoughts to concentrate on the fire's bright flames and soothing hiss. What he endured was no different than what he had suffered in Gazir's dungeon. A different kind of physical torture, aye, but one he would survive. This torment was necessary if he wished to have Rexana body, heart and soul, and to win her love.

He exhaled against the pillow. If only his loins understood that if he took her virginity this night, he might lose her forever. He would not allow resentment to build an emotional barrier between them, or for her to claim that he had forced her against her wishes.

She must be handled with care, dignity and honor. With all the courtesies she expected of a civilized English nobleman.

Only one little detail remained. A matter he must settle in the morn, to protect his own manly honor.

He watched the fire for a long time. His breathing slowed. Deepened. The lust in his blood dimmed, but it would never disappear. Not when Rexana lay in his bed. Not when he pictured her lips pursed in slumber and the rise and fall of her breasts.

Dragging up another dose of willpower, he sighed.

He prayed morning came soon.

# Chapter Eleven

SOMEONE NUDGED REXANA'S SHOULDER. She grumbled, tried to snuggle deeper into the warm cocoon of bedding, and savor the remnants of a dream. The vision resurfaced. Her, dancing naked in a verdant meadow that smelled of violets, while in the nearby shadows, a man watched.

"Wake up, love."

Fane's voice shattered her reverie. As her eyes flew open, memories of the previous night flooded back to her. His incredible kisses. His refusal. The craving that had taunted her until her eyelids became so heavy, she could no longer deny sleep. She bolted upright. Remembered, at the last instant, to drag the sheets with her and clutch them to her bosom.

He stood beside her, his mouth a taut line. He had dressed. A hunter green tunic hugged his torso and fell to his thighs. A belt defined his waist, and his legs were encased in snug black hose tucked into leather boots. She cleared an appreciative purr from her throat. Dismissed the renewed tingle of wanting. She had no wish to couple with him.

Not the slightest. Not one.

Not when her brother was a prisoner in the dungeon, and his life depended upon her.

Not when she intended to stay virgin, so when Rudd was free, she could annul her marriage.

Rexana shoved the inconvenient hunger to the back of her mind, along with stinging regret. Saving Rudd was far more important than dangerous delusions of pleasure between her and Fane. She must not let desire interfere with what must be done.

Raising her lashes, she looked at Fane. Shadows darkened under his eyes. He looked as though he had slept as little as she. A tiny, foolish thrill comforted her. Mayhap he had not been as unaffected by the kiss as he wanted her to believe?

"Have you looked your fill, wife? If so, I ask that you get out of bed."

Her cheeks stung. She thought to remind him how long *he* seemed to spend looking at her breasts, but a sudden yawn curtailed the words. " 'Tis dawn already?" she asked.

" 'Tis before daybreak. The servants have not yet begun their duties."

She swallowed an exasperated grumble. A draft chilled her back and she pulled the bedding tighter around her. "Why must we rise so early? Is this some strange eastern custom?"

"I want the sheets."

Her sleepy mind refused to enlighten her. "Sheets?"

He dragged his hand over his chin. Scowled as though he would rather not have to explain himself. "Little fig, if you do not rise this instant —"

She sighed. "You need the bedding that urgently, milord?"

"Aye." As though barely restraining his impatience, he shifted his stance. Set one hand on the bedside table. Metal glinted close to his fingers. A dagger. An exotic looking knife with a jeweled sheath and handle. The hair at her nape prickled. She did not doubt he knew how to use such a weapon.

Why had he brought it? Her muzzy mind leapt with possibilities. Had she annoyed him somehow? Would he threaten her with the dagger if she did not obey? Her breath quickened to nervous pants. She looked from the knife, to him. "What . . . Oh, my . . . Would you —"

"Love?"

She tore back the bedding. Scrambled off the mattress. As her feet hit the cold floorboards, she gasped.

Fane caught her elbow and steadied her with a firm grip. His potent male scent encompassed her. Her cravings revived full force, and her whole body quivered, as though he had just kissed her with the exquisite skill he had shown her last eve.

Reproach glinted in his eyes. "I have frightened you."

Her head spun. *Frightened?* Fear did not account for the shivers shooting through her, or the sluggish warmth settling low in her belly.

" 'Twas not my intention to scare you." His thumb massaged her arm through her shift's fabric. "I would never intentionally hurt you, Rexana. You must believe me."

A draft swept across her ankles. Startled her back to her senses. Reminded her she stood before him in naught but her thin undergarment. Reminded her that until moments ago, she had happily enjoyed the bed's warmth.

She shook off his hold. Crossing her arms, she curtailed his wandering gaze. "I am not afraid, milord, but confused. Why do you need the sheets?"

Did a flush stain his cheekbones, or did her eyes deceive her? Before she could insist upon an answer, he turned, grabbed the coverlet and top sheet, and yanked them off the bed. Withered violets swirled in the air and scattered near her feet. He dropped the bedding into a heap, then whipped the bottom sheet off the mattress.

"Milord!"

"Watch. You will understand." He snatched up the knife, then strode toward the hearth, dragging the sheet behind him.

He squatted before the fire and smoothed the creased linen until he found a portion near the middle. Unsheathing the dagger, he cut his little finger.

She hurried to him, her feet pounding on the floorboards. "Stop! God's teeth, are you mad?"

"Nay," he said calmly. "Determined."

He set the knife on the hearth tiles. Relief shivered through her. Thank the saints he would not cause himself further injury. Curse her soft heart, but after seeing his scars, she could not bear to think of him enduring more pain.

Yet, what did he intend? His actions were very deliberate.

The fire's heat reached to where she stood only a few paces from him. She moved closer. Blood glistened on his cut.

"I will fetch you a bandage and salve," she soothed. "Then we will discuss what made you take a knife to your flesh."

Tilting his head, he looked at her. "No need, love. The cut is tiny and will soon cease bleeding." He glanced back at the sheet and smeared his finger on the linen. "There will be no question that we are man and wife."

Cold realization struck her. Plunged into her stomach like a chunk of ice. Mocked her moment of sympathy. Her ambitions of freeing Rudd, then annulling her marriage, shattered to bits like an ice-covered puddle smashed by a rock.

"Virgin blood," she whispered.

Fane nodded. "The servants will look for it when they change the bedding. 'Tis proof our marriage was consummated."

Her mouth soured with a vile taste. " 'Tis not my blood."

His narrowed gaze shot to hers. "Only you and I know that. The truth will remain between us."

Angry tremors shook her body.

Grabbing the stained linen in his fist, he shoved it nearer the fire. "I will not have the servants whispering I could not bed my wife on my wedding night."

"You do this to prove your prowess?" she hissed.

His eyes sparked with dark fire. "A warrior's strength is judged not only by his valor on the battlefield, but his skill in bed."

She threw up her hands. "What a selfish, pigheaded —"

"I do not think only of myself." He shifted his grasp on the sheet, and his gaze softened a fraction. "Do you wish to become the subject of cruel gossip? To hear the maidservants' hushed giggles as you walk past? I spare you that indignity."

She ground words between her teeth. "Our marriage, namely the reasons for it, have already incited plenty of gossip."

"With any nuptials, there is speculation."

Frustration heated the skin across her throat. "One stained sheet will not end the speculation about us, milord. Do you really believe that by convincing the servants of our wedded union, that tongues will stop wagging?"

"A naïve hope, mayhap. Yet, one day, 'twill come to pass." He smiled and in one breathless swoop, his gaze traveled over her shift. "I only prove with a little of my blood what is inevitable between us, Rexana. I *will* have you."

His words ended on a velvety growl. Need and anticipation swarmed within her. Even now, she craved him. What wretched weakness. She turned to face him with her back.

Her gaze locked upon the mussed bed, even as soft words warmed her lips. "Your reasoning is flawed, milord. I can visit a physician. An examination will prove I am virgin."

His boots squealed on the floorboards, her only warning. His hands closed upon her shoulders, and he spun her around. Fury etched his mouth and knotted his brow.

"You will do no such thing. We made an arrangement. You signed the consent to marriage."

"I remember."

"Then why speak of a physician?" As though catching the thread of ambition in her gaze, his eyes narrowed. "What plot spins through your mind, that you have not shared with me?"

She steeled herself against the urge to break his gaze. She must not imply her guilt, or give away her intentions of an annulment. Her mind scrambled for a convincing answer that would swiftly diffuse his suspicions.

Tipping up her chin, she said, "I do not plot, but think of Rudd. You vowed to do all in your power to save him, if I wed you. I have seen no evidence you intend to do as you promised."

Fane's hold gentled. "Ah. You threaten me, so I will begin helping your brother." He laughed. "You are cunning."

"Determined," she corrected.

He grinned at her reminder of his own words, but his smile quickly faded. "Know this, Rexana. Your plan to see a physician would fail."

Warning flared within her, yet she could not halt the rash words. "You could not stop me."

"I could." His gaze hardened. "I would."

He would, indeed. A man of his authority had means far beyond hers. Why had she been so foolish as to provoke his suspicions? When she wished to secure an annulment, she might need to get a physician's examination.

She forced a careless shrug. " 'Twas only a silly remark. Naught more."

His hands skimmed down her arms and caught her fingers. "I will keep my vows. All of them."

His touch rekindled the forbidden fire in her blood. "Will you?" she whispered.

"I will." He leaned close. His hair brushed her cheek. Of its own cursed will, her body stretched to greet his lips. The remembered taste of him flooded her mind and tongue and drowned her senses. How she craved his kiss!

Yet, at the last moment, he drew back, placed a chaste kiss on her brow, and stepped away.

To her shame, she could not halt a disappointed blush.

He shook his head and growled low in his throat. "Later, love, we will explore our passions. Aye?"

Her flush deepened. Before she could reply, he turned and crossed the chamber. He snatched up the stained sheet, tossed it onto the bed, then dropped the remaining bedding on the mattress. Hands on his hips, he swung back to face her.

"I will wake the maidservants and send them with water, so you can bathe."

A sudden thought trapped the air in her lungs.

"Will you also bathe?"

His lips twitched. "When you have dressed and quit the chamber. If we climbed into the tub together, love, we would do far more than wash."

She frowned. "What do you mean?"

A rueful groan burst from him. "One day, soon, you will understand." He spun on his heel, returned to the hearth, and collected his knife. Shoving it into his belt, he strode for the doors. "I have duties I must attend. Later this morn, we will ride. Be ready when I summon you."

"Ride? Where —"

The door clicked shut behind him.

Fane strode across the landing toward the great hall's stairs. He could not move fast enough. His blood pulsed with an earthy rhythm that warned if he had stayed in the solar with Rexana for one more moment, he would have yanked her into his arms. Kissed her. Carried her to his bed. Made love to her until they both collapsed with exhaustion.

How could he have felt otherwise, when she stood before him wearing only a shift? The wispy garment had barely shielded her from his view. The linen's swells and shadows had tempted him more than if she had been naked.

His boots thudded on the staircase, and he stifled a raw laugh. She had wanted his kiss. With the sensual grace of a skilled courtesan, she had raised her lips to him, arching her body to fit against his. How easily he could have slid his arm around her back and drawn her close. Pressed his mouth over hers. Smothered her protests until her virgin passions bloomed.

He scowled down into the darkened hall. Easy to win her body, mayhap. Far more challenging to win her heart.

Snores rattled in the hall. As he stepped down onto the rush-strewn floorboards, he looked across the rows of straw pallets and slumbering bodies. Maidservants. Men-at-arms. Noblemen who had collapsed in a drunken stupor. Dogs.

Sidestepping a hound and a pool of ale, Fane wove toward the hearth. He smiled. One advantage to Winton's bright red tunic. Fane could always find the steward, even in the dark.

Winton lay on his side, squeezed up against a buxom maidservant, his chin resting on the crown of her tangled brown hair. His face held an expression of utter bliss.

God's teeth. Even the old steward had enjoyed carnal pleasure last eve.

Fane nudged Winton with the toe of his boot, a little harder than intended.

The steward groaned. "Not again, sweetum." He waved a feeble hand. "Three times in one night —"

"Winton."

The steward's eyes flew open. "Milord?" He pushed

the young woman aside, sat bolt upright on his pallet, then yanked at his creased tunic. "Lord Linford, you woke early." He ran his hands over his balding head. "After your nuptials last eve, I did not think —"

Fane bit back a rush of irritation. "Lady Linford wishes to bathe. Rouse the servants. Make sure she has all she needs."

Winton nodded profusely. The maidservant beside him stirred and shoved hair out of her eyes. As she turned sleepily to reach for Winton, her gaze met Fane's.

She scrambled to her knees. "Milord!" She winced, clutching her brow as though enduring a fierce headache.

As the woman fumbled with her gaping bodice, Fane glanced across the hall. The first blush of dawn tinged the sky beyond the high, horn-covered windows. Today was his first day as a husband. His first day married to Rexana. He would not waste a single moment. Today, he would make her his.

He turned away. "Winton, see that our guests break their fast and leave. I want the hall and bailey cleared by midday."

"I will see it done. Personally. First, I will arrange the lady's bath."

"Good." Fane took two steps, then spun back. He curled his fingers against a pressing surge of emotion. "Lady Rexana may do as she pleases in my household.

She is to be shown all the courtesies and granted all the privileges due to her as my wife." Fane held Winton's gaze. "She is not, however, allowed to visit the dungeon."

"As you command, milord."

"If she wants to see her brother," Fane muttered, "she must come to me."

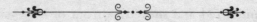

Rexana was leaning out of the solar's open window, peering up at the lightening sky, when a knock rattled the door.

She jumped and fell back against the stone embrasure. Pressing a hand to her throat, she laughed at her skittishness. How foolish to startle. Fane would not return until after she had bathed and dressed.

She hurried across the chamber to open the doors. Three servants stood in the passage. A middle-aged woman with graying hair and arms as thick as trees stepped forward. Barely visible behind her, the other two maidservants looked scarce older than girls. They clutched towels and stood with downcast eyes.

"Me name is Tansy, milady." The older woman tipped her head to the girls. "Nelda. Celeste. We were sent ta help ya with yer bath."

Rexana motioned them inside. Tansy plodded around behind the screen, pulled out the tub, and set it near the fire.

She clicked her tongue. " 'Is lordship skipped his bath this morn? 'Tis the first time since 'e came ta Tangston."

Rexana wet her lips. "I believe he will bathe later, when I am done."

Tansy grinned, revealing the gap between her front teeth. "Mayhap this day, 'e will ask me to scrub his back again. Scarred or no, 'tis a fine bit o' male flesh."

Annoyance skittered through Rexana. This woman bathed Fane? Touched his skin? How often?

"I did not realize he had help with his daily bath." She could not school the tartness from her voice.

Tansy's wrinkled face flushed. "I do not wash 'im every day. Only when 'e asks me. 'Tis usually the morns when 'e's tired. Did I tell ye I was in charge of helping Tangston's previous lord with his baths, afore the king sent 'im off to another keep?" Her bosom swelled with pride. "I do me job well. Sheriff Linford said."

Inwardly, Rexana groaned. She could not brush aside an image of Fane sprawled in the tub, with Tansy's soapy hands sliding over him. Jealously flared. How ridiculous. Mayhap the bath was not such a sound idea, after all.

Another knock shook the doors. Tansy's eyes brightened. "The water." Her shoes slapped on the floorboards and she yanked open the doors. Boys staggered in with filled, steaming buckets. "Be quick now. We do not want 'er ladyship ta catch a chill, especially the day after the weddin.' 'Is lordship wants 'er good and hale fer a few sennights, at least." Tansy winked.

The young girls glanced at the mussed bed, then smothered giggles behind their hands.

Rexana's eyes narrowed. Were the servants privy to information of which she was unaware? Why was she, the lady of the keep, not told? "Why the next few sennights?"

Tansy smiled. "Why, ta get ye with child, milady."

Rexana gasped. "With child!"

The boys, emptying their buckets into the tub, glanced up and scurried away. More young men appeared with water. As she stared at the water's glinting surface, a tremor shot through her.

Of course Fane wanted a child. An heir of noble blood. A son. He wanted to secure his claim to his lands and keep, as quickly as possible.

Foolish, giddy joy unfurled within her at the thought of bearing a babe. She snuffed the thought. No wonder Fane was so determined to couple with her. She must work harder than ever to resist him, to ensure she did not receive his seed.

She would never win an annulment if she carried his babe within her womb.

Shuffled footsteps approached. Tansy patted her arm. In a motherly tone, she said, "Do not fret, milady. I pray I do not speak out of station, but there are many women at Tangston who have birthed strong and 'ealthy sons. I myself 'ave lived through three husbands and eight squawlin' babes. I will gladly help ye with questions and the like."

Rexana drew a shaky breath. "I . . . ah . . . Thank you."

With a sharp cluck, Tansy sent the boys scampering into the corridor. She ordered Nelda to shut the doors, then caught Rexana's hand. "Let us wash ye clean and ready ye for the day."

Protest bubbled in Rexana's throat. The spicy tang of Fane's soap surrounded the tub as though the essence had seeped into the wood, a reminder she was about to partake in one of his private rituals. Yet, as she approached the steaming water, need blossomed within her. She loved leisurely soaks. She always felt refreshed afterward, as though she had revitalized her spirit. Since her parents' deaths, there had been few moments to savor a bath.

She allowed Tansy to whisk off the shift and help her into the tub.

"No bruises," Nelda whispered.

"No marks at all," Celeste said, sounding astonished.

Rexana looked at the girls, who quickly lowered their gazes. Frowning, she sluiced water over her arms and throat. "Bruises? Marks? Whatever do you mean?"

Tansy grunted and knelt beside the tub. When the girls did not answer, she snapped, "Tell her ladyship. What nonsense do ye chatter?"

Nelda fingered a washcloth. Her cheeks stained pink. "His barbaric lust —"

Rexana's shock quickly transformed to sadness and regret. The maids had expected to see that Fane had mistreated her. She stared at the ends of her hair, dripping water like tears. How could these women think aught else? They knew only hurtful gossip. They did not know he had spared her virginity last eve, or of the gentleness he had shown through his kisses.

Tansy's palm slapped the water. "Ye have upset her ladyship. Ye will get a whippin', if ye are not careful."

Nelda's shoulders shook. "I am sorry, but others said —"

Tansy wagged the soap in the air as though it were part of her fleshy hand. "I have known all kinds o' men in me two score and four years. While the sheriff may look fierce, I vow 'e has a gallant heart." Shaking her head, she plunged the soap into the tub. "Look at 'er ladyship. Does she not look hale? She had color in 'er cheeks, until ye spoke so."

"Milady," Nelda whispered, "I apologize."

The maidservant's quivered words poked at Rexana. She might only be married to Fane for a brief while, until her brother was free, but she would not allow her relationship with Fane to be stained by rumor and falsehood.

She raised her chin and held Nelda's gaze. "We will not speak of this matter any more. You will also tell the others — whoever they may be — that the sheriff has shown me only courtesy and respect. Do you understand?"

"A - Aye, milady."

Tansy snatched the washcloth from Nelda. As water sloshed over Rexana's back, followed by the slightly abrasive cloth, she closed her eyes. Soap glided over her back. With a sigh, she leaned into Tansy's skilled scrub.

The familiar scent of lemon and spices enveloped Rexana. Coaxed. Tantalized.

Tansy used Fane's soap.

Rexana's belly tightened. She would smell him on her skin for the rest of the day. The clever woman branded her with his scent. Had Fane asked her to?

She scooted out of reach. "There is no other soap?"

"Only the coarse one the servants use. 'Tis not fit ta use on yer delicate skin." Tansy's brow creased with a puzzled frown. "Ye do not like this one, milady? 'Tis 'is lordship's, and a fine quality."

Goose bumps prickled on Rexana's skin. She tried to ignore the image of Fane sliding into the tub beside her. Of his tanned hand touching her damp skin. Of his mouth, lowering to hers for a kiss. "The scent is a man's, not a lady's."

Tansy's eyes glowed with years of womanly wisdom. "Ye want a perfume ta entice 'is lordship? Next market day, I will send one of the girls ta buy ye some pretty smellin' soaps. Mayhap gilly-flower or lavender?"

"Aye," Rexana said.

"Very well, milady." Her lips pursed, Tansy resumed scrubbing.

Smothering a groan, Rexana closed her eyes, blocked the soap's scent from her mind, and focused on finishing her bath as quickly as possible.

Fane sensed the moment Rexana stepped into the bailey. Just as he relayed final orders to Kester, awareness thrummed through Fane's body. His words vanished mid-sentence. He turned, slowly, to look toward the forebuilding.

Rexana stood with one hand on the open door. The morning sunlight seemed to brighten, as though she were a precious jewel which caught its light. The breeze stirred her loose, damp hair and the hem of her cinnamon colored gown. Dogs barked across the bailey and, as she turned to glance in their direction, the sapphire on her finger glowed.

Warmth rushed through him. Appreciation. Lust.

Now, and forever, lovely Rexana would belong to him.

Kester cleared his throat.

Without looking back, Fane muttered, "You know what to do?"

"Aye, milord. I will get the information you seek."

"Good. I await word of your findings," Fane said. Today, in keeping with his pledge to Rexana, Kester and the men-at-arms would question the local tavern owners and cotters about Rudd.

Yet, when the men returned, Fane expected the evidence to prove not that Rudd was guiltless, but that he was involved in the rebellion.

As Rexana watched the dogs chasing a stick, she tucked hair behind her ear. Fane felt the gesture like a caress upon his skin. His gut tightened. Whatever his men found, he would not allow her brother's actions to undermine her budding sexual interest or the rich, soul-deep love the marriage promised.

He would not allow her untamed passions to wither like a thirsty flower.

Fane headed toward her, gravel skidding under his boots. With each stride, his anticipation heightened. Rexana still had not seen him. She now seemed to be assessing the bailey and its slate-roofed buildings and working servants. Her gaze shifted to the children splashing in a pool of muddy water by the well, and her mouth softened into a smile.

As he approached, her gaze darted to him. She stiffened, as though she gathered up her fortitude like a battle shield.

He pretended not to notice. "You look well, love. You enjoyed your bath?"

She nodded. "Tansy will draw yours, when you are ready."

"I will bathe now. I do not wish to delay our departure."

Rexana turned more fully toward him. Sunlight played over her cheek and her lips' rosy sweetness. "Where will we ride?"

He smiled. "A special place." *A place where you and I can be alone. A place where I can woo you, and begin to sway your heart. A place where you will become mine.*

"While I bathe, will you go to the kitchens? The cook is waiting. He will show you the cooking area and storerooms, then will ask your favorite dishes so he may prepare them. He also has a package waiting for us." Holding her gaze, Fane raised her fingers to his mouth to place a slow, wet kiss on her palm. "I will meet you at the stables."

She shuddered and withdrew her hand. "Very well."

Mischief pricked him. He wanted to see her eyes flash with spirit. To see her cheeks pinken with awareness. To prove she was not immune to her desire.

He trailed his fingers across her shoulder, was rewarded by her ragged intake of breath. "Before you go," he murmured, "we must seal our arrangement. I shall kiss you."

A faint grin curved her lips. "I am out of kisses today."

Before he could draw her into his arms and prove her wrong, she spun away and headed across the bailey.

He laughed. "We shall see," he called after her.

She flicked her hand at him, as though whatever tactics he tried, he would not be able to change her mind. As his laugher faded, he folded his arms over his chest. Leaned a shoulder against the forebuilding's rough wall. Watched sunlight dance over her hair and her hips sway beneath the well-cut silk.

Pleasure stirred within his soul. Knowingly or not, she had taunted him. Challenged him. Dared him to try to get another kiss.

He intended to have it.

And a whole lot more.

# Chapter Twelve

REXANA FINGERED HAIR FROM HER BROW and looked out across the fields that stretched either side of the road like folds of sumptuous green silk. A stream glinted amongst the grass and wildflowers. Excitement quickened her pulse. What a glorious place. She itched to jump from the mare's saddle and run to the sparkling water. To plunge her hands into the swollen pool caught between large rocks. To lie back in the cornflowers and daisies and feel the sun shine on her face.

As though sensing her mood, Fane swiveled in his saddle to look back at her. "This place pleases you?"

She nodded eagerly.

He smiled. "I thought you would like it. We will stop at the stream."

As he turned to relay orders to the guards riding ahead and behind them, Rexana glanced back at the fields. His gaze had held a heat even bolder than the sun's, a fire that had rippled through her like light on water. Would she ever become immune to his sinful looks?

Birds twittered from the grove of aspen and birch ahead. The bright song called to her. Tugged at the wildness in her soul. The part of her that vowed she would never belong to Fane.

She tightened her grip on her mare's reins. "I will meet you at the stream," she called.

Fane looked over his shoulder. "Rexana?"

She kicked her heels into her mount's sides. The horse bolted, plunging into the sea of grasses, flowers, and floating dandelion spores. With a delighted laugh, Rexana bent against the horse's damp neck and let the animal canter.

Grasses swished against her ankles and her bliaut's hem. Seed pods snapped. Yellow butterflies and honeybees whizzed into the air. Rudd's brooch, pinned to her bliaut, thumped against her skin. With her palm, she pressed it against her heart. She inhaled the scents of crushed grass and rich earth and sighed with pleasure.

Filtering out the meadow sounds, she listened. She expected to hear Fane's bellow. Anticipated the thunder of his destrier's hooves as he pursued her. Yet, she heard only her own rasped breaths and the mare's pounding hoofbeats. She shrugged off unexpected disappointment.

With encouraging words and pats, she guided the horse to the stream bank. Drawing the sweat-lathered animal to a halt, she dismounted, then led it down to the water for a drink. The muddy shore was sprinkled with stones, worn smooth as old coins. The horse walked into the shallows and drank. Loosening her hold on the reins a fraction, Rexana stooped to pick up a pale pink rock. It glittered in the sun's light, as though peppered with stars.

Hoofbeats and a horse's breathy snort came from behind her. She glanced at the field. Fane rode toward her. Alone. The guards, she noted with a quick glance, stood in the birch's shade and watched the road.

She braced herself against the fury she expected to see in Fane's gaze. Yet, he regarded her with wry amusement. Before his mount even came to a complete halt, he kicked his leg over and slid from its back.

He landed in the grass with effortless grace. The grace of a hardened warrior who had spent half of his life upon a horse, and who knew victory in battle. The grace of a man who believed himself in complete control of a situation.

Fane caught his horse's reins. As he led the destrier down to the stream, his boots crunched on the stones. The huge beast splashed into the water beside the mare, bent its head, and drank.

"You ride like a meadow sprite," Fane said, not looking at her. "I would be wise to remember that."

His hair, stirring in the breeze, lifted from his forehead in shiny strands. She resisted staring at his handsome profile. Resisted the glow of pleasure that his words sparked. "I ride as I please." She dropped the pink stone into the mud, then wiped her hands on her skirt. "You are not angry that I rode off?"

"Why would I be?" He looked at her. "My horse can easily outrun yours. I could have caught you, if I had wished."

The peculiar disappointment returned. "You had no wish to pursue me?"

"You did not wish to be caught." His voice lowered. "When you want me to capture you, little fig, I will."

His words shivered through her. She laughed, a harsh sound. "When will that be? Today? Tomorrow?"

His smile became a sensual grin. "I do not know, love. Yet, I vow 'twill be soon. Your body, heart, and soul cry for our union. Aye?"

Fie! How could he read her so clearly, as though she laid herself bare to his scrutiny? How did he spy upon her feelings?

Her face burning, she turned her back to him and tugged on the mare's reins. She led the animal out of the water and up to the grass where it began to graze.

Fane chuckled.

Refusing to look at him, she stomped back to the

water's edge to glare down at her reflection. She wrenched up her bliaut's hem to keep it out of the mud, hunched down, and rinsed her shaking hands.

"Come, Rexana," he said, laughter in his voice. "Shall we call a truce and eat?"

Out of the corner of her eye, she watched Fane lead his horse up alongside hers. After giving the beast a pat on the neck, he reached for the bulging sack tied to the saddle.

She stood, drying her hands on her skirts.

When he glanced at her, one eyebrow raised in expectation of an answer, a little voice inside her sighed. She could not easily forget his arrogant words. Yet, the morn's ride and fresh air had given her an appetite. She nodded.

Fane strode up to where the grass met the stream bank. She followed. He reached into the sack, withdrew a woolen blanket, then spread it on the grass. They could still see the guards, she realized, but also enjoy the beauty of the stream, the rocks, and the endless fields. She hugged her arms over her chest and squeezed. How lovely.

Fane dropped down onto the blanket. He stretched one muscled leg out and bent the other. Resting an elbow on his raised knee, he looked inside the bag. He whistled. "I hope you are hungry."

She knelt on the blanket's edge. "Cook would not tell me what he stuffed into the sack. He said he was forbidden."

A grin curved Fane's mouth. "I threatened him with a wretched punishment if he told you."

"Why would you wish harm upon that poor man?" She frowned. "What did you threaten him with?"

"Ten poisonous spiders in his bed."

She shrieked. "How could you?"

"Rexana, I tease you."

He patted her arm. Sensation buzzed across her skin. Swift. Undeniable.

"I did order him not to tell you, though," Fane said, as though she had not jumped at his touch. "I did not want him to ruin the surprise."

She busied her fingers with smoothing her skirts around her legs. "Surprise?"

"I asked him to prepare foods with more . . . bite than usual. I did not think you would mind a culinary challenge."

Mischief gleamed in Fane's eyes. He looked like a cheeky little boy with a sack full of naughty secrets. She could not keep from laughing.

"I do enjoy a challenge, milord." She grinned. "Let me see what you have."

"First, you must promise to have a taste."

Warning stirred inside her. She sensed he spoke of more than food. Yet, with the sun warming her back and the sweet whisper of wind through the long grass, she could not deny the wild urge to play along with him.

If she grew weary of his game, she could simply walk away to explore the stream, and leave him to his meal.

"I promise," she said.

He winked. "I hoped you would not disappoint me."

Reaching into the sack, he took out cloth-wrapped bundles. She lifted the fabric from the treasures inside. Honey-glazed dates sprinkled with cloves and ginger. Roasted chicken encrusted with fat lumps of garlic. Meat pies dusted with cinnamon and herbs. A loaf of rye bread. And figs.

She inhaled the heady aroma. "You woo me with spices?"

"Amongst other temptations."

Her heart fluttered. She cast him a quick glance, but he had turned his attentions to the wine flask at the bottom of the sack. With a snap, the flask opened.

He offered it to her. "Drink?"

She shook her head. "I will eat first." The voice inside her applauded her restraint. She would be wise to get fare in her belly, so the wine did not addle her senses.

Or sway her reason.

Rexana took a meat pie and bit into the flaky crust. Fane's gaze fixed upon her mouth. He stared as though he, too, tasted the light, buttery pastry, chicken and spicy gravy flooding her tongue. Disquiet tingled through her. She touched a finger to the corner of her mouth. Caught a stray bit of pastry.

"Allow me."

Before she could wipe her finger on a cloth, Fane caught her hand. Drew it to his mouth. His breath warmed her fingertips. She tensed . . . yet somehow could not pull away. He smiled before he licked her finger clean. "Delicious," he murmured, then released her hand.

Her breath shivered from her lips. Awareness whooshed through her, from the tips of her fingers to the secret place between her thighs. She could scarce keep her eyelids from sweeping shut. Saints above, did he know he had this effect upon her? Did he woo her with his tongue, as well as the fare?

With effort, she finished chewing the mouthful of pie. She struggled to control her rampant imagination, which had leapt from him suckling her fingers to pressing her down in the grass and kissing her witless.

Shame on her foolishness. Fane might have licked her fingers because, in the east, this was considered a courtesy between husband and wife.

Or, he tried to seduce her.

She did not understand him well enough to know for certain.

Rexana dared another bite of the delicious pie, careful this time not to miss a bit. He smiled, dragged hair from his eyes, then studied the unwrapped bundles.

"What shall I eat first?" he said, as though to himself. "Chicken? Dates? Mayhap a little fig?"

His sensuous voice resonated through her. An icy tingle pooled in her belly as she fought a delicious shudder. Did he woo her with clever words too? Did he infer he wished to taste more than her fingers, or did her imagination again cloud her judgment? "Since the figs are sweet," she said, proud of her unwavering voice, "mayhap you should eat those last?"

"My thoughts exactly." With a brazen grin, he picked up a chicken leg and tore off a strip of meat with his teeth.

Perspiration beaded on her upper lip. The devilment in his gaze had sharpened. He had a definite purpose to his teasing. Why did he look at her as though he found her more tempting than all of the delicacies spread out before him? Did he?

His lips moved as he chewed. Sensual, firm lips, shiny from the moist chicken. He bit down again on the meat, his bite deft. Elegant. Restrained. Not at all the way she imagined an uncivilized barbarian ate. Uncertainty swept through her. She forced her gaze from his tantalizing mouth that tempted her to lean over and kiss him, and nibbled the pie.

She had dined with many nobles of rank, including Garmonn, at her parents' feasts. Few had eaten with the courtesy Fane showed at this simple picnic. And Garmonn . . . She closed her eyes against a memory. He had delighted in playing with the fare while boasting to Rudd how much he could stuff into his mouth all at once.

Once, Garmonn had choked on an enormous mouthful of stewed cabbage and had turned a violent purple color before he spewed the mangled shreds all over the table. Rudd had laughed. Her parents — a blessing upon their departed souls — had ordered fresh table linens and dismissed the incident as the unfortunate result of poorly cooked cabbage.

Raising her lashes, she cast Fane a glance. How little she knew of him. Yet, she could not imagine him gorging himself or making a public spectacle of retching.

As though sensing her gaze, he tossed aside the gnawed chicken bone and looked up. He gestured to the blanket. "You like the fare?"

"Aye, milord."

"Why do you not eat, then?" He pushed the bread toward her. "We cannot let Cook's work go to waste."

She laughed. "I doubt you will allow that to happen."

"True." His eyes softened with a hint of admiration. "I am glad that this meal pleases you, as it does me."

"Indeed, I enjoy learning what pleases my husband." As soon the words left her lips, she gasped. She had not meant to sound so provocative. As though she tried to woo him.

His brows raised in unquestionable interest.

"I mean," she added, unable to defray a blush, "what *fare* pleases you. Spicy. Not spicy. Sweet. As lady of

Tangston, I expect my duties will include ordering the food, wine, and spices." Before she embarrassed herself further, she bit off a gigantic mouthful of pie.

Fane tore off a chunk of bread. "Your duties may well include such things. Yet, your words raise an interesting point. I would like to know what pleases my wife."

She swallowed. "Oh." Traitorous warmth, licking through her like greedy flames, thawed the icy pool in her belly. *Your kisses please me,* her mind cooed. *Your touch pleases me. Your wet tongue upon my fingers —*

She looked at the horses and schooled her bawdy thoughts.

"Horse rides," she said, "They please me."

"Ah." He chewed the bread. "And?"

Her frantic gaze darted about the meadow. She would not betray her lustful thoughts or yield to the reckless impulses taunting her. Not when she must remain virgin. "Flowers," she said brightly. "All kinds. Especially roses."

"You have a romantic heart. Good."

"Also swimming." Rexana stared down at the stream's blue-green pool. "'Tis wondrous to splash in cool water on a scorching summer's day."

"You can swim?"

She smiled at the incredulity in Fane's voice. "I learned when I was a child. My parents did not know until years later." With a soft laugh, she added, "My mother would have screeched in horror to see me frolicking in the water wearing only my shift. I always made sure my hair was dry and braided again before I returned to the keep."

His jaw tautened mid-chew. His gaze flicked over her once, as though he imagined her clad in the wet slip of linen. "If your parents did not teach you to swim, who did?"

"Rudd."

Fane's lips curled. "I should have guessed."

His gritty tone pricked her unease. She remembered the brooch pinned to her bliaut and resisted the urge to touch it. "Rudd taught me many things, including how to ride a horse without a saddle, and to hold a dagger."

"A dagger?" Fane threw up his hands. "Why? You wished to do battle like a man?"

"We cut up sticks, then made boats to float on the water. I was glad to do more with my hands than straighten my skirts or push a needle through silk."

His eyes narrowing, Fane leaned toward her. "Your brother has been a disruptive influence for years, it seems."

Air shot from her lungs. The last bite of pie fell from her hand and landed on the blanket. "My brother is an intelligent young lord who —"

"He is a hellion."

She fought to restrain her temper. "Rudd is head-strong and . . . outspoken, aye, but he was not always so. He was very close to my father. He grieved terribly when my parents died."

"You did not?"

The healing wound deep inside her hurt. She fought tears, while forcing calmness she did not feel into her tone. "He is still my brother. I have no other family left." Her chin tipped up a notch. " 'Twould please me above all else, milord, to see him."

Fane looked across the meadow. His gaze darkened to the murky brown of a fathomless pool. She sensed his fierce resistance to the idea, and the anger simmering within him.

"Please," she whispered.

A muscle in his jaw twitched. "Nay."

"I must know Rudd is all right. That he is not hurt. That he has enough to eat. That he has a blanket at night to ward off the dungeon's chill."

"He is not harmed. He is being treated well enough."

She choked back a scathing retort. She would gain naught by shrieking, crying, and insisting upon Rudd's innocence. She must approach this disagreement with care. With civility.

As she swept crumbs from her skirts, she said, "Were you not a prisoner once? I have heard the tales. I have seen your scars."

A growl rumbled between his teeth. His steel-hard gaze flicked back to her. "Beware, love. You tread a forbidden path."

"Do I?" Her body quivered like a frightened hare's, but still she plunged ahead. "Would you not have been grateful to see your family? For a visitor to soothe your fears, and reassure you when you thought your cause was lost?"

His expression clouded with warning. "Enough."

"Would you not —"

"I said *enough*, wife."

His voice's desperate edge silenced her. Touched her, with a raw potency she did not expect.

The set of his jaw held grief and self-condemnation. She had wounded him. What had she said to affect him so? What memories, buried within his soul, had she awakened? Somehow, she had roused the demons lurking inside him.

She touched his arm. "Fane?"

He shook off her hand, tossed aside the bread, then picked up the wine flask. "I will not discuss my imprisonment. Do not compare my experiences with your brother's. I did not conspire against my king."

"Neither did Rudd."

Fane shook his head and exhaled a hissed breath, as though he struggled to leash a curt reply.

Tension hummed in the air between them.

Tension, aye, but also a seething undercurrent of

desire.

Even in this fragile moment, desire drew her to him. Yearning tugged at her conscience. Challenged her quest to stay pure. Challenged who she really was, and what she had vowed.

Her stomach did a sickening turn. How could she want Fane, when he refused to let her see Rudd? How could she even think of lying with Fane, in hopes of changing his mind?

Huffing a breath, she shoved to her feet.

"You have eaten your fill, love?"

"I am no longer hungry." Ignoring his offer of wine, she shook the last crumbs from her gown and stomped into the sea of grass.

"Rexana."

She paused in a swath of daisies, her back to him. "Aye?"

"I will . . . consider . . . your request."

Her pulse kicked against her ribs. Joy and anticipation rushed through her. Her hands fisted into her wrinkled skirts as she blinked away the first sting of tears. "I thank you, husband. Your consideration pleases me."

*Your consideration pleases me.*

Rexana's words circled in Fane's mind like hunting hawks. He scowled, tipped his head back, and downed a mouthful of wine. The tart liquid rushed down his throat and burned all the way down to his gut. A distinctly uncomfortable experience. Yet thankfully, it robbed his attention from his throbbing loins.

The battle of words had not driven an anvil between them, as Rexana may have expected or even intended. It had only whittled away the restraints he had managed to impose upon his sensual hunger. Ah, God. Such a fine line lay between the past and the present. Between restraint and mindless intent. Between anger and desire.

A laugh rumbled in his chest. What irony. He sat among a tantalizing orgy of food, yet he starved. Craved. Wanted.

He stared at Rexana, strolling through the grass toward the stream. Her hair gleamed in the sunlight, a luxurious fall of golden honey-brown. His fingers itched to plunge into her silky tresses and haul her back against him. To turn her around and cup her head. To hold her firm, while his lips and tongue showed her exactly what in hellfire pleased him.

Swatting aside a gnat, he drank again. He could not take his gaze off her. Her body swayed with each stride, a natural movement, as though she intuitively sensed the rhythm of the breeze through the grass. She had moved with such grace when she had danced for him in veils, bells and smoky shadow.

A shiver ran through him. If he closed his eyes, revived that titillating memory, he could still see her lithe body arching, spinning and swaying, a look of pure abandon on her face.

Leaning forward, he watched her step down onto the stony bank. She hesitated, then headed toward the large stones half submerged in the water. Caution flickered at the back of his mind. He dismissed it. Foolish to worry about her, when she seemed capable of taking care of herself.

He set down the flask, then began to rewrap the fare. None of it would go to waste. Memories of old women and children begging for scraps in the squalid eastern markets still haunted his dreams. The leftover food would feed Tangston's beggars.

Or even the traitors in the dungeon.

His fingers tightened on the linen enfolding the chicken. He had been right to deny Rexana a visit. Of course he had. She would not appreciate his reasons, even if he explained that he was required, as High Sheriff, to deal harshly with suspected criminals.

Would she call him barbaric, for using the prospect of a visit from her as leverage to make her stubborn brother confess? Nay, she would call him heartless, manipulative and cruel. Yet, she knew naught of real cruelty, of stinging whips, gouging metal instruments, and taunts that would strain even a holy saint's sanity. Indeed, he would have lost his mind, if not for Leila's visits and her healing touch.

A shudder crawled down Fane's spine. He would never apply brutal torture to prisoners in his dungeon.

Yet, that meant he must use other means of persuasion. Including denial of what his prisoners wanted most.

Rexana now stood on the third rock, peering down into the water, one hand pressed to her bodice. She touched that wretched brooch. She wore the gold arrow every day. It seemed to mean more to her than her own happiness.

"I will have you, Rexana," he said under his breath. "I will."

He reached for the saddlebag, shoving in the chicken and the stoppered wine flask. As he reached for the figs, water plunked behind him—the sound of a small stone plummeting into the pool.

Rexana shrieked. "Nay. Oh, nay!"

Her distress slashed through Fane like a double-edged knife. He shoved to his feet, one hand on his dagger's jeweled hilt. Danger? The meadow seemed deserted. The guards had not shouted a warning.

She was down on all fours on the rock, her face close to the water. Her body shook as though she scarce had the strength to stand.

"Rexana?" He tore through the grass, smashing stalks and daisies. A bee hurtled over his head, its drone as sharp as a whizzing arrow.

She plunged her arm into the pool. Soaked her silk bodice up to her shoulder. Grabbed for an object in the water.

"Rexana!"

He stumbled on the stony bank, regained his balance, and lunged toward the nearest rock. Why did she not answer him? What could be so important that she risked falling in?

Sobbing, she leaned farther into the water, as though the object were just out of reach. Her cheek flattened against the pool's surface, and her hair floated behind her like a silky golden veil.

"Stop!" He leapt onto the first stone. "Be careful—"

Her free hand skidded on the smooth rock. Clawed for a handhold. Slipped.

Head first, she tumbled into the water.

"God's teeth." Water splashed over Fane's boots. He jumped to the third wet, glistening rock and stared at the silk floating on the pool's surface. Rexana flailed her arms. Her foot slapped the water. Spitting, choking, she surfaced, then stood.

Rubbing water from her cheeks, she blinked down at the mud-swirled pond that came to her waist. She was trembling. Her eyes welled with tears. She looked utterly bedraggled and as vulnerable as a soggy baby rabbit.

Fane's heart twisted. Hunching down, he extended his hand. "Come out, love. I will help you."

She sniffled and shook her head. "The brooch fell in. I must find it."

A groan stirred within Fane. His gaze dropped to her bodice. The little arrow no longer winked and taunted him from its esteemed place above her left breast. A gleeful laugh welled inside him.

As he silently snuffed away his ridiculous thoughts, his gaze drifted lower. His throat thickened. The wet silk dragged down the neckline of her gown. Revealed the enticing cleft between her breasts. Molded to her luscious swells. Her hardened nipples poked against the bodice like two fat, juicy grapes. What a magnificent sight.

"I must find the brooch." She squinted down into the pool's clouded depths.

Clearing the lustful haze from his mind, he said, "Stand still. You are stirring the bottom."

She froze. Her mouth crumpled. "If 'tis lost —"

He caught her icy fingers. "We will find it. Together."

Another groan rumbled inside Fane, this one born deep in his soul. *We*. Lovesick fool. He could not refuse to help Rexana, no matter how much he resented her brother and that accursed brooch.

Her face warmed with hope. He released her hand, unlaced and removed his boots, then slid off the rock into the pool.

The chill water sucked the air from his lungs and the heat from his loins. He inhaled once, twice, until the initial shock subsided. As his breaths slowed, he became aware of her warm nearness only a touch away. Of her quickened breathing. Of a sense of expectation humming between them.

He ran his hand across the water's surface, brushing aside her floating skirts. Her fingers touched his. She did not pull them away.

Anticipation shivered through him. He clenched his teeth. Fought the wanton thoughts that leapt into his mind. Focused on the murky swirl of mud and water around him. His nostrils filled with the scents of damp cloth, mud, and sun drenched water. And with Rexana's tantalizing scent.

Down near his bare feet, where the sunlight just reached, he spied a glint of gold. He ducked beneath the water. Dragged up a handful of mud. As he rose, shaking hair from his face, he sluiced the mud from his fingers.

The brooch winked in the light.

"You found it!"

"I vowed that we would," he said.

Her eyes shone with gratitude. With her free hand, she wiped tears from her cheeks.

He extended his dripping palm toward her. Her fingers brushed across his skin. Touched the brooch. Then, on a sob, she wrapped her fingers around his and squeezed tight. The little arrow nestled between their wet palms.

Pride and pleasure leapt to life within him. He held her gaze. Questioned, without words, her desires. Strong, sure, her gaze did not falter.

Realization shot through him with the echo of a thunderclap. She wanted his kiss.

Expectation throbbed through every part of his body. He savored the press of her flesh against his. Gently swept his thumb across her knuckles, even as he planned how best to give her what she asked.

"Thank you," she whispered.

He smiled. Raised their joined hands. Kissed the backs of her fingers. "Come here, Rexana."

She tilted her head up, as though startled by his boldness. Sunlight played over her throat and the matted strands of her hair streaming down her bodice. Her lashes dropped on a shiver.

A shiver of interest.

He pulled her toward him. Water lapped against his wet tunic. Chilled his cold flesh. He did not care. He wanted her kiss. Needed it. Craved it.

Closer, closer, she came. Her drifting skirts brushed against his groin. His senses flooded with her. Rexana. His wife. The woman of his heart and soul.

Her tongue darted between her lips, dampening them. His patience fled. Burying his hand into her wet hair, he cupped her head. With a groan, he lowered his mouth and kissed her.

He expected resistance — a cry of protest, or her hand, tearing free of his, to press against his tunic. Yet, with a breathless moan, she melted against him. Opened her lips like a sweet, blooming flower. Kissed him back.

Desire roared to life in his veins. She tasted wild. Eager. Like a woman whose fierce hunger matched his own. With his tongue, he deepened the kiss. He had sensed her rich passion, the untamed desire hidden deep within her. At last, he had unleashed it.

He kissed her until his body thrummed with need, and his soul cried for physical consummation. He tore his lips from hers. Shook his hand free of hers. As she curled her fingers protectively around the brooch, he reached into the water, locked both hands on her waist, and raised her up. He set her upon the closest rock.

Eyes glazed, her mouth reddened with kisses, she braced her hands upon the weathered stone and stared down at him. Expectation shone in her gaze. Shimmering droplets on the ends of her hair dripped into the water. She was beautiful. A water Nereid, gifted to him by some ancient pagan deity.

He set his hands upon her damp, silk-covered knees and parted them. A breath wrenched from her lips. He stepped forward. Claimed the water between them.

Gazing up at her, he trailed one hand up her right calf, shielded from his touch by wet silk. "I want you, Rexana."

Her breasts rose and fell on a sharp inhalation.

"Tell me you want me. Tell me you want our union."

Her eyes closed. She pressed her lips together, as though to quell an urgent, impulsive 'aye.' "I want you, Fane, but —"

"But what?" His patience broke like cracked stone. He grabbed rock handholds either side of her hips. Bracing his foot against the slick, submerged portion of the boulder, he heaved himself up. His thighs slid between hers. He hovered over her, his arm and shoulder muscles screaming with tension, his body hard and straight as an arrow.

She scrambled backward.

Shaking hair from his cheek, he dropped to his hands and knees. Pulling his sheathed knife from his belt, he tossed it onto the rock. He crawled toward her like a hungry, prowling lion, until he trapped her at the other side. With a low, husky growl, he straddled her.

She lay flat on her back. She stared up into his face. Her wide-eyed gaze shadowed with desire, yet also uncertainty.

The stone's rough warmth seeped into his palms. In contrast, he imagined the soft, pliant texture of her skin. His hands itched to touch her. Explore her. Free her breasts from the mass of soggy, confining fabric. Bare her beautiful body to the sunlight, so at last, he could see and touch all he desired.

As though reading his thoughts, she pushed up on her elbows. "Fane, cease."

"Why?" He dipped his head to kiss her brow.

Nose. Mouth. Tempted her with slow, deep, persuasive kisses, until her head fell back and she whimpered. "This is what we both want," he said against her lips. "You cannot deny it. You cannot deny *me*."

"I cannot," she agreed with a helpless gasp, "but —"

"You worry we will be seen?" He laughed against her creamy neck. "The guards will turn their backs. They will be watching the road" — he nibbled her earlobe — "though there will be few travelers this day. Most of the locals celebrated our wedding feast. They will be lying abed, nursing sore heads."

His mouth skimmed lower, to the fragrant hollow of her throat. She jerked sideways, thwarting his kiss. " 'Tis not . . . being seen."

He paused. "You wish to lie on my tunic? Is the stone uncomfortable?"

She bit her lip and shook her head.

"Good." He smiled, then reached one hand behind him. Caught the sodden fullness of her skirts. Tugged.

"Oh!" She struggled to rise.

With gentle persistence, he pressed her down on her back. Kissed her again. Seduced with his tongue, even as the silk dragged against his wet hose. "Relax, love," he whispered. "Let me lead this dance."

Her breaths quickened. Her brow furrowed into a frown, yet before she could answer, he kissed her again. Coaxed her, with nips at the corner of her mouth and down the side of her neck.

"Fane . . . oh. . . .what . . . Oh, mercy."

One swift tug, and he bared her almost to her thighs. He looked between their bodies at her pale skin and slender legs, lying between his own. A shudder tore through him. He must be patient. He must soothe her virgin uncertainties, to ensure that even her first time, she found pleasure.

She squirmed as though self-conscious, then tried to wriggle free of his hold. As he caught her lips in a reassuring kiss, he reached down to brush his fingers over the smooth swell of her knee. "You are beautiful, Rexana. I will make you feel beautiful. I promise."

She moaned. Her lashes fluttered, and he slid a hand under her calf. Raised her leg. Guided her bent leg onto his back.

Her body tensed. "Fane."

Shifting his weight, he eased down to his forearms, until his mouth hovered above hers. His hair brushed her throat.

He kissed her. Slowly. Tenderly.

Then lowered his full weight upon her.

A raw groan ripped through him, the sound of a starving man gifted with a bounteous feast. At last, they lay chest to chest. Belly to belly. Hardness to womanly softness. Despite layers of damp cloth still separating them, sensual fire blazed through him. His loins tightened. As he expected, her body fit well to his. Their union would be perfect.

He looked down at her lovely face. Her eyes were closed. A blush stained her cheeks. "Fane," she said thickly. "You must not tempt me like this."

"You complain, wife?"

"You are most wicked."

Laughter warmed his throat. "I know."

She half laughed, half sobbed. "Let me up. I can bear no more."

He did not answer. Words could not convince her like his body could. Pressing a kiss to her brow, he flexed his hips.

She gasped. Her lashes flicked open. He caught the self-reproach and regret in her gaze. Why did she feel so? She treasured her virginity? Or, did she fear the moment of pain that initiated her into womanhood and fully made her his wife?

Before he could ask, a primitive cry warbled in her throat. A sound that voiced his own wanting, need, and hunger.

As though the last of her restraint had fled, she clawed her hands into his hair. Hauled his mouth closer to hers. She kissed him hard, a tempestuous clash of lips and tongue.

Her body shifted under him. Arched against him. Fitted him more fully into her body's curves.

He shuddered. "Rexana."

Gasping, panting, he reached between their bodies.

Yanked up his wet tunic. Found the points of his hose and tore them free.

Over her urgent kisses, he thought he heard shouts. His imagination. Had to be. Now, of all times, fate would not be so cruel.

He buried his face against her neck. Pulled the last of his points free. A moment more, then he could ease himself inside her. Plunge into her tight warmth and make her his.

His hardened flesh pulsed with excitement.

Her hands, sliding up under his tunic, stilled. "I hear voices," she said.

The shouts became insistent.

Hoofbeats drowned out the meadow's seductive hum.

Fane cursed. He would threaten whoever interrupted with a punishment far worse than ten deadly spiders.

He raised his head.

And froze.

# Chapter thirteen

A MAN'S BELLOW ECHOED ACROSS THE MEADOW, jolting Rexana from the haze of desire. Her pulse lurched into a sickening *thud-thud*. She had heard a cry like that once before. It still echoed in her nightmares.

Scrambling off her, Fane rose to his knees. His expression grim, he fastened his hose, shoved his knife into his belt and pulled on his leather boots.

A foul, metallic taste flooded Rexana's tongue as horrible memories invaded her mind. Swallowing hard, she sat up, pushing her gown back down to her ankles, even as her gaze flew to the meadow.

Riders were silhouetted on the road. Two of Fane's guards stood on the outskirts of the grove, yelling and waving at him. The other two, their horses at a full gallop, were half way to the stream, pursuing a lone man on horseback. Ahead of the guards by several paces, he kicked his mount as though he were possessed.

With another angry roar, he whipped a sword from its scabbard. Steel gleamed in the sunlight.

Sweat dampened Rexana brow. Her hand, pressed to the rock, curled around the gold arrow. Her nails scratched on the stone.

Her mind had not played tricks on her.

Garmonn was near enough that she saw the fury contorting his mouth and his jaw's ugly set. Her chest tightened. It hurt to inhale. She heard a strange, wheezing sound, and realized it was her own breathing.

Fane glanced back at her, his visage partly hidden by his snarled hair. "Stay here. Do not move from this rock."

She shivered at the controlled fury in his words. Memories of Thomas's anguished cry, of bloodstained snow, whipped through her mind. This time, Fane's blood would be spilled.

Panic welled between her ribs. She could not let Fane suffer at Garmonn's hand.

She grabbed Fane's leg. "Be careful."

His lips tilted in a grim smile. "He will not harm me. 'Tis time he learned a lesson or two."

"Nay! He —"

"Later, love, you will tell me. Stay on this rock. Do not cross to the shore until I say you can."

His boots clipped on the rocks. He leapt off and onto the stony shore. He stooped, collected a few pebbles, then set his hands upon his hips.

Fingers pressed to her mouth, she watched Garmonn tear toward Fane. The guards behind him shouted for him to stop. They kicked their lathered mounts faster.

They would not catch him. He was too far ahead. He was skilled at eluding pursuit. Many times he had boasted of outrunning murderous Saracens in battle, when they tried to corner his mount and cut his head from his body.

As his horse bore down on Fane, the ground seemed to shake. The air pulsed with tension. Her body stiffened. Quivered. A scream burned for release.

Garmonn leaned over his horse's neck. Adjusted his hold on his sword's grip. Aimed the blade straight at Fane's heart.

The horse's hooves clattered on the bank. Closer. Closer.

Garmonn's battle roar ripped through the air.

She lunged to her feet. "Naaayyy!"

His face twisted in surprise. The blade wavered a fraction. At the same moment, Fane darted aside. His arm snapped back. A stone whizzed through the air and smacked into Garmonn's temple.

Garmonn jerked upright. The horse skidded to a halt, reared, and flailed its front legs.

Blood trailed down Garmonn's forehead to the side

of his face. With a jerk on the reins, he steadied his
horse. He rubbed his brow with his sleeve. Stared at
the crimson stain. Pointed the sword at Fane. "God
damned *barbarian*!"

"You wish to kill me?"

Garmonn's face reddened. "Why should I not? You
forced yourself upon Rexana."

Fane laughed. The sound held no warmth, only
warning.

Garmonn flicked his sword in her direction.
"Rexana's bliaut is ruined. Her hair is tangled. You
must have dragged her kicking and screaming through
the water."

Rexana hugged her arms across her bodice. If only
she had a cloak to draw around her to shield her from
Garmonn's roving gaze. Yet, naught could buffer her
against his knowing eyes, or the deadly chill that rippled through her. When she saw the anger etched into
Fane's features, the chill deepened.

*Oh, Fane. Beware.*

Out of the corner of her eye, she saw the guards
reach the stream bank. Fane motioned for them to
halt. They hesitated, but obeyed.

"Your words are false," Fane said. "Rexana —"

"I saw." Garmonn's eyes narrowed to slits. "She
pushed you away. She tried to flee. You would not let
her. You forced her down beneath you, yanking up her
skirts as though she were some cheap tavern slut. She

would not willingly lie with you, so you forced her to rut with you."

Rexana gasped. How could he accuse Fane of such savagery?

A blush stung her face but, holding her place upon the rock, she met Garmonn's accusatory stare. She ignored the fear crushing her innards, and prayed that he heeded her. "Please, listen to me. Fane did not —"

"Our affairs are no concern of yours, Garmonn," Fane interrupted, "but I have never forced Rexana. I have no need."

Garmonn's hand tightened on the weapon. "Liar!"

In her mind's eye, Rexana saw Garmonn's arm thrust forward. Fane's face whiten with agony. Blood spatter, thick and red, on the stones.

Oh, God. *Oh, God!*

As though from a distance, she heard Fane growl. "Lower your sword, Garmonn. Now."

"Go to hell."

The pebbles in Fane's hand clicked together, a grim sound. "You are on my lands. You disturb my privacy and make threats upon my life. You have frightened my wife. Do you wish to spend time in my dungeon?"

"You have suffered no harm. You have no reason to arrest me." Garmonn's mouth twisted into a sneer. "My father will convince you that your judgment is flawed."

"You cannot hide behind your sire's position, or his goodwill, for the rest of your life."

The thud of approaching hoofbeats underscored Fane's last words. Sucking in a painful breath, Rexana dared a glance. Lord Darwell drew his horse up beside the guards, tossed aside the reins, and dismounted in the grass with a loud grunt.

Hope flooded through her. Darwell was one of the few people who had influence on Garmonn. Mayhap he would be able to prevent bloodshed.

Mopping his forehead with the edge of his mantle, Darwell hurried down the bank. He slipped and skidded on the stones before halting beside Fane.

"Garmonn, what are you doing? Lower that sword before you cause injury."

"Lord Darwell," Fane muttered. "I did not expect to see you this day."

Darwell's gray head bobbed. "Good day, milord. Milady. We are on our way home."

Fane's brow arched. "Ah."

"I met up with Garmonn at a tavern last eve. We decided to stay the night, as my son was . . . ah . . . unfit to ride." Darwell cleared his throat, then glared at Garmonn. "Put the sword away. You are making an idiot of yourself."

Garmonn's mouth flattened, but he did not move. "Linford assaulted Rexana."

"Neither you nor I can be certain of what we saw."

Darwell adjusted the belt at his waist. "I am sure there is a reasonable explanation, if his lordship desires to tell us. Which, of course, he may not."

Fane shrugged. "Rexana fell into the water. I offered her comfort. I did what any civilized, warm blooded, newly wedded husband would do."

Darwell wiggled his eyebrows. "I see."

"Do not believe him, Father. He lies like a slippery tongued Saracen." Garmonn raised the tip of the sword. His gaze darkened with menace.

Rexana's belly roiled. She ignored Fane's earlier words, forced aside the warning cries within her, and stepped onto the next rock. "Fane did not harm me. I swear, he did not. There is no reason to draw blood on my behalf. None!"

"You speak true, Rexana?" Garmonn muttered. "Or do you try and protect his miserable life?"

"I speak true."

Fane's fingers closed over the pebbles. "I have told you twice to sheathe your weapon, Garmonn. Do it. If you refuse, my men will arrest you."

"Arrest my son?" For a moment, desperation gleamed in Darwell's gaze. Stretching his arm up in a plea, he strode closer to Garmonn's mount. "Do as Sheriff Linford commands, son. We do not want more trouble, do we?"

Garmonn's jaw tightened. He swore, lowered the sword, and rammed it back into its scabbard.

Catching his horse's reins, Garmonn looked at Rexana. Her pulse suspended for a painful beat. His stare reminded her of that winter day, and warned her anew of the threat he had made if she ever told what happened. She had told Rudd that poor Thomas was wounded in an accident. Rudd did not know the whole truth. He could not, or his life would be in terrible danger.

Garmonn's gaze slid to Fane. Brutal promise shone in Garmonn's eyes. "We will meet again, Sheriff."

After wheeling his horse around, he spurred it back toward the road.

Rexana's legs threatened to buckle. Before she collapsed upon the rock like a spent flower, she wobbled across the remaining stones and stepped down to the muddy bank.

Darwell shook his head. His mouth pursed in disapproval. "I apologize for Garmonn's behavior. Since his return from Crusade, he has been . . . unmanageable."

As though he noticed she had left the rocks without his permission, Fane drew himself up to his full height. "He and I have crossed twice. I respect he is your son, but I will not tolerate his rudeness or his threats. Next time, I shall have him arrested."

"I will tell him." Darwell's smile held sadness. "Thank you, milord, for your generous warning. He will not bother you again."

Fane signaled his guards to ride with Darwell back

to the road, where Darwell's men-at-arms waited. As the men cantered through the meadow, Fane glanced at Rexana. She walked the flattened grass path back to the blanket. With each step, her drying skirts hugged her body and reminded him, with potent urgency, of all he had touched, tasted, and almost had.

Lust swiftly melted into the anger still burning in his blood. She had disobeyed his order to stay upon the rock. Why? Did she not realize he wanted her out of the fray? Did she not realize he tried to protect her from harm? Her safety meant more to him than his own.

His gaze narrowed on the set of her shoulders and her rigid back. Her movements were stiff, deliberate, not at all carefree, as they had been when she strolled to the water.

An unwelcome sting flared in his gut. She moved like a woman plagued by her conscience. What could weigh upon her that she would react so, after Garmonn's insolent bravado?

Fane's brow furrowed into a frown, and he shifted the pebbles in his fingers. His mind shot back to the feast at Tangston, to his conversation with Darwell before Rexana's dance. Darwell had practically begged for approval of Garmonn's marriage to her.

He wondered what Rexana had thought of wedding Garmonn. Women of her station oft had little say in marriage, but had she pined for him? When she listened to the minstrels' *chansons*, had she dreamed of

Garmonn's kiss? Of his embrace? Of his making slow, sweet, sweaty love to her?

Jealousy lashed through Fane. Her fear for him moments ago had seemed very real. Yet, mayhap she had not worried so much for his well-being, but for what he might do to hot-headed Garmonn.

Fane's throat tightened, as though a snake had somehow coiled around his neck and begun to constrict. He had thought, after her disagreement with Garmonn before the wedding, that she disliked him. Had she acted her disdain?

Mayhap, at last, he had found the reason why she hesitated to consummate their marriage.

Ah, God. Nay.

His fingers curled so tightly around the pebbles, his knuckles snapped. He forced himself to loosen his grip. Turning, he swore and hurled the rocks into the pond. They landed with a hollow *plonk, plonk, plonk*.

He spun back, to find her watching him. Her face shuttered with an odd blend of longing and wariness, before she resumed clearing away the fare.

Frustration ran hot in Fane's blood. He would have an answer from her. She would not secretly crave another man.

He stomped across the bank, through the grass, and dropped to his knees in front of her on the blanket.

Rexana glanced at him. As though sensing his volatile emotions, she averted her gaze and pushed a wrapped package into the sack.

She would not evade him. Not now. Not ever.

As she withdrew her hand, he caught her wrist. Her pale skin reminded him of her soft, silky thighs. With effort, he stifled the urge to press her fingers to his cheek and kiss her palm. "You have not been honest with me, Rexana."

Her bones jerked in his grasp. "Milord?"

"Tell me what is between you and Garmonn."

Panic shone in her eyes, before her gaze turned cool, cooler even than the water at the bottom of the pool. The invisible serpent around his throat squeezed tighter.

"There is naught between Garmonn and me," she said at last. "Why do you ask?"

"I do not believe you."

She stiffened. Her fingers splayed, like a cat baring its claws. "Release my hand, Fane. You hinder my work. After what happened moments ago, I do not wish to speak of Garmonn."

"Nor do I." Fane brushed his thumb over her wrist in a deliberate caress. "Yet, I was almost run through by his sword. I believe I am entitled to the truth."

He felt the shiver that coursed through her body. She twisted in his hold, but he did not relax his grip.

Her eyes blazed. "What can I say that you do not already know? He is Rudd's friend. He is arrogant and reckless. He is good with a sword, and he despises you."

"He desires you."

Anguish shivered across her face. "His interest in me is of no consequence any longer, now you and I are wed."

Fane's gut wrenched. *Ah, love, but you and I are not fully man and wife. We have not yet consummated our marriage.*

"Do you desire him, Rexana?"

An incredulous laugh burst from her. She shook her head, as though struggling to make sense of what he had asked. "You are jealous of Garmonn?"

Fane's cheekbones stung, but he refused to look away. "I am jealous of any man who dares to lay claim to what is mine. *You* are mine. Until the day I die. I will tolerate no other man in your heart."

A sad smile curved her mouth. Her hand relaxed in his hold to curl like a blossom against his. "I could never hold Garmonn dear."

Pleasure unfurled within Fane. He resisted a smile. His blood screamed for him to pull her close and kiss her. Yet first, he must have answers to the questions that ate at him. "Why not? Once, did you not consider marrying him?"

She looked out across the shifting sea of grass and flowers, as though she saw into the past. "When he and I were younger, marriage was discussed between us, but we were not officially betrothed. My parents were friends of Lord Darwell. He encouraged the marriage. At first, my family supported the idea. I imagine there were many benefits to a union between our two families." With her free hand, she swept away windblown hair. Her gaze shadowed. "After Garmonn returned from crusade, he was a different man. Cold. Ruthless." She paused. "Frightening."

Fane nodded. "War oft changes a man. It can shrivel a soul. Turn it cold."

She looked at him, an intense stare, as though she saw far more than his sun-bronzed skin and disfiguring scars. "You are not cold. In your years of imprisonment and torture, I vow your soul suffered worse than his."

Fane started, for her words touched a protected, tender place in his heart. A howl ripped through him, echoing again and again in his mind, as though he yelled into a fathomless cave. How dare she speak of his soul in the same breath she spoke of Garmonn's? She had no right to pass judgment, when she did not know what Fane had endured, or the decisions he had been forced to make in the name of God and king.

"We do not speak of me," he bit out. "We speak of Garmonn."

Moisture glinted in her eyes, and she blinked before she looked away. Did she weep for Garmonn? For the man he had once been, before battle, bloodshed, and death had changed him? Mayhap she missed the respectable, prominent marriage of which she had dreamed and which never came true.

Fane fought to keep his tone civil. "When he returned to England, did he expect to wed you?"

Her head dipped in a jerky nod. "He made many visits to Ickleton. He courted me. Brought me flowers and gifts. Spoke of the day when we would be man and wife. He was . . . persistent."

"Persistent?"

She shrugged. "He wanted me to press my father for a formal betrothal. When I refused, he tried to kiss me. I pushed him away. He got angry. Father told him not to return until he could control his temper." Her throat moved with a swallow. "I told my father I did not want to marry Garmonn. Father understood. He, too, did not like how Garmonn had changed. Nor did he appreciate the dangerous, foolish pranks Garmonn coaxed Rudd to take part in."

She paused to flick an ant from her gown. "I believe Father intended to tell Lord Darwell there would be no wedding. Before he could, both he and Mother fell ill. They died."

Her words faded to a whisper. With a muffled sniff, she tugged at her hand. "Release me now, Fane. I have told you all you wished to know."

Nay, she had not told him all. She had convinced him she did not lust for Garmonn, but she left a great deal untold. Tension still lined her eyes, while her posture held a hint of caution.

If he drew her into his arms, would she soften against him? If he offered her kisses and caresses, if he coaxed her to confide in him, would she yield what she knew? Would she then let him press her down on the blanket and ease her tension with slow, tender love-making?

Fane's heated blood urged him to touch her. His mind scorned him. He had not wooed her enough. She was not yet completely his.

With a last caress, Fane released her. Wiping her eyes, Rexana pushed to her feet. She exhaled and thrust her shoulders back, as though, despite all that had occurred, she would not fail to carry on.

Fane stood. "Some day, love, you will tell me the rest."

"The rest, milord?"

He smiled.

In the brilliant sunlight, her face paled. Her gaze sharpened. He braced himself for her retort. Instead, she grasped her skirts, turned away, and marched toward the grazing horses.

Her posture told him what her luscious lips had not. *Never.*

Fighting the scream welling in her throat, Rexana reached her mount. As the mare shook off a fly and stepped forward to nibble more grass, Rexana retrieved the dangling reins.

*Some day, love, you will tell me the rest.*

With a firm mental shake, she forced aside Fane's words. She would *not* be ruled by the disquiet pulsing in her blood, or the looming sense of entrapment. She had told Fane what he wanted to know. She had confessed her dealings with Garmonn, yet she had not told of Thomas. Thank God.

The sweetish, comforting smell of horse filled her nostrils. She set both hands upon the mare's warm hide, then shut her eyes. As a child, she had often streaked through the fields on horseback, at one with the animal and the wind, Rudd not far behind. In those irreverent rides, she had escaped her boredom and tiresome duties.

If she leapt onto the horse, kicked it to a gallop, and rode as far as the dusty road took her, would she recapture that exhilarating sense of freedom?

Would Fane thunder after her, or let her go?

Over the sighing breeze, she heard him cinching the leather sack. A moment later, he shook out the blanket with a brisk snap.

She scowled. Her foolish thoughts corrupted her reason. She could not leave Rudd in the dungeon. She could not shirk her responsibility to find the missive, free him and see the treason charge dismissed. She could not ride away, because her duty to Rudd would draw her straight back to Tangston Keep.

The subversive voice in her mind taunted her. She could never flee, even if Rudd were free, because her body, as well as part of her heart and soul, already belonged to Fane.

Grass crunched behind her. Fane strode toward her.

She felt his gaze wandering down her back. Her blood heated in response.

*Some day, love, you will tell me the rest.*

Nay! She would not. The risk was too great.

Her hands curled around the mare's reins, and her mouth pinched with resentment. Why should she tell him? He had given her little insight into his past. He wanted her heart, yet the gossips whispered he had a passionate affair with a Saracen courtesan. Some said he had loved her.

Had he?

As he approached the destrier, Rexana glanced at him. She was his wife, yet even she did not know the truth. 'Twas not fair she had to reveal her past, when his remained cloaked in exotic mystery.

Even more unfair, she found she wanted to know what had happened between him and his eastern lover.

Fane slung the sack over his horse's saddle. Muscles shifted beneath his tunic as he tied the bag in place, and she tore her gaze away.

"We will leave now."

"Aye."

"I realize you do not trust me enough yet to reveal all you know of Garmonn. For some reason, you are afraid. Yet, I promise you this. He will never hurt you.

I will not let him."

She adjusted her saddle. As Fane's words wrapped around her like an embrace, part of her wept with relief. For months, she had kept the truth of that winter day to herself. Did she dare confide in Fane? Would it ease the hurt inside her?

Another part of her shrilled a warning. With gilded promises, Fane coaxed her to tell him all. Yet, if he knew the truth, he might be duty bound to investigate. Garmonn would know what she had revealed. Rudd's life would be in jeopardy.

"I have told you what I can of Garmonn. Why do you press me?"

Fane's head swiveled. "I can protect you best if you trust me, and share what you know."

"*Trust* you? A difficult task, when you hold my brother prisoner. Indeed, milord, I hardly know you. You are my husband by law, yet most of what I have learned about you has come from rumor and gossip."

He shrugged. "In time, you will come to trust me."

"Will I?"

His gaze turned assessing. "Do you believe all the rumors about me, Rexana?"

"Nay, but —"

"Does part of you worry what Garmonn will tell others about today? Do you fear what the gossips will say about us?"

She worried about far more deadly matters than

gossip. Yet, as she stared at Fane, a grin warmed her lips. He had just given her a way to divert his suspicions.

Nodding, she said, "Garmonn will not speak well of us to his peers."

Fane laughed. The vibrant sound rolled across the meadow, borne on the breeze. "We can thwart the tongue-wagging, love. We will prove Garmonn's words are false. He may tell his friends that I forced myself upon you, but 'twill be clear to all who see us that we are in love."

"Milord, I am not in love."

He grinned. "That, too, is only a matter of time."

# Chapter Fourteen

FANE SHIFTED IN HIS SADDLE to ease a cramp in his scarred thigh. He looked at Tangston Keep, directly ahead on the pitted dirt road. The sun's rays had begun to lengthen, casting parts of the mortared wall and watchtowers in shadow. Intriguing, the contrast of light and dark. His relationship with Rexana was the same — moments of brilliance, as well as moments of uncertainty.

She rode several yards behind, followed by the guards. He imagined her as he had seen her moments ago, when he dared glance over his shoulder. Her hands clutched the leather reins. She sat stiff and proud upon the mare, looking elegant despite her creased, water stained gown. Her hair fell over her shoulders in an unkempt mass. Her chin jutted at a stubborn angle. Her eyes flashed with warning, before she turned her head to stare across the fields of wheat and barley.

Earlier, he had attempted polite conversation, yet she had discouraged him with a frosty stare that could have tempered newly forged steel.

She did not like his assertion she would come to love him.

She did not care to admit the truth.

Warmth lightened Fane's heart. Her passions ran strong and deep. One day, she would care as much for him as she did for her brother.

Fane smiled. He could woo her stubborn pride. He could woo her tender heart and passionate soul. He had successfully wooed her body. He remembered her gasped cries, her lips' welcoming urgency, the way she had trembled when he flexed his body against hers.

In a matter of days, she would be completely his.

Mayhap he would have her tonight.

The destrier clopped down the final approach to the keep. The drawbridge was already lowered, the wood and iron portcullis raised. A different sort of excitement stirred within him. He wondered if Kester and the men-at-arms had finished their mission, and what they had discovered about Rudd Villeaux.

Fane hailed the sentries standing guard in front of the drawbridge. The men bowed, then stepped aside to let him pass.

"Have Kester and the patrol returned?" he asked.

"Not long ago, milord," one replied.

The destrier's hooves thudded on the drawbridge. Fane spurred his mount under the gatehouse and into the bailey. Dogs scampered out of the way. He guided the horse around a pile of wine barrels, remnants of last eve's celebration, then headed for the stables.

Five horses, lathered from a long ride, drank at the water troughs.

A dirty-faced young lad hurried out of the stable, dumped his armload of straw onto the ground, and caught the destrier's reins.

Fane dismounted. "Where's Kester?"

"In the great hall, milord." The boy lowered his gaze. " 'E went ta parch his thirst afore ye returned."

Fane ruffled the boy's hair. "Good lad." He heard horses behind him and turned.

Rexana halted the mare. Frowning, she looked at the drinking horses.

As a boy hurried over to her horse with a mounting block, Fane followed. He set a hand on Rexana's leg, covered by yards of stained silk. Did she start at his touch, or had he imagined her reaction?

He stretched his arm up to her. "Place your hand in mine, love."

She refused to look down at him. "Thank you, but I can dismount on my own."

He bit his tongue, resisting a laugh. Anger would

not keep them apart. She misjudged his determination, if she believed 'twas so.

He rubbed her leg. "Can I not be chivalrous?" He infused his tone with a teasing lilt. "I must assist my lady wife. 'Tis my husbandly duty."

She huffed a breath. After a pause, she curled her hand into his. More to quell the inquisitive glances of the servants around them, he vowed, than to please him.

As their flesh connected, a sigh rippled through him. She must have felt the physical connection too, for her gaze shot to his. Tightening her grasp on his hand, she slid down off the mare's back to the mounting block.

Yearning tore through Fane. He pressed closer. As her shoes hit the block, he trapped her between his body and the mare. He curled his arm around her waist. Yanked her against him.

They stood almost nose to nose, her breasts squeezed against his chest. She shivered in his hold, while her lips formed a tense smile. "What are you doing?"

He nuzzled her ear. Her hair smelled of sunshine and meadow air, and his blood instantly heated. "Shall we give these lads something to talk about?" he murmured. "Kiss me, Rexana. Kiss me with all the passion ruling your heart."

Her gaze was cool, yet he saw a hint of the wildness he had enjoyed in the meadow. "A deception, milord?" she said, her voice soft.

"Not at all, wife." He nibbled the corner of her mouth. "You may be angry, but you crave my kiss. Show me how much."

Her smile turned sly. "If I refuse?"

Fane grinned. "I will have to devise other, far more wicked ways, to bend you to my will."

Her eyes darkened. He anticipated her hot refusal, but instead, she smiled. Her expression rivaled that of any of Gazir's ambitious courtesans.

She pressed a slow, slippery kiss to his cheek. "Let me visit Rudd," she whispered, "and I will kiss you with a passion you will never forget."

He laughed, then caught her mouth in a thorough kiss. The stable lads hooted and clapped. Cheers erupted from across the bailey.

With a groan, Fane released her. He stepped away, forcing his thoughts from the temptations she posed. When he had done his duties, he would have time to play. "I will send Tansy to the solar to tend you. I know you are eager to bathe and change your gown."

She lifted her skirt's hem to step off the mounting block. "Will you not bathe and change your garments?"

He shut his mind to the invitation in her words. Did she realize how seductive her question sounded? Did she realize he had dreamed, more than once, of climbing into the tub with her and exploring, with soap and water, every bit of her luscious body?

Clearing the roughness from his throat, he said, "My garments are dry enough. I have important matters to attend."

She looked at the horses. "You will question the riders?"

He nodded. "I will see you anon. If my duties permit, I will join you at the evening meal. If not, I will see you later in our bed." Turning on his heel, he started toward the keep.

"Do your duties involve Rudd?"

Challenge rang in her voice. She confronted him in front of the stable hands and the rest of the folk working in the bailey. If she hoped to win sympathy for her brother's cause, she trod dangerous territory.

Fane turned, narrowing his gaze. "You know I am responsible for law and order in Warringham. 'Tis my duty, bestowed upon me by our king, to capture the rebels who threaten peace. As your brother is involved with these traitors, then aye, my duties concern him."

"I will come with you. Rudd —"

"Nay, love." Aware their disagreement had made them the focus of the bailey, Fane softened his tone to a sensual rumble. "You are weary after our long journey. Let Tansy tend and refresh you." He raised one eyebrow. "No man will consume your energies today but me."

Bawdy titters rippled through the bailey. She scowled, then planted her hands upon her hips. 'Twas clear she prepared to do battle.

"I will come."

"You will not, Rexana. That is my final word." He strode across the bailey, aware of her glare scorching his back, and her most unladylike curse.

As Rexana stared at Fane, annoyance swelled inside her like a bubble about to pop. If she stomped her feet, shrieked, or had an unseemly tantrum, would Fane change his stubborn mind?

Most likely not.

Master of clever words, he would probably convince all who watched that she had caught too much sun, throw her over his shoulder, and carry her straight to the solar.

She kicked at the dirt. Why did Fane keep her from Rudd? Was Fane reluctant to have her accompany him because he had no intentions of proving her brother's innocence, even though he had vowed to help Rudd?

The mare's bridle clinked, and the stable hands' lowered voices reached her. Aware of their stares, she started off across the bailey toward the forebuilding. Her gown, stiff from drying, snapped at her heels.

She would not allow Fane to ignore their agreement. She might not be able to escape the marriage until Rudd was freed, but she could be persistent and determined.

A daring thought took form in her mind. With Fane busy for the rest of the day, 'twas the perfect opportunity to search the solar.

She would find the missive that named her brother a traitor — and she would destroy it.

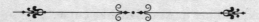

As Fane strode into the great hall, Kester looked up from a trestle table near the hearth. He set down his ale mug, stood, and bowed. "Milord."

"I trust you were successful?"

Kester grinned. "Very."

Fane slid onto the wooden bench opposite Kester before glancing at the wax tablets laid out on the scarred oak. He accepted a mug of ale from the servant hovering nearby, then dismissed her.

He studied the tablets' marked surfaces. The scent of ale, musky and bitter like unwelcome secrets, rose from the mug. The earthenware warmed to his touch, as heady anticipation fired within him. A wealth of information lay before him. Kester's men had done well.

Fane sipped his drink. He willed himself to be patient and let Kester tell of the day's success. "What did you learn?"

Kester's eyes lit with pride. "We visited four taverns. Several of the owners recalled seeing Villeaux over the past months. He came after dark with a group of men. Not always the same men, mind you. They usually sat in a quiet part of the room, ordered several rounds, and seemed like any other lads out for a night of drinking."

Fane scratched his chin. Meeting his friends did not prove Villeaux guilty of treason. He stifled an impatient sigh. "Did the tavern owners overhear the conversations? See aught happen during their meetings?"

"One told of a near fight a few sennights ago. There was a disagreement over who was to pay for the ale. One lord drew a sword. Looked eager to draw blood." Kester shrugged. "Apparently Villeaux intervened to stop the argument."

Fane blew a breath. He had not expected to hear of Rudd's heroics. He shoved aside an unwelcome prick of conscience.

Kester picked up a scored tablet. "This account is from Master Jones, of the Cock and Hen. He witnessed Villeaux and his friends passing a small, rolled parchment between them."

A triumphant growl rumbled in Fane's throat. At last, what he wanted to hear. "What of this parchment?"

" 'Twas clearly important, for there were serious discussions."

"The missive?"

Kester smiled. "Mayhap, though the traitors likely drafted other documents. Letters to fellow lords to join their cause, for example."

Fane nodded his agreement.

"Jones said it appeared each man was to sign. Some were hesitant, but in the end did. Once they had all done their part, the parchment vanished."

Fane sipped his drink. An image of Rexana, her eyes glowing with love for her brother, flashed through Fane's mind. How would she react when he showed her evidence that proved her brother was not innocent, as she insisted, but guilty? How could he tell her the truth without hurting her? He could not.

Shrugging tightness from between his shoulder blades, Fane said, "We must know what missives are circulating, and find them. Unfortunately, Villeaux still refuses to cooperate."

"As you know, he has revealed naught to my men who have interrogated him twice a day." Kester's mouth tilted in a grin. "Though that may soon change."

Satisfaction rang in Kester's voice. Almost gloating. He sounded like an ambitious servant who knew he had well exceeded his lord's expectations.

"Indeed?" Fane sipped another mouthful of ale. The cool liquid flowed over his tongue and down his throat, as Kester slid near several tablets.

"Here, I have accounts from the cotters. Most knew of Villeaux because they had heard of his parents' deaths. Many recounted seeing him and his sister in the village on market day, or him in the taverns." With a lazy half shrug, Kester said, "there is much here that may not be of interest—personal statements of his character, past sightings, and such — but one of the villagers, in particular, knows Villeaux well."

Fane wiped his bottom lip. "His name?"

"Thomas Newland. He is a farmer. He lives with his wife and five children not far from the river that runs between Tangston and Ickleton. Not long ago, Villeaux visited Newland's home. Villeaux asked to use his barn for a meeting."

Fane struggled to keep from lunging to his feet and whooping with elation. "Meeting?"

"Villeaux paid Newland a bag of silver in advance, and said he would arrange the exact day later. Newland did not suspect Villeaux's intentions, for he had no reason to. He also was glad of the money, for he has a game leg from a bad wound he got last winter. Since he cannot work, he needed the coin to feed his family." Kester shook his head. "He had heard of Rudd's arrest for treason. He hated to speak ill of the lad — he wept as he talked — but his conscience plagued him."

Fane's eyes narrowed. "Newland's account can be trusted?"

Kester nodded. "His family is highly respected. His brother is a talented goldsmith. You may have seen his work for sale in Tangston's market."

*Goldsmith!*

Fane's mind spun, but not from the ale. He thought again of Rexana. Of her cherished brooch, pinned above her heart. The detailed little arrow was not the work of an amateur, but a talented artisan. His hands squeezed tight around his mug. Could the links in the treacherous chain be so simple?

"Does this craftsman design brooches?"

"Aye, milord, as well as jewel boxes, rings, crucifixes, and other ornaments."

Enlightenment pulsed through Fane in a slow, stunning throb. With care, he set down his ale. He could scarce think past the hammering at his temple. "Tell me more of Newland and his goldsmith brother."

Humming under her breath, Tansy finished fastening Rexana's midnight blue silk gown. "There now, milady. Come sit near the fire, so I can dry your hair."

Rexana walked around the bathing tub, through the orange-red sunlight pooling on the floorboards, and bit back a groan. True to his word, Fane had summoned Tansy. The woman had arrived at the solar moments after Rexana. With a bright smile and endless chatter, Tansy had ordered a hot bath, a soothing mint and chamomile tonic, plus a bowl of sweetmeats for Rexana to nibble.

Irritation crackled in Rexana's veins. While she appreciated the luxurious bath, and the extraordinary time Tansy had spent lathering, scrubbing, and rinsing, Rexana had to wonder if her wicked husband had ordered the pampering to keep her occupied. To keep her from getting in the way as he completed his "duties."

Blowing a sigh, she dropped onto the stool near the

hearth tiles. She clasped her hands in her lap and, as Tansy smoothed a towel down her hair, did her best to sit still. Rexana's fingers twitched. What was Fane doing at this moment? What had Kester discovered? Had they found information that implicated Rudd?

She had to find the missive.

Thoughts whirled around and around in her brain. She shut her eyes. Forced her mind to calm. She would accomplish naught by working herself into a tizzy. She must focus. Concentrate. Plan.

Beside her, the fire snapped. She inhaled the smoky odor of burning wood along with the tang of hot pitch. As Tansy set to work with a wide-toothed ivory comb, a yawn warmed Rexana's throat. She resisted the fatigue. Resisted the temptation to relax into Tansy's care. Resisted the urge to set aside all worrying and searching until the morrow.

If the missive were hidden in this room, she would find it.

"Thank you, Tansy. That will be all."

The maidservant clucked her tongue. "Yer hair is not quite dry. Just a little more —"

Rexana trapped a yawn with her hand.

Tansy chuckled. "Ye must keep awake fer the evenin' meal, milady." The comb whispered through Rexana's hair again. "There. 'Tis the best I can do fer now." Tansy shuffled around to face Rexana, and said, "Will ye come ta the hall, then?"

Ignoring the woman's coaxing, toothy smile, Rexana rose and ran her hands over her wind-chapped cheeks. "After today's long ride, and the fresh air, I am weary. I think I will go to bed."

Tansy winked like a cheeky child. "Forgive me if I speak plainly, but I was a newlywed meself a few times. I know 'is lusty lordship kept ye up late last eve."

Despite her determination not to, Rexana blushed. Fane had indeed kept her awake until the wee hours, though not with coupling. She glanced at the bed, for her skin tingled with the memory of lying beside him, her blood sluggish and hot, her body yearning in a manner she had never felt before.

Rexana cleared a knot from her throat. "How did you guess?"

The giggling maidservant waved her plump hand in the air. "I will tell 'is lordship ye retired early, and that ye are warm and snug in the blankets. Restin' up," she added, "for the next time 'e desires ye."

"Ah . . . thank you."

Tansy plodded to the solar doors. She yanked them open, leaned into the hallway, then clapped her hands. Young lads hurried in to drag the sloshing tub out into the passage. Tansy quickly dried the floorboards and collected the towels and soap. "I will ask the lads ta leave the empty tub outside, so they do not disturb ye." She dropped into a wobbly curtsey. "May ye slumber well, milady."

The doors clicked shut.

Rexana listened as Tansy snapped orders to the boys. The voices faded down the hallway. As the quiet settled around Rexana, warning tingled down her spine. She must not be caught searching the solar. Not when Fane moved like a silent, stalking cat. The last time she had explored the chamber, days ago when she was disguised as a dancer, he had caught her unawares.

She picked up the rectangular stool and set it against the doors. Fane would not be able to enter without it scraping across the floor, or him tripping over it. She brushed her palms together and smiled. Now, to search.

Her gaze narrowed on Fane's wooden chest, set beside hers along the wall. While he had not forbidden her to look at his belongings, she sensed he did not wish her to. She dropped to her knees, sucked in a shaky breath, then raised the lid.

His lemon-spice scent filled her nostrils. She resisted the delicious shiver that rippled through her to settle low in her belly. Her fingers brushed a cloth wrapped package tucked to one side. By its shape, she guessed it held many soaps. She shifted the layers of folded tunics and shirts and found a glittering sword shaped like a half moon. A weapon unlike any she had seen before.

In the east, had Fane learned how to wield such a sword? Had he killed men with such a barbaric looking instrument?

A shudder tore through her. She pushed the sword away to work her way down to the bottom of the chest. Blank parchment. A pot of ink. A quill. Woolen hose. A sheathed hunting knife. A bag containing coins and jewels.

Her fingers brushed an item hidden under the hose. A rolled parchment.

Her mouth went dry as stale bread.

Had she found the missive?

# Chapter Fifteen

HOLDING A RING OF KEYS AND A TORCH, Fane strode toward the dungeon cell. Kester followed close behind. Smug satisfaction blazed inside Fane, as hot as the sputtering torch flame. This time, he would extract answers from Villeaux.

The lad slumped on the ground against the cell's far wall, his back pressed against the stones, his knees bent and his scruffy head resting on his arms. Misgiving, sharp as a spiny lizard's tail, flicked through Fane. He squashed the emotion. He would not think of the days he had sat huddled so, mentally withdrawn from his smelly prison, as he forced his desperate, fevered mind to focus on survival.

And, above all, duty.

As light broached the cell's darkness, Villeaux looked up. "Back again, Linford?"

Despite the sense of victory sluicing through him, Fane ground his teeth. Still, the lad refused to address him by his proper title, and thereby show him a measure of respect.

"I am, *boy*," he said. "We have much to discuss."

Rudd snorted, a sound of utter repugnance. He stretched out his legs and brushed dirt from his filthy hose. The rattle of chains competed with his arrogant chuckle. "You will get no more from me than you did in the last interrogation."

Fane smiled. The iron keys jangled in his palm. He fitted the correct one into the door's lock, and it opened with a click. With his foot, Fane shoved the door open.

Rudd's gaze slid to Kester. "The captain has come to hold your hand?"

"Nay," Fane said lightly. "He will torture you."

Panic flashed in the boy's eyes, before he shook his head and laughed. "With wax tablets? I quake with fear."

"You should." Fane stepped into the cell. "He brings proof of your guilt."

His back to the bars, keeping well out of the boy's reach, Fane stepped to one side to let Kester enter. The smells of mildew and sweat filled Fane's nostrils. He fought to keep his memories submerged. The past had no bearing on here and now. None.

Pushing hair from his grubby cheek, Villeaux rose to standing. Stubbornness tightened his jaw. Fane resisted the urge to grin. At times, Rexana's face held exactly the same determined expression.

As though he could read minds, the lad said, "How is Rexana? Why do you not let me see her?" Anger rumbled in his voice. "If you are ill treating her —"

"She is well," Fane said. "She enjoys all the privileges of a High Sheriff's wife. She does not visit, because I do not permit it."

"Why?"

"You do not confess."

Rudd's throat moved with a swallow. "I will not."

Fane shrugged. He quelled the roar that burned inside him. "Whether you admit to your conspiracy or not may not matter to the King's Court. Kester has eyewitness accounts of your tavern meetings. And" — he paused for effect — "a signed statement from Thomas Newland."

The boy's face paled. "Newland? What did he say?"

Fane took the tablet from Kester. "He made many interesting comments. A barn you paid him to lease. A meeting you planned to hold there." He ran a thoughtful hand over his mouth. "I did not realize Newland's brother is a goldsmith."

A harsh sigh flew from Rudd. His wrist chains clinked. The tension in the cell thickened.

"Newland's brother made Rexana's brooch. Aye?"

Words rushed from Rudd as though he could no longer restrain them. "The brooch was a gift, no more. She has no part in the rebellion. Do you hear me? She is guilty only of a tender heart."

Fane arched a brow. What did the lad mean? Mayhap his words foreshadowed his willingness to speak of his treachery. "Is that so?"

Villeaux's eyes blazed. "She knows naught. I was careful to keep my affairs from her."

Crossing his arms, Fane leaned his shoulder against the cell's bars. "I must be certain of Rexana's innocence. She is, after all, my wife. The future mother of my children."

Rudd swore.

Fane pushed away from the bars. "You will tell me of your connection to Newland. You will tell me all I wish to know. Your future depends upon your answers."

Rexana withdrew the worn sheepskin from Fane's linen chest. A frisson of foreboding shot through her. If this was the missive she and Henry had sought, she must burn it.

Casting a nervous glance at the closed doors, she untied the strip of leather binding the parchment. As she unfurled the document, her hand shook.

Her gaze skimmed the awkwardly penned lines. She had not found the list of lords sworn to betray the crown, but a letter.

*My dear son,*

*My stiff hands fail me so I will speak plainly. Your father quit this earth two nights past. A painful sickness of the belly took him, and I thank God he did not suffer long.*

Rexana gnawed her lip. She should not go on. She should not pry into Fane's past. Yet, she could not resist reading more.

*I, too, am unwell. My body pains me, thus I have little strength to write. Yet, I must. I pray, my son, that you are hale. I pray that wherever you may be, you will know I never ceased loving you. I pray that you will one day receive this and know, with all my heart, how I regret how your father and I wronged you.*

*I should have been stronger. I should never have allowed his cruel tongue to wound you or banish you from this keep. For that, I am eternally sorry.*

The signature blurred before Rexana's eyes. She blinked away tears. Of all the things she thought to find, 'twas not this.

She had heard rumors that in a fit of rage, Fane's father had disowned him. What had happened between Fane and his sire? What had Fane done? How could a man banish his own blood son? She had known Fane's emotional scars ran deep, but she had not imagined finding proof of how pitiless his father had been.

She wondered if Fane had ever known love. Genuine affection, as she had shared with her parents and Rudd. His mother had loved him. Had he known? Had he loved her in return, or had he always yearned for acceptance?

Was that why he succumbed to an eastern courtesan's charms?

Rexana sighed. Such musings accomplished naught, and spun a dangerous web of emotions. She could not grow to care deeply for Fane. She wanted an annulment.

Of course she wanted her marriage to end. She had wed Fane for one purpose only, to help her exonerate Rudd.

She would not fall in love.

After retying the parchment, Rexana set it beside her on the floorboards. She, too, would reject Fane. Just like his family. Was that not cruel?

Steeling herself against that thought, she searched the rest of the chest. Frowning, she sat back on her heels. Either he carried the missive with him, or he had hidden it elsewhere.

Rexana stared down at his mussed garments. He did not trust her. He expected her to search the solar, and so he had put the document where she could never find it. No doubt he could claim 'twas his crown duty to keep it from her.

Well, he would not thwart her, for she would find where he had hidden it. She would not fail Rudd.

After replacing the items in Fane's chest, she shut the lid and stood. Hugging her arms to her bodice, she strolled to the solar window. Dusk had fallen like a gray blanket. Stars twinkled, tiny winking pinpoints of light. Sparks of hope in the vast stretch of blackness.

Rexana closed and latched the shutters, curtailing the cold breeze. She had sought to save her brother's young life. She had found proof of the bitterness in Fane's.

How foolish, that she wished she could share some of her love with Fane.

Fane raked his hand through his hair as he started up the landing's stairs. Below, in the shadowed hall, castle folk slumbered. Weariness made his steps heavy, and he willed away the fatigue. He would not allow it to impair his judgment, or allow Rexana to glean answers from him that she would no doubt demand. Answers his duty forbade him to reveal.

He had no wish to do battle with her. 'Twas well past midnight, yet he had not obtained all the answers he sought from Villeaux. The lad refused to tell all he knew about the traitors or outright confess his guilt, but the link between Rexana, Newland, and Rudd was clear.

Fair Rexana had acted with rare courage the day she risked her own life to save Newland's. If the events had transpired as Rudd said, she had selflessly accepted responsibility for the life of a man well below her station, whose death few would have noticed.

Yet, Fane had to wonder . . . Why had she fought through the driving snow to save Newland? Why had she risked her life? What bound her to the humble farmer, whom, Rudd claimed, she had not met until the day she saw him floundering in the snowdrifts, wounded by his own arrow which had bounced off a rock and buried deep in his leg?

"She is guilty only of a tender heart," Villeaux had said. He had repeated this several times during the questioning. A grudging smile touched Fane's mouth. Mayhap, indeed, she had not wished to see the man die.

He strode into the passage and hailed the guards on duty. When he looked at the solar doors, his gut clenched. She had accepted a similar responsibility for saving her brother. Yet, the evidence Kester had collected and Rudd's own words proved 'twould be nigh impossible for her — or even a High Sheriff — to prove him guiltless.

Unless Villeaux withheld information that would illuminate his innocence, and explain why his signature came to be on the list of traitors.

Fane frowned. Why would the lad refuse to talk? He knew he faced the King's Courts and grave punishment. Even death.

Unless he had a very good reason to remain silent.

A draft skimming through the passage set the wall torches flickering. Fane rubbed his brow, which pounded with the beginnings of a bad headache. His big, comfortable bed, behind the doors, beckoned.

He hesitated outside the solar. As soon as he stepped in, Rexana would cross to him, demanding to know what his men had discovered about Rudd. Fane knew his wife well enough now to predict the tight pursing of her lips and her narrowed eyes.

He did not want to discuss Rudd. He did not want to argue. He wanted to crawl between the sheets, draw her into his arms, and thoroughly woo her. Make her his. Though the way his eyelids drooped, he doubted he had the stamina to make love to her with any kind of finesse, as she deserved.

A wretched, embarrassing thought.

He depressed the door's handle. The panel did not swing inward. With a tired grunt, he pushed harder. Inside the dark room, an object scraped across the floorboards.

Astonishment slammed through him. Rexana had blocked the doorway. Did she intend to keep him out? Was she still miffed by their earlier disagreement in the bailey?

He shoved harder. Stepped forward. His calf knocked against solid wood, and he yelped.

Across the chamber, the bed ropes creaked. Sheets rustled.

Squinting down, he spied a stool. "Hellfire!"

One of the guards strode to him. "All is well, milord?"

"Aye," Fane snapped. The man's footfalls receded.

As Fane kicked aside the wooden stool, Rexana hurried to his side, her shift flapping about her legs. Eyes wide, she pressed a hand to her mouth.

"I . . . Oh, I am sorry. Are you hurt?"

He scowled down at her. Did she blush, or did the fire lit shadows play tricks on his weary gaze?

He shoved the door closed. "You set this stool here?"

She gave a sheepish nod.

"Why? You intended to send me sprawling to the floor? Or even unman me?"

"Of course not. I planned to return it to the hearth after I had disrobed, but —"

"You forgot."

She crossed her arms. "Aye, I forgot."

He closed the space between them. Stood close enough that her arms brushed against his tunic. Her tousled hair tempted him. So did her unique scent. He longed to take her in his arms to pleasure her . . . yet, God help him, even his loins were too exhausted to manage more than a feeble stir.

He brushed past her. Strode to the side of the bed.

Sat and began to unlace his boots.

Clasping her hands together, she padded to his side. "We must speak, milord. I must know of Rudd and —"

"Not now." As Fane yanked off his tunic and shirt, he prayed his gruff voice was enough to dissuade her. He reached for the points of his hose.

She swallowed. Yet, she did not avert her gaze. In fact, she stared at his loins with undisguised hunger.

Ah, God, 'twas his own fault. Had he not promised, as he left her standing in the bailey, that he would see her later in their bed? Had he not implied that he would couple with her?

He groaned. To his shame, he sounded like a camel with a rotten bellyache. "Rexana."

"I have not uttered one more word. You will not let me."

He sighed. " 'Tis late. I am weary."

"Please. Rudd is all I have."

"You have me."

She nibbled her bottom lip. To his surprise, she did not challenge his statement, but nodded. "I have you."

He rose, the points of his hose gaping. His pulse thumped. Had he finally won her? Had she accepted him?

Had she realized that they were destined to be together?

His loins warmed. As he reached out to touch her

cheek, his hand trembled.

Pressing her lips together, she turned away. He listened to her walk around the bed. The bed shifted and squeaked. She lay still.

Running his tongue around his suddenly dry mouth, he stripped off his hose and tossed them on the carpet. He climbed between the sheets to lie staring up at the beams overhead.

The dryness spread to his throat. He felt parched, like desert sands after months of no rain. Rexana was like cooling, soothing water. He would perish without her.

He must find a way to win her heart. He must make her believe, with all the fire in his own soul, that no matter what happened to her brother, she would forever be Lady Rexana Linford.

Rexana awoke with a start. Her cheek pressed to the pillow, she blinked in the watery light filtering in through the open window. The smoky tang of the blacksmith's fire carried on the breeze, borne up from the bailey. Zounds! She had not intended to sleep so late. Last eve, as she had yielded to a restless slumber, she had vowed to rise with Fane, to demand to know what he had discovered.

A knock sounded on the door. The same noise, she realized muzzily, that had interrupted her sleep. She pushed up to sitting. The sheets on Fane's side of the bed were cold. She inhaled his scent clinging to the rumpled linens and scowled. He had managed to rise, wash and dress without her hearing. He had clearly made an effort not to rouse her.

Anger surged inside her. He had slunk away like a slick fingered thief, before they could discuss what he had learned from his men. Mayhap he never had any intentions of revealing what he had learned about Rudd.

Yet, she had every right to know.

The knock came again. Rexana glared at the door. Fane, being chivalrous? Nay. He would not bother to rap, but would stalk in. She shoved aside the bedding and set her feet on the floor. Well, whoever stood on the other side of the door would not prevent her from doing what she must to free Rudd.

She would begin this morn, by visiting him in the dungeon.

She opened the door to see Tansy, Nelda and Celeste. They carried cloths, along with water for washing, and a trencher of bread and cheese accompanied by an eating dagger.

With a polite smile, Rexana ushered them in. The sooner she ate and dressed, the sooner she could see Rudd.

Celeste and Nelda hurried to the bed and began to straighten the sheets. Humming a familiar love song, Tansy set the trencher, water, and cloths on the nearby table. Then, she eased a rolled parchment from her bodice. "For you, milady."

All trace of sleep vanished from Rexana's mind. A message? From whom? Dear Henry? Rudd? Had her brother managed to acquire parchment and ink? She smiled. Her brother had always been resourceful.

She snatched the parchment from Tansy's fingers. "Who gave this to you?"

"Winton." Tansy turned back to the cloths. Humming again, she dropped one into the water.

Rexana ignored Celeste and Nelda's inquisitive whispers. A frown tugged at her brow. Rudd would not have given a message to the steward, who was loyal to Fane. Yet, the efficient little man did get to all parts of the keep in his daily duties. Mayhap one of the other servants had handed it to Winton, and asked that it be delivered.

The missive was sealed with wax, but did not bear the imprint of a crested ring or other identifying marks. Of course not. Rudd would not be so foolish as to announce he had penned the note. How remarkable, though, that he had obtained wax.

She broke the seal and unfurled the parchment.

*I am the randy bee. I cannot wait to suck your nectar.*

Rexana gasped. She quickly rolled the document closed.

Tansy looked up. "Milady?"

Heat flooded Rexana's face. Her most secret of places tingled with a shocking, thrilling tension. Fane had written those bawdy words. She recognized his bold, elegant script from his signature on the marriage contract.

Nelda and Celeste hurried to her side. "Milady? Are you hale?"

Tansy elbowed the girls out of the way. She caught Rexana's arm, then steered her toward the made bed. "Here. Sit. Ye look flushed. Do ye feel queasy?"

Rexana sat. She clutched the parchment between her damp fingers. Her every nerve buzzed. Her pulse thumped at a dizzying pace. How did he affect her so, with only a few words?

"The note," Celeste whispered behind her hand to Nelda. " 'Tis foul news."

Tansy's mouth crumpled in sympathy. With a motherly cluck, she plopped down on the bed beside Rexana. The bed ropes groaned and sagged in violent protest. "There now. I pray the news is not too awful."

" 'Tis not bad news. 'Tis —" She bit down on her lip as the fire in her cheeks intensified. What did she say now?

Tansy and the girls leaned closer. "Aye?"

Rexana looked into their bright, curious faces, and laughed. " 'Tis a love poem."

"Ooohhhh. From 'is lordship? How romantic." Tansy's fingers twitched. "What does it say?"

"Do tell, milady!" Celeste squealed. Nelda elbowed her in the ribs and she added in a hushed voice, "Only if you wish, of course."

As Rexana unfurled the missive again, her face burned. "*I am the randy bee,*" she read. "*I cannot wait to suck your nectar.*"

Celeste frowned. "Suck what?"

Tansy rolled her eyes. "Nectar, you silly girl. From flowers."

Bewilderment clouded Celeste's gaze. "Aye, but . . . Milady is not a flower."

"Sheriff Linford is trying to write a *chanson,*" Rexana said. "He uses the extravagant language of the courtiers to express his . . . feelings."

With a loud snort, Tansy got to her feet. "We are all aware of those feelings, milady. Even a blind woman would see his lordship's affection for ye." She scowled down at Celeste and Nelda. "If the rest of the poem is as bawdy, ye'd best read it in private. Would not wish ta give these girls any notions."

Celeste and Nelda wailed in dismay. "But —"

"'Er ladyship is not even washed or dressed," Tansy said. "We must not forget our duties, must we?"

*And I must not forget mine,* Rexana reminded herself. The excitement in her blood dimmed. As enticing as Fane's missive was, she must not dally. She must focus on seeing Rudd.

As soon as she had broken her fast, Rexana quit the solar. As she walked, her braided hair swept against her lower spine. A yellow bliaut, cut from the softest wool, brushed her ankles and a gold cloth girdle pressed upon her hips.

As Rexana's shoes tapped on the stairs down to the hall, unease rippled through her. What if Fane learned of her visit to the dungeon? He would be angry. Yet, she could not sit idle, and let her brother be punished for a crime he did not commit.

She hurried down the forebuilding's steps, then out into the sunny bailey. Murmuring hello to the children drawing pictures in the dirt with sticks, she approached the slate-roofed building that housed the kitchens. She dried her hands on her gown and opened the door.

Steam wreathed the huge pots hung over the cooking fires. Servants stood nearby, stirring in handfuls of vegetables and spices. The scents of stew and baking bread wafted to her.

The cook chopped onions at a nearby table. Setting down his knife, he smiled at her. "Milady, ye look lovely this morn." He wiped his fingers on his stained apron and crossed to her.

"Thank you." Keeping her voice light and steady, she said, "I thought the prisoners in the dungeon might like some bread and cheese. Will you get it ready?"

He frowned. "They ate well earlier this morn."

*Hellfire!* "Ale, then," she said.

With a puzzled smile, the cook shook his head. "They had ale too. His lordship asked me to make sure they have enough food and drink."

She sighed, scarce able to control her rising impatience. "When is their next meal?"

"Midday." With a corner of the apron, he dabbed his sweaty nose. "Surely you do not wish to deliver food to the dungeon yourself? From what I have heard, 'tis not a place for a lady." Raising his hand like a claw, he hissed, "Spiders." He shuddered as though he saw one crawling across the floor.

"I am not afraid of spiders."

The cook's mouth tilted into a reluctant smile. "I do not mean to offend, milady, but I cannot help you. His lordship chose the servants who will deliver the meals each day. No one else is permitted."

Rexana resisted the urge to stamp her foot. Fane had outwitted her. Yet, if he thought she would be deterred, he was very wrong. She would find another way to access the dungeon.

As she stepped out of the kitchens, she spied Winton. He stood near the forebuilding's door, speaking to one of the laundresses. Rexana skirted a flock of geese waddling across the bailey and marched to Winton, a new plan already buzzing around in her mind.

With a brisk nod, the steward dismissed the laundress. He smiled as Rexana approached, and bowed. His head shone like a newly minted coin. "Good morn, milady."

"Good morn to you."

"Did you get the missive I sent with Tansy?"

She flushed at the reminder of Fane's note, tucked into her girdle for when she had time alone to read the rest of the poem. "Aye, thank you." She cleared the blush from her voice. "I realized this morn I have not yet completed a tour of Tangston Keep. There are several places I have not seen. I feel that in order to properly fulfill my role as lady of this fortress, I must know it with utmost thoroughness. Do you not agree?"

He blinked. His expression turned grave, as though he blamed himself for erring in his duties. "I will see that you finish the tour at once. Where —"

"The dungeon."

Winston shook his head. "I am very sorry, but —"

Summoning her sternest tone, the one that made even Rudd pause, she said, "You refuse my request?"

The little man's face lost color. His hands fluttered as though he did not know quite what to do with them. "I would be glad to accommodate you, milady. However, first, Sheriff Linford must give his permission. I have strict orders. So do the guards in the dungeon."

She growled. "I should have known."

Winton's shoulders raised in an awkward shrug. "Mayhap if you asked the sheriff for a visit —"

"Thank you, Winton. That is all."

Rexana spun on her heel and marched across the bailey. Dust swirled at her feet. The breeze blew her hair into her eyes, and with an angry hand, she swept it away. Frustration threatened to choke her.

She passed the well, the stables, the kitchens, and the blacksmith's, only slowing her pace when she reached the keep's gardens. A riot of herbs and greenery tumbled from earthen beds and popped up in the stone path under her feet. In the far corner, distinct from the rest of the garden, rose bushes grew in profusion. Climbing roses wove through a long, arched trellis and draped down in a curtain of leaves and pink petals. Inhaling a breath of the sweet perfume, she skirted the trellis to sink onto a weathered wooden bench.

Her eyes smarted. Rubbing her hands over her face, she vowed not to despair. She must think of another way to visit Rudd. A ruse. God forgive her, another deception.

The wind whispered through the scented curtain. Honeybees droned as they ambled from bloom to bloom. The sound reminded her of Fane's poem.

Rexana sighed. She might as well read the rest of his words.

She withdrew the parchment from her girdle and unrolled it.

*I am the randy bee. I cannot wait to suck your nectar.*

*I know you will taste sweet*

*Your dewy essence fills my mouth, quickens my wings,*

*Heats my body like a summer breeze*

*I am lost in your delicious taste, your fragrance*

*I am lost to all but my quivering need*

*Bzzzzz!*

*Love me, fair flower, with all the passion in your heart,*

*As I will love you.*

She wiped her mouth with a shaking hand and dropped the poem onto her lap. How she yearned for Fane. Quivered, like an eager flower.

How could she keep fighting what she desired?

"Bzzzzz."

She jumped. The sound, too low and masculine to be a bumblebee, came from behind the trellis. A flush seared her face, even as she crumpled the parchment. "Who goes there?"

Fane strode toward her, turning a delicate pink rose in his fingers. " 'Tis I, love. Did I startle you?"

She wadded the poem tighter, hiding all traces of it in her curled hand, as she shook her head. "You did not sound at all like a bee."

He laughed and dropped down onto the bench beside her. He tossed the bloom into her lap. Then, as though he had seen the movement of her fingers, he caught her fist. She tried to pull away, but he gently pried open her hand.

Disappointment shadowed his gaze. "You did not enjoy my poem?"

His fingers upon hers, and the nearness of him, threatened to pluck the last petals of her restraint. Fie!

She should be furious with him, not longing to curl into his embrace and kiss him with all the fervor pounding in her blood. " 'Tis a most seductive poem. You woo my heart and body with words."

His heavy-lidded gaze locked with hers. "Did I succeed?"

Rexana was suddenly aware of how alone they were. "Aye." She expected him to draw her into his arms, to begin seducing her right there on the bench, but he made no move toward her.

His callused finger trailed over the back of her hand, as though he wrote his name upon her sensitized skin. "I meant every word, Rexana. I want you, in all ways, and intend to have you." His tone softened. "Yet, I realize the choice is not as simple for you, because part of your heart belongs to your brother."

She looked at him.

"I know you tried to visit the dungeon. Cook and Winton told me."

She fought a renewed blush. "You are wrong to keep me from seeing him, and to imprison him. He is not guilty of treason."

Fane sighed. His eyes narrowed before he looked out across the rose garden, as though reading an answer to an impossible question amongst the blooms and greenery. "I have come to a decision. One that will, I hope, be productive for both of us, and break this impasse in our marriage."

"Decision?" she echoed.

He nodded. His face shadowed with an unreadable expression. "Your brother refuses to tell me all he knows about the traitors. I promised you that I would do all I can to help him. Yet, 'tis impossible, without complete information. All the evidence I have collected so far proves not that he is innocent, but that he is guilty."

Cold sweat broke between her breasts. She swallowed the awful taste in her mouth. "Why will he not tell you?"

Fane shrugged. "He does not trust me. Or, he is afraid." Tilting his head, he looked at her. "But he trusts you."

Fragile hope grew inside her. "Do you mean —"

"Aye, love. I permit you to visit him."

"Today?"

"Now, if you wish."

A delighted gasp burst from her. Without a moment's thought, she threw herself into Fane's arms. As her cheek crushed against his tunic, his strong embrace enveloped her. "Oh, thank you," she whispered. She fought a rush of tears.

His breath ruffled the crown of her hair. He chuckled, and the sound rumbled though his chest and against her ear. "I am glad my words please you."

She squirmed free of his hold. Her bliaut felt scratchy against her skin. Saints above, she could scarce sit still, her blood pounded so fast. She wanted to whoop with joy. Jump and throw her arms toward the sun. Dance and dance and dance, until she could not take another step.

She scrambled onto the bench. Pushed up on her knees. She stared into his handsome face, then leaned closer, until their noses touched.

Rexana kissed him full on the lips. "Aye, husband. Your words do please me."

# Chapter Sixteen

HIS FINGERS LINKED THROUGH HERS, Fane hurried along behind Rexana. He could scarce keep up. She plowed down the garden path like a cog in full sail, spurred by storm winds.

"Rudd will still be there," he said, "no matter how soon we arrive."

She glanced over her shoulder and grinned, her face lit by a rare warmth. "You cannot keep up, husband?"

He grunted, then gave her a crooked smile. "I can keep up, love. I have plenty of stamina, as you will soon learn."

Blushing, she looked back at the keep. "How do we get to the dungeon?"

With a swift, efficient tug, he hauled her backward into his arms. She squawked, struggled, until he slid his arm around her waist, turned her to face him, and silenced her with a thorough, wet kiss. She responded eagerly, as though the joy welling up inside her could never be silenced. His loins hardened. Ah, for a bed. Now. Now!

Mint carpeted the ground near his feet. If he pressed her down amongst the piquant leaves, covered her with his body, devoured her lips —

Her muffled protest pierced his lust-hazed brain. "The dungeon?"

Fane clenched his teeth against his burning arousal. He straightened his tunic and caught her hand again. "Follow me."

He led her into the keep. As they descended the musty stairwell to the fortress's lowest level, her fingers curled tighter into his. He felt the shudder rippling through her, and his jaw tightened. He would not apologize for the unpleasantness she would experience here. Tangston's dungeon was far better than General Gazir's.

Still, he prayed under his breath that he had not erred in judgment by letting her see Rudd. That her tender spirit would not be wounded by what she saw. That she would glean from her brother details which would lead to the traitors' capture and help crush the stirring rebellion.

Fane halted at the bottom of the stairs. She stopped beside him. Hesitated. In the shadowed light, her face looked tense. She glanced at the iron barred cells, her eyes gleaming with anxiety, yet also hope.

A guard crossed to him and bowed. "Milord."

"Lady Linford wishes to see her brother," Fane said. "I have permitted her a short visit."

As he looked back at her, she tugged her fingers free. He sensed her withdrawing into herself, steeling herself for what she might encounter. She ran a hand over her gown, then said in a calm, quiet tone, "Where is he?"

Admiration flooded through him. She might be unsettled, but she would show a strong front to her brother.

Fane pointed across the dungeon. "There."

Chains rattled from the farthest cell. Rudd's strained voice came from the darkness. "Rexana? Is that you?"

A cry broke from Rexana. She tore across the dungeon, her breath lodged tight between her ribs. She flung herself at the bars, wrapping her hands around the cold metal. "Rudd!"

He pulled at the end of taut chains fastened to his wrists and ankles. Oh, dear God. His hair was matted, his fine garments filthy and torn. The odors of mold and misery wafted from the cell. A painful sob welled in her throat, but she swallowed it down. She must be strong. He must not see her despair.

Rage roiled in her belly, and it growled like an angry fox. How dare Fane treat her brother this way? How dare he?!

"Rudd," she whispered. She stretched her arm through the bars. Tried desperately to reach him. Clawed against air.

He jerked hard against his chains, but their fingers did not meet. "I cannot reach," he said, his voice cracking.

She heard Fane's clipped footfalls. Sensed his presence behind her. He touched her shoulder, a small gesture of comfort, but she shook it off. Hands clamped into fists, she spun to face him. Her body shook with the storm of fury churning inside her.

"Why do you treat him this way?"

"He is a traitor."

Fury turned her tone shrill. "He is the son of an earl and lord of his own keep, yet you hold him like a beast. Is he so dangerous that you must chain him?"

Fane's eyes narrowed to angry slits. His mouth opened, as though he intended to reply. Then his gaze slid past her. He nodded.

Keys clinked. She whirled to face the cell. A guard strode to the door, unlocked it, and pulled it open.

She ran inside and threw herself into Rudd's arms.

With a ragged moan, he caught her in a rib-crushing hug. He smelled as though he had not bathed in days. The manacles at his wrists pressed into her back. Dust from his garments stung her eyes. She did not care. It felt wondrous, truly wondrous, to hug him.

"Come away," Fane muttered.

"Never." She shook her head against Rudd's shoulder.

"The guard will remove his chains, if you allow him."

Fane's gritted words pulled at her like invisible hands. She drew back a fraction. "Do you speak true?"

"I do."

Gratitude warred with her simmering anger. Fane had made this concession for her. Rage quickly snuffed the idiotic sentiment. Her brother did not deserve to be chained at all.

She stepped back, catching Rudd's cold fingers, then releasing them. At the terse wave of Fane's hand, the scowling guard strode forward, hunkered down, and unlocked the manacles at Rudd's ankles. The metal sprang open. The chains clattered to the ground. Rudd stood motionless, his moist gaze locked with hers, as the guard freed his wrists.

The instant the chains fell away, he stumbled to her and hugged her tight. The guard strode away.

After a long moment, Rudd held her at arm's length. His gaze shot to the doorway, then back to her.

"You are well?" His voice sounded unsteady.

Smiling, she nodded. "Better now I have seen you."

"I asked to see you. Linford refused."

The scrape of a boot from the doorway warned her

Fane stood nearby. Close enough to hear their conversation. Resentment flamed inside her like burning oil. Still, she would not waste her precious moments with her brother. "I asked to see you too." She pressed her hands over his, felt the tremor that ran through him.

"I cannot believe you are his wife." Rudd drew a harsh breath. "How did this come to be? He has not harmed you, has he? Mistreated you? God's holy teeth, if he —"

"He treats me well. How do you fare?"

"I cannot wait to quit this wretched place."

Anguish underscored his words. He obviously tried to be brave, but he was only ten and five. Far too young to spend the rest of his life locked behind bars, or to be executed for treason.

She looked up into his unshaven face. "I know you are innocent of treachery. Tell me how I can prove you are not guilty, and I will do it. I promise."

His mouth curved in a shaky, almost regretful grin. His gaze dropped to the brooch pinned to her bliaut. "You wear it. I am glad."

Smiling, she touched the little arrow. "Of course I do. I treasure its beauty, and wear it every day. I shall wear it even when you are free and cleared of all wrongdoing."

As she fingered the gold, an idea blazed into her mind. Zounds! Why had she not thought of it before?

Thomas would be able to vouch for Rudd's honor

and integrity. Rudd had visited Thomas with her every week as Thomas recovered from his arrow wound. Her brother had given Thomas's family coin to pay for a healer and to buy food. Had not Thomas's brother made her brooch, as a token of thanks?

Exhilaration flowed through her, hot as molten metal. She must visit Thomas as soon as possible, and see her brother freed from this horrible imprisonment.

Rudd leaned closer, until his tattered sleeve brushed her wrist. "Rexana?"

"Do not lose hope," she murmured. "I will not fail you."

He shook his head. "I fear I have failed you."

His strangled words cut like a sharp-edged stone. What, exactly, did he mean? He had failed to prevent her marriage to Fane? He had failed to live up to her expectations? He had failed a promise he had made to their parents? Stifling a pang of uncertainty, she wrapped her arms around him. Told him, with her snug embrace, that she believed him innocent. That she loved him.

Tears filled her eyes. Her resolve was slipping. She would not cry in front of Rudd. Not now. Not when she might have found a way to save him.

She blinked away the wetness. "I must go now," she said against his grubby shoulder.

As she drew away, he turned his face into her hair, as though he meant to kiss her. "Keep the brooch safe," he whispered against her ear, so quietly she almost did not hear.

She straightened. Shock pounded in her veins. Her palms coated with sweat. She glanced at him — she could not keep from looking — but his face remained in a tender smile, as though he had not whispered those few important words. But he had.

Keep the brooch safe.

Why? What was so important about the little gold arrow? Rudd had whispered, so Fane did not hear. There must be a reason why Rudd wanted his words to be private.

She felt Fane's assessing stare upon her back. Disquiet slid through her to settle in her stomach like a lump of ice.

Her lips had turned stiff and wooden, yet she managed a smile. She nodded once to Rudd. "We will speak again soon, dear brother."

"Goodbye, Rexana."

Fane watched the guard secure Villeaux's cell door, then followed Rexana into the stairwell leading out of the dungeon. She ascended with brisk strides, her shoes tapping on the uneven stones. He watched her bottom's luscious sway. Her skirts rustled, a familiar sound, yet something was amiss. His mouth filled with a foul taste, like the tart residue from an unripe lemon. A voice inside him whispered he had been deceived.

He had witnessed her visit with her brother. He had listened, assessed, and committed details to memory, like the occasions when he had been dragged in chains to Gazir's palace hall and displayed as a prized war trophy to visiting Saracens. Rudd had not slipped Rexana any messages. Nor had he spoken words or phrases that suggested hidden meaning or a brother to sister code.

Rexana reached the top of the stairs. Her head jerked, and she glanced down the corridor toward the hall. Torchlight played over her bound hair and rigid shoulders. Anger vibrated from her, potent as a hooded cobra poised to strike.

He would know what had transpired. His duty demanded it.

Before she walked away, he loped up the last steps, caught her arm, and pressed her against the wall. When she cursed and tried to shove him away, he thrust his hips forward, until her body was pinned between him and the mortared stones.

She looked up at him, her lips set in a mutinous line. "Fane, move."

Trailing one hand down her hair, he caught her braid. "You have not spoken one word to me, little fig, since we left your brother."

Fury glittered in her eyes. "What is there to say? I cannot bear to see Rudd so. 'Tis unjust, disagreeable and —" Her body shook.

Fane gently turned his hand. Her braid, soft as a silken cord, wrapped around his fingers. "Are you not pleased that I released his chains during your visit? Despite your worries, you have seen he is hale, and not being tortured or beaten."

Rexana swallowed. "Aye, I am pleased. 'Twas most generous of you, and I thank you for the visit. Yet, it changes naught. Now I have gone, he is once again chained. A prisoner. An innocent man condemned."

Misgiving raced down Fane's spine. She told him what he expected to hear, not what he wanted to know. Pressing his lips to her brow, he said, "What else runs through your pretty head?"

Squeezed against him, her breasts rose and fell on a huff. "Naught I wish to tell you."

He chuckled. "At least you do not feed me a falsehood."

"Fie! There is naught to tell. You saw and heard all that occurred in my visit with Rudd."

"Did I?"

Her furious gaze locked with his. "Aye."

The braid pulled taught. Her head tipped back against the wall, exposing her creamy neck and bringing her pink mouth closer to his. The lust that had blazed between them in the garden rekindled. 'Twould be easy to woo her into coupling with him, and 'twould all begin with a kiss.

She tried to shove him away. "Release my hair. I

am in no mood to play."

"I am." He nibbled her lips, felt her quiver. "I gave you what you desired, a visit with your brother. Now, you will grant me what I wish. What we both wish," he amended on a rasp.

"Fane —" Her plea warmed his mouth.

He kissed her. "Aye, love, you will cry out my name when I make your body soar." He flexed his hips and relished her shuddered gasp. "Come with me to the solar. Lie with me, naked, willing, so I may show you this pleasure." His tone roughened with need. " 'Tis our destiny, Rexana, as husband and wife. You know it, as well as I."

Her blazing eyes shadowed with longing and — God above — indecision.

Frustration gusted through him like a winter gale. "Come."

She looked away. When she spoke, her words were calm, yet held a residual edge of anger. "I need a moment alone to gather my thoughts. Then, I will."

"Nay, love. Now."

Her lips curved in a wry smile. "You will not force me. You have had the chance, but have not done so." Pressing her hand to his cheek, she whispered, "A moment is all I ask."

Her thumb swept over his skin in a light caress, and his pulse leapt. His fingers loosened, then he released her braid. "Do not make me wait long, Rexana, or I shall come fetch you."

He balled his hands into fists, the only way he could keep from lifting her into his arms and carrying her to their chamber. He fought the hunger wailing in his blood, turned on his heel and stalked away.

Exhaling a held breath, Rexana stepped out into the sunlit bailey. She had little time, so she must be convincing. Her acting skills had fooled a High Sheriff once. With luck, she should be able to deceive the stable hands.

Forcing herself to take unhurried strides, to ignore the fury fizzing inside her, Rexana skirted a group of pecking chickens and walked toward the low-roofed stables. She glanced at the lowered drawbridge, then beyond, to a horse drawn cart rumbling on the dirt road.

A shiver ran through her. Fane would thunder through the hall, bellowing and searching for her, when she did not arrive at the solar. He would be furious.

As she imagined Fane's handsome face, dark with rage and disappointment, her conscience pinched. She shoved aside the inconvenient emotion. He could never understand her deep bond to Rudd. Seeing her brother in tattered garments and chains had made her quest to clear his name and free him even more urgent.

In the sunny patch beside the stable, a man groomed a white mare. His tongue stuck from his lips, a sign of intense concentration, as he ran the brush down the horse's glossy coat.

She cleared her throat. He looked up, saw her, and dropped into an awkward bow.

Careful not to rush her words, she asked, "Is my horse ready yet?"

The man hesitated. "Milady?"

"I asked one of the maidservants to come to the stable, to tell whoever was here to ready a mount for me. I need to ride into Tangston village." Rexana sighed. "Did she not relay my message?"

A frown creased the man's brow. "I . . . Nay, milady." He called into the stable, and two young boys poked their heads out. "Did one of the maids tell ye ta ready the lady a horse?"

They shook their heads.

Rexana prayed that the shouts had not carried up to the open solar window. She resisted the urge to glance over her shoulder to see if Fane stood there watching. "Mayhap the maid told one of the other lads." She waved an impatient hand at the mare. "This one will do. Please find a saddle. I wish to leave now."

The groomer's gaze sharpened with worry. "Does 'is lordship know of your journey? 'E must be informed. 'E told us 'e must know all who enter or leave the keep." Thrusting back his shoulders, the man added, "I will not 'ave poisonous spiders in me bed."

She ignored her belly's nervous swoop and forced a titter. "I plan to buy his lordship a special gift. A surprise. Come, now. I am in a hurry."

The man mulled her words, then fetched a saddle and bridle. As she waited, tapping her foot in the dirt, she prayed Fane's patience would last a bit longer, and that he had not looked out the solar window and seen her.

After what seemed an eternity, the mare was ready to ride.

Scratching his head, the man glanced about the bailey. "Where is yer armed escort, milady?"

Rexana stepped up on the wooden mounting block and swung onto the mare's back. "They will be along soon. Tell them I am on my way to the village. They can catch up with me."

"Ye cannot —"

She snatched up the reins and nudged the mare's side. The horse trotted forward.

"Milady! Wait."

The man's voice was drowned by the rhythmic clop of the horse's hooves. A moment later, she crossed the drawbridge. As she coaxed the horse to a canter, she smiled.

She could not wait to speak with Thomas Newland.

Hands on his hips, Fane scowled down at the stable hand. "She *what*?"

The man's face crumpled. Bowing his head, he turned the grooming brush in his fingers. "She told me she 'ad ta ride into Tangston, ta buy ye a gift."

Fane bit back a string of vile curses waiting to explode. Anger thumped in his veins. Rexana had deceived him. Deliberately. She had never intended to come to the solar and taste passion. As she had pleaded for a few moments to collect her thoughts, she plotted to take one of his horses and flee.

Did she try to avoid the consummation? To escape their marriage? Did she truly believe that after all his careful wooing, he would ever let her go?

Between his clenched teeth, he said, "Ready my horse."

The man bowed, then scurried into the shadowed stable. Fane flexed his fingers and shrugged away knotted tension. She might run, but he would catch her. Heart, body and soul, she belonged to him. She was *his*.

The captain of the guard strode across the bailey toward him. "Milord."

"Find three of your best men. I need an escort."

"Aye, milord."

Fane glanced at the drawbridge and the winding road beyond. Disquiet fueled his fury. She traveled alone. To his knowledge, she did not carry a weapon. The roads were dangerous enough for armed knights, but a beautiful woman riding alone . . .

He cursed again. Had she no care for her own safety? Why did she take such a senseless risk?

The stable hand returned with a saddle.

"Hurry," Fane growled. "I have no time to waste."

His hand settled on the jeweled dagger tucked into his belt. He turned and stormed back to the keep, almost tripping over a dog chewing on a bone. He must take his sword. Before he gave Rexana a well-deserved tongue lashing, he might have to save her pretty neck.

Through the stand of sun-drenched alders ahead, Rexana spied the thatched roofs of Thomas's cottage and barn. She urged the lathered mare to a faster trot.

Not far, now. She could not wait to speak with Thomas. He would help her prove what a grievous error Fane had made in arresting and imprisoning her brother.

As the mare clopped into the dirt space before Thomas's home, two girls, busy milking a cow, glanced out of the barn. They dried their hands, waved, then ran to the house. Excited shrieks drifted to Rexana. "Mama! Mama."

Thomas's wife Mary stepped out, a swaddled baby in her arms. The scent of cooking food wafted from the open doorway. She smiled, waved, yet the welcoming gesture seemed hesitant. Her face, too, held a wariness that had not been evident in earlier visits.

Ignoring a twinge of unease, Rexana slid from the mare's back and smoothed the creases from her bliaut. "Hello, Mary."

The woman dropped into a deep curtsey. "Good day, Lady Linford. 'Tis an honor to see you."

Rexana suppressed a frown. Mary's voice quavered. Why? Did she feel differently about Rexana now that she was married to the county's High Sheriff? Surely Mary did not believe that the marriage had changed Rexana.

Offering a warm smile, Rexana swept hair from her brow. " 'Tis good to see you. Is Thomas about?"

Mary stiffened. "He is. Ye wish ta speak with 'im?"

"Aye."

Mary's gaze darkened with trepidation, yet she motioned Rexana inside. As Rexana stepped over the cottage's threshold, her belly tightened. Why did Mary seem so unsettled, even frightened?

The shadowed interior, softened by candles and a crackling fire, soothed Rexana's frazzled nerves. Mary must have heard of Rudd's arrest. Such news would no doubt have caused the family uncertainty, since Rudd had been generous in helping them and ensuring they did not go hungry.

Thomas sprawled in a rickety chair near the fire, his chin drooping to his chest. His game leg stretched toward the warmth. His open-mouthed snores competed with the pot bubbling over the flames. Stepping over a sleeping mongrel, Rexana touched his weathered hand.

He blinked. When his gaze focused upon her, he sat up with a start. "Milady!" He struggled to stand.

"Do not trouble yourself. I know your leg pains you."

With a frustrated grunt, Thomas dropped back into the chair. "After many long months. One day, soon, I pray I will be able to walk like a man again."

"The healer said your wound would heal," Rexana gently reminded him, "but 'twill take a while. You must be patient."

One of the girls hurried forward with a battered wooden stool. With a nod in thanks, Rexana took it and sat down beside Thomas.

"May we fetch ye some ale, milady? A bowl of pottage?" Mary asked.

Rexana's stomach gurgled. She had not thought to pack any fare before she left Tangston, and the steam from the cauldron smelled delicious. Yet, Thomas had five children to feed — including two sons who worked long days in the fields and in the village — and his family had little enough. She could not take their food and drink. "Thank you, but nay."

Thomas looked at Mary. He flicked his hand, as though signaling her and the girls to leave. Mary lingered, as though questioning the wisdom of his decision, but Thomas gave a sharp nod. She ushered the girls outside. The cottage door banged shut behind them.

Rexana breathed in, trying to quell her racing pulse. Her stomach tightened even more. She prayed Thomas would give her the information she needed.

"You have come to speak of Rudd," he said, before she had a chance to speak.

She nodded. "Sheriff Linford has arrested him for treason. The sheriff refuses to believe he is not guilty. Please, Thomas, I need your help. You can tell him of Rudd's honorable character. You are a faithful subject of the crown, and you know Rudd is loyal too."

Thomas looked at her brooch, then stared down at the fire. His face shadowed with an odd expression.

"Thomas?"

Low, rumbled voices intruded, coming from outside the cottage. She recognized Mary, speaking to her children. Mayhap her sons had come home early, so she told them to stay out of the cottage.

Rexana closed her mind to the distraction. She leaned forward, her hands clenched into her skirt. "Please, Thomas. You must help me save Rudd."

The cottage door crashed open.

A tall, broad shouldered man blocked the light streaming in from outside. The hair on her nape prickled. Awareness and shock rushed through her, a moment before Fane spoke.

"You are foolish to come here, wife. Thomas knows Rudd is guilty. As do I."

His blood pulsing hard against his temple, Fane watched Rexana rise to her feet. As her body straightened, her bliaut smoothed over her hips, the simple yellow gown provocative in the smoky shadows.

Her gaze shone bright with anger. "You followed me."

"Nay, love. I hunted and found you."

She continued as though she had not heard him and did not care that Thomas overheard. Her words flew like chunks of ice. "Did you go to the solar, after we spoke? Did you look down from there, see me at the stables, and decide to pursue me? Or did you simply watch from a distance to give the illusion that I had freedom to go, so you could entrap me?"

He took a step forward. His arms shook with the fury pounding through him. "I did not see you at the stables. If I had, I would not have allowed you to ride out of Tangston's gates. Not when you had promised with such sweetness to come to my bed."

She flushed. "You could not have stopped me."

Lust pulsed hot within him, yet he resisted the urge to march forward, grab her arm, and haul her flush against him. To claim her mouth in a kiss. To feel her body quiver with desire and want. He would not take her here, in this humble dirt-floored dwelling, and the next time he touched her, 'twould be to couple with her.

Aware her defiant stare had not wavered, he said, "You will not leave Tangston on your own again. I will not allow you to recklessly endanger your life. Do you understand?"

Her lips flattened with resentment. She did not answer.

Thomas shifted in his chair, while the dog near the

fire tucked its tail between its legs and scurried under a table.

Fane strode closer. He stood near enough now to catch her arm, if he wished. "You will heed me, Rexana."

Her chin thrust up a fraction. "Answer me this, husband. How did you know to find me here? How did you know of my friendship with Thomas?"

Fane smiled. How cunning, that she changed the subject and avoided agreeing to his demand. Yet, he would have a compliant 'aye, milord' from her before their conversation was through. "How? I am a High Sheriff. I have my ways."

Uncertainty flickered in her eyes, but her chin nudged higher. "Rudd told you?"

"I did not ask your brother. My men spoke to Thomas yesterday when they questioned the tavern owners and villagers. He freely admitted he knew Rudd. 'Twas difficult for him to tell of Rudd's treachery, yet Thomas is loyal to the king. He felt honor bound to do so."

Her stunned gaze flew to Thomas, then back to Fane. She blinked, as though unable to believe what she had heard. "Naught you have told me proves my brother is guilty. Did Thomas explain how Rudd supported him and his family over the past months? How Rudd visited every sennight to make sure his leg wound was healing?"

Thomas's head moved. "I told them, milady."

With deliberate patience, Fane folded his arms over his chest. "Did he tell *you*, love, that Rudd asked to use his barn, and paid a sack of coin for the privilege? Your brother planned to meet there with his fellow traitors."

She gasped.

Bowing his head, Thomas moaned. "Milady, I am sorry."

"I do not believe it!" Anguish glittered in her eyes.

Fane saw the effort it cost her to keep her head held high. "Love, you must accept the truth. Rudd is a traitor."

"He is not!"

"I have detailed eye witness accounts of the meetings held in local taverns. Over a score, to be exact. I also have the missive which bears his signature."

Her lush mouth trembled. " 'Tis forged."

"The signature is his. Rudd admitted to me, the first time I questioned him, that he signed the document." Fane held his hand out to her. He willed her to place her fingers in his, to accept, at last, what she must. "Come with me back to Tangston. I will show you the evidence."

"I will not —"

He loosed a low, warning growl. "Come, wife. My patience wears thin. I have waited long enough for you to accept this." *And me*, his heart roared. *And, by God, me*!

Her breathing became ragged. Her hands clenched and unclenched. She looked down at Thomas. Torment etched her face, yet she graced him with a stiff nod. "Good day."

"Good day to you, milady," Thomas whispered.

She swept around the far side of the fire, her gown bright as the leaping flames. She moved well out of reach, as though she believed physical distance could keep her from him.

"Rexana," Fane called.

Half way to the door, she faced him. Her loosened braid flipped back over her shoulder. Like a potent physical caress, he again felt its glorious silk wrapped around his wrist. Binding him to her. Her to him.

"You will never stop me from leaving Tangston alone," she said. "Nor will you keep me from proving my brother's innocence."

A rough laugh burst from him. "Foolish words, little fig."

"I mean them."

He started toward her. She yanked open the door, strode out, and slammed it behind her.

Spitting a curse, he crossed to the door to wrench it open. She did not even glance back. Her braid swaying side to side, she marched past Thomas's bewildered family and Fane's armed guards, untethered her mare, and swung up onto its back. Even in anger, she moved with sensual grace.

She would move with such beauty beneath him as he brought her to writhing, moaning pleasure.

Fane halted and planted his boots in the dirt. "Where do you think you are going?"

She coiled the leather reins around her wrists. Her eyes glittered with rebellious intent.

"If you run from me now, you are forever mine."

She smiled, a disbelieving turn of her lips. With a sharp cry, she wheeled the mare around and spurred it toward the road.

"We will stop her, milord," a guard yelled, running to his horse.

"You will follow at a discreet distance, but you will not interfere."

Frowning, the men glanced at each other. "Milord?"

Fane swung up onto his destrier. As though attuned to his heightened state, the horse whinnied and sidestepped. Fane's blood roared. He struggled to keep a clear mind, to keep his desire in check for a little longer.

He fixed his gaze on Rexana. "Obey my orders. The only man to catch Rexana will be me."

# Chapter Seventeen

REXANA GALLOPED PAST FIELDS, down pitted dirt lanes, and through groves of sun-dappled trees. She rode until the sun had slipped from the midday sky. Until her wind-whipped hair felt like straw against her cheek. Until the sweaty mare stumbled and, with a reluctant groan, Rexana knew she must stop to let the horse rest.

As she slowed the animal to a walk, a shiver rippled through her. She had traveled many leagues, yet still, she sensed Fane's presence. Rexana stole a glance over her shoulder again, as she had numerous times during her ride, but saw only distant riders, too far behind and moving too slowly to be pursuing her.

She shook off her unease. Fane had not come after

her. He had only chased her for a league or two. To her amazement and relief, the mare had outrun his destrier, and he had fallen back. At times, she had thought the breeze carried the clop of hoofbeats or the snort of nearby horse, yet each time she swung around, she found herself alone.

Her imagination toyed with her. Fane had let her go.

At last, had he accepted that she would never surrender her fierce loyalty to Rudd? That whatever Thomas, the eyewitness accounts and missive implied, she would always believe her brother guiltless? That she could not rest, now more than ever, until she found undeniable proof of his innocence?

Fane must have. He had let her go.

Yet, even as her mind offered reassurance, a wild tingle trailed down her spine. A simmering anticipation she could not dismiss.

Her imagination, again.

Rexana studied the road ahead, recognizing the familiar stretch near Ickleton. How fitting that her heart had brought her here, to the place that gave her solace. She guided the mare into the ancient trees' cool shadows, then took the winding deer path to the secluded pool.

As the glade opened before her, she sucked in the calming scents of loam, grass and violets. Her breath rushed out on a half sob. Here, as she had so many times before, she would stretch up her arms to dance.

Here, she would defeat the anxiety warring within her. Here, she would vanquish the nagging voice that warned Fane was not one to forget a promise.

Or leave it undone.

Resisting another shiver, Rexana slid from the mare's back. The horse began to graze. Smoothing her hands down her bliaut, she strolled to the center of the glade. She halted in a shaft of sunlight. Closed her eyes. Called to the ancient place to inspire and enlighten her.

Reaching her arms up to the sky, she dipped and whirled. Grasses tugged at her bliaut. Butterflies and bees whizzed from the heads of wildflowers. Birds flitted through the tree boughs overhead. Leaves rustled.

Her soul shuddered. She begged for answers. Resolution.

*If you run from me now, you are forever mine.*

Her inhalation snagged in her throat, like delicate silk caught on a rock. Her body twisted, turned, and arched.

*I have waited long enough for you to accept this.*

Confusion flooded through her. Yearning. Desire. Need.

She spun faster. Faster.

Her back arched. Her arms stretched.

She twirled, faster again.

"Rexana."

Had she imagined Fane's voice? Panting, she stumbled to a halt. Her pulse thundered like a galloping horse. As she swept hair from her face, she saw him.

Fane walked at the glade's edge, holding the destrier's reins in one hand. With unhurried strides, he led the horse toward the pool. Sunlight gleamed on his windswept hair and touched the firm set of his mouth.

His head tilted, and his gaze locked with hers. His expression held not anger or scorn, but acceptance. Knowing. A promise that what happened now, between them, was inevitable.

"W - Why did you come here?"

A faint smile touched his lips. "You brought me here."

Resentment gnawed at her. "This is my place. I never wished you to find it."

The destrier's hooves sank into the soft muddy bank. The horse dipped its head to the water to drink. Fane chuckled, released the reins and looked at her. "You speak false, love. You wanted to be chased. I have caught you."

She gasped. "I did not —"

"Now, you lie to yourself."

A fierce trembling racked her body. The leaves overhead shifted, as the little voice inside her murmured in agreement. He spoke true. A secret part of her had wanted him to catch her. A part of her had led him here to fulfill his promise.

As she struggled to control her thoughts, his gaze

flicked around the glade, then settled on her. " 'Tis a fine place to make love." His voice sounded almost reverent. "I could not have chosen better myself."

Tangled emotions warred inside her. "I did not bring you here to fornicate," she cried. "I meant to run from you."

With a laugh that sounded almost tender, he set his hands upon his hips. "You really thought you could run from me and our marriage?"

"Why not?"

"Where did you think to go? You are my wife. Our marriage is legal, and we are well known throughout this county. Wherever you tried to hide, I would find you."

She fisted her hands. "I could seek refuge in a nunnery."

His grin widened. "You would make a rotten nun."

She arched an eyebrow. "Indeed?"

"You are not a woman who would enjoy endless hours of prayer, or a life constrained by religious rule. Not to mention celibacy." He winked. "You are a woman of passion and wild joys. A woman to be loved, cherished, and treasured by a man."

His words warmed her like molten sunlight. Pleasure shimmered through her.

Shaking her head, she fought the traitorous pull. "Milord, you are a rogue." Despite her intended scorn, her words came out in a breathless rush. She sounded like a woman intrigued. Tempted to the point of desperation.

He took a step closer. "I mean every word."

Her pulse skittered, then pounded at a faster rhythm. "Do not play with me. You married me for my noble blood. You wanted the prestige of my family name."

"I cannot deny that is true, but—"

"You never wanted me for who I really am."

A sigh exploded from his lips. "Rexana, I wanted you from the moment I saw you dance." His gaze sharpened with a hunger that shot deep inside her. "I saw your soul that night in my hall. I wanted you then. I want you now. God's teeth, have you any idea how much I desire you?"

Warmth flooded between her thighs. Her legs quivered. She struggled against her melting, yielding body. "My brother —"

"Nay. You will not hide behind your loyalty to him. He has no part in this. He made his own choices. He is responsible for his own fate. This matter is between you and me." As Fane spoke, he moved closer again. He halted before her. His breath warmed her brow. He did not touch her, yet she felt his body's powerful sexual aura. It wove itself around her. It drew her, like a vine, to him.

Her body screamed for his touch.

Oh, God. One touch, and she would be his.

He stared down into her face. Softly, so softly, he

said, "What do *you* want, Rexana? Do you want to run? Do you want out of our marriage? Or are you curious to see how wondrous it can be between us?"

Her last, unraveling shred of reason warned she should not heed his entreaty. That she should stay true to her goal of an annulment. That she should resist the sensual web his words wove around her, grab her skirts, and run.

Yet, reason faded in the wake of another, more vibrant cry. One that tempted her like a potent nectar. It said that Fane was her destiny. All that had happened since Rudd's imprisonment had led to this one, pivotal moment.

A primitive rhythm seemed to flow up from the ground beneath her feet. The same rhythm echoed in the breeze, pushed up through every stalk of grass, quivered in each tiny, fragrant violet. It pulsed through her veins, heady as sap, to pool in her womb. The ancient magic coaxed. Tempted. Enlightened. She had not realized before now that every time she had danced in despair and loneliness, she had danced for him.

"What do *you* want?" he whispered again, his words hot on her skin. "What does your heart say?"

Tears dampened her eyes. Did she dare tell him that she desired him, with a passion that excited yet frightened her? How could she want him, when he sought to persecute her brother?

Yet, the spell of the ancient place pulled at her.

Wooed. Infused her with hunger.

He raised his hand, so his fingers hovered over her heart. "Here, now, your lineage does not matter. You are not a titled lady, fettered by tutoring and civility. You are the untamed, stubborn, incredibly beautiful woman who lives in your soul."

His fingers brushed her bliaut, just above her cleavage. "That is the woman I saw in your dance. The woman I love."

"Love?" Joy swelled within her.

He nodded. "Let me show you how much."

His fingers slid across her breast. Heat blazed on her skin. Her eyelids fluttered. As her body arched into his caress, he pulled her into his arms. His hard loins thrust against her womanhood, and the wanting inside her flared.

"Oh, Fane. Aye!"

"Rexana, how I love you."

"Show me," she whispered. "I am willing."

His lips swept down on hers in firm possession. He squeezed her tight. He held her as though he feared she might slip away. As though he would never let her.

A sigh rushed between her teeth. His mouth left hers to nibble a path across her jaw.

She shivered. "You tease."

"I seduce," he growled against her tingling skin.

His hands skimmed down to her bottom, and she wriggled against his hardness. He groaned and inhaled sharply.

"I shall seduce too," she murmured.

"Careful, love. Our dance will finish before it has properly begun."

"Why?" She squirmed out of his arms. "You must take the lead in this dance?"

His words rumbled low in his throat. "After the first time, you may lead. Aye?"

"If you wish."

"Good." He reached for her, his face stark with need. On instinct, she stepped backward. Grass heads brushed against her hands. He pursued, and she laughed.

She had taken no more than two steps, when he pounced. He pushed her down, cushioning her fall. She landed on her bottom in the lush grass. She half giggled, half squealed, as he dropped to his knees, prowled onto her, then pressed her onto her back. Nibbling the side of her cheek, he rolled her over, his limbs entwined with hers. The sweet scents of crushed grasses, flowers, and the spicy musk of man filled her senses.

Over and over they rolled. Kissing. Touching. Laughing. At last, she fell still, her head pillowed in a patch of violets.

Breathing hard, he settled himself over her. He grinned. "You are a fetching sight with your hair full of grass."

She feigned a frown. "And you are a barbarian, husband, for tossing me to the ground."

He chuckled. His mouth caught hers in a slow, wet kiss.

Moaning, she reached up to tangle her fingers through his silky hair. The kiss deepened. His tongue meshed with hers in a steady, sensual rhythm. Her womb pulsed with a similar beat.

He shuddered. "I cannot wait much longer."

"Nor can I."

He smiled. As his fingers slid to her bliaut's ties, a tremor rippled through her, rattling the haze of pleasure. What did she have to do? Would her first experience hurt?

She shifted beneath him. "Will it —"

"Shhh, love. I will be gentle." He shook. "Though, by God, 'twill be a valiant effort."

The last tie whispered free. His hand slid underneath her yellow gown to her linen shift, and closed over one of her breasts. She gasped.

He groaned. "Ah, love."

His thumb rubbed over her nipple. Heat shot down between her legs. Sensation so sharp and urgent, she cried out.

He bowed his head. Swore between his teeth.

He caught her gown, pulling it up to her thighs.

"Fane?"

"Let me lead," he begged, even as his fingers

searched through the layers of bliaut and shift. "Let me give you pleasure. Let me show you this dance between man and woman."

A draft, then his hands, brushed her inner thigh. She started. As he touched her sex, she jumped again. "Oh!"

"You like this? 'Tis only the beginning." His skilled fingers worked the nub of nerves. Each sensation was more delicious than the first. Saints above. She could scarce breathe. Her eyes squeezed shut.

Through the exquisite haze, she became aware of him shifting to one side. He fumbled with his garments. The points of his hose popped. He shifted again, and then his warm maleness brushed the place where his hand had been.

Her eyes flew open.

His snarled hair hung down beside his taut jaw. His gaze smoldered. His mouth tensed, as though it took great restraint to hold still above her. Leaning forward, he brushed his lips over hers in a rough kiss. He nibbled her bottom lip and his hardness glided against her. Teased. Tempted.

An intense thrill seared through her. His flesh felt smooth against hers. She wanted more. She wanted to taste the wildness his body promised. With a greedy moan, she tilted her hips up.

He pressed forward.

Pain stabbed between her legs. Pressure. Her entire

body tensed, and her breath jammed in her throat.

He groaned. "You feel wondrous. Perfect."

*Perfect*? "Ouch. Fane?"

With utmost tenderness, he kissed her and nuzzled her cheek. "The pain will fade, I promise." He slowly withdrew, then gently eased forward again. "At last, love, you are mine."

His strangled tone washed through her. Reassurance and pleasure warmed her soul as she blinked away tears. No man had spoken to her with the desperation, honesty, and love she heard in Fane's voice.

"And you are mine," she murmured and touched his cheek.

He stilled, as though surprised by her words, then smiled. "I am."

He thrust again. The pain dimmed, fading to an elusive craving.

He began a slick rhythm that erased all memory of discomfort. Delicious heat filled her hips, belly, and limbs, right to the tips of her fingers.

It grew. Grew. Grew.

A new, intoxicating pressure built between her legs. Fane's breath hissed between his teeth. His hair brushed her face. She tossed her head and curled her hips into his thrusts. Restless. Needy.

Her fingers clawed into the grass and violets beneath her.

"Do you feel the wildness, Rexana?" he rasped

above her.

"Aye." She stared up into his dark, hungry eyes.

Heat flared.

She dragged in a breath. Once. Twice.

"Fane . . . !" Sensation exploded.

He stiffened above her. A growl wrenched from him. The harsh, primitive sound filled her with wonder.

Her body throbbed, again and again. As the pulses faded, she unclenched her hands from the crushed grass. The fresh glade air filled her lungs. She smelled the musky scent of aroused male, sweat, and violets. Bittersweet pleasure stirred within her.

Now, she was his. Body, heart and soul.

Fane dropped his face into the warm cradle between Rexana's neck and shoulder. He listened to the wind sigh around them, the birds chatter, and her slowing breaths.

Rexana smelled wonderful. Sated.

His blood cooled. His body purred.

He lay there for some moments, savoring the scent of her. Contentment flooded through him. He had succeeded in wooing her. She had finally accepted the rightness of their marriage. He prayed she did not have virgin regrets.

She swallowed.

Steeling himself against her tears, he braced himself up on one elbow to look down at her. A blush stained her face. The enticing rosy hue ran all the way down

her throat to her gown's neckline. With a sting of regret, he realized they were both still fully clothed. In
the mad rush to have her, he had not even taken the
time to undress her.

She looked away, so he brushed a finger down her
cheek.

"Are you well?"

A smile touched her mouth. "Mmm."

" 'Twas pleasurable for you, our coupling?"

She stirred beneath him. "Most pleasurable."
Frowning, she added, "Though I did not expect to be
dressed."

Heat warmed his cheekbones. "I was impatient."

"Indeed?" Her smile turned wry before she pressed
her hands against his shoulders, an entreaty for him
to move. He rolled off her into the violets, and she
sat up.

She righted her creased gown and fumbled with the
loosened ties, then threw up her hands in dismay.

"The birds do not care that your bliaut is unfastened."

She flipped her straggly braid over her shoulder and
looked at him. "They would not care if I were nude."

He wagged his eyebrows. "True."

Her flush deepened. A spark lit her eyes, a moment
before she stood. "I am going down to the water to
bathe."

"I will come too."

She did not answer, but walked toward the glinting pool. He pushed to his feet, fastening his hose.

As Rexana trampled a path through the grass, her body swayed. He smiled. She moved like a woman who had experienced her own sensual power. Who had tasted love, and knew it to be good.

Raking a hand through his snarled hair, he followed her. She kicked off her shoes and stepped barefoot into the mud. She hesitated, stared down at the gray-green water, then hugged her arms over her breasts.

Sunlight washed over her profile. She looked ravishing, yet also vulnerable. Fane stepped down into the mud and, before he cautioned himself, wrapped his arms around her waist. A tremor rippled through her.

He nuzzled the back of her neck. "Love?"

She sighed.

"You cannot regret our coupling."

"I do not. 'Twas what I wanted. Yet —"

He looked down at the glassy reflection of them together. "Here, in this glade, we think only of our pleasure. Not what has been, or what must be."

Her body tensed. " 'Tis not so simple a decision for me."

Pushing aside her braid, he nipped her skin. "Nay?"

She shuddered. Heat shot through his loins. His manhood pulsed. Hardened. Again, he craved the luscious taste and feel of her, the velvety warmth of her body encasing him.

Before he could kiss her again, she wiggled free of his arms. She reached down, caught her bliaut and shift, and whisked them over her head. Light played over her naked back, and the fetching curves of her bottom.

The air shot from his lungs. In his wildest imaginings, he had not come close to her true beauty.

Sweeping wispy hair from her cheek, she partly turned toward him. A mischievous smile touched her mouth. "You are impatient again, milord. This time, you must wait."

He growled. "I will not."

She laughed. Ran into the water. Dove under with a splash.

His blood thumped with challenge. He groped for his clothing. Cursed his clumsy hands. He yanked off his tunic and shirt and, as he hopped out of his hose and boots, saw her surface at the far edge of the pool near a cluster of rocks and a fallen, gnarled tree.

She blew water from her lips, then brushed hair from her face. As she turned to glance at him, he charged, roaring, into the pool.

Her eyes widened. She submerged.

Fane opened his eyes in the water. She swam ahead of him, past a school of fish that darted in and out of the light, their backs glinting like bits of silver. He kicked hard. Pulled his arms through the water. Closed the space between them. Caught her ankle, and yanked her to him.

She surfaced in his arms. Splashing. Squawking. Water droplets glinted on her eyelashes.

"Fie! How did you cross so qui —"

He smothered her words with a kiss. She resisted for an instant, then, with a mewl, softened into his embrace.

He gently propelled her backward, against a semi-submerged rock. The water lapped just below her breasts. As he broke the kiss, he pressed his forehead against hers and stared down at the luscious swell of flesh so close within reach.

*His.*

Knotting his fingers into her hair, he tipped her head back. She laughed, and he sensed her heavy-lidded gaze upon him as he laved and kissed her satiny neck, her collarbone, the hollow of her throat. Little gasps burst from her lips. When he cupped her breasts in his hands, she groaned.

Madness shot through him. He had to have her. He coaxed her up out of the water. Followed her, dripping, onto the sunny rock. Urged her to lie on her back. This time, she smiled up at him with understanding and anticipation. When he thrust into her, she cried out with her own need.

He took her with care. Thoroughness. Watched the pleasure bloom on her face. Cherished each of her cries and moans, before taking his release. He loved her, as his soul mate deserved to be loved.

Afterward, he lay beside her on the rock, his eyes closed, one hand splayed on her belly. He lost himself in the lap of water, the drone of dragonflies, and his utter contentment.

She sighed, a thoughtful sound. "Tell me about her."

Fane roused from near slumber to crack open one eye. A chill skittered through him. Did she ask about Leila?

"Who, love?" He feigned a yawn, and prayed his sleepiness would deter her questions.

"The Saracen courtesan. The one you met in the east."

A silent oath exploded in Fane's mind. He had no wish to discuss Leila with Rexana. Not now.

The chill slipped deep into his soul. If he told Rexana the truth, it might change how she felt about him. He might lose her.

He wet his lips with his tongue. "Rexana."

Turning onto her side, she braced her head on one hand. Her legs brushed against his. "I wish to . . . I must know if the rumors are true."

He fought to keep the edge from his voice. "Why? The past is the past."

Looking down, she traced a furrow in the rock. "I still want to know."

He rolled onto his back. The rock's warmth seeped into his skin. The earthy scent of sun-baked stone filled his nostrils, taunted him with memories of merciless desert heat and what seemed a lifetime ago.

His gut whined. He did not have to tell her. He could fabricate a tale, tell her only what he thought she wanted to hear. Yet, he hated the thought of deceiving her. His soul mate, of all people, deserved to know the truth.

"She was very beautiful," he began. As he spoke, Leila's olive-skinned, dark-eyed image filled his mind. He remembered her fragrance, sultry as incense. "She was General Gazir's favorite courtesan."

Rexana's gaze darkened. "And yours?"

Fane smiled, but could not ignore the sadness piercing through him. "Your jealousy is ill placed, love. Leila is dead."

As though sensing his inner turmoil, Rexana fell quiet. Yet, he saw countless questions burning in her eyes.

"General Gazir ruled a fortress not far from Acre," Fane said. "He paid allegiance to Saladin, whom King Richard defeated at Acre."

She nodded. "I heard of Saladin."

"I went to the holy land long before King Richard. I had joined his crusade, but was starved for adventure." A tight laugh broke from him. "As you have probably heard, my father disowned me. I had no land, no coin, so I could scarce feed myself. I could not wait to leave England."

"Oh, Fane," she whispered.

"I proposed that some fellow crusaders and I go on ahead to spy on the Saracens, and gather information for when the king arrived at Acre. He agreed. We left soon afterward. After many setbacks, we reached the shores near Acre, but were attacked. Most were slaughtered. A few of us were captured and sent to Gazir's dungeon." The stench of the eastern hell pit roused in Fane's mind, and he shuddered. "We were chained. Beaten. Tortured."

Her gaze softened. She stared at his scars, and inside, he curled up into a ball. He felt exposed, as though he bared not only his marred flesh, but his soul.

"Go on," she said gently.

Steeling emotion from his voice, he said, "One by one, the others went mad or died. I refused to surrender. I refused to abandon faith in my king or hope of escape. There were nights, though, that I longed for oblivion."

"How did you survive?"

Fane looked up at Rexana. Her fair skin glowed. Her loosened hair, flowing over the rock, had almost dried in the sun's heat. She looked fresh, innocent, the very opposite of Leila's blatant sensuality.

"Without Leila, I would not have lived." Rexana's eyes flared with shock, but he pressed on. "The first time I saw her, she had come to the dungeon out of sheer curiosity. She wanted to see the Christian knight who was too stubborn to die. I remember lying in my cell and hearing bells. I thought angels had come for me. I opened my eyes to see her outside the bars. Her costume glittered like stars on a clear winter night." He rubbed his lips together. "Soon, she visited every day. She brought ointments and oils and tended my wounds."

"General Gazir let her?"

Brutal shivers raked down Fane's spine. "As the months passed, I grew in value to him. In his own twisted way, I vow he admired my struggle. He ordered Leila to treat me so I would survive." He fought the memory of Gazir's mocking laughter. "On the days he met with visiting dignitaries, he ordered me brought to his chambers, chained like an animal. He gloated. Called me the pale skinned English beast. Hauled me around by my chains and showed me off like a prized trophy."

"How cruel!"

Fane struggled to shut out Rexana' pity, and his own suppressed rage. "Gazir did not realize Leila and I had learned to communicate. One day, when I was strong enough, she would help me escape. I would take her with me, so she would be free from Gazir."

"Word by word, she taught me Arabic. While she treated my scarred body, she kept my mind focused on survival. Soon, I understood what my prison guards

were saying. And, I understood the conversations between Gazir and his peers."

Rexana smiled. "An advantage, for a spy."

He nodded. "One day, I heard my guards talking
about a Christian king's boats being sighted near Acre.
I wept with relief. Yet, I also realized I could best serve
my king from within the dungeon. I wrote down what
I heard on scraps of parchment Leila smuggled beneath
her veil. She delivered these to secret messengers who
in turn took the information to the crusaders. Many
of Gazir's subjects, I learned, despised him." Fane
pointed to Rexana's hand. "The sapphire ring you
wear was Leila's. She used it to identify herself to her
messengers."

Rexana turned the gleaming ring on her finger. "I
see."

"When King Richard's forces advanced on Acre,"
he continued, "my position became very dangerous.
Gazir threatened to cut off my head and deliver it to
the king as proof the crusaders would never win. Gazir
summoned his armies to support Saladin, and plotted
an attack. Each time Leila left to deliver a message,
I feared for her life. I knew if she were caught, she
would die a horrible death. We agreed I must escape.

"One night, she drugged the guards and unlocked
my cell. She helped me don eastern robes, then led me
through the servants' passages. I could hardly walk,
but she urged me on. We hurried into the city. There,

we heard the shouts of alarm."

He swallowed, the desperation of that night pulsing afresh inside him. "We ran through the market into the streets. We could not stop or we would die. Leila took me to the house of one of her contacts. We hid in a tiny, secret room under the floor for two days, until Gazir recalled his guards from the city." He exhaled. "Escaping the dungeon was a tremendous moment in my life, yet I was also scared beyond reason. Gazir could still find us. He would not be merciful. Leila . . . understood."

Rexana's lashes flicked down. "You mean, you coupled."

Fane stared down at the rock. He had never told anyone what had happened between him and Leila. Yet Rexana, of all people, deserved to know. He prayed she would not loathe him.

"She begged me to lie with her. I will not speak false, Rexana. I desired her. I had not been with a woman in months, and I owed her my life. Would you not have done the same, if you thought you might not live one more day?"

To his relief, Rexana's gaze did not harden with disgust. She swallowed and looked out across the water, as though deciding what to make of his words.

"We coupled only once. 'Twas not love." He caught her fingers, picking at a ridge of stone. " 'Twas not at all what I shared with you."

A breath shivered from her. "I will try to believe you."

" 'Tis the truth."

"Please, tell me the rest."

He squeezed her hand, forced himself to tell the story to its wretched end. "At dark, Leila and I left for the city gates. Half way there, she handed me her ring and a dagger she had stolen

— the jeweled one I still use — and told me where to find a horse. She told me to ride to my king, for she would come at dawn. I tried to stop her from returning to Gazir's castle, but she refused to listen." He paused, his throat raw. "She kissed me, then ran into the darkness. That was the last time I saw her alive."

"Gazir found her," Rexana said, her words hushed.

Fane nodded. "When she did not appear the next day, I asked to speak with the king. He had received my missives and knew of the threat Gazir posed. He assigned me an army of knights and we thundered into the city. We besieged the fortress. In the main hall, I found Gazir holding a knife to Leila's neck. She had freed the other courtesans and poisoned his wine before trying to flee, but he had caught her. He knew that she had freed me."

A violent tremor tore through Fane's body. "I tried to save her. I could not stop him. He slit her throat." His voice shook. "I cut his head from his shoulders."

Rexana touched his arm. "Fane."

Bitterness tore through him. "I held her as she died. She made not a sound. She smiled up at me as her life's blood ran onto the tiled floor, and the light left her eyes."

He did not realize Rexana had snuggled herself against him until he felt her hand curling around his neck. "I am sorry," she whispered.

Drawing her close, he said, "As am I."

"You must not blame yourself for her death. Leila made the choice to return to Gazir's castle."

He blinked wetness from his eyes and kissed her hair.

"She acted of her own will."

"True." Fane breathed in Rexana's scent, the essence of his life now. Locking his heart against the past's pain, he caressed her satiny arm. "In the same way, love, you cannot be responsible for your brother's deeds."

Rexana stared at him, then pulled out of his embrace. Before Fane could tug her back, she dove into the water with the barest splash.

She drifted to the surface, and he scowled down at her. "Why did you run away?"

She blew a stream of bubbles. "I wished for another swim, 'tis all. I know we will begin the journey back to Tangston soon." Crooking a finger, she murmured, "Will you join me?"

Fane sighed. She avoided giving him an honest answer. Yet, no matter how she felt about her brother, she could not escape the truth. Her destiny, and Rudd's, forged separate paths.

Fane jumped into the water. The murky depths co-cooned him before he rose at her side. He kissed the tip of her nose, and she giggled.

The musical sound touched deep in his soul, rousing the joy, desire and love buried there. Rexana belonged to no man but him. He would die before he let her suffer for her brother's treachery.

He would die before he ever let her go.

# Chapter Eighteen

BLINKING AWAY TEARS, Rexana tossed the wax tablet down on the bed. Yesterday, on the ride back to Tangston, Fane had promised to show her the evidence against Rudd. True to his word, Fane had brought the accounts and documents to the solar the next morn.

She stared at the tablets, laid out upon the coverlet and lit by the sunlight streaming in through the open shutters. The words taunted her. The accounts Kester had carefully documented reinforced what Fane had told her — that Rudd met in local taverns with known conspirators to plot treachery.

Equally damning was the missive Fane had shown her. He had not let her touch it, but had held it out to her. Once she had seen Rudd's unmistakable, scrawled signature, Fane had tucked it into his belt. She shivered, remembering his shuttered expression. Despite his feelings for her, he took no chances she might snatch the parchment and toss it into the fire.

She rubbed her lips together, silently praying for strength.

Dragging her gaze from the tablets, she said, "I cannot believe it."

"Why not?" Fane lounged with one hip against the trestle table, holding a half eaten block of cheese. He wore black hose and a russet tunic, the shoulders still damp from his hair. They had bathed together earlier, but the wash had quickly progressed to lovemaking in the tub.

His eyebrow arched. Wanton sparks shot through her. He had quirked his brow before he cupped her wet breasts in his hands and seduced her. He had been very attentive since telling her of his past, as though he feared she now despised him. Yet, how could she, when she had no doubt he cared for her and Leila was long dead?

By the saints, how could she, when he knew how to spin her body into a wondrous sensual whirl?

"Well, love?" With an eating dagger, Fane sliced some cheese and slid it between his teeth. "What more proof do you need? 'Tis more than sufficient to convince the King's Courts of your brother's guilt."

She drew her legs up under her chin, adjusted her

gown, and dropped her forehead to her knees. "I know what the accounts and his signature imply. Yet, I know my brother. He would not betray the king."

Fane sighed. The eating dagger clicked on the table before he strode to the bed. He rubbed his hand over her shoulder, a skilled touch that fired her every tingling nerve and made her burn for him. "Come. Break your fast. You will feel better, and your thoughts will be clearer."

A bit of bread, cheese, and fruit would not change her mind about Rudd. Yet, Rexana slid off the bed and walked to the table. Grabbing the dagger, she cut into the peel of an orange. The zesty scent burst into the air.

Fane retrieved the tablets and stuffed them into a leather bag. "I have matters of estate to attend this morn. Duties I should have addressed yesterday, except I was delightfully occupied." His mouth curved in a roguish grin. "If only I could set my High Sheriff duties aside yet another day."

His smile flooded her with sensual anticipation. She swayed her body in brazen invitation. "I shall await your return."

"I am counting on it." He crossed to her. His mouth danced over hers in an arousing rhythm. As his scent mingled with the orange's, loyalties warred within her. Her fingers itched to drop the fruit and grab the missive, while her mind scorned the hope that she would reach the hearth in time to toss the parchment into the flames. Her heart screamed that Fane would consider such actions the worst betrayal. He would never, ever forgive her.

Why did the thought of betraying him hurt so much? He had come to mean as much to her as her own brother.

Before she had a chance to resolve her dilemma, he groaned, then pulled away. "Think of me, as I will think of you. I will see you anon."

He slung the bag over his shoulder and strode toward the door.

"Wait." She hardly dared ask, yet she must. "May I visit Rudd?"

Fane looked at her. "Why?"

"I must speak to him about this evidence you have collected. Please."

His gaze sharpened, as though he considered the wisdom of her visit. Then, he nodded. "When I return, I will go with you."

Relief filtered through her. "Until then, may I send him clean garments? Surely that is not too much to ask."

"I had thought to see it done myself. Speak with Tansy. She will help you find clothes to fit him, and will see them delivered."

Rexana smiled. "Thank you."

He smiled back. "Thank you, love, for the pleasure you have given me. Our marriage will only get better."

He winked and opened the door.

Dropping the orange and knife onto the table, she hurried to the doorway, her silk gown brushing at her ankles. As Fane turned onto the landing that led down to the hall, she waved. He disappeared from view, and she ordered one of the guards to send for Tansy.

Rexana closed the solar doors and leaned back against them. Her gaze fell to the half eaten food. Anticipation drummed to life in her blood. A plan, hovering at the edge of her consciousness, coalesced in her mind.

Could it succeed?

With slow strides, she crossed to the table. The eating dagger glinted in the sunlight. 'Twas a common knife, devoid of fancy patterning like Fane's. The dagger was one of several brought up by the kitchen staff, used by the chaplain and steward, and made available to visiting dignitaries who had forgotten their own.

She fingered the small knife. Nausea churned inside her. She had no choice. If she did not seize this opportunity, her brother might end up beheaded. She knew him to be innocent, but the evidence she had seen against him was overwhelming.

Oh, God. Could she conceal the dagger in the clothing she sent to Rudd? Could she betray Fane's trust?

Her stomach clenched. She could. She must.

A knock sounded on the door. Tansy.

"One moment." Rexana grabbed the knife, slashed

an opening in her sleeve's cuff, then pushed the dagger inside. She forced herself to ignore her conscience's warning cry and the ache consuming her heart.

She could. She must.

As Fane climbed the forebuilding's steps to the hall for the midday meal, his strides lightened. He had investigated a dispute between neighboring cotters, collected overdue tithes from a nobleman, and dismissed baseless accusations of stealing brought against a peasant girl. Fane smiled. That afternoon, he would have time to spare, and would spend it with Rexana.

Their coupling in the bathtub had been extraordinary. What would it be like to make love on the garden bench?

He imagined Rexana's bared breasts, shimmering in the sunlight like pearls. Her pale skin flushed and damp. Her nude body, stretched out on the stone, writhing against him. He could not remember desiring a woman with such hunger.

As he took the last step, he forced his mind to neutral territory. He smiled at the matrons and young children waiting patiently beside their tables, nodded to the men-at-arms, and crossed to the dais.

Rexana sat in her usual place, beside his.

She looked up, smiling as he approached, yet the warmth did not completely reach her eyes. She looked a little pale.

A pang of disquiet jarred through him, but he

shrugged it aside. After the evidence he had shown her that morn, she had every reason to be unsettled. No doubt she had thought about Rudd's fate all morn. No doubt she was realizing she had misjudged her brother.

Fane dropped down into his chair and kissed her cheek. "Love."

"Milord."

He poured wine into the silver goblet set before her. "You had a good morn? You found plenty to amuse you, and did not get into mischief?"

He spoke in jest, yet she visibly tensed. Her expression softened, and she laughed. "Milord, the only mischief I entertain is with you."

He chuckled. Leaning close, he began to whisper a naughty secret in her ear.

Footfalls rose above the hall's chatter. "Milord!"

Fane halted mid sentence to glance toward the commotion. Armed guards hurried toward him, their weapons drawn.

Silence fell in the hall.

"What has happened?" Fane snapped.

"Villeaux," a guard said. "He and the prisoners escaped the dungeon."

"*What*?" Fane slammed down the jug. Wine sloshed over the rim to stain the tablecloth.

"They are in the bailey. Villeaux has a knife. They have hostages."

Rexana gasped. "Nay!"

Barely holding back the fury scalding his lungs, Fane rose to his feet. "How did this happen? I gave orders —"

"I do not know, milord."

He exhaled on a growl. He looked down at Rexana, her face ashen. Anger and dismay roiled in his gut. Curse Villeaux for provoking a confrontation. Curse Villeaux for choosing to take hostages. The situation did not bode well for a quick recapture, for it could only lead to bloodshed.

How in hellfire had the traitors escaped their cells?

He yanked his jeweled dagger from its sheath.

Rexana's hand flew to her mouth. "What will you do?"

"Whatever I must."

Her chair squealed back. "I am coming with you."

"You will stay here."

Fane skirted the table, stepped down from the dais, and marched across the hall. The armed guards fell in behind him. He took the forebuilding's stairs two at a time, and threw open the door to the bailey.

Clad in a loose-fitting brown tunic and hose, Villeaux stood near the stables. His right arm was wrapped around a young boy's neck. Fane recognized the lad as one of the stable hands. A knife glinted at the boy's throat.

An eating dagger.

Fane scowled. He had forbidden implements of any kind to the prisoners. Who had dared to defy his orders? Rage blazed through him. He would find out, and they would pay dearly.

A pained grunt drew his gaze to the other three traitors who stood near Villeaux. They wielded swords, stolen from the dungeon guards. They stood over one of the guards, whom they had forced to kneel in the dirt. Blood ran down his face. He swayed from side to side, as though on the verge of fainting.

With measured strides, Fane crossed to Rudd. "Let the boy go."

Rudd smiled. The knife edged higher. The lad's eyes flared with fear. "He comes with me. I will not release him and let you kill me."

In the near distance, Fane heard a woman's scream. The boy's mother. Her cry became hysterical sobs.

"Mama." The lad's face crumpled. Tears welled in his eyes.

Fane sensed Rexana step into the bailey. For an instant, no more than the space of a blink, Rudd looked at her. Then, his gaze shot back to Fane.

Awareness of Rexana whooshed through Fane, even as his anger surged. He had told her to stay in the hall. He had tried to shield her from the inevitable fight. Did she really want to watch him subdue her brother with brute force?

Frustration pressed like an iron fist against Fane's

ribs. Forcing his emotions aside, he weighed his options. The archers on the battlements could shoot the three men, but could not wound Villeaux without harming the boy. Tangston's men-at-arms could overpower the escapees, but again, the child could be injured or killed. So could the guard.

The knot in Fane's belly tightened. Did he risk harming a defenseless child to recapture Villeaux? Did he risk the guard's life, when the man was newly wed and his wife expected a babe? Did he risk killing Villeaux, likely one of the rebel leaders and thus a key prisoner Fane wanted alive?

Were such choices not barbaric?

A grim smile hardened Fane's mouth. Villeaux might not have the stomach to murder a child before a score of witnesses. Villeaux might be bluffing.

Yet, he did not know Villeaux well enough to know for certain.

As though sensing his dilemma, Rudd tipped his head to the stable. "I want four horses. You will clear the guards from the gatehouse and let us pass."

"If I refuse?"

Rudd's expression darkened. He no longer looked like a misguided youth, but a determined man. "I will slit the boy's throat. My friends will kill your guard. Their deaths will be on your conscience."

"You would kill a child?"

For the briefest moment, hesitation flashed in

Rudd's green eyes. His fingers curled tighter around the knife's hilt. "Do not force me, Linford."

"Rudd," Rexana cried. "Nay!"

Fane heard her skidded footsteps a moment before she reached his side. She looked at him, her gaze frantic. "Let me go to him. I can reason with him."

"You will go no closer." Fane looked back at Rudd. "He is armed and trapped."

"He will not harm me."

Fane's jaw tightened until it hurt. His stomach twisted, as though a knife had plunged into his flesh. It was not mere coincidence that the day she delivered Rudd clean garments he escaped the dungeon. Had she slipped him the dagger? Had she brought about this wretched dilemma? He would ask her, as soon as he resolved the imminent danger.

Fane signaled to the men-at-arms who had moved into the bailey. Two approached. "Escort Lady Linford to safety," Fane muttered. "Keep her well away from these ruffians."

The men guided Rexana back toward the forebuilding.

"Fane!"

He shut out her indignant shrieks. Strode closer to the rebels. A decision consolidated in his mind. One he despised, but the only choice to avoid bloodshed.

Yet, his decision might lead him to the rat's nest of traitors.

"You will have your horses." He ignored the shocked gasps that rippled through the onlookers. "Let me send stable hands to ready them."

The tension in Villeaux's face eased. "A wise decision."

Murmurs rose behind Fane. Biting back his fury, he ordered four horses saddled and readied. He sent a man-at-arms to the gatehouse, with orders for the armed guards to leave.

The rebels abandoned the wounded guard to mount their horses. They grinned in triumph.

Rage boiled inside Fane and threatened to explode.

Yet, if his plan developed as he hoped, he would be the victor.

As Villeaux forced the terrified boy onto the horse, determination burned in Fane's blood. Villeaux might think he had won, but this battle was far from over.

With an insolent whoop, Rudd urged his horse toward the gatehouse. The other traitors followed. Hoofbeats thundered on the drawbridge.

Fane turned to the servants nearby. He pointed to the injured guard. "Get him to the healer. See that his wounds are tended, and find his wife." He looked at his soldiers. "To your mounts. Now."

"You let them escape," the mother wailed. She swooned into the arms of two young girls, a hand clutched to her breast. "My son."

"We will bring him home safely," Fane said. "This

I promise."

Shouting to their squires, knights hurried to the stables. Bridles jangled. Men-at-arms and stable hands led out horses, including Fane's destrier, which snorted and flicked its tail. The air hummed with anticipation of battle.

Fane set his hands on his hips. He glanced at the dust rising on the road beyond the drawbridge, then looked to where the guards had taken Rexana. She would answer to him now.

She was no longer in the guards' care. She stood a hand's span away, her hair mussed. How hauntingly lovely she looked. He cursed the appreciative groan that even now rumbled inside him.

Her guards hovered at a discreet distance. With a nod, Fane dismissed them.

He stared at her. Hard.

"Rudd would not have harmed that child," she said with quiet conviction.

"You do not know that for certain."

"I do."

Fane snorted. "I vow the brother you once knew no longer exists."

Anguish shivered across her face. She glanced away, as though fascinated by the noise and activity at the stables. His mouth tightened. She would not escape so easily.

"You gave Rudd that eating dagger. Aye?"

Her chin nudged up, even as she sucked her bottom lip between her teeth. She had done that the last time they coupled, just before she climaxed around him and sent his pleasure soaring.

Emotions warred within him, the desire to yank her close and kiss her, as well as the urge to shake her. Instead, he cupped her chin, forcing her gaze back to him. "I want an answer."

She swallowed against his fingers. "Why ask me? A servant may have delivered the knife to him along with his food."

"They were warned against such folly. None of them would dare to disobey me." His thumb brushed her petal soft jaw. "The only one who might defy me is you."

After a silence, she said quietly, "I gave him the knife."

"You concealed it inside the clothes?"

Her head jerked in a nod.

Fane swore. His hand fell to his side. "Foolish, wife."

"I know what you believe. I know what your evidence implies." She trembled. "I tell you, Rudd is not a traitor. He cannot confess his crimes because he has done naught wrong."

A sigh hissed between Fane's teeth. "He is a criminal. If you will not accept the evidence I showed you, his actions today prove it." His voice thinned to a dangerous growl. "Your actions also make you suspect, love. I trusted you. I granted you a kindness, by sending your brother clean clothes, and you betrayed me."

She shook her head. Tears misted her eyes. They turned as green as the glade's lush grass. Despite his fury, despite what she had done, he hated to see her cry.

His voice shook. "We enjoyed such passion, Rexana. We began to trust. Why did you betray me in this way? *Why?*"

She did not speak, yet he glimpsed an answer in her watery gaze. She had deceived him to save her brother, yet she had also acted out of self-interest. His soul screamed, as though she had ripped it from his chest. In her heart, she did not really trust him. Like so many others, she saw him as the misfit barbarian who had bedded a Saracen courtesan.

No matter how he tried, he could never completely win her.

*I do not love you. I never will*, she had said the day he had proposed marriage.

She had spoken true.

Painful words ground between his teeth. "After what you have done, I should imprison you."

She wiped tears from her face. "I am no traitor. Yet, if I must be imprisoned for my actions, so be it."

Fane glanced over his shoulder. "Guards."

As the men-at-arms approached, she tensed. Yet, her head remained at a proud tilt.

"Escort Lady Linford to the solar. She is not to leave it. I also want guards posted under the window. From this moment on, no one enters or leaves the solar without my permission."

Her gaze turned as cold as sleet. "Why not throw me in the dungeon and chain me to the wall, as you did to my brother?"

He looked at her, a deliberate stare that began at her mouth and traveled down the slender length of her body, then back up to her pursed lips. Ah, God. Even now, he wanted her. Even now, she stubbornly held his gaze, taunting his mangled patience. Even now, she radiated insolence and utter conviction in her wretched brother.

With cool purpose, Fane arched an eyebrow. "You are still my wife, Rexana. Have you forgotten that I may do with you as I please?"

Fighting a hurt she had never before known, Rexana walked with the guards to the solar. She stood in the silent chamber, her hands fisted by her sides, as the men pulled the door closed behind them.

She was alone. Her husband's prisoner.

Fane's words taunted her. *Have you forgotten that I may do with you as I please?*

A sob caught in her throat. She tried to swallow,

but her throat refused. Her breath gasped between her lips and, clasping her hands, she pressed them over her heart. It hurt as though tearing in two. One half loyal to Rudd, the other to Fane.

Stumbling past the bed, she struggled to shut out memories of her and Fane together, naked, rolling, and kissing in their lovemaking. Despite his lust, he had always been gentle. She knew without a shred of doubt that he would never do her physical harm. Yet, his words stung.

Rage had roughened his voice, yet also anguish. He had taken her actions as a personal rejection. Like a trapped animal, he had lashed out. She had wounded him in a way no swords or arrows or physical scars could, though she had never meant to.

"Oh, Fane," she half sobbed, half whispered.

A cold shiver snaked through her. She approached the fire, hugging her arms to her chest. How could she have avoided hurting him? She had been right to free her brother. He did not deserve to languish in the dungeon and face punishment for treason he did not commit.

She hoped Rudd used his freedom wisely. She hoped he stayed hidden until he could prove beyond doubt he was not guilty. Under her breath, she prayed for his safety and that of the hostage child. As soon as he reached a safe haven, Rudd would let the boy go. The child would not be parted from his mother for long.

Of course he would not.

On the heels of that thought, Fane's furious expression blazed into her thoughts. He had worried for the boy. He had feared for the child's life, as well as that of the other wounded hostage. For those who still believed him a heartless barbarian, his honor and integrity was laid bare for all to see.

How proud he had made her in that moment.

Exhaling a tortured breath, she knelt by the fire. How could she choose between Rudd and Fane? Would she forever be torn by her loyalties? Chills ripped through her, colder and deeper than before. Sobs burned her throat. Tore from her. She clutched her belly and let the anguish weep from her soul.

The fire's heat wrapped around her like an embrace. Her body ached for Fane's touch. For his whispered words. For his kisses filled with love, that lightened her spirit and whisked her to a realm of wonder, joy, and pleasure.

Did he still want her? Would he ever make love to her again with the passion that touched her soul, or had she destroyed all chance of happiness? Would theirs become a marriage in name only, a legally binding union that became an invisible, loveless trap?

She squeezed her eyes shut. She loved her brother, but she could not bear to live without Fane's love. She would not be wed to him, while he took a mistress to his bed. With a low moan, she sat on the warm hearth tiles and drew her knees up to her chin. She must find a way to resolve this dilemma. Oh, God, she must.

Or she might lose Fane forever.

The twilight breeze stirred the destrier's mane as Fane rode into the bailey. His men-at-arms followed several yards behind, and the clatter of armor and horses' hooves rang in the open courtyard. His gaze shot to the guards standing by the keep's wall, as he had ordered earlier, then up to the shuttered solar window. What new betrayal had Rexana plotted in his absence?

Hurt welled up inside Fane in a violent storm. He still could not believe what she had done—and that he had been fool enough to trust her so completely.

All afternoon, his heart had throbbed with a terrible pain. It had devoured him. Robbed him of concentration. Corrupted his logic.

Was that why he had failed to find Villeaux and his cohorts?

Fane swore into the breeze and stared at the solar window. He would not allow distractions to undermine his responsibilities. Somehow, he would smother the inconvenient angst. He had survived worse torment in Gazir's dungeon. As he had vowed then, his crown duty took priority.

It still did.

He would recapture the traitors.

He would not fail his king.

Fane guided his horse to the stable, and, without waiting for a mounting block, slid from its back. He tossed the reins to a waiting stable hand.

"You caught the traitors, milord?" The lad's question seemed to be what all the folk lingering around the shadowed stables wanted to hear.

Fane shook his head. "Not this day. We will search again on the morrow." Managing a smile, he added, "We did find the boy. The traitors let him go."

A woman moved out of the throng. The hostage boy's mother. She gasped and, with a curtsey, bolted past. She hurried to Kester who was assisting the boy down from his horse.

"Mama!" The child ran forward and threw his arms around his mother's waist. She hugged him.

Fane tore his gaze from the joyous scene. He shut out the mother's laughter, the celebratory cheers, as well as his own sense of relief. Too many questions remained unanswered. Why had Villeaux released his hostage? Did Villeaux fear being held responsible for the boy's death? Or, now Villeaux was free, had he set into motion a treacherous plan for which he did not need a hostage?

Mayhap he aimed to plunge Warringham into rebellion.

Fane groaned, brushed through the crowd, and

headed for the keep. His head pounded, the discomfort as intense as the torment eating at his soul. He struggled to maintain focus.

Duty was more important than his happiness.

Duty would sustain him when his heart shriveled to dust.

He strode through the great hall, growled a greeting to Winton, then loped up the stairs to the solar. His hand hovered over the doors' handles. Bracing himself to face Rexana's anger along with demands for word on her brother, he depressed the handles and strode in.

She lay with her back to him, stretched out on the hearth tiles. Her head rested on her bent arm. Her hair spilled over her shoulder in a tangled swath. Firelight danced over her slender figure, gilding her silk gown in light and shadow. Her rib cage rose and fell on the gentle rhythm of sleep.

She looked incredibly lovely.

He paused, yet his jaw hardened with resolve. He quieted his boots' tread, crossed the chamber, and knelt beside his wooden chest. Opening it, he withdrew parchment, ink, and a quill, then lowered the lid, being careful not to make a sound.

Fane returned to the solar doors and glanced back at Rexana. She slept on, oblivious to his deeds. His fingers curled tighter around the blank parchment. At dawn's first light, the missive she had danced so bravely to get would be on its way to the king's ministers, along with an official report. In wretched detail, her brother's treachery would be revealed to the crown.

Rudd Villeaux's fate was sealed.

Through the muzzy haze of slumber, Rexana heard the solar doors open and close. Footfalls approached.

"Rexana."

*Fane.* Her mind shot instantly alert. Her pulse quickened with a rush of joy, anticipation, and dread. She raised her head from her numbed, bent arm. Through a snarl of hair, she blinked up at him.

Firelight limned his scuffed boots, muscled legs encased in snug hose, and tunic hazed with dust. He looked tousled. Tired. Desirable.

His gaze sparked with irritation. "Why do you lie on the floor? I have not banished you from our bed."

Concern rang in his voice. Pressing her palms to the floorboards, she pushed to sitting, then pulled her hair from her face. "I do not remember falling asleep."

He carried a small pot, a quill, and rolled parchment. Black ink stained his fingers. When her gaze fell to his hands, he crossed to his linen chest, tossed the items inside, and slammed the lid.

Confusion swirled inside her. Had he fetched the quill and parchment from the solar? When? She drew a breath, yet before she could ask, he spoke.

"I expected the wooden stool against the door this eve. Mayhap even the trestle table."

"I am sorry I disappointed you." As soon as she

spoke, she realized her words' double meaning.

His hands, plowing through his hair, stilled. "As am I."

Anguish stabbed through her again. Rebellion surged inside her in a boiling wave. She may have disappointed him by helping Rudd escape, but she had just cause for her actions. When Rudd proved himself guiltless, would Fane at last accept what she did was right? Mayhap not. Fane's disdain for Rudd seemed complete.

Defiant words filled her mouth, yet she could not voice them. The bond between her and Fane seemed so fragile. Rising to her feet, she smoothed her wrinkled gown and fought to hold together her shattering heart.

He, too, seemed eager to avoid an argument. Looking away, he unbuckled his sword belt. "Have you eaten?"

She shook her head.

He frowned, tossed the weapon onto the bed and crossed to the table. He looked at the untouched plate of bread and cheese. "You did not drink the wine either. Why?"

"I was not thirsty."

Wine pattered into two silver goblets. "You will achieve naught by denying yourself sustenance." He strode back to her and pressed a goblet into her hands. "Drink. You look terrible." When she frowned, the faintest grin touched his lips. "Ah. I see your spirit is unharmed."

"You are unwise to insult me, milord," she said with biting heat. "You look wretched yourself."

"I pursued your brother for many miles."

Half way down, the wine lodged in her throat. She forced herself to swallow. "Did you capture him?"

"I regret we did not. We found the boy, though, huddled under an oak on the outskirts of Tangston village."

"Unharmed?"

Fane nodded. "He wore your brother's tunic. It seems he was given it to stay warm."

She cheered. "I told you! Rudd —"

"The boy likely became a burden. Your brother did not want the extra weight on his horse to hinder his escape."

Scowling, she said, "I vow he intended to let the boy go."

"Think what you will. The truth remains. With your help, your brother broke out of my dungeon, took hostages, and escaped. For those crimes and all his others, he will be captured, tried, and punished."

Fane's steely voice grated on her nerves like rough stone. He spoke as though Rudd's fate was predetermined. Arching an eyebrow, she said, "What if he is innocent of treason?"

Fane turned his back to her and pulled off his tunic.

He tossed it onto the floor by his side of the bed. She watched, unable to look away, as he yanked off his ivory lawn shirt. The muscles across his back flexed, rippled. With her fingers, lips and tongue, she had memorized every one of his scars. She had come to love his unique physical beauty.

Yet, their intimacy seemed years ago.

When he did not answer her, she said in a tight voice, "Well? Will you answer my question?"

"He is guilty, therefore you know my answer." When she shook her head, Fane sighed, a sound of torment, and swept his sword off the bed. It thumped onto the carpet. " 'Tis a senseless debate, and I am weary. Go to bed, Rexana."

"Fane —"

A groan tore from him. "God help me, I cannot stop loving you. But I am angry."

Her belly did a painful somersault. She stared at his rigid back, her eyes dampening with tears. "I had no choice."

His hands stilled on the belt of his hose. He looked at her, before his rough laughter raked over her like an icy draft. "You had every choice. You made the wrong one."

"We shall see."

Muttering a curse, he yanked off his hose. Naked, beautiful, he climbed into bed and pulled the sheets up to his chest. He lay on his back and closed his eyes, one tanned arm draped over his brow.

She moved to the bedside. Silence stretched taut as a length of silk cord. She sensed his gaze upon her, studying her, as she untied and removed her bliaut.

Desperate hope sparked within her.

Despite his fury, he still wanted her.

Her need flared, along with a desire to make him yearn as intensely as she. To seduce him beyond anger to raw, undeniable lust. To bridge the vast chasm between them with sensual pleasure.

She removed her shift and let it slide with a whisper to the floor. Her skin cooled. Tingled. Raising her arms over her head, she stretched her nude body in slow, sinewy movements that echoed her brazen dance. She coaxed him to touch her, kiss her, and love her as he craved.

He drew a breath. Then, as though battling his self-control, he rolled onto his side to face the fire.

Her body trembled with unfulfilled desire. Fresh tears stung her eyes, yet with a calm she did not fully understand, Rexana drew back the sheets and lay down. As the darkness soothed her burning eyes, she understood.

It was not calm inside her, after all, but emptiness.

# Chapter Nineteen

THREE DAYS LATER, Fane sat at the lord's table in the great hall, swirling the dregs of his ale. He pushed aside the pile of parchments he had been reviewing — complaints of thefts in the market, disputes between villagers over livestock and crops, and other matters of law that required his scrutiny — and stared at the wax tablets Kester had set out before him, fresh reports from the men-at-arms who continued to search roads, towns, and taverns for Villeaux.

"Well?" Fane muttered.

Dropping into the chair beside him, Kester shook his head. "Villeaux has disappeared."

"A man cannot simply vanish."

"Agreed." Kester's mouth pursed in thought.

"Mayhap we should extend the search beyond Warringham county."

Fane's fingers tightened around the earthenware mug trapped between his palms. Lord Darwell's lands were the closest to border his own. Fane smothered a groan. If he contacted Darwell and asked permission to send men onto his estates, Darwell would want to know why. Despite past loyalty to the Villeaux family, Darwell might offer his own forces to assist in the hunt, and would want to be involved in all the decisions.

Yet, involving him was a risk. Word of the traitors' escape was not yet common knowledge, and Darwell's loose tongue could not be trusted. In no time, half of England would know that High Sheriff Linford, crusading spy hero, had failed to capture escaped prisoners on his own lands. That did not speak well of his abilities as sheriff. It bode far worse for his efforts to win his noble peers' respect.

Most galling of all, Garmonn would know. He would no doubt use the opportunity to his advantage. If he had ties to the traitors, as Fane strongly suspected, this could prove disastrous. Fane did not fear for his own life, but if the traitorous bastards got to Rexana —

Kester shifted in his chair. "Milord?"

Fane snapped his attention back to the tablets. A ruthless pain pounded at his brow. "Villeaux may be well hidden, but he cannot remain so for long. If he is not sighted in two days, I will order the search extended."

"Very well, milord." Kester rose. Then, as though reconsidering, he sat again. He cleared his throat. "I mean no disrespect, milord, but I must ask. Might Lady Linford know of her brother's whereabouts?"

With effort, Fane eased his crushing grip on the mug. "I have asked her. She refuses to cooperate."

"Still?" Kester said.

"Aye, still."

Fane rubbed the heel of his hand against his forehead. He remembered her frosty gaze as he quit the solar that morn. Her defiance gleamed as bright as the sunlight flashing off her brooch, which she had pinned to her fitted gown of blue wool. She looked ravishingly beautiful standing at the window, her hands clasped on the stone ledge.

Three days of confinement had not softened her resolve. Yet, after long, lonely nights of watching her sleep, burning for her body's sweetness, he had barely leashed his desire to cross to her, sink his hands into her hair, and seduce her. Despite the ache in his loins, he had resisted. Just as she, with infuriating stubbornness, resisted giving him any useful insights into her brother's character or favorite haunts.

He drained his mug and banged it down on the table. Why did the crux of his thoughts always return to her?

He froze. Why, indeed?

Kester stood, his chair scraping on the floorboards. "Have you finished with the tablets, milord?"

Fane nodded and waved a dismissive hand. The idea drifting through his thoughts gathered momentum like a spinning whirlwind. Why had he not realized such an option before now?

The answer to his dilemma was within his grasp.

Specifically, she was confined to the solar.

Rexana, of all people, could lure Villeaux out of hiding. She, of all people, could lead her brother into a well-laid trap, or lead Fane to him.

Yet, she would not do so of her own will. If she learned of the plot, she would fight it with every ounce of her willpower.

For that reason, she must not know. She must believe she acted of her own initiative.

Regret tempered Fane's excitement. He would have to deceive her. Betray her trust.

Bitter frustration cut through him. Had she not betrayed his trust by freeing her brother? Had she not chosen loyalty to her brother over loyalty to her faithful, wedded husband?

His anguish sharpened with an edge of fear, for his plan entailed danger, most of all for her. Yet, despite the rift between them, he would never let her come to harm. He would plan well, protect her life from a distance, and with his own life, if need be.

A hard smile curled Fane's mouth. When she realized he had used her to bring about her brother's capture, she would hate him. Yet, he had no choice. He had few options left, and he would not fail his king.

Fane shoved to his feet. He looked at Kester. "How soon can you arrange a meeting of the men-at-arms?"

Kester's eyes widened. "Reasonably soon, milord."

"Do it. Now."

Rexana drew the wrinkled parchment from her sleeve and unrolled the tattered edges. As she reread the bold words, which she had long ago committed to memory, her vision blurred.

*I am the randy bee. I cannot wait to suck your nectar.*

She swiped at her damp lashes. How ridiculous to torment herself with Fane's poem. Yet, each day she found it harder to fight her misery. In her enforced solitude, longing taunted her. Yearning for what she and Fane had shared, his wondrous touch, and the pleasure he had shown her.

Irritation rubbed her raw nerves. She would accomplish naught by yielding to tears.

Footfalls and voices sounded beyond the solar door. If Fane found her weepy eyed over his poem . . .

Her face burned. Rising from the stool set near the window to catch the afternoon sunlight, she hurried to the bed and shoved the parchment under her pillow.

As she smoothed her sleeve, the door opened. Fane strode in, his face a mask of cool politeness. She saw no trace of the heat that had smoldered in his eyes before he left that morn.

The door slammed. "You are hale, wife?" His tone held an odd hint of foreboding and resolve.

"I am, husband."

"You looked flushed." He scanned the room, as though searching for what had consumed her attention before he entered. "What were you up to?"

She would not tell him a moment ago she had sniffled over his words of love. Pointing to the wooden stool, drowned in a pool of light, she said, "I am warm from sitting in the sun."

His lips twisted into a smile. "You watched the bailey?"

"I have few ways to pass my day." Resentment tightened her voice, yet she held his gaze. "Do you bring word of Rudd?"

When Fane's eyes flashed, relief rushed through her. He had not captured her brother. There was still a chance for Rudd to prove his innocence.

Fane spun on his heel and strode to the wooden chest. He bent down, flipped the lid, then rummaged through the contents. A leather belt slapped against the side. Coins jangled.

The clatter of horses' hooves rose from the bailey. Many riders were leaving the keep. Before she could hurry to the window to look down, a rolled parchment flew out of the chest and rolled across the floor toward her.

The list of traitors?

Rexana lunged forward, snatched it up, and whisked off the strip of leather binding it. She glimpsed scrawled handwriting before Fane grabbed her wrist and yanked the parchment away.

Her skin burned beneath his fingers. She jerked back. With a mirthless grin, he released her.

"Sorry, love. 'Tis not the document you seek."

The bitter taste of disappointment flooded her tongue. "I know."

His gaze sharpened. "You do? How?"

Tremors shook her. Crossing her arms, she tried to warm the ice cold fist that had curled fingers around her ribs. She would not lie. "I saw it when I searched this chamber for the missive. 'Tis a letter from your mother."

His dark eyes flashed with fury and disapproval. "Another betrayal, Rexana. Did you mean to tell me you had read my private letter, or keep that trespass to yourself?"

Rage blazed in his eyes, yet she stood firm, refusing to avert her gaze. She had good reason for looking through his belongings, and would not apologize for trying to save Rudd.

Fane crumpled the parchment. He pivoted toward the fire, swung his arm back, and looked about to hurl the document into the leaping flames.

"Do not!" Rexana darted forward.

He turned part way to face her, his profile framed by tangled hair. His teeth gleamed in a warning snarl. "I should have burned it long ago."

His unsteady voice quelled her anger. She could not bear to hear his torment. "Your mother loved you. From her words, she regretted what happened. She cared enough to write to you, despite her failing health."

Spitting a foul curse, Fane faced her. He stared down at the crushed letter. "This reminds me that everyone I have ever loved shunned me. Except Leila."

His words stuck like a physical blow. Rexana pressed her hands to her stomach and stifled a moan. "I did not shun you."

"Nay, you betrayed me." Shaking his head, he tossed the wadded missive into the chest.

His anguish wounded her like an invisible battleaxe. How she yearned to cross to him and soothe his hurt, yet he seemed unapproachable. He had erected a high emotional wall, one she could not scramble over, no matter how hard she tried.

Desperation welled inside her, along with an awful fear they would never again enjoy the precious intimacy they had built together. She had to broach the awful barricade, to bond with him again in friendship and love. To show him that despite all, she still cared.

He knelt before the chest. As he searched the objects inside, she said, "Tell me about your parents. Tell me why your father banished you."

Fane's head jerked up. "Why?"

"I am your wife. I would like to know. Please."

"So you have another means to betray me? So you can feed the rumors with details of my wretched past?"

His callous words stung, but she held his gaze. "The gossips have already voiced their thoughts on what happened between you and your sire. If you do not wish me to reveal what you tell me, I will not."

He stared at her for a moment, then shrugged. "Most of the rumors are true. My father never liked me. He saw me as more of a nuisance than a son. When I played pranks on the servants or pointed out ways to improve running the keep, he beat me."

"Oh, Fane," Rexana whispered.

"He was always shouting and ordering me to be obedient. I tried, for a while, but I still made him furious. The day I killed his favorite destrier, he sent me away for good."

Rexana could not imagine Fane injuring an animal out of spite or carelessness. "What happened?"

He brushed aside a rumpled garment, and resentment tightened his features. "In front of a hall filled with important guests, my father insulted me. He said I would never be man enough to ride his new, high strung stallion."

"How could he?" Rexana choked out.

A terse chuckle broke from Fane. "I was angry. I stormed off to the stables, saddled and bridled the destrier, then climbed onto its back. It tried to throw me, but I hung on. It bolted out of the keep's gates and I rode it for leagues. When it began to tire, we started home. I was proud to have proven my sire wrong." Fane paused, as though he could not bear to remember. "The destrier jumped a broken wall. I did not know peasant children were playing behind it. As the stallion soared over, it sensed the children and startled. It landed at an awkward angle, and its right front leg snapped."

A sob burned Rexana's throat.

"My sire and a contingent of men-at-arms found us by the wall. The horse lay with its head in my lap, shivering. It could not walk, thus it had to be killed." He exhaled a shuddered sigh. "My father dragged me back to the keep, whipped me, then told me never to come back."

" 'Twas not your fault!"

"It does not matter." He snatched a bag of coins and a dagger out of the chest, slammed the lid, and stood.

Shaking her head, Rexana said, "It does matter. You did not deserve to be treated so." How she yearned to hug him and murmur comforting words for the injustice he had suffered.

Yet, Fane's flinty gaze warned he would not accept her succor.

The emotional wall between them remained intact. He seemed to believe she had rejected him just like his father. Oh, if Fane only knew how she truly felt.

His gaze slid down her bodice to her brooch, and the corner of his mouth turned up. "After the midday meal, I will come to fetch you. Be prepared to ride."

Astonishment jolted through her. "Ride?"

"We will journey to Tangston market."

Excitement sped her pulse. "Am I no longer a prisoner?"

His brittle laughter scratched down her spine. "I have not forgiven your misdeed, love. I wish to question the goldsmith about your brooch, and I want you with me. I do not trust you here alone while I am gone."

A disbelieving sigh burst from her. "You have ridden from Tangston several times in the past days. You left me alone then. Why, now, is the situation different?"

His gaze shadowed. "I hoped the journey might encourage you to reassess your loyalties. If you heard of your brother's treachery from someone other than me, you might reconsider your foolish faith in him." His shoulders rose in a stiff shrug. "I regret I was mistaken."

He turned and strode toward the door.

Oh, what she would give to be able to leave this chamber. She craved freedom. Sweet, fresh air. The cacophony and smells of market day.

And the chance, no matter how slim, to make contact with her brother.

Schooling all eagerness from her voice, she said, "I do need soap, milord. If I may, I would like to choose some of a pleasing fragrance. I have my own coin to pay for it."

His hand on the iron door handle, he glanced back at her. He seemed about to declare that since she was his wife, he would buy the soap for her, but then nodded. "You may."

As soon as the door closed behind Fane, she ran to her wooden chests of belongings. She tossed aside the folded gowns, shoes, and hose, until she found the small leather coin pouch. It held less silver than she had hoped, but 'twould be enough. Dropped into the right hands, she could easily persuade a vendor or street urchin to whisper what he had heard of her brother.

She could even pay for a message to be delivered to him.

Rexana fought a tremor of unease. How she hated to deceive Fane again.

Yet, she must. Oh, God, she must.

As Fane strode out into the sunlit bailey, Kester left the men-at-arms by the stable and crossed to him. " 'Tis set, milord?"

"Aye." Fane glanced up at the solar window. Rexana stood with her arms folded, staring down at him. Their gazes locked before she turned away and disappeared from view.

His voice lowered to a fierce murmur. "She must not come to any harm. No matter what she has done, she deserves —"

"The men know what to do, milord. They are already spreading the word that you and your lady will visit the market this afternoon. Your plan is sound."

A bitter smile touched Fane's mouth. " 'Tis not the least bit barbaric?"

Kester grinned. "Nay, milord. I vow 'tis very clever."

Her coin purse clutched in her hands, Rexana halted in the crowded market square.

Fane stopped beside her and tipped his head. "The soap maker is that way."

She strained to see past crates of hissing geese, a wagon filled with vegetables and flanked by shouting peasants, and the blacksmith forging a horseshoe near his blazing fire. As the smoke dissipated, she spied the table of small, wrapped parcels. Would the soap seller know of her brother's whereabouts?

She had not yet had the opportunity to ask questions, for Fane had escorted her from her horse into the market. He walked close at her side, followed by armed guards — though fewer guards, it seemed, than had ridden with them. The others must have dispersed through the market. Mayhap they ensured no unsavory villains tried to harm or rob them. Mayhap they kept an eye upon her from a distance.

Fane might have ensured she was closely watched, but she would find a way to get the answers she sought.

Tightening her hold on her purse, she nodded to him. "I will fetch the soap."

"When you are done, come back here. Then, we will see the goldsmith."

Surprise rippled through her. "You are not coming with me?"

His eyes clouded with a strange, almost bleak expression. "I must speak with the spice merchant about recent thefts from his stall. Do not worry. These guards" — he gestured to four men-at-arms — "will ensure your safety, and that of your coin purse. They will also make certain you do not escape." He strode away, stirring up dust beneath his boots.

Rexana drew in a nervous breath, sharpened with the smells of horse and wood smoke. She wove her way through the milling throng, aware of the guards' gaze upon her and their strides several paces behind. What luck, that Fane had decided not to escort her. She would not have been able to complete her deception with him nearby.

Ahead, two boys scampered through the crowd. One followed a puppy at the end of a rope. Young though they were, such urchins often knew as much gossip as the vendors. For a bit of coin, would one of them be willing to help her? With discreet glances, she tried to catch their attention, but they ran on.

She stopped at the soap maker's stall. The mingled scents of rose, lavender and almond oil rose from the variety of soaps arranged on an old cloth. She fingered a cake sprinkled with dried rose petals, hoping to attract the attention of the hunchbacked woman behind the table.

A solid weight barreled into her.

Rexana gasped and grabbed the table's edge.

"Sorry, milady."

She righted herself. The boy with the puppy stood in front of her, his dirty face red and his eyes round. His gaze darted behind her, as though he saw her guards storming toward him.

"Sorry," he blurted again, as though he expected a beating.

" 'Tis all right." She waved her guards away. They hesitated, obeyed, then spoke to one another in muttered tones.

As she looked back at the boy, her mind raced. She must ask him. Now.

Before she could speak, he brushed past her.

Something rough scratched against her fingers. A note. She curled her hand around the slip of parchment.

Her pulse thundered. Who knew she would be in

the market? Who tried to contact her? She quickly chose two rose-scented cakes, paid the merchant, and waited as the woman wrapped them in a swath of fabric.

As Rexana strolled to the end of the table, she pretended to examine vials of scented water. With careful fingers, she unrolled the tiny parchment.

*I know where your brother is.*

Shock tore through her like a sprinting hound. Who had penned the note? The scruffy peasant boy certainly had not. The lettering looked too precise to be a child's.

She glanced at the next stall, the first in a line of cloth merchants. She looked further down, and saw a familiar face.

Garmonn.

He met her gaze, then resumed speaking with a merchant.

A shiver raked through her, cold and then hot. Bile burned her throat. She would sooner trust a rat than Garmonn.

Yet, if he could take her to Rudd . . .

She mentally squashed her fears. Her fingers tightened around the message. Rudd's life was too important. She had risked much to get to market, and could not let this chance slip away.

Even if Fane found out. Even if Fane tried to stop her.

Ignoring the nagging ache inside her, she glanced

at Garmonn. He fingered a length of green silk. Arching an eyebrow in silent inquiry, he met her gaze. When she gave a slight nod, a smile touched his lips. He tilted his head toward the part of the market where the horses were stabled, then stared back at the expensive cloth.

Tension whipped through her body. Her limbs stiffened, as though her flesh had turned to wood, yet she forced herself to stroll on to the next stall, then the next.

"Milady. Halt."

The guards had realized her intent.

She quickened her pace.

Someone caught her arm and yanked her into the shadowed doorway of a crowded tavern. Struggling, she tried to pull free. She looked up into Garmonn's flushed, triumphant face. The odors of sweat and ale surrounded him.

"Do not worry. My men will take care of your guards."

Where his fingers pressed, her skin crawled with goose bumps. "Where is Rudd?"

"In a safe place, a short ride from here."

"Please tell me where he is."

Garmonn pulled her into an alley that reeked of moldering vegetables. " 'Tis too dangerous. Come."

Rexana stumbled along behind him, barely able to match his strides. Her foot skidded on a mound of rotting apple cores. As she regained her balance, the little voice inside her screamed she was a fool to go with him.

She prayed she was not making a terrible mistake.

Part way through questioning the gruff-voiced merchant about some vagrants he had seen days ago, Fane heard shouts. He spun on his heel. Rexana's guards approached at a run.

The nearest one staggered to a halt. "She rode off with Lord Darwell's son, Garmonn."

"Garmonn!" A brutal chill whipped through Fane. "When did they leave?"

The guard wiped his brow. "A moment ago. We pursued Lady Linford, as you ordered, so she would not suspect your plans. Garmonn's men confronted us, but we defeated them. We came straight here."

Anticipation clutched Fane's gut like a cruel hand. He struggled not to yell and slam his fist through the nearest wall. He had suspected Garmonn was involved with the rebels. His instincts had rung true.

Today, he would learn Garmonn's part in the traitorous plot.

Yet, now Garmonn had Rexana. She had gone with him of her own free will. What had he promised her to lure her away?

Under his breath, Fane prayed for her safety.

If Garmonn dared to harm her —

He shut his mind to the worry flooding through

him. "You have done well," he said to the guards. "To the horses."

He shoved two silver coins into the merchant's hands, then loped to the market's outskirts. His destrier stood tethered in the dappled shade of large oaks. There, thirty armed men watched the peasants, merchants, and travelers who passed by. As he neared, the knights mounted their horses and looked at him, awaiting his command.

Fane leapt onto the destrier, then took his iron shield from one of the knights. Over the metallic jangle of his horse's bridle, he heard the *clop, clop* of a cantering mount. He wheeled his destrier around. Kester rode toward him.

"They took the north road," he called.

Fane nodded. Rexana and Garmonn were not far ahead. At a brisk clip, Fane and his men would soon catch up to them.

He looked back at the knights. "Keep your weapons ready. The lady's safety comes above all. She must not be harmed."

Kester quirked his brows. "Lord Villeaux?"

"He, like Garmonn, has two choices: surrender or die."

The verdant forest, not far from Ickleton Keep, was familiar to Rexana. Memories prowled through her mind, rousing a nest of torment. Fane striding out of the trees. Fane telling her in his husky voice that at last, they would make love. Them rolling over and over in the sweet-scented glade and making wild, passionate love.

Why had Garmonn brought her *here*?

Her chest tightened until she could scarcely breathe. Yanking on the reins, she halted her horse on the shaded road.

Garmonn glanced over his shoulder. He scowled and wheeled his horse to face her, its hooves ringing on stones. A muscle ticked in his jaw.

Dread skittered through her. That dangerous unpredictability gleamed in his eyes. It had been her only warning before he had grabbed his bow and shot Thomas. Yet, he did not have a bow with him today, and she doubted he had brought her all this way to kill her. "When will we see Rudd?"

Garmonn tipped his head toward the trees. "Your brother is waiting in the glade."

She bit back a dismayed cry. How could Rudd have told Garmonn of the special place? Long ago, when children, they had promised to keep the forest pool their secret.

As though sensing her disappointment, Garmonn shrugged. "Rudd vowed we would be safe from Linford's men here. Come." He did not wait for her to reply, but turned his horse and rode into the woods.

Unease plummeted into Rexana's belly like a rock. Who did he mean, when he said "we"? How many others had he brought to her sanctuary? What would she find when she rode into her beloved glade?

Part of her shrieked that she did not want to know. Part of her insisted that she turn around and ride like demons from hell chased her.

Yet, she could not turn back. Not when she would see her brother.

Not when she was honor bound to help him.

Garmonn melted into the trees' shadows. Guiding her horse onto the trail, she followed. Beneath the shifting canopy of boughs, the air seemed oddly silent. No birds flitted in the branches overhead or welcomed her with their bright chirps. She squinted up into the trees and gasped.

A stocky man in green garments dropped from the branches a few yards ahead. He landed on the trail near Garmonn, a bow in one hand and a quiver of arrows slung over one shoulder. There were other armed men in the trees. Watching her.

The burly archer looked at Garmonn. "Milord."

Garmonn laughed. "Keep watch. Do not let anyone pass."

"My pleasure."

As the archer looked at her, Rexana shivered. She recognized him from some of Lord Darwell's feasts. If her memory was correct, he was the son of a lord who had misruled his estate and owed a huge sum of unpaid tithes to the crown.

Was he a traitor?

She held his gaze as she rode past. He sneered, his head dipped in the barest attempt at a bow, then he stomped away. Mutters and coarse laughter rippled through the forest behind her. Did they mock her because she had married Fane, or because they did not expect a lady to visit their lair?

Squaring her shoulders, she stared at the thinning trees ahead. Let them laugh. Once she had found Rudd, they would ride away from this place together. If he had not yet gathered proof of his innocence, she would help him do so.

As she rode into the sun-slanted clearing, her heart lurched. The grasses and wildflowers were trampled flat. The scent of crushed violets hung in the breeze. Her beautiful glade was overrun with armed men and their mounts.

There were at least twenty ruffians. They groomed horses tethered nearby, bathed in the pool, and sat in the shadows sharpening their weapons. Many turned to look at her, their gazes wary.

Anger and fear swarmed in the pit of her stomach.

A sense of imminent danger hummed in her mind.

She must leave here as soon as possible.

"Rexana?"

Rudd's shout carried above the low chatter. She glanced at the pool. He strode from the bank, shaking water from his hands. His expression held astonishment and a trace of worry. She smiled, and, when he smiled back, some of the tension inside her melted.

He loped up the muddy bank toward her. Someone had given him new clothes. His tunic and black hose looked more of the fine garments he normally wore. Vestments that befitted a titled lord, not a prisoner.

She slid off her horse and ran to him. He embraced her, his breath ruffling her hair. "Zounds, Rexana! How did you come to be here?"

"I saw Garmonn at Tangston market. He said he knew where you were."

Rudd's body tautened. " 'Twas dangerous to bring you. Linford —"

"— does not know I am here." She sighed against her brother's shoulder. "How could I not come? I have worried about you. I had received no word of your fate for days."

Rudd pushed her to arm's length. She sensed tension drop between them, invisible yet tangible. "Rudd?" she said softly.

Nearby, Garmonn halted his horse and dismounted.

"I did not expect to see Rexana," Rudd called to him, "but I thank you."

Garmonn shrugged. " 'Twas no trouble. After all, she will soon be —"

Rudd abruptly shook his head. "Later."

Chuckling, Garmonn patted his horse's lathered neck.

Unease rooted deep within Rexana. Yet, before she could ask Garmonn to clarify his unfinished statement, he clicked his tongue and led his horse toward the tethered mounts.

Rudd caught her hand and drew her to a quiet part of the glade, where hazy sunlight slanted through the oaks. He released her, then dragged his fingers through his hair.

Frowning, she planted her hands on her hips. "What did Garmonn mean when he said —"

"Listen to me," Rudd said in a strained voice. "You must get away from this place. 'Tis not safe. I will convince Garmonn to take you to the main thoroughfare and —"

"You will come with me."

"I cannot."

"Why? What holds you to these men?"

He did not answer. Yet, the glint of his eyes bespoke fierce loyalties, and vows made in secret.

Oh, dear God.

She pressed trembling fingers to her lips. "Who are these men?"

His mouth twisted. "They are who you expect them to be. Traitors."

Her words rushed out on a strangled moan. "Are you . . . a traitor?"

Rudd looked away. Shadows slanted over his handsome face, casting part in grayed darkness. Her fingers curled against her skin, and she fought the dizzying pull of emotional chaos.

Why did he not answer her? Why?

"I want the truth. Tell me." Her tone sharpened. "Tell me you are innocent of treason."

"Rexana —"

Fury shrilled inside her. "I have risked a great deal to try to help you. I have risked my life, my marriage —"

"Marriage? Ha! You are glad to be free of Linford."

Her innards constricted with a hurt so deep, it snatched her breath. A sob wrenched from her. "Rudd."

"You do not care for Linford. He forced you to wed him."

"He did. Yet, I have come to know him well. He is a just and honorable man."

Rudd cursed. He stared off across the glade, before his angry gaze returned to her. "If you have come to convince me to surrender, I refuse. I would rather die than rot in his dungeon."

"Fie! I do not believe you are guilty of treachery. I came here to help you."

His expression softened a fraction, even as he shook his head. "What happens now, I must do on my own." He touched her arm. "Leave here. Please. I beg you."

"I will not leave without you."

He closed his eyes, as though fighting for patience. When bold footfalls approached, his voice roughened. "I must stay. My task —"

"— is not yet done." Garmonn came to Rudd's side and clapped him on the back. "I have brought fare for Rexana. We must make our lady guest welcome."

His queer grin made her shudder. She glanced at the sliced meat and bread set out on a metal plate, and forced a polite smile. "Thank you, but I will not be staying."

His smile thinned. "Of course you will."

Rudd scowled. "Nay, she —"

"Rexana goes nowhere, until you have done as you promised."

"Promised?" Rexana echoed. Fear tightened the word to a rasp.

"Rudd did not tell you? Why, he is going to kill High Sheriff Linford. Your accursed husband."

# Chapter Twenty

REXANA GASPED. "MURDER FANE? You will never succeed."

"Rudd's plan is sound," Garmonn said. " 'Twill work."

Horror coiled up inside her. Clutching a hand to her breast, she covered the aching heart of her that hurt more than she could bear. She stumbled back a step. How could her brother plot such a terrible crime?

Now that she knew of it, she could not let him succeed.

Longing and love for Fane sang through her every vein. She would never allow her brother to kill Fane. Never!

She stared at Rudd. Anguish honed each of her

words. "You are a man of honor. Will you prove yourself a criminal?"

"My plan is the only way —"

"Nay! I know you are innocent. Together, we will prove it. I will help."

Garmonn laughed. "Aye, you will help." His eyes gleamed with a hideous fervor as he smirked at Rudd. "She cannot leave now she knows the plan."

"A pity you were careless and told her," Rudd snapped.

Rexana's skin prickled with a sickly heat. Did Garmonn mean to hold her prisoner? What did he intend to do with her? Forcing a brave tone, she held his stare. "I have no intention of staying here. You cannot stop me from leaving."

She turned on her heel to stride toward her horse.

Garmonn whistled. The men in the glade grabbed their weapons and sprang to their feet.

They blocked all routes out.

She whirled and glared at Garmonn. "Let me go."

He sauntered toward her. His mouth slanted into a hideous smile. "You still do not understand, do you, Rexana?"

"I understand you have corrupted my brother's vision until he no longer thinks clearly." She saw Rudd flinch, but she refused to meet his gaze. "You, Garmonn, are a heartless manipulator. I know for certain you are a criminal."

His face took on a merciless cast, the look she had seen before he wounded Thomas. As Garmonn strode toward her, grasses snapped. The sound seemed louder than arrows shot from a bow.

She shivered. Cold. Hot.

"Garmonn," Rudd shouted. "Stop."

Garmonn's pace did not slow.

Her legs threatened to buckle, but she held her ground.

"You speak with such a rash tongue, Rexana. Why do you provoke me?" Before she could jerk away, his hand sank into her hair. He held the back of her head firm, and brought his mouth close to her ear. His angry scent flooded her nostrils. "I warned you once what would happen if you spoke of that day."

Fear screamed through her. She would never forget.

*"I shot him for you, Rexana. When we marry, these worthless peasants will be our people. We can do with them as we please."*

*"Nay!" she had said, her voice barely audible over Thomas' agonized cries. "You should not have done this. How could you be so cruel? I will see you punished!"*

*"How he screams. I should have shot him dead." Garmonn's face had hardened into a sneer. "If you tell anyone — anyone — I will kill Rudd. I know many ways to slaughter a man, Rexana. I learned well on crusade."*

Rudd came to Garmonn's side. "Release her."

As she struggled to snuff the memory, fear plunged into her gut. If Garmonn wished to harm Rudd in this glade, 'twould be desperately easy. Despite his skills with a sword and crossbow, Rudd could not defend himself against twenty men.

Would Garmonn hurt Rudd in order to make her cooperate?

As though sensing her thoughts, Garmonn relaxed his hold. He stepped away, his hand dropped to his sword, and he smiled.

Foreboding rushed through her. She forced herself to speak with calm, to find logic despite her fear. "What do you want of me? Why did you lure me here? You had a reason for bringing me. 'Twas not to see Rudd."

Admiration lit Garmonn's eyes. "Mayhap you do understand. You see, you are the one thing that will lure Linford to us."

"*What?*"

"You will lead him into a trap. You will watch him die as a barbarian deserves to die."

*Oh, God!*

Rudd frowned. "Wait a momen —"

"He manipulated our king with tales of imprisonment and heroic escape," Garmonn muttered. "He convinced King Richard to appoint him High Sheriff and grant him a rich keep." He thumped his chest.

"I, too, fought in the east. I, too, battled Saracens and spilled blood for my king. What did I get in reward? Naught."

Anger burst inside her.

"Garmonn —" Rudd said.

"You returned home from Crusade alive, thanks to Fane's bravery," Rexana bit out. "Is that not a reward?"

Garmonn's face turned scarlet. "I will have what is owed to me. What was promised to me long ago. What will lead me into the king's honored circle." He reached out to cup her breast. "I shall have you."

She slapped his hand away. "Your plan is flawed. I am already wed to Linford."

Laughter ground between Garmonn's lips. "Soon, he will be dead."

"I will not let you kill him. I will stop you."

"How?" He gestured to the armed men surrounding her. Coarse chuckles rippled through the throng, and she fought a suffocating wave of anxiety.

Rudd swore. He shoved Garmonn's arm. "What are you doing? This plan is not what we discussed. You agreed she would not be involved or harmed. You promised."

"I changed the arrangements."

Worry shone in Rudd's eyes before his gaze narrowed. "Escort her out of Warringham if you are concerned she will tell of our plot, but let her go. Do it, or

I will not kill Linford."

Garmonn's jaw hardened. His hand on his sword's grip, he turned to Rudd. "If you value your sister's life, you will do as you agreed."

Rudd's eyebrow arched. "You threaten me?"

"Linford must die. We both know 'tis so." With a twisted smile, Garmonn looked back at her.

Panic reared inside Rexana like a frantic horse. She fought her stomach's violent lurch. Never would she let him use her as a pawn to destroy both her brother and Fane.

Rexana caught up her skirts. She bolted for the nearest trees. Men shouted, running for her. She darted from side to side, lunging through gaps between her pursuers.

Rough hands caught her arms. Hauled her back.

She broke free. Tripped on her bliaut. A man catapulted into her from behind. She fell face first onto the grass. Gasping, she spat seeds out of her mouth, pressed her hands flat, and tried to rise.

"Nay, woman." Garmonn sat on top of her, panting. His thighs framed her bottom. She shuddered at the hard, warm weight of him crushed against her. She squirmed. Tried to wriggle free. With a grunt, he caught her arms and wrenched them behind her back. "Rope," he bellowed.

She struggled. Kicked. Screamed. Men knelt beside her to pin her down. The hemp rope scratched her fingers and hands. The binding tautened. Dug into her wrists. She bit her lip against the discomfort.

Garmonn tested the ropes, then hauled her to her feet. He shoved her toward a group of men. "Watch her."

She blinked, fighting tears. She stared at Rudd. With her eyes, she pleaded for him to help her, to defy Garmonn, to rebel against the horrible plan he had devised.

For an instant, her brother's gaze flickered. Then, his expression changed to stony determination. As Garmonn passed, he looked at Rudd. Rudd nodded. Together, they strode across the glade.

Her tears welled. She had not misjudged her brother, had she?

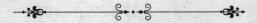

Fane fought the painful oath that rose in his throat. He stared at the forest visible on the road. Remembered.

Ah, God, how he remembered.

With effort, he suppressed the tantalizing memories. Rexana's cries. Her delicious scent. Their wild, glorious consummation. He would not be distracted in this vital time. He must fulfill his duty.

Tightening his grip on his shield, he glanced back at his men. "If the traitors do not yield, kill them."

Fane fixed his gaze upon the road ahead and spurred

his horse to a canter. The breeze cooled his face and tangled his hair. As he plunged into the forest's shade, his blood pumped fast and hot. He reached for his sword. The blade hissed out of its scabbard.

In the gray-green shadows, he imagined the earthy smell of sand. Blood. The Saracens' savage war cries. His body thrummed with battle fervor. This time, he would spill English blood in the name of his king, in the name of justice and duty. He would fight to save the woman he loved.

An arrow whizzed past his ear and *thunked* into a tree trunk. He spied the archer in the trees.

"Surrender to me, or die," he shouted.

Laughing, the man nocked another arrow. Before Fane sheathed his sword and grabbed his bow, an arrow launched from behind him. With a gurgled cry, the man plummeted into the undergrowth.

"Thank you, Kester," Fane called.

"My pleasure, milord."

Arrows flew like rain. With a lusty roar, Fane raised his bow. His first arrow flew straight and true. His mouth set in a determined smile. He pitied Villeaux. He pitied all of the damned traitors. Their time had come.

Rexana twisted her bound hands. Broken grass stalks scratched her skin, and she groaned. Cursed ropes. Garmonn had tied them tightly. Her fingers were beginning to go numb.

She fought tears. She must not despair. She must escape.

She must warn Fane.

Drawing in a shaky breath, she pondered her options. Garmonn had forced her to sit on a saddle blanket in the center of the glade, in clear view of his men. As she moved her leg a fraction, easing a cramp in her thigh, her gown rustled. A ruffian near her stopped polishing his dagger, and watched until she settled. She could not even burp without the men knowing.

Indignation heated the anger simmering within her. Earlier, with nauseating courtesy, Garmonn had pushed her down on her knees upon the blanket. "I cannot have you running away, can I?"

She sat, turning her face away.

He chuckled, crouched next to her, and swept a hand down her hair. "One day, lovely Rexana, you will want me."

"Never. My heart belongs to Fane." How easily the words flew from her lips. Her heart almost burst with the rightness of her declaration.

Garmonn spat in the grass. "You care for him?"

*Aye!* The answer soared inside her like a dancer leaping for the sky. "I love him. Body, heart, and soul."

Garmonn's eyes flashed with fury. He had withdrawn his hand, shoved to standing, then stormed off to speak with his cohorts.

Voices carried on the breeze. She spied Rudd standing near the horses, deep in conversation with Garmonn. Anguish slashed through her, so intense she almost cried out. Her brother had made no effort to help her. On occasion he glanced at her, as though to be sure she was well treated, but when she met his gaze, he looked away.

He nodded at something Garmonn said, and her throat tightened. Why did Rudd continue to aid Garmonn? Did he believe Garmonn's threat to do her harm? Did he try to protect her? Or, did he intend to help her escape later, mayhap when darkness fell?

She wriggled her hands again. She would not sit idle and wait for rescue.

A few yards away, men began sharpening their swords. The rasped sound grated on her frazzled nerves. Zounds! If only she could loosen her bindings. Or create a distraction.

A strangled cry came from the woods.

Garmonn froze. The men near her ceased their sharpening.

Another cry. A scream.

Mutters ripped through the glade. The men around her picked up their weapons.

Hope swelled within Rexana, and she tugged on the knotted ropes. Had Fane and the guards somehow tracked her to the glade? Had they come for her? Foolish hopes, yet she could not quell the burgeoning excitement.

She braced herself to run. Any moment now, there would be a chance —

Garmonn stared at her. Hard.

He gestured to the men nearby. "Go check on the others."

They nodded, then disappeared into the woods. Garmonn's gaze remained on her. Rexana trembled. *Look away,* her mind cried.

His lips curled, and he crossed to her. Hellfire! If she tried to bolt now, she would not get more than a few steps. She swallowed crushing disappointment.

As his footfalls approached, she pointedly stared off in the opposite direction.

He kicked shredded grass over her gown. "Get up."

"Why?"

He grabbed her upper arm, and she winced. "Up. Now."

Pushing her heels into the blanket, she rose on unsteady legs. She straightened, just as a man crashed through the underbrush into the glade. Blood stained the front of his tunic and soaked his right sleeve. His eyes rolled in their sockets.

"Linf —" With a grisly thud, the man fell face first to the ground. Arrows protruded from his back and shoulder.

Garmonn cursed.

Rexana gasped. Joy, then terror, whirled inside her.

Fane had come. Yet, he did not realize the glade harbored armed traitors who planned to kill him.

A scream tore from her lips. "Fane. Beware!"

Garmonn's fingers dug into her flesh with punishing force.

"Fane!"

Garmonn yanked her in front of him, shielding his body with hers. "Go on. Scream again." His mocking laughter burned her ear. "Bring him here so we can kill him."

Her rising cry fizzled in her throat.

His arm slid around her neck, and he dragged her flush against him. Her back bumped against his torso. Her bound hands pressed near his pelvis, close to his groin. Revulsion snaked through her.

"Ready your weapons," Garmonn called from behind her. He drew his sword, and the blade glinted. " 'Tis not as we planned, but Linford has come to us. He must not leave here alive."

She struggled, shaking her head.

"You" — Garmonn's arm tightened on her — "will stay with me."

He hauled her forward, closer to the forest's outskirts. Quiet spread over the glade and trees like an invisible blanket. Deadly quiet, as though a predator waited in the shadows. She hardly dared breathe.

"Linford!" Garmonn raised his sword. "I know you lurk in the woods."

No answer. The silence dragged.

She felt an exited shudder ripple through Garmonn. He wanted this fight. He craved the chance to kill. Her skin crawled with horror.

"Show your face, Linford," Garmonn shouted. "Come forth, for I have your wife."

Out of the corner of her eye, she saw Rudd edge closer. She prayed he would help her. She prayed that when the battle ended, he would be alive and hale.

Snapping twigs drew her attention to the forest. She heard hoofbeats. Leaves stirred.

A rider emerged from the shadows. He sat upon a huge, gray destrier and carried a shield.

Her pulse froze, then drummed a desperate beat. *Fane.*

At the forest's fringe, he drew his horse to a halt. His loose black hair drifted in the sunlight, and his angry brown eyes blazed almost the same inky shade. His beautiful mouth flattened into a line.

"Linford," Garmonn muttered.

"Let her go." Fane spoke softly, yet his words carried through the glade like an icy blast.

Garmonn's rough laughter stirred her hair. His arm squeezed in mock affection. "Rexana is mine now. She has sworn her love to me. She will wed me and bear my sons, as promised long ago."

Fane's gaze narrowed.

"He lies," she cried. "Do not believe him."

With a growl, Garmonn jerked his arm back. The glade spun before her in a painful blur of color.

"Let her go," Fane repeated, this time with more force. His lip curled back from his teeth. Her skin prickled with the realization how close his fury was to exploding.

"Ah, Linford," Garmonn crooned. "Man to man, crusader to crusader, at last we will settle this matter between us."

"Drop your weapons and surrender. Your fellow traitors are to do the same. I command you, in the name of our king."

A breath hissed from Garmonn. "Come nearer, fool."

Rexana squirmed in his hold. "Do not!" she choked out. "They mean to kill you."

"The glade is surrounded." Fane's voice carried a calming edge. "No man will leave here alive, unless he surrenders to me. If you do not believe me, ask those who were keeping watch in the trees. They are all dead. All but two, who are now my prisoners."

"You, too, are a dead man," Garmonn snarled.

"We shall see." Fane kicked his heels into his horse's sides. The animal surged forward.

Straight for her and Garmonn.

"Kill him!" Garmonn shouted.

At the same moment, arrows zinged out of the woods and into the glade. The air swarmed with steel-tipped bolts. Men shouted. Screamed in agony. A man near her collapsed, clutching at the arrow embedded in his chest.

The destrier's hooves thundered. The animal's path did not waver. It would trample her and Garmonn into the grass.

His arm a band around her neck, Garmonn dragged her backward. She struggled. Kicked his shins. Swearing, he pulled her toward a fallen tree.

Fane's horse pounded closer. Its breath seemed louder than the scream burning her throat.

Garmonn would never reach the tree.

As though he reached the same conclusion, he halted. Light flashed on his sword. He aimed for the destrier's legs.

If he wounded the horse, Fane would fall to the ground. He might be injured. He might even be crushed under the dying animal.

Rexana frantically twisted her hands, pressed against Garmonn's pelvis. A plan shot into her mind, tainted by disgust. Yet, if she could save Fane's life, she must do it.

She rammed her fists into Garmonn's groin.

He yelped. Jolted forward. The sword's tip listed to the ground. His hold relaxed for the barest instant.

Breaking free, she ran. One step. Two.

Hoofbeats rang in her ears. The ground shook under her feet. She pitched to the side. Staggered.

A muscled arm caught her waist. *Garmonn!*

"Nay!" she screeched.

"Hold, wife." Fane lifted her onto the galloping horse and seated her sideways in front of him. He shifted his shield to his left hand. With a sharp tug on the reins, he wheeled the destrier around. His left arm settled against her lower back, supporting her, as he urged the horse to a canter.

An arrow streaked past his head. More arrows pinged off the shield. Muttering a foreign sounding oath, he held the shield higher. "Keep your head down."

She slumped against Fane's chest. Fear, relief, and gratitude flooded through her. Her bound hands itched. She longed to touch and kiss him. To tell him how foolish she had been to go with Garmonn. To ask him to forgive her. To tell him she loved him.

As they entered the forest, shadows cooled her skin. Branches tugged at her clothing. Kester edged out from behind a tree, along with several men-at-arms. She recognized other knights from Tangston in the undergrowth, bows raised, skulking toward the glade. With a nod to Fane and her, the knights moved past. Moments later, their attack roars joined the battle's cacophony.

Fane halted the destrier. After handing his shield to Kester, Fane dismounted. Looking up at her, he set his hands at her waist and drew her down. His gaze locked with hers.

His possessive hold soothed her shattered nerves. His hands' warmth flooded through her flesh to the very core of her. She leaned back against the destrier's warm side. It felt wonderful to be near Fane again. Her husband. Her beloved. Her soul mate. Her eyes moistened with tears.

Wiping sweat from his lip, Fane stared down at her. His eyes held a violent storm of emotions, among them fury, hurt, and concern.

She did not know what to say first, or how to begin. Yet, she must. "Fane," she said on a ragged whisper, "I —"

"Later." He dipped his head. Caught her lips in a deep, thorough kiss that shot straight to her soul and melted her into sheer bliss. Then, he turned her slightly, whipped his dagger from his belt and slashed her ropes.

She rubbed her sore wrists. "Thank you."

Fane looked at her bruised, reddened skin. His expression darkened to a forbidding scowl. "Stay here with Kester. I cannot be worrying about your safety."

"I can help. I can shoot a bow —"

"You have done quite enough, love."

He took his shield from Kester, drew his sword, then stalked toward the glade.

She watched him go. Watched the light slant over him and illuminate his muscled physique. Anguish knotted her insides. He was angry, yet he still cared for her. She had seen it in his gaze before he turned away. When he returned from battle, she would tell him she loved him.

An arrow thudded into a tree not far from her. She jumped.

Kester hurried to her side, pointing to a tall patch of ferns. "Milady, hide there. Keep down. You will be safe."

She shoved her torment to the back of her mind, nodded, and crept off in the direction he had indicated. Weapons littered the ground, likely taken from men they had killed. She glanced over the bows, swords, and knives, then snatched up a dagger. She would not be unarmed.

Hunkering down, she peered through the ferns. She could not see the glade. She rose up to see past the outlying trees and bushes, and gasped. Many of the traitors lay dead. Others, wounded, were surrendering to Fane's men, who were cautiously stepping out of the forest. Fane and Garmonn stood facing each other, their swords raised in challenge. Fane had dropped his shield into the grass, as though to even the fight.

Her fingers flew to her brooch. Where was Rudd? Was he among the dead? Oh, God. Nay!

She crawled forward. Rudd's head popped up from behind the fallen tree. Arrows peppered the log's peeling bark. More arrows whizzed over the tree, yet he did not return fire. Why?

Did he intend to surrender, or run?

As she watched, he slunk down the log's length to where it almost touched the water. An arrow flew through the air . . . and plowed into his left shoulder.

He cried out in pain.

"Rudd!" She bolted from the ferns.

She heard Fane curse. Heard the arrows whistling past, so close the air burned her skin.

"Rexana," Fane bellowed. "Get back." Sweat glistened on his brow. His face contorted with rage as he circled in a lethal dance with Garmonn.

"I will not leave my brother."

"Do not risk your life for him." His gaze trained on Garmonn, Fane jerked his head. "Obey me. Now."

His tone brooked immediate compliance. She ducked a flying arrow. "I cannot."

"Rexana!" Fane glared at her.

A skin-crawling laugh burst from Garmonn. He lunged.

Rexana screamed.

Snarling a curse, Fane darted aside. Metal clanged. Garmonn yelled, thrusting again. The swords squealed, locked together. Fane's arm shook. As she watched, unable to look away, he jerked back and attacked. He met Garmonn's onslaught with cold, efficient grace.

Fear slashed through Rexana. She glanced from Fane to the fallen log. How could she choose between him and Rudd, when she loved them both?

She prayed for Fane's safety, even as she ran to the tree.

Rudd emerged. Gripping a broadsword, he stood and threw a leg over the log. With an awkward turn, he slid to the ground. He had yanked the arrow from his flesh. His left arm hung limp at his side, blood streaming down his sleeve.

As he straightened, he stared at Fane and Garmonn.

Oh, God. Did he mean to kill Fane?

Rexana crossed to him. She gestured for him to follow her into the trees. "Come. We must tend your wound."

Shaking his head, he muttered, "I am not done."

Rexana snuffed welling panic. "Do not be a fool. Save yourself, so you may tell Linford the truth. Tell him you are innocent."

Rudd's fingers flexed on the sword. He grimaced, as though he fought agonizing pain. "Aye, he will know the truth."

He strode toward the two men.

"Stop!" she shrieked.

Garmonn grinned at Rudd. "Kill Linford. Go on!"

The barest smile touched Rudd's lips.

Choking down her terror, she caught up with Rudd to plant herself between him and the fight. "Do not. I beg you, as your sister."

Garmonn leapt out of Fane's reach. Their swords clashed. "Kill him! Now. He cannot fight us both."

Rudd sidestepped her, and horror clawed up inside Rexana. "Rudd, you are not a murderer."

Steel shrieked. Fane cast her a furious glance. "Get to safety. Go!"

"Aye, go," Garmonn mocked. His blade slashed down, almost catching Fane across the stomach. "Or watch me disembowel your husband."

Rexana looked at her brother, poised to step into the fray, and fought a crushing wave of despair. "Rudd will not fight."

Garmonn laughed. "Does the clever sheriff know Rudd planned to murder him?" As Fane's gaze sparked with wrath, Garmonn's tone turned triumphant. "Rudd's plans for rebellion are under way. Once you are dead, Sheriff, Warringham will be ours."

"Rudd is not guilty of treason," Rexana shrilled. "You forced him to obey you. You wanted Fane killed for your own selfish interests. You wanted to marry me to gain access to the crown's privileged circles. I vow you planned to overthrow the king's trusted men."

Fane growled. "Is that so, Garmonn?"

"Tsk, tsk, Rexana," Garmonn muttered.

Her nerves jarred. The murderous intent in his eyes promised he might turn his sword on her too when he had finished with Fane.

Stepping forward, Rudd raised his weapon.

She clutched at her brooch.

Fane might die. Her brother might die.

A last, desperate hope flared within her. She stumbled forward. Fought for words. Fought to interrupt the inevitable combat in any way possible, as her fingers closed on her dagger. "I know what you confessed to me, Garmonn. I know *you*. I remember your unspeakable cruelty last winter."

Garmonn flinched. His merciless gaze shifted from Fane to her, then back to Fane.

She shut out the inner voice that screamed for her not to speak, the fear gusting inside her like a blizzard. "I will no longer be silent about what you did to Thomas."

"Thomas?" Fane and Rudd said together, sounding stunned.

"Garmonn shot him like an animal and left him in the snow to die. You will answer to Sheriff Linford for your barbaric crime. You will be punished by law."

"I warned you, Rexana, what would happen if you told." Garmonn's pitiless gaze slid to Rudd. "I keep my promises."

"And I will see you pun —" Before Fane finished speaking, he tripped on a fallen bow.

Garmonn roared. His blade arced down, straight for Fane's ribs.

Rudd darted forward.

Rexana screamed and plunged down the dagger.

The blade buried deep in Garmonn's forearm.

With a blood-curling howl, he dropped the sword.

She froze. Her shaking hand flew to her lips. She stared at the knife's hilt, protruding at a grisly angle. "I —"

"Well done, love." The flat of Fane's sword crashed down on Garmonn's head. The howling stopped. Garmonn's eyes closed and he slumped to the grass.

Blinking back tears, Rexana stared at Garmonn's limp body. Bile flooded her mouth. At last, 'twas over.

She raised her head and looked at Fane.

Shock wrenched through her.

His expression grim, Fane pointed his sword at Rudd's chest. "I have waited long for this moment."

# Chapter Twenty-one

FANE IGNORED REXANA'S DESPERATE WAIL. His blood pumped with resolve. Need. Fury. Her brother would no longer stand in the way of their marital happiness, or elude justice.

To Fane's surprise, no foolish arrogance shone in the lad's eyes. Only resignation. Mayhap he realized this would be a hard and bitter fight.

As he adjusted his sweaty grip on his sword, Fane drew a breath. He steeled his concentration and waited for Villeaux to make the first strike. He would not underestimate the lad's murderous intent.

Rudd dropped his blade. It thumped on the ground near Garmonn's unconscious body. "I will not fight you."

Rage slammed through Fane. "You will dishonor me? Do you dare me to attack when you are unarmed?"

Rexana clutched Fane's arm. "He is innocent. Rudd, tell him."

Scowling, Fane shook off her hold. He shut out her plea and the painful war of emotions it roused. He lunged forward, so his sword's tip pressed against Rudd's tunic. "Aye, tell us. Tell how you plotted to undermine the king and rule Warringham with the traitors."

"Wait. I —"

The glade blurred around Fane in a haze of angry red. "Your sister deserves answers. Tell her how you deluded her with lies and deception. Tell her how you betrayed her pure, unselfish love. Speak! She will hear it from you."

Rudd swallowed, then looked at Rexana. "I am not a traitor."

"You *lie*!" Fane bellowed.

Rudd shook his head. He stepped backward, stumbled, and fell to the ground. Crying out, he clutched at his bloody arm. Fane followed him down. Straddled him. Tossed aside his sword, drew his jeweled dagger, and held it to Rudd's throat.

Choking a breath, Rudd said, "I surrender!"

"Tell her the wretched truth," Fane snarled. "Now."

The lad's green eyes, so like Rexana's, blazed. "I did. I am not guilty of treason."

Fane heard the rustle of footfalls. His heightened senses buzzed a warning, an instant before steel pressed against his neck. Rexana had found another knife.

"Let him up," she rasped.

"I do not wish to hurt you, love, but God help me—"

Her hand did not waver. "Let him up, and let him speak." Her tone softened. "If you look, you will see the traitors are defeated. Kester and his men surround the glade. They are tying the prisoners. Rudd cannot escape."

Fane's face stung. His wife had outwitted him. He doubted she would use the knife, yet her feelings for her brother ran deep.

Muttering an oath, Fane rose. She eased away. As he straightened, he glared at her, but she quirked an eyebrow. Saucy wench. Later, he would deal with her willfulness.

Rudd shoved to his feet, rubbing his neck, and smiled at Rexana. "Thanks."

"Rudd, please. I want the truth."

"I swear I did not lie." As though he sensed the rebuttal burning on Fane's tongue, Rudd raised a hand. "There will be eye witness accounts that imply my guilt. Those could not be avoided. I could only collect evidence against the traitors by pretending to be one of them."

A disgusted laugh shot from Fane. "What trickery do you speak?"

Rudd looked sheepish. "I admit, I went along with Garmonn's ideas at first. I, like many others, did not want a crusader barbarian as sheriff of our lands."

"Rudd!" Rexana gasped.

"When I realized that Garmonn planned to overthrow the king . . ." He dragged his fingers through his tangled hair. "I could not withdraw from the plans. I knew too much. Also, I could not risk Rexana being threatened or harmed." His face reddened. "I knew Garmonn had wounded Thomas, and that he would hurt or kill others to get his way."

Her eyes widening, Rexana said, "How did you know? Thomas told me he did not see who wounded him. Snow was falling."

"Garmonn told me one night, when he was very drunk. He laughed and thought it great sport. He told me he had shot a peasant to impress you. I had helped you save Thomas a month earlier, and guessed he was the man Garmonn wounded."

Loathing blazed through Fane. He vowed to see Garmonn punished for his ruthlessness and manipulations.

Rexana crossed her arms. She looked worn, as though the day's turmoil had overwhelmed her. As Fane drew her against his side, she shuddered. "Oh, Rudd. He said he would kill you if I told anyone of that day."

Rudd's gaze hardened before he stared down at Garmonn's motionless body. "The night he told me, I knew I had to stay with the traitors until I could prove their deceit."

"This is a fascinating tale," Fane muttered, "but you plotted to kill me."

"I devised a plan, aye, but did not intend to follow through. Garmonn began to suspect me, so I had to defray his distrust." Rudd shrugged. "I joined the fight earlier not to kill you, but to ensure Garmonn did not win."

Irritation thinned Fane's temper. He could have defeated Garmonn on his own. "Naught you have told me proves your innocence, Villeaux."

"I have documents. I planned to send them to the king, but I will give them to you."

"Where are they?"

Rudd's gaze flicked to Rexana. "I will need your brooch."

She fingered the gold arrow, clearly reluctant to part with it. "Why?"

"You, dear sister, hold the key to the truth. I did not trust anyone else."

A puzzled frown furrowed her bow, yet she unpinned the brooch and handed it to her brother. Fane followed them to the fallen tree. Cradling his hurt arm, Rudd eased over the log. Fane assisted Rexana over. Rudd walked down to the end of the tree, which drooped into the pool, then reached into a hollow in the rotting wood.

Warning pricked at the base of Fane's skull. Pulling Rexana aside, he raised his dagger. "If you try to trick me —"

Rudd sighed. "No trickery, I promise."

Leaves rustled. Bark dropped from the hollow. A moment later, he brought out a small box. The metal lock was an odd shape. He set the box atop the log and pushed the fletching end of the brooch into the lock. With a click, it opened.

As Rudd raised the box's lid, Fane strode closer. Rolled parchments lay inside, many bearing wax seals.

Rudd wiped his sweat-beaded brow. "There are records of meetings, signed promises of military support, as well as letters I said I would deliver but never did. I also have a statement of the traitors' purpose, penned by Garmonn. Enough evidence to imprison him and the other traitors for years."

Rexana's face glowed with pride.

Tearing his gaze from her, Fane smothered an oath. If the box did indeed hold this trove of documents, Rudd had fulfilled an extraordinary duty for the king. He had risked his life to work amongst men who would have killed him if they knew his true purpose. With honor and discretion, he had shielded Rexana from the danger, and fooled even a crown appointed High

Sheriff.

Yet, 'twas also possible the lad had made up his account to save his neck, and the documents were forged.

Fane closed the box with a snap. "I will consider what you have told me, and review these parchments."

"I expected as much." Rudd slumped against the fallen tree. In the stark sunlight, he looked wan.

Sliding her arms around her brother's waist, Rexana hugged him. His eyes closed, and he hugged her back.

Fane ignored a jealous pang. He looked at his men, herding the traitors to the glade's center. "We will return to Tangston Keep. There, Rudd, I will decide your innocence. Or guilt."

Some time later, Rexana stepped into the passage outside the solar, closing the doors behind her. As she nodded to the guards, smoke from the wall torches wafted to her like veiled secrets. Anticipation swirled up inside her.

Fane had promised to summon her once he had studied the box's contents and questioned Rudd. She had bathed, dressed in an embroidered pink gown, and dried her hair by the fire. Fane had not come. Was he still mulling her brother's fate? Or, had Fane deemed Rudd guilty and was reluctant to tell her?

They had arrived back at Tangston just before dusk. Fane had been quick to get her away from Rudd and the prisoners. As soon as Fane had dismounted, he shouted for Tansy. "Refresh yourself, love," he had said, pushing her toward the beaming servant. "I will fetch you when I have made my decision."

"I want to stay with you."

Fane touched her cheek. "I will fetch you." After silencing her protests with a kiss, he had ordered the traitors taken to cells and begun discussing dungeon security with Kester.

Pausing at the end of the shadowed passage, Rexana braced a hand against the wall. Fane's rumbled voice carried from the hall below. He did not sound angry. A woman murmured before an object clunked on a table. A chair scraped on the floorboards.

Rudd spoke, his tone strained. What had he said? Rexana moved closer.

Her brother gasped, then groaned. He sounded in agony.

The hair at Rexana's nape prickled. Her imagination filled with grim images. Fane did not approve of torture, but if Rudd refused to talk, mayhap he had found another means to —

Her brother yelled. "Zoundchs, that shurts."

His words were slurred. Drugged? Shock and outrage

slammed through her. She grabbed her skirts. Her feet pounded on the wooden landing, and she stared down over the rail.

Fane glanced up from where he sat at the lord's table. The brooch and box sat near him, the documents scattered within his reach. "Ah, Rexana. I planned to come get you soon."

Her gaze flew to her brother, seated at a table below the dais. His tunic and shirt lay rumpled on the floor. Celeste stood beside him, peering down at his bare, bloody shoulder. She held something between her fingers. What?

Rexana thundered down the stairs. A biting herbal scent assailed her, and she wrinkled her nose. "What goes on here?"

"Rexshana." Rudd stretched a hand out to her, then winced. Shaking her head, Celeste bent over his wound. He flushed. "Ousssccchhh."

Rexana ran to his side. He reeked of ale. A full pitcher and mug sat next to his good arm. "He is besotted!"

Fane pushed up from his chair. "No man would have his arm stitched without downing a few stiff drinks first."

"Stitched?" she repeated in a weak voice. Celeste held a bone needle. Near her on the table was a bowl of pungent, greenish-colored herbal water, no doubt used to cleanse the needle as well as Rudd's mangled flesh.

Rexana's stomach churned and she looked away.

Fane crossed to her, his expression somber. "His wound is deep. Yet, with stitches, it should heal well enough." A faint grin touched his lips, igniting warmth within her. "I had not summoned you yet, because I hoped to spare you having to watch."

She stared up into his dark, mesmerizing eyes. "I thought you had forgotten me."

"You were impatient, wife."

His acute assessment rubbed her frayed nerves. She sighed. "Well? Have you reached your decision? Are you convinced of my brother's innocence?"

Fane's gaze lowered. Frowning as though struggling with difficult words, he said, "It seems I may have been mistaken."

"Indeed?" She smiled.

"Rudd's collection of documents is impressive." Fane shook his head. "I can think of no reason for him to have gathered them, but that he planned to send them to the king."

"Riyghto, Linford." Rudd's fist thumped on the table. He slurped more ale, then loosed a loud belch.

Rexana drew a shaky breath. "Do *you* believe, beyond doubt, he is not guilty of treachery?"

Fane nodded.

"Oh!" Joy filled her, along with love so intense, she thought her heart would soar free from her body. Throwing herself into Fane's arms, she snuggled against him to hug him tight. At last, they could be together without any hindrances to their happiness.

He returned her embrace, yet his hold seemed loose and reluctant, his posture tense. Doubt nibbled at her elation.

Before she could ask what was wrong, Fane said, "There is another, Rudd says, who will vouch for his innocence."

She raised her head from Fane's tunic. "Who?"

"Thomas."

She gasped and glanced at Rudd. "Why did you not tell me?"

He did not answer. His mouth drooped and his eyes were closed. A snort rattled in his throat as his chin slumped to his chest. Celeste continued her stitches.

"He is oblivious," Fane muttered.

"Is he all right?" Breaking free of his embrace, Rexana ran to the table. When she nudged her brother's good shoulder, he did not stir or awaken.

"Your brother will be fine in the morn, apart from a sore head. He is old enough to look after himself now." Wry laughter warmed Fane's words. "He is a man, Rexana, not a boy."

As she looked down at her brother, her cheeks warmed. "You are right."

"Of course I am."

She rolled her eyes toward the shadowed trusses overhead, then straightened. Fane had crossed to the lord's table. His gaze held residual mirth, yet also wariness.

He kept something from her.

Resisting a rush of uncertainty, she said, "Please advise me what he told you. I cannot wait until the morrow to ask him myself."

Fane rubbed a hand over the back of his neck. "Very well. If you remember, Rudd paid Thomas for the use of his barn. Rudd planned to schedule an important meeting there and invite all known traitors to attend. He also intended to send a missive to the king's ministers. If the crown forces attacked during the meeting, they would snare most of the traitors. The rebellion would be all but snuffed."

"But before that meeting could be set, your men captured Rudd at the tavern."

"Correct."

Frowning, she said, "I do not understand. When you came to Thomas's house, the day I rode off to visit him, Thomas claimed Rudd was a traitor."

"Rudd made Thomas swear not to reveal the truth, not even to you. Rudd feared being discovered and what Garmonn, the traitors' leader, might do. Your brother worried not only for himself, but for you. Brave Thomas even hid some documents for Rudd for a time."

"Until Rudd had the box and brooch made," she guessed.

Fane nodded. "Yet, Thomas is a loyal subject. When

Kester arrived at his home and began asking questions, Thomas would not lie before his lord's men. He admitted he loaned the barn to Rudd and had heard of Rudd's involvement with the traitors. After all, this is what Rudd wanted him to say. Your brother wanted to appear guilty."

"I see." She blinked. "I think."

Fane's expression shadowed. " 'Tis a convoluted tale, I agree. No doubt Thomas's account will flesh out Rudd's. I plan to visit Thomas in the morn."

Rexana glanced at her brother, whose chest rose and fell in sound slumber. Just days ago, he was chained to the dungeon wall, condemned as a criminal. If the events of the past few days had unfolded in a different pattern, he might not have had the opportunity to prove his innocence and clear his name. Shutting out the dark thoughts, she said, "If Rudd was working in secret for the king, why did he not tell you during his imprisonment?"

"He feared the traitors in the other cell would hear, and that word might somehow leak to Garmonn." Fane's shoulders moved in a stiff shrug. "He also knew I had coerced you into marriage. Your brother did not trust me, for he thought me a ruthless barbarian, just like the rest of his peers."

Bitterness underscored Fane's words, yet as she stared at him across the distance separating them, fierce pride surged inside her. With his capture of the traitors, he had proven the king's wisdom in appointing him High Sheriff. Fane's triumph would soon be lauded throughout all of Warringham. He had fought with chivalry and honor, and proven himself worthy of the greatest respect. She could not wait to prove to him, in the solar, how much she admired him.

How she loved him.

With slow, loose-hipped strides, she crossed to him. "What will happen to Garmonn?"

As she neared, Fane's gaze narrowed. "He will answer for his crimes in the King's Courts, along with the other traitors."

Caution hummed in his tone, but she dismissed it. Fane might think she disagreed with his harsh intentions for Garmonn, but she did not. "As you know, milord, Lord Darwell is a powerful man. He may use his influence to free Garmonn."

She reached Fane's side. He stared down at her, determination gleaming in his eyes.

"Darwell will not succeed, Rexana. Trust me."

"I do, husband." Arching against him in sensual invitation, she slid both arms around his waist.

He tensed, as though her caress brought physical discomfort. He did not return her embrace. "Do you, Rexana?"

Disquiet whipped through her. "Aye, husband, I do." She drew back. Their hips and bellies touched, yet he seemed distant. Remote. Tipping her head up, she looked into his eyes. They gleamed with misery. A violent chill tore through her, like she had plummeted into the midst of a winter storm.

Forcing a sultry smile, she murmured, "At last, we can be together."

His eyes closed. A sigh shuddered through him, so harsh it seemed ripped from his very soul. "Celeste, leave us."

"Aye, milord." The maid picked up the bowl, and with hurried strides, left the hall.

Silence settled like a smothering fog. Rexana stared at her fingers, curled into the front of his fine-spun tunic. Fear stabbed through her. "What is wrong?"

"I wish you did trust me. Above all, you should have told me Garmonn had threatened your life."

Fane's outraged, disappointed tone stirred the loneliness which had lived with her for the past few days. "I could not. He might have killed Rudd."

A bitter smile twisted Fane's mouth. "You told me when I first proposed marriage that you did not love me, and never would. I realize now you spoke true then."

"Nay," she choked out. "I did not realize I would care for you as I do."

He caught her elbows and pushed her to arm's length. "The past days have shown me much, Rexana. Our marriage is not grounded in trust, but deception, a rotten foundation for a lifetime together." He shook his head, and his words became as rough as grating stone. "I had hoped to win your affection, yet I see that I dreamed of what will never be. I must accept our marriage will be a civilized but empty dance, not one of soul deep meaning, passion, or . . . love."

Hurt clawed into the torn, bleeding shell of her heart. "I do love you!"

Moisture shone in his eyes. "I want to believe you."

"Oh, Fane." Distress racked her, clouding her vision with scalding tears. "You are no barbarian. You are a kind, honorable, and loyal English lord. A man of whom I am very proud. A man I lo —"

"— have deceived, more than once."

"With Rudd cleared, I have no reason left to beguile you." She pleaded with all the torment churning in her soul. "Please believe me. I love you. I love you!"

A sound like a sob broke from him.

He released her. Turned away.

Wiping tears from her cheeks, Rexana stared at the rigid line of his back. Her womb throbbed with an intimate pain. She craved to kiss him, to prove how much she had missed him over the past difficult days. Yet, that intimacy seemed impossible.

"My body, heart, and soul are yours. Until the day I die," she croaked on a ragged whisper. "Tell me what I must do to prove my love, and I will do it."

Setting his hands on his hips, he bowed his head. The tunic shifted over his buttocks, and memories wounded her. The slow, wet mingle of lips and tongues. The thrust of his hard, skilled hips. The rush of desire that seemed to burn hotter in her veins now than ever before.

If she coaxed him, reminded him of all the wonder they had shared and the unhindered future that lay before them, would he come with her to the solar? Could they vanquish the hurts of the past days, to begin their dance anew?

Stretching out shaking fingers, she touched his shoulder. As he glanced up, his profile taut with anguish, she heard footfalls, then the squeal of a servant coming to a halt. "Milord."

Fane swept a hand over his face. " 'Tis important, Winton?"

"Lord Darwell is here."

Shuffled footsteps echoed in the hall. Quelling a curse, Rexana turned to see Darwell hurrying toward them, his face sweaty and flushed.

"Sheriff, I bring important news. I —" Darwell halted, gaped at Rudd slumped at the table, then at her and scowling Fane. "Oh, my. Have I interrupted?"

As Fane strode toward Darwell, Rexana's hand listed to her side. Sadness crushed her. How composed Fane appeared after their conversation, while her eyes smarted and her soul seemed to be shattered into a thousand bleeding bits.

"I am glad you are here," Fane said, his tone brisk. "I planned to contact you in the morn. There is a matter we must discuss."

Darwell grinned like a delighted child, and a shiver tore through Rexana. It seemed he did not know of Garmonn's arrest.

What had him so excited?

"Milord," he whispered, "that crown secret that you — that I promised to —" With a gasp, he covered his mouth. "I know I vowed not to speak of it, but this eve, a messenger for the king's minister rode through my gates."

Rexana froze, even as Fane said, "Messenger?"

Darwell nodded. "He said to tell you the king's minister received the documents you sent. He and his army will arrive at Tangston on the morrow." Tugging on his beard, Darwell beamed. "The poor messenger looked exhausted from his long ride, so I promised to bring word straight to you."

"I see," Fane said.

Darwell's fingers wiggled like fat worms. "Milord, I must know. The visit concerns the crown secret, does it not?"

A faint flush colored Fane's cheekbones. "I fear, my friend, there is no crown secret. Never was. The king's minister has come for Warringham's traitors. And for Garmonn."

"No secr — Garmonn?" The glee drained from Darwell's face. "My son is in trouble?"

Rexana fought a stab of pity.

"Aye." Fane clapped him on the shoulder. "I will tell you all. I am afraid I must also investigate your involvement in the matter. But first, is there any other news from the messenger?"

Darwell's bewildered gaze slid to Rexana. Closing his eyes, he shook his head, and her broken heart clamped into a brutal knot.

"I am sorry, milady," he said. "I believe the king's minister intends to charge your brother with treason."

# Chapter Twenty-two

LEANING OUT OF THE SOLAR'S WINDOW, Rexana stared up at the night sky. Stars, bright as tears, glittered against the inky swath. A breeze whispered up from the bailey, bringing with it music, chatter, and the smells of cooking food. A reminder that down in the great hall, the castle celebrated the visit from the king's minister.

She fingered windblown hair from her lips. Part of her celebrated too, rejoicing in the traitors' capture and her brother's exoneration. Yet, her wounded soul wept that she had lost Fane's trust and love, mayhap forever.

That afternoon, looking tired yet determined, Rudd had presented his box of documents to the king's men and explained his actions. Fane had also asked Thomas and Lord Darwell to attend. Dressed in his finest clothes, battling an unsteady voice, Thomas had given his account. Afterward, the king's minister praised his bravery, and awarded him a plot of prime land, at which Thomas flushed with pride.

Darwell seemed shocked to learn the extent of Garmonn's treachery. Blubbering into his sleeve, he had disowned Garmonn, affirmed his family's loyalty to the crown, and offered Thomas a rich payment in compensation for Garmonn's cruelty.

Closing her stinging eyes against the breeze, Rexana remembered Fane lauding her brother's actions. Pride throbbed inside her. Fane had called Rudd a hero. The king's minister had agreed, absolving Rudd of all suspicion of treason. Rudd was a free man.

Tears rolled down her cheeks. She had tried to thank Fane, to tell him how she appreciated his words, but he had looked at her with such regret and longing, her words had jammed in her mouth. He seemed determined to keep the emotional barricade between them, for she had seen little of him since Darwell's arrival yesterday. Fane had not come to bed last eve until very late, as though he had waited until he believed she was asleep.

Oh, how she loved him! How could she have possibly known that on a night similar to this, when the castle celebrated and she danced for Fane, her life would change forever?

The doors to the solar clicked open. Drying her face, she turned. Fane entered the chamber, closed the doors, and stared at her. "You are not joining in the celebrations, love."

Had he missed her? Her pulse kicked into a foolish patter. "I grew weary, so I decided to retire early. I thought you would be entertaining the king's minister until dawn's first blush."

"He understood that the past days have been busy for us. Your brother offered to stay and drink with him."

"Oh."

"In truth, I, too, am weary." Fane's tormented voice tugged at her bruised emotions, coaxed her to go to him, to plead with him to give their love another try. Yet, before she had taken two awkward steps, he crossed to her. His thumb traced the damp path of her tears, and he shook his head. "Ah, Rexana."

Her lips quivered. "Fane."

His grave gaze held hers. "I have thought much about our talk yesterday. I once vowed never to let you go. Yet, with the king's minister here, if you wish to ask for an annulment —"

"Never!" The refusal flew from her without the slightest hesitation. "I will not forsake you, Fane. I love you."

His expression softened. "Are you certain you want our marriage?"

Smiling through her tears, she nodded. "There is no other man for me. Only you."

Relief and pride lit his eyes. "I am glad, wife. For I have come to realize I cannot live without you."

Her hands flew to her mouth, and she smothered a gasp.

"From this day forth, we begin a new round of our dance together — one spun from trust and love. Aye?"

"Aye!" she cried. "Oh, Fane. How I have missed you."

His arms slid around her, drawing her to his broad chest. She inhaled his spicy essence. His potent, male aura surrounded her, filled her, courted the very essence of her being. Joy flared, along with the urge to dance, wild and fast.

As the music drifting into the chamber quickened, she swayed from side to side.

"Rexana?"

She pulled free of his arms. A bemused frown darkened his face. Laughing, she circled him, her strides long and loose, her hips swaying in invitation.

"You tempt me, little fig?"

"I do, husband."

A growl rumbled in his throat. He reached for her. She twirled out of his grasp. Darted around to stand in front of him. With a gentle shove, she propelled him backward.

He resisted. She clicked her tongue and shook her head. With a tortured groan, he obeyed. She pushed him to the edge of the bed, then to sitting. The bed ropes creaked.

As she whirled away, her skirts flaring, his gaze sharpened. "Come here, little dancer."

"Not yet."

His eyes blazed. "You forget, wife, I was celibate for days. I am starved for you." He licked his lips. "Ravenous."

A wicked thrill ran through her. Spinning in a circle, she reached her hands up to the shadowed ceiling. The familiar cry swirled inside her. Brilliant. Beautiful.

*Dance, Rexana!*

She sucked in a breath, turned, and dipped. She peeked at Fane through her fingers. He watched like a man who could not look away. Like a man seduced.

*Step. Whirl. Step. Sway.*

She spun faster. Faster. Her skirts rustled like dry grass. Yearning, longing, and need spiraled up inside her.

And then he was there. Catching her in his arms. Kissing her with heart-pounding passion.

Breathless, grinning, she leaned back in his embrace.

He dropped a final heated kiss on her lips, then lifted her into his arms. He carried her to the bed and laid her on the lion skin spread atop the coverlet. "I love you, Rexana."

"I love you." Her eyes wet with tears, she drew him down beside her. "Let us make a child tonight. A son."

"Or a daughter." He winked. "A wild little hellion like her mother."

She giggled and, with a calculated shove, rolled him onto his back. Straddling him, she stared down into his mischievous brown eyes. As she arched her body against him in a teasing, sensual rhythm, he inhaled sharply.

His hands slid to her gown's ties.

"Aye, husband," she purred. "Let us dance."

— *THE END* —

# A Knight's Vengeance

## *A quest for revenge . . .*

Geoffrey de Lanceau is a knight, the son of the man who once ruled Wode. His noble sire died, however, branded as a traitor. But never will Geoffrey believe his father betrayed their king, and swears vengeance against the man who brought his sire down in a siege to take over Wode.

## *A quest for love . . .*

Lady Elizabeth Brackendale dreamed of marrying for love, but is promised by her father to a lecherous old baron. Then she is abducted and held for ransom by a scarred, tormented rogue who turns out to be the very knight who has sworn vengeance against her father.

## *A quest for truth . . .*

The threads of deception sewn eighteen years ago bind the past and present. Only by Geoffrey and Elizabeth championing their forbidden love can the truth - and the lies - be revealed about . . .

A Knight's Vengeance

ISBN#1932815481

$6.99

2006

Jewel Imprint - Sapphire

www.catherinekean.com

For more information
about other great titles from
Medallion Press, visit

www.medallionpress.com